ring of truth

new york times bestseller
ciji ware
diana dempsey
kate moore

Ring of Truth Novellas

The Ring of Kerry Hannigan by Ciji Ware

On the eve of a move from New York to San Francisco, classically trained chef and respected food blogger Kerry Hannigan's world turns upside down the instant she puts on an Irish Claddagh ring rescued from the rubble of 9/11. A gift from her godmother, the emerald gemstone reputedly offers life-changing guidance and counsel—but only for seven days, and only to those who *listen*.

A Diva Wears the Ring by Diana Dempsey

Veronica Ballard, adopted from Russia at birth, sings opera and longs to understand where she comes from. One fateful day, she receives both a life-changing letter and the Ring of Truth, and embarks on a journey to answer her heart's deepest questions. Little does she know her quest will lead to love.

Once Upon a Ring by Kate Moore

Boutique hotel concierge Tara Keegan finds the perfect way to deal with the woes of modern dating—invent a boyfriend. As long as Tara clings to her Mr. Wright, she can't take the first real step toward happiness—opening her heart. It takes the Ring of Truth on Tara's finger to discover that she wants more than fiction. Now her heart prompts her to risk all and tell the humiliating truth to a man who's suddenly very present in her life.

Cover design 2014 by **Streetlight Graphics**
Colophon design by **Kim Killion**
Formatting by **A Thirsty Mind Book Design**

ISBN: 978-1500461126

Published by Lion's Paw Publishing, a division of Life Events Media LLC, 1001 Bridgeway, Ste. 224, Sausalito, CA 94965

First print edition: July 2014

In This Anthology

The Ring of Kerry Hannigan
by Ciji Ware

A Diva Wears the Ring
by Diana Dempsey

Once Upon a Ring
by Kate Moore

The Ring of Kerry Hannigan

Ciji Ware

Chapter One

The cab door nearly blew off its hinges when its harried passenger prepared to step out of the taxi and on to the curb at 83rd and Park Avenue on a blustery, rain-soaked December afternoon. Kerry Hannigan was late by nearly a half-hour and feared she was about to disappoint her favorite person in the world—again.

Drenched by the downpour in the time it took her to sprint to the elegant front door of her godmother's co-op building, the thirty-three-year-old nodded politely to the uniformed doorman who ushered her across the hushed lobby's black-and-white marble squares leading toward the familiar set of brass-trimmed elevators. She'd been riding up to the fourteenth floor ever since the day her mother and grandmother selected Angelica Fabrini Doyle to serve as Kerry's legal guardian, should anything happen to her parents. Their choice for the only Hannigan daughter had occurred long after their beloved friend had met and happily married their cousin Brian Doyle, a successful corporate lawyer who had not only shocked his Irish friends and colleagues "by marrying Italian," but had also changed the former seamstress's life forever.

As the elevator lifted smoothly toward the higher floors, Kerry could almost hear her godmother repeat a mantra she had lived by all her life: "'Friendship, loyalty, and love,'

Kerry, my pet. That's what my darling Brian taught me about being happy. If you have that, you have all of life's riches!"

Oh, how she would miss Angelica's wisdom and the love this woman had lavished on her since birth! She dreaded the moment when she had to explain to the octogenarian how long she would be away from New York, but there was no avoiding a full disclosure this afternoon about what was happening in her life—and that moment was *now*.

The elevator doors slid open and Kerry padded toward Number 3 at the end of the hall where her godmother's four-bedroom palace overlooked Park Avenue. Her late godfather had not only been a loving, sweetheart of a guy, recalled Kerry fondly, but he had managed to be both hugely successful *and* ethical, representing wealthy clients suing certain wayward money managers for fraud.

Even so, her godparents' lives had not *all* been a perfect fantasy, had it, she reflected? Kerry tried not to let thoughts of Maggie Doyle add to the jumble of emotionally-charged issues she had already been wrestling with from the moment Charlie excitedly burst into her office cubicle with his big announcement, "Pack your bags, kiddo...you're gonna be a millionaire!"

She drew closer to Angelica's front door at the end of the hallway, hoping that her boots weren't leaving discernible puddles on the expensive carpeting. She paused, inhaled a deep breath, and pushed the buzzer. Within seconds, she heard footsteps and the door to the Doyle's abode swung open.

"Kerry, pet!" Angelica held her arms wide and then noted how soaked from the rain her visitor was. "Oh, my goodness! Look at you, you poor dear! I'll hug you in a minute. Come in, come in, and let's get you out of that dripping raincoat! Molly's got the tea brewing for us in the living room."

Kerry couldn't help but feel her spirits lift as the sprightly, ageless Angelica, stylish as ever in pleated grey wool trousers and a matching grey cashmere sweater set, hung up her visitor's coat in the hall closet, chaffed her goddaughter's cold hands, and led her briskly into the elegantly appointed front room that almost seemed like a movie set.

Kerry's glance absorbed the well-remembered peach-colored, Thai silk matching sofas and Louis XIV chairs gathered around a glowing fireplace whose ornate marble mantel was graced with a ceiling-high, gilt-framed mirror reflecting back the beauty of the entire chamber.

Angelica patted the sofa cushion next to her to indicate her godchild should sit down beside her.

"I'll take things from here, thank you, Molly, dear," she bid her maid of many years. Angelica turned to her goddaughter. "Even though it's nearly five o'clock, you prefer good, strong, Irish Breakfast tea with a little milk, if I remember, yes, Kerry?"

"Yes please, and I'm so sorry I was late," Kerry replied, hoping she didn't sound too defensive. "The crosstown traffic—"

"The point is you're here, now, and that's all that matters."

Kerry adored her godmother, but lately, there had been long periods between their visits and she'd missed sharing confidences with Angelica in ways she'd never been able to do with her busy, preoccupied parents. As long as she could remember, she'd basked in the warm glow of affection that she'd always felt whenever they were together. Charlie never seemed to understand how indebted she felt to the older woman for having gifted her with a very expensive certificated course at the Culinary Institute of America in Hyde Park, outside New York City. When Kerry had protested the $53,000 price tag for the program, her godmother had scoffed.

"It's the Harvard of cooking schools, for pity's sake, and you are far more the chef than your mother or father ever were! I merely want to offer you an alternative to life at Hannigan's Bar and Grill!" she'd teased the year Kerry was poised to enter her sixth season as sous chef to her mother since graduating from a local community college. "This degree will be your ticket to working in the finest restaurants anywhere...and maybe even to opening one of your own someday. There are lots of successful female chefs nowadays, my dear...and I think *you* could be one of them!"

And yet what did I do with all that knowledge....?

In her mind's eye, a cascading image of endless late nights at her desk in the CookChic.com's office in Brooklyn flashed before her. During the two years since she'd graduated from the CIA, she had slaved away in her tiny, three-sided cubicle creating new, up-to-the-minute blog posts about New York's culinary scene. As for cooking itself, she hadn't tried anything new or ambitious in months, and—

Her guilty thoughts were interrupted by her godmother handing her a steaming cup of tea in eggshell-thin, Irish Belleek chinaware that had belonged to Brian Doyle's late mother.

"So tell me, Kerry, dear," her godmother said, forcing the younger woman's thoughts back to the present, "I want to hear all about the new development you mentioned on the phone. You hinted it might involve spending some time in California? It's all happened so quickly."

Kerry explained in as little detail as possible that Charlie Miller, her classmate at the legendary culinary academy, had helped her launch a food blog for the serious home chef who occasionally likes to dine out.

"Charlie knew how to drive tons of traffic to my blog because he is, as he calls himself, 'King of the Key Words'— thanks to a series of tech jobs before he enrolled in the CIA."

"That can't be the only reason your blog has been so successful," Angelica protested.

Her godmother's staunch loyalty brought a grateful smile to Kerry's lips.

"Well, his knowledge of how social media works, combined with a pretty great recipe of mine at the end of every post, apparently made a good combination," she allowed. "We formed a fifty-fifty partnership in our little start-up business, and suddenly, we were getting thousands and thousands of hits and—"

"Hits? That doesn't sound good," Angelica interrupted.

"In the Internet world, hits are a *very* good thing," Kerry assured her. "In fact, the number of daily visitors to our site got so impressive that a company called LifestyleXer in San Francisco made an offer for us to become part of a bigger site that provides my age group everything from online apart- ment listings to home furnishing tips to...well...guidance and recipes from me for the busy home chef, along with my recommendations about the best places to dine out when amateur cooks don't feel like cooking."

"Well, how exciting, dear," Angelica complimented her mildly.

"Yes, it is...and now, as part of this bigger company, I'll be expanding to *two* blogs a day, Monday through Friday. The new company also wants us to find and manage other bloggers in ten major cities around the country, based on my template."

"That sounds like quite an additional challenge,"

Angelica commented, regarding Kerry closely.

"Our deal with them, though," Kerry replied, not meeting her godmother's steady gaze because this was going to be the hard part of what she had to tell her Angelica today, "is that we have work in San Francisco. Starting tomorrow."

There! She'd finally said the words: she was moving away...

"But it's three weeks before Christmas!" Angelica protested.

"I know...I tried to get that changed, but...they said no."

Angelica remained silent and then took a slow, measured sip of her tea. Finally she said, "And has the company that bought yours at least made it financially worth going through this rather major upheaval in your life?"

It was Kerry's turn to stare into the milky depths of her teacup.

"Well...we're considered a start-up division within LifestyleXer, so we'll still be earning a modest salary, *but,*" she emphasized with all the enthusiasm she could muster, "the company is paying for our move and Charlie and I are due half a million dollars, each, in vested stock options, at the end of two years—"

"Two *years!*"

Kerry could understand how—for an eighty-one-year-old—the thought of far fewer visits and coping with different time zones was...well...unsettling.

"Two years," she repeated, "if the IPO goes through this January."

"The IPO?" Angelica echoed. "Your new company is going to make an Initial Public Offering of its stock?"

Angelica Doyle read *The Wall Street Journal* religiously and was certainly no neophyte in business.

"Yes. The San Francisco dot com is going to offer its stock

to the public in a few weeks," she disclosed. "And we'll be granted *more* shares, down the road, if the food blogging part of the business continues to do well after the two years."

"Hmmm, stock *options*," mused her godmother. "So your pay-out as a result of this move is not a sure thing?"

Angelica Doyle had been the consummate businesswoman in the interior design firm she had founded and run for many decades and was no pushover, as Kerry could plainly see.

"It's a fairly sure thing, as these things go," she replied carefully. "The IPO is all teed up for the first of the year, so once that happens, all we have to do is wait for our stock to vest and then sell it in batches of twenty-five percent a fiscal quarter after that two-year date."

"*If* the stock price retains its value all that time, yes?" Angelica pressed. "Sometimes these ventures don't, you know."

"Charlie thinks that all indications are that LifestyleXer might be another LinkedIn."

The tiniest frown had appeared between Angelica's eyebrows.

"I take it that meanwhile, *you're* the one busy writing all those blogs and managing the compatriots you find and hire?"

"Well...right."

"And will you do any hands-on culinary work for your new employer?"

"Well, no...but—"

"And what is your...business partner, Mr. Miller, going to be doing during the two-year waiting period?"

Kerry could tell that Angelica couldn't quite bring herself to call Charlie Miller her godchild's "boyfriend" or even her "beau." Kerry had never described to her godmother the way in which Charlie had swept her off her feet from the first day of class with adulation both for her person and her cooking. And despite the fact that Kerry and Charlie had lived together for nearly a year, Angelica had met him only once on an occasion when Charlie's one-syllable answers to her godmother's polite attempts to draw him out had been less than inspiring for either of them. Angelica was a wildly creative, visually oriented person. Kerry wasn't surprised her godmother couldn't appreciate a tech-focused guy like Charlie, and she felt impelled to defend him.

"Oh, he'll share his Internet expertise with the larger company and will still be pushing traffic to my blog and the other ones we're going to establish around the country," she assured her with a bright smile. "Charlie's work should make the stock even more attractive to potential investors."

"I see..." murmured Angelica. "So that's why the move to San Francisco. And what about any face-to-face connecting for you with experts in the food world out west? Will you have time to do some of that?"

Angelica's probing questions hung in the air several moments before Kerry answered.

"Well, I'll certainly be interviewing those sorts of people on the phone for my blog, and as far as cooking, we've been so busy, we usually eat out. For research."

Her godmother paused and then asked pointedly, "And is this move what *you* want to do?"

Kerry hesitated, and then replied, "As you just said, it's all happened so fast, Angelica. The sudden sale of CookChic...and then, as part of the deal, the west coast execs subsequently insisted that we move to San Francisco to be close to headquarters. But it's only for two years—" she reiterated.

"It's been two *years* since you got your degree from the

CIA, pet," Angelica reminded her quietly—as if she needed to.

Kerry felt a rush of warmth invade her fair skin and she wondered, suddenly, if her black hair and blue eyes conjured up for her wise, perceptive godmother a vision of an embarrassed Irish Snow White, indeed, mortified that she hadn't put her acknowledged culinary talents and training to practical use in the real world of top-flight food production, which was, after all, her true passion. She leaned forward and put her hand on the older woman's sleeve.

"Angelica, I will never be able to thank you enough for paying my tuition at—"

"Kerry!" she interrupted in the sharpest tone of voice Kerry had ever heard her use. "That is not *at all* what I'm talking about here! Just as I did with my darling Maggie," she continued, referring to her late daughter, "I will always support you in whatever path you wish to follow. It's just I would hope it is *your* path. Not one that someone else has chosen *for* you."

Before Kerry could reply, her godmother thrust her hand between the sofa's silk cushions and withdrew a scuffed, burgundy leather ring box.

"The other reason that I asked you to come here—besides wanting to see you—is that I have a present for you. I guess, now, we can call it an early Christmas gift."

"Oh, Angelica…you've given me so much and—"

"I gave this to Maggie back when she was a bit older than you are now. I will try once more to pass this on as it was passed to me."

Kerry stared, dumbfounded, as Angelica opened the leather box in whose depth was nestled a ring every self-respecting Irish-American would instantly recognize. She remembered that Maggie Doyle had worn the gold Claddagh ring every day since her mother had given it to her. How in the world did Angelica have it in her possession *now*...after...

From the small leather box, her godmother gently lifted the ring featuring two cupped, gold hands embracing an emerald gemstone cut in the shape of a heart and topped with a tiny, golden crown.

"You know," Angelica said softly, "the New York City police chief told me that one in five people who died in the Twin Towers on September Eleventh was of Irish extraction." She gazed somberly at the beautiful ring. "The numbers vary, depending on who you talk to, but twenty-three members of the NYPD, along with three hundred-plus firemen, and more than *six hundred* employees of the Cantor Fitzgerald firm died that day. Many who worked there were Irish-Americans, like Maggie. When the recovery teams finally finished going through those acres of rubble, more than two hundred Claddagh rings similar to this one were found..."

"No!" exclaimed Kerry, stunned by this revelation.

"Well, I suppose it's not too surprising, since these rings are traditionally exchanged at Irish weddings and given as tokens of kinship and friendship."

Kerry's throat began to close and she could see tears edging into the corner of her godmother's eyes as well. It had been more than a decade since Maggie went off to work that sparkling Tuesday morning, a member of the legal staff at a prosperous bond brokerage house. Despite the young woman's earlier leanings toward a career in clothing design, she'd ultimately chosen law school, dark pinstripe business suits, and a penchant for "Ice Men"—as her mother once described the males that her daughter had occasionally brought home to dinner.

"I gave the ring to Maggie for her thirty-seventh birthday

when she told me they were going to promote her to the top job in the legal department at work. I thought, perhaps, if she took advantage of the ring's...rather unusual powers, she might change the way her life was—"

"What do you mean 'unusual powers?'" Kerry interrupted, taken aback by what she'd thought she heard her godmother say.

"Maggie was conflicted," Angelica disclosed. "She wanted to please her father, even though he never urged her to follow in his footsteps. Brian was a wonderful husband, but his law practice demanded so much of his time that, looking back on it all, I think Maggie's going to law school instead of design school, and her taking that horrible grind-of-a-job in the Twin Towers, was just a way of asking for more of his attention."

"Oh, Angelica..." Kerry said, feeling tears about to spill down her cheeks. "I can't imagine how hard it's been for you with both Maggie and Brian gone." She seized one of Angelica's hands. "And if *I've* disappointed you, I feel just horrible—"

"No!" Angelica said fiercely. "You haven't disappointed me one bit! I just don't want you to disappoint *yourself*! I want you to have this ring that was among those given back to the surviving relatives after that ghastly day. The victims' families were asked to list anything that might identify their loved ones, and one day I got a call and..."

Her godmother closed her eyes briefly and Kerry squeezed her hand, holding it tightly. Angelica bowed her head, and then continued to speak in a low voice.

"I can only assume that Maggie chose not to...to listen to what the ring had to teach her." She cast her goddaughter a piercing gaze. "Now, you can say I should be committed to a lunatic asylum if you want to, but you must trust me when I say *this* particular Claddagh ring can help you know what's truly in your heart!" Kerry stared at the object in Angelica's hand, her godmother's aged fingers slightly swollen with arthritis.

"But *how*?" Kerry murmured, amazed to think the ring Maggie Doyle once wore had survived the devastation of that day and had eventually been returned to her mother. "How can a piece of jewelry—"

"*My* mother," Angelica began, "died years before you were born. She was a new Italian immigrant working at the Triangle Shirtwaist Factory in 1911. One of the young women who toiled beside her ten hours a day—an Irish girl—took Mama aside as they were walking home together late one night and gave her the ring, saying it had told *her* to quit her job that day and to pass the ring on to someone else who needed it."

"Oh, now, Angelica...how could—"

"Hear me out!" commanded her godmother. "The co-worker told my mother that the ring had originally been made in the town of Claddagh on Galway Bay in Ireland. Mama swore to me that as soon as she put the ring on her finger, a voice in her head said to turn around and go home only a few minutes after she'd arrived at work at the shirt factory the next morning—which meant she was fired, of course."

"So what happened? Did the ring tell her where to find a better job?" Kerry teased.

Angelica shot her a stern look.

"That same day in March, 1911, the factory burned to the ground, killing 146 of the two girls' co-workers. Three days later, wandering into Hannigan's Bar and Grill—which was only a pub back then—Mama met your grandfather's cousin and married him." Angelica smiled faintly. "That man drinking Guinness that evening became my father."

"The ring *talks?*" Kerry asked, unable to keep the skepticism out of her tone.

"Not exactly. Not out loud. In my own case, I simply had *thoughts* surface in my mind. Thoughts that contained much wisdom, I might add."

"You're saying *you've* heard this ring speak to you?" Kerry queried. "Those were probably just your *own* thoughts!"

Angelica shrugged. "Maybe so, but the ring only spoke to me for one week. After that, the guidance ceased...but of course by then I'd met Brian Doyle."

Kerry couldn't refrain from teasing her once more. "Well how do you know it was the *ring* 'speaking?' From pictures I've seen of Brian in his youth, he was a pretty dishy guy. It wouldn't have taken anybody else to tell you that."

Angelica pointed to the heart-shaped emerald clasped between the ring's two golden hands.

"When certain thoughts popped into my head, the emerald pulsed and turned opalescent...and when that happened, I knew it was the ring offering a message of guidance."

"Make it glow, then," demanded Kerry.

"Oh no, dear," protested Angelica, "I can't do that. Its powers only last for seven days, starting from the moment a new wearer puts it on. That still, small voice of counsel and guidance is offered on a temporary basis only. The wearer can choose to follow the suggestions or not...and at the end of the week, the ring reverts to being simply a lovely piece of jewelry which one can wear as long as one likes until prompted to give it to another woman who needs it."

Kerry reached out and gently rested a finger on the emerald.

"Maggie was wearing this on September Eleventh? Why didn't it protect her, then?"

"Yes, she was wearing it. She loved the ring because it was beautiful and a gift from her father and me...but she told me flat out she thought the whole 'guidance thing' was ridiculous and a bunch of Irish hooey and she certainly didn't want to hear any advice to quit her job and go back to her first love—designing clothes."

"She told you the ring said to do that? To go back to the field of clothing design?"

"Whatever thoughts came into her head when she first put it on she just...ignored. Weeks went by. She was waiting for the retirement party of her mentor and the official announcement about her huge promotion. She was ambitious, you remember, which was *fine*, but I know she was lonely, which is why I had decided to pass on the ring to her that summer. Her job in those towers was all-consuming. She never seemed to have time for close relationships, except for those wolves of Wall Street she dated from time to time. She kept telling me 'I don't have the bandwidth to go out for lunch or drinks with people.'" Angelica shook her head, murmuring almost to herself, "Imagine saying that about friends and family..."

A wall of misery Kerry had learned to keep mostly at bay was threatening, now, to engulf her godmother and her as they both fought off the terrible memories of those days following 9/11.

Desperate to guide the conversation in another direction, Kerry asked her, "So, what did the ring tell *you* to do when you were given it?"

"Me?" Angelica smiled at the memory, which was exactly what Kerry hoped would happen. "Back in those days, I was working two jobs to earn the money for interior design school...days doing clothing alterations at my parents' dry cleaners and nights at Hannigan's Bar and Grill on West 44th Street, smack in the middle of the theatre district. Your father, Patrick, was starting to take over the management—the fourth generation in the food business, you know, making *you* the fifth—" Angelica paused, and then amended, "Well, maybe not anymore..."

"Doesn't *writing* about food count?" Kerry demanded.

Angelica merely shrugged again.

"At any rate," her godmother continued, "one night, about two days after I'd been given the ring from my mother—who knew I wanted to be more than just a seamstress in a dry cleaner by day and a waitress by night— in walked Brian Doyle, dressed to the nines. That particular night, I had worn a lovely outfit that had been unclaimed at my parents' shop for a year and so I was put on duty up front, checking in the guests. The dapper Mr. Doyle had an extra ticket to a Broadway show and offered it to me as soon as he saw me there."

"What about your manning the reservations desk?"

"I was quite shocked when a voice in my head said, *'Say yes to Mr. Doyle!'* so I ran to your Grandmother Hannigan, cooking in the back, and she made your father take over for me out front. From that moment on," Angelica added with a girlish giggle, "I listened carefully to every thought that came to me whenever the emerald turned into a glowing opal— even though most people I knew thought I was crazy, getting engaged in a month."

"Only a *month*?" Kerry replied, aghast.

"Actually, I accepted Brian's proposal on the seventh day I had the ring...we just didn't *tell* anyone for a month!"

Kerry laughed and shook her head. "Well, it was a love match, that's for sure." She glanced around the beautifully appointed living room, adding, "And look what a wonderful career you had."

"Brian made all that possible. Encouraged me to get the best training there was in interior design and bankrolled tuition at Parsons and my first few years in the business."

"But you barely *knew* the man when you married him!" Kerry protested. "Didn't you feel you were mighty lucky that it actually worked out? Who would have bet back then that you and Brian would turn out to be so well suited?"

"No, it wasn't luck!" her godmother replied emphatically. "We just *knew.*" She glanced at the ornate clock on the mantel. "Well...it's getting late and I'm sure you have a million loose ends to tie up. I'm terribly sorry Mr. Miller couldn't come with you today, but...do give him my best."

Kerry had tried to persuade Charlie to join them for tea, but he'd begged off, as usual.

"Now put this in a safe place," Angelica said, securing the ring in its box and closing the lid. "You can choose to put it on whenever you like—or not at all. It's totally up to you, pet. Just remember, though, I give it to you with the greatest love."

Kerry's eyes grew moist again as she wrapped her arms around her godmother in a hug. Then, she slipped the ring box into the bottom of her handbag, wondering, suddenly, what her life would be like in California without Angelica close by? Her godmother was right to suspect that the new job might not allow the time to do more than search the Internet for artisan food entrepreneurs to interview by phone. Kerry had wondered lately if it was her destiny only to *read* about farm-to-table cuisine in Northern California—not experience it? Given her increased blogging schedule of two posts per day, and recruiting all those new writers, she seriously doubted she'd get to meet many of these food devotees in person. In fact, CookChic's only other female employee, Sally, had called their enterprise in Brooklyn "an electronic sweatshop." What would LifestyleXer prove to be?

Triangle Shirtwaist Factory indeed…

She glanced down at her purse and speculated about the choices she'd made since graduating from culinary school—and about a ring that could put thoughts in a person's head. By this time, she and Angelica had reached the apartment's front door. Her godmother enfolded her in her arms one last time and then kissed her on both cheeks.

"Goodbye, Kerry, pet. I'll miss you *molto, molto*."

"Goodbye, Angelica. I'll miss you, too. I love you," she added, as she had every time she'd said farewell to her godmother since the events of 9/11.

"I know that, darling girl, and it's been a great comfort, believe me."

A hollowness filled Kerry's chest. How long would it really be before she saw Angelica again? Her godmother had always been her rock, the person she could turn to. For months ahead, Kerry's work routine in San Francisco at the bigger company on the eve of an IPO would rule out even quick trips back to New York. As for speaking together on the phone, that three-hour time difference between coasts would be a killer. And how long, she wondered, would Angelica be as spry as she was these days?

The clock in the living room tolled the hour, its delicate brass pings reminding her that Charlie was probably waiting impatiently at their apartment for her to fix him something to eat.

Kerry summoned a cheery smile. "Now, don't forget to read your email!"

"No," her godmother said firmly. "Do the old fashioned thing and call me once in a while, will you? *Slàinte,*" she said, offering the Irish word for "To your health," instead of her usual *"Ciao, bellissima!"*

"Ciao, Angelica," Kerry replied, and walked swiftly down the hall as her godmother closed her front door.

The elevator swished to fetch her on the fourteenth floor, and in less than a minute whisked her down to the lobby where the doorman found her a cab for the ride across Manhattan in the pouring rain.

Chapter Two

By the time Kerry's cab pulled up in front of the apartment that she and Charlie Miller shared on 87th and West End Avenue, the rain had tapered off and her stomach was rumbling. She waited impatiently for the vintage elevator to arrive, wracking her brain about what to whip up for dinner.

Or maybe just send out for Thai…unless Charlie's already ordered in.

Hoping for the latter, she slipped her key into the lock and opened the front door. She gave a sniff, but detected no scent of dinner wafting from a bag of cardboard cartons waiting to be revived by the microwave in their minuscule kitchen.

"Hey, hi…I'm home!" she called. Her words had a hollow ring, now that the movers had loaded the van with their furniture.

Charlie's slender, brown-haired figure was hunched over his laptop sitting on a packing carton in the middle of their bare living room.

"Did you bring food home?" he said without looking up as he continued to type furiously.

"No, did *you*?" she retorted, annoyed it was always assumed *she* was responsible for putting food on the table every single night.

"You're an hour later than you said you'd be. I thought you must have stopped somewhere to get us something to eat."

"You were here all day," she protested. "Couldn't you have run down to—"

"Cool it, Kerry," he snapped. "I had a few more pressing things than to drink tea on Park Avenue, you know what I'm saying?"

Stung, Kerry turned abruptly and marched into the four-foot-square kitchen and opened the refrigerator that barely came up to her waist. She proceeded to throw together two omelets with the four remaining eggs, a tired green onion, and a wilted half of a red pepper that she diced into tiny cubes with a vengeance. She dished this hurried fare onto the paper plates they'd been using since her dishes had been packed.

"Here you go," she announced, and left the food on a nearby suitcase they'd be taking with them in the morning.

She waited a millisecond for a "Thanks" and when it wasn't forthcoming, she headed directly for the bedroom. She ate her eggs while sitting on the bed that they'd previously sold to their neighbor who would move it across the hall once they'd left. In twenty-four hours, this room would be empty of any trace she'd ever lived here, and, for some reason, that thought brought a huge lump to her throat.

She rose to her feet, swiftly shed her clothes, and hopped into the shower, allowing a fierce stream of hot water to drown the sound of her soft weeping. She cried once again for the loss of Maggie Doyle and the generosity of the gallant, lonely woman living directly across Manhattan whom she would miss terribly during the next two years. And she mourned, too, the sudden, sorry state of her personal life.

***

Kerry slept fitfully beside Charlie, who had finally come to bed in the wee hours. She was already awake before the alarm on her cellphone was due to ring. She turned it off and bolted for the bathroom, thinking of a myriad of last-minute To Do's before the car service to the airport arrived.

She stared into the medicine cabinet mirror at her tousled head of shoulder-length, ebony hair and the royal blue eyes that distinguished her "Black Irish" ancestry, and wondered how, at thirty-three, she'd somehow lost her sex appeal? She glanced through the half-opened door at Charlie lying, face down, his head buried beneath his pillow. She realized, with a start, that they hadn't made love in—what? A month? Two? Could it be since Charlie first mentioned the possibility of selling CookChic to LifestyleXer, a deal that now sealed their joint fate?

That was it!

They'd ceased being intimate almost three months ago, right after all the negotiations to sign over their start-up to the bigger company began, and their new boss, Beverly Silverstein, insisted they make a move to San Francisco. What had appeared a solid personal-professional relationship between Charlie and her just seemed to unravel.

Kerry searched her memory for the exact moment it all seemed to go awry. Perhaps it was when her expression disclosed her dismay about the "offer they couldn't refuse"— moving to San Francisco.

At first, she'd been as excited as he was at the prospect of making some serious money for the first time in her life. But then, the thought of leaving her family, and—most of all— Angelica, now that she was both widowed and childless, plus the reality of the increased workload of writing more daily posts, along with supervising an army of bloggers around the country, began to weigh on her, and she'd summoned the courage to voice her misgivings.

"Look, Charlie…this offer sounded pretty great, at first, but when you really look at what our new bosses want from us—their demands are huge, and besides, it's really pushing me farther and farther away from what I love: which is *making* food, not writing about it!"

Charlie had been angry when she'd pointed out these negatives and responded, thin-lipped, "Look…you don't *have* to do this, you know. We can tell Beverly you just want to do your little blog from New York, and I'll recruit and manage the other blog teams from out there. We'd have to adjust the fifty-fifty deal between you and me, but—"

"*You*?" Kerry challenged, hurt he'd dismiss their relationship so casually. "You've never written or edited a piece of copy in your life."

"Exactly!" he'd replied. "See how you're about to *screw up* everything? If you really want to grab that brass ring, Kerry girl, you'd better suck it up and head west to the new Gold Rush going on out there in Silicon Land." When she'd remained silent, he'd grown impatient. "It's only for two years, for God's sake! Once the stock goes public and we vest, you're free to live wherever you damn please!"

"Can't we just say no to moving out there? Do it all from New York…and yes, I could *use* your help recruiting new bloggers!"

She could tell that Charlie had become even more exasperated with her, but he'd simmered down and merely gave a slight shrug of his black, T-shirt clad shoulders.

"Well, if you don't show them your good faith with the acquisition of CookChic before the company goes public, your *not* moving to company headquarters could actually be a deal-breaker…and wreck things for both of us."

Recalling the conversation, now, only made her feel

worse, so she turned on the water in the bathroom sink and began to scrub her face.

She'd ultimately come to realize that for Charlie, it was all about the score...the "Big Bucks," as he always termed it. And it didn't really seem to matter to him how he or she got to the big pay-off. Or, in her case, whether it felt right or made her happy. Just that he put a notch on his dot-com belt and that she was dumb not to do the same.

To be fair, she conceded silently, leaning over the bathroom sink to brush her teeth, Charlie Miller had taught her everything she knew about social media and building a business from scratch. She should at least give the guy some credit for that.

"Hey, you might eventually have enough money to invest in your own restaurant, kiddo!" he'd said, once the discussion was over and she'd agreed on the move. "Or you can buy out your mom and dad so they can retire"—though Charlie knew perfectly well that being partners with her brothers, Liam and Connor, at a beer and grill joint was not exactly what she had in mind.

Heaving a sigh for all the other things she *hadn't* said to Charlie to make a more convincing argument about her emotional obligations to Angelica and the other good reasons for remaining in New York, Kerry resignedly applied her lipstick and a touch of mascara to her already dark lashes. She donned the clothes she'd laid out to wear on the plane and headed through the bedroom with her remaining toiletries to pack them in her suitcase waiting in the living room.

"Charlie...wake up," she called over her shoulder. "The car will be here in twenty minutes."

By this time, Charlie had flopped over on his back, the overnight stubble on his slack jaw making it appear as if he hadn't washed his face in a very long time. His thinning brown hair had been flattened against his skull by the pillow he'd slept under, revealing a receding hairline that would be a serious detriment, one day, to his rather ascetic good looks.

"C'mon!" she repeated. "Up-and-at-'em. California here we come, right?" She was startled by her sarcastic tone. She was starting to sound just like Charlie.

Not good, she thought glumly.

She tucked her cosmetic bag into her suitcase and then spotted the airplane boarding passes Charlie had printed out after she'd gone to bed. She opened her purse to stow them where they'd be easily accessible and noticed the vintage leather ring box her godmother had given her, wedged next to her wallet.

She could hear Charlie pad toward the bathroom and soon the water was running in the shower, full blast. Meanwhile, she slowly lifted the box's lid and withdrew the Claddagh ring, her breath catching as she read the inscription engraved inside the gold band.

Know Thy Heart.

Tucked tightly against the red silk lining inside the box lid was a small, yellowed piece of paper that she unfolded, revealing a message penned in spidery script.

Be brave!—for the ring of truth will test you. Once on your finger, its power to speak endures but seven days. Listen and learn, lest you lose its wisdom and your heart's desire. When seven days pass, prepare to give the Claddagh as a gift. Once her face you see, you'll know the one who must the ring receive. On her bestow the ring of truth...

Kerry stared at the ring as she slipped it from its silk nest and onto her finger. Despite the jewelry's age and what the metal must have been subjected to on 9/11, its surface remained smooth and unblemished and the gemstone in the perfect shape of a heart. She'd put it on her right hand with the point of the heart facing outward—the age-old Irish symbol for an unmarried person who was "open to love." Within seconds, an odd tingling began to radiate up her arm as she vaguely heard Charlie humming off-key in the bathroom.

Is Charlie Miller open to love?

Startled by the suddenness of this thought, she stared at the heart-shaped emerald, but the gemstone remained its lovely green hue. Apparently, she thought with a cynical grimace, the ring hadn't warmed up yet.

Tucking the empty ring box back into her purse, she noticed Charlie's laptop sitting on his suitcase, its battery charger plugged into both the computer and the wall. When she reached to unplug it for him, inadvertently touching the keyboard, the screen sprang to life. A glowing page from his Inbox displayed a long series of emails with the same name repeated nearly all the way down the page. Why were there so many communications these last days in New York from b.silverstein at lifestylerXer dot com that Kerry had never been copied on?

Beverly Silverstein was the executive that had let them know that closing their deal was on shaky grounds unless they agreed to move out to California until the public stock offering was final and their shares in the company fully vested.

Kerry was curious why it would have taken so many emails to Charlie to convey the facts they'd already agreed to? Or were there other elements of the new relationship between their buyer and CookChic she should have been told about? She would have been embarrassed to admit to

Angelica that she'd left working out the details of their deal to Charlie and their lawyer—*his* lawyer, actually—and now she regretted not knowing much about the contract she'd signed.

Click on that name...the last entry at the top of the page...

Kerry heard her own sharp intake of breath and glanced down at her right hand. The emerald had taken on a glowing, pulsing opalescence, and a strange warmth had begun to spread up her right arm.

She shifted her gaze to Charlie's laptop and obediently clicked on the most recent email. A message instantly displayed across the screen, its date and time confirming that it was sent late the previous night.

Charlie Boy...

One last thought before u go to sleep...I cannot believe u will actually arrive in San Francisco tomorrow! Have u told KH yet? I'd just as soon have that dealt with b4 u walk into the Howard Street offices, please.

I'll have someone from r HR staff sit her down as soon as she is assigned her cubicle and explain how things r to b...

Meanwhile, lol & xoxo
Beverly

Kerry tore her gaze from the laptop as she heard Charlie's footsteps heading out of the bathroom. A jumble of emotions swinging wildly between suspicion, shock, and embarrassment for being caught reading somebody else's email propelled her across the living room to busy herself zipping up her carry-on bag.

Charlie called out, "You left a lipstick on the sink. If you want it, better come get it."

"Yeah. Right. In a minute."

Tell him what you've seen!

She didn't have to look at the Claddagh ring to know where *that* thought came from, but a quick peek confirmed it. The emerald stone now glowed a pearly white.

Then another notion floated through her head. Perhaps she was totally reading too much into that email—and only imagined that the ring had changed color since the stone had resumed its deep green hue once again. And she would have given anything to have had the time to click on some of b.silverstein's previous missives before launching any accusations at her lover and business partner. Didn't half the universe sign off "lol" and include the shorthand for "hugs and kisses?"

Charlie appeared at the doorway to the living room just as the laptop's screen reverted to sleep mode.

"C'mon!" he demanded, irritation lacing his words. "Let's move it! I just got a text that the car service is waiting downstairs. We can't be late *this* time, Kerry!"

Kerry raced into the bathroom to collect her last personal possession, chucked it into her purse, and rode in silence to the ground floor.

Don't shoot yourself in the foot, Kerry. You've got a lot riding on whatever you decide to do...keep your mouth shut until you're sure you know what's going on...

Then a louder, more insistent voice in her head declared:

Don't be daft! You know what's going on!

Kerry spent the entire early morning, five hour and fifty minute flight to California pretending to be asleep while her mind was whirling with a variety of scenarios about what all those emails from Beverly Silverstein meant—and none of her conclusions were good.

The central question spinning around in her head was their boss's query: "Have you told KH yet?" And why was the *tone* of the email so chummy? No...*intimate*, which was odd, given that Charlie had rarely mentioned the woman's name, once their deal papers had been signed. And what, exactly, was LifestyleXer's Human Resources Department going to inform Kerry about "how things are going to be?"

Even when she roused herself to pick at the pre-packaged airline fare of crackers and cheese, her frosty silence had the effect of keeping her seat companion mum until a sleek Lincoln Town Car, sent by their new employers, pulled up to the curb just as they came out of the Virgin America baggage area at San Francisco Airport.

Kerry watched silently as the limo driver loaded their luggage into the trunk. With the three-hour time change, it was just past ten in the morning and she was vaguely aware of the mild December sunshine freshened by a breeze off kidney-shaped San Francisco Bay which they'd flown over on their approach to the airport. They were barely settled into the luxurious black leather seat when Kerry uttered words that she'd been dreading to say all day.

"You need to know that your computer was still turned on this morning and I saw all those emails from Beverly Silverstein."

Even in the dim light inside the car with its smoke glass windows, Kerry could see Charlie literally blanch.

Before he could respond she continued, "What is it she wanted you to *tell* me before we arrived at the LifestyleXer office today?"

Charlie's jaw clenched. "I don't exactly appreciate you

snooping through my emails!"

Kerry was amazed how calm she felt and how steady her voice sounded in the hush of the back seat.

"Only one email," she corrected him. "I accidentally bumped your laptop and a full page of entries came up from her, so I clicked on the last one she sent you last night. What did that women mean about 'how it's going to be?' What gives, Charlie?"

"You had no right to read my private mail—"

"What *gives*, Charlie!" she repeated more sharply.

"What *gives*?" he mimicked her. "What gives is…it's over."

"What is?"

"Us. You and me." He was watching her closely to gauge her reaction to this bombshell. "Be honest, Kerry…we both know it's been over for a while, now."

She gave a small shake of her head.

"No, I did *not* know it was over," she said, her calmness suddenly evaporating. "I just began to feel something was rotten in Denmark…or should I say rotten on West End Avenue!" She seized her handbag and shoved it as hard as she could into his narrow chest. "You bastard!" she cried. "This deal would have gone through whether I moved out to California or not!"

"Not true," Charlie replied coolly, placing her handbag on the floor of the limo. "*My* deal wouldn't have gone through, according to Beverly, because you're the so-called 'talent'…the hot-shot blogger. I'm just the tech guy, and techies are a dime a dozen out here. She and I…well, she said the only way I was guaranteed a fifty-fifty position in this thing was if her boss thought you and I *both* wanted to be part of the west coast company. She let them think…that without me, they couldn't have *you*."

Charlie was looking amused now, as if he was proud of how he'd pulled off the charade that had turned her life upside down.

"So you and Beverly are...already *acquainted* with each other, am I right?" she said, stating the obvious with a biting sarcasm she'd learned from the man who'd betrayed her in such colossal fashion.

"Yeah. Beverly and I hooked up again on Facebook a couple of months ago after not seeing each other for years since Bronx Science, back in the day. She'd...well...apparently she—"

"Had the hots for you in Coding 101," Kerry interrupted. "Spare me the boring details of this pathetic romance. The point is you *used* me to get a half of what I could probably have gotten on my own, and then didn't even have the decency to tell me you were pretty much faking our little toe-dance the entire time we were working and sleeping together, correct?"

"In the beginning, I thought you were pretty cool, you know?" he replied with a shrug. "Different, you know, from my usual type. But I got tired hearing about the great tragedy of 9/11 and your poor, downtrodden Irish and Italian relatives, and how obsessed you are with cooking only 'healthful, local, sustainable' food, you know what I'm saying? Frankly, all that stuff got kinda old."

She ignored the barbs that she knew, somehow, he was employing to insult and denigrate her, thereby giving him the upper hand. Oddly, knowing it was over with Charlie Miller produced a strange sense of relief. Even so, what a lying son-of-a-bitch!

In a low, angry voice, devoid, now, of the slightest hint of tears, she said, "And *your* usual type is your duplicitous little lab partner who's become an ace exec in the digital frenzy out here—and a convenient stepping stone to Silicon Valley for your next big score? *Nice.*"

"Hey, look, Kerry—" he began, but she hardly heard him.

"And what if I tell Ms. Silverstein's *boss* what you two have cooked up here? That she just made you part of the package so she could get her old Bronx boyfriend back?"

Charlie paused and she could tell he was choosing his words carefully.

"Listen, Kerry," he said in a conciliatory tone, "sure…I should have told you that the thing I once had with Beverly had heated up again, but when she read your blog and thought that CookChic was a perfect acquisition for her company *and* a way for her and me to be together—giving all three of us a pretty big boost, by the way—I figured it was cool since you and I would both make a nice chunk of change, and—"

"That is just *crap,* Charlie Miller!" she exploded. "You figured you'd get me out here so *you* wouldn't miss out grabbing that proverbial brass ring you kept talking about. I should have known you were a taker from the shitty way you treated Joe and Sally at our old office. Why should *I* be any different, except as your ticket west?"

"Hey, wait a minute," he countered. "You didn't know the first thing about promoting yourself as either a chef or a food expert, and you knew less than zero about driving the kind of traffic you're now getting on that blog, thanks to me! I've given you the chance to make a half million bucks or more so you can write any ticket you want in your precious food world, so don't make *me* the villain here!"

"You're not worthy of being a villain," she retorted. "You barely rise to the level of *creep.*"

Kerry could see that Charlie was genuinely shocked to

hear his usually polite and well-behaved former girlfriend lash back so effectively. But by this time, her initial outrage had morphed into deadly calm.

"You're right, though," she continued. "You did do all those things to promote my blog. It's just that how you've gone about it is pretty slimy, Charlie Boy."

Gazing across the limo's wide seat, she wondered how in the world she had slipped into an intimate relationship with a man who should have remained a business partner—if that, even—given the dishonest troll that her CIA classmate had turned out to be. Out of her lack of confidence in her talents as a newly-minted chef, along with sheer fear about living on her own, she'd ignored all the signs that Angelica had obviously picked up on.

Kerry glanced down at the ring on her right hand. *Know Thy heart* the Claddagh's inscription advised

She wondered, now, if she knew the first thing about hers. And if she were brutally honest, she'd learned today that she had never been in love with Charlie Miller, any more than he had been with her. She had *wanted* to be in love, but that definitely wasn't the same thing.

Then, much to her amazement, the Claddagh ring's deep green stone began to radiate an inner light until it appeared white hot.

Keep the faith, Kerry...wanting to be in love is the same thing as being open to love...but next time, listen to your heart, instead of your head.

The moment the limousine arrived at the Howard Street lobby of LifestyleXer.com, Kerry watched, dumbfounded, as Beverly Silverstein immediately took Charlie's arm, led him into an elevator, and disappeared without more than a curt nod in her direction. Meanwhile, a trim, toned young woman in tight-fitting, straight-legged, two-hundred-dollar jeans and a boat-necked coral cashmere sweater that barely reached her midriff sashayed over to Kerry and swiftly ushered her down a deserted hallway and into a vast bullpen of wall-to-wall cubicles.

"Here is where we've set it up for you to work," announced Kerry's 'minder' who'd introduced herself as Tiffany Gergus, Assistant Director of Human Resources. "People in here are at their desks by eight o'clock, by the way," she added with a thin smile, as if she greatly enjoyed informing new hires about strict company rules.

Kerry's assigned cubicle was positioned in the middle of perhaps fifty others, all jammed cheek by jowl into the enormous room with track lighting overhead and a row of windows facing the back of the building.

"I plan to work at home a few days a week," Kerry said in a firm tone of voice. No twenty-six–year-old was going to treat her like a minor little worker bee, given the deal she'd signed with this company.

Ms. Gergus arched an eyebrow.

"We've tightened up the WAH rules, so I'm afraid we expect you to be in that chair *every* morning by eight."

"WAH rules?" Kerry repeated, furrowing her brow. "Oh…you mean 'working at home.' WAH."

Ms. Gergus cast her a look of disdain as if everyone in the Universe knew that WAH stood for working-at-home. Then she pronounced with steely officiousness, "And also, Kerry, I see there was an addendum to your contract last week that stipulates you're to blog 500 to 800 words on food, travel, and restaurant subjects twice a day, and once on Saturday."

"*What?*" Kerry exclaimed, and sensed her cube-mates

were all ears. "I never agreed to posting on Saturday!"

The young woman smiled primly.

"You certainly did. I just read your personal services contract word-for-word this morning, before you arrived. Mr. Miller, as president of your former company, signed that addition and said you'd okayed it."

"Well, I didn't," Kerry retorted.

The HR assistant narrowed her gaze.

"Well, then I suggest you'd better speak to Beverly about it."

Beverly, is it? It was definitely more than "casual Friday" if a lowly assistant spoke of a company vice president in such a familiar way.

"Also, the vice president wants a full report by a week, tomorrow, on how many new bloggers you've recruited in the major markets, as outlined in your deal."

She had a week to find food bloggers in ten cities as experienced as she was?

Impossible.

Tiffany Gergus pursed her lips and said by means of farewell, "And a final few things you should know...I want to be sure it's clear to you that your stock options do not vest for a full two years after this company tenders its announced Initial Public Offering three weeks from now and, after that, you can only sell your shares in twenty-five percent increments—"

"Yes, Tiffany," Kerry interrupted, deliberately calling the little twit by her first name. "I'm sure Ms. Silverstein told you to emphasize that fact, but I'm well aware of standard, boilerplate regulations about selling company stock."

As if Kerry hadn't uttered a word, the HR representative continued, "And, I hope you are aware that your contract also stipulates that if Ms. Silverstein doesn't find your blogging up to par, you could be out-placed before that date."

Kerry stared at the assured young woman, unable to mask her astonishment. She *hadn't* realized that little feature must have been in the fine print somewhere.

Tiffany slapped down on the empty desk something that looked like a credit card with Kerry's photo on it that LifeStyleXer must have scraped off the CookChic website.

"Here's your ID that will also serve as your cafeteria card. You get the first hundred dollars of food free every month."

Before Kerry could reply, the young woman handed her a thick manila envelope. "And just so you won't bother a busy executive like Beverly about any of the other details in your revised employment agreement, I made you a copy and I suggest you read it very carefully…line by line."

Without so much as a farewell, Ms. Tiffany Gergus turned on her Kate Spade wedge heeled sandals and marched toward the exit. Kerry noted that the Human Resources assistant was not offered a single friendly wave from anyone encased in the other cubicles that the tight-assed woman walked past on her way out.

Chapter Three

Alone in her cubicle, Kerry stared at the contract she'd trustingly signed on Charlie's assurances that it was "practically a free giveaway," reeling from the shock of having read it thoroughly and understanding, now, that the terms were far more advantageous to the parent company than to CookChic. Unable to think clearly about what she should do next, she made her way to the company cafeteria with the desperate hope that wine was sold with lunch.

The ultra-modern steel-and-glass expanse featured food stations with every imaginable cuisine provided to fuel workers who toiled the long hours that employment at LifeStyleXer apparently required. Sometimes, according to a cynical cube-mate named Jason who'd provided directions to the cafeteria, he slept under his desk when a new feature of the website was due to be launched. "It's way cool that it's open twenty-four/seven."

Kerry noted the variety of ethnic choices: Thai, Chinese, Japanese, to say nothing of fragrant Indian curry and the heavenly aroma of Tandoori chicken, along with the sweet scent of steaming jasmine rice. Kerry had begun to feel queasy from her sleepless night and the flight across the country—to say nothing of the full scope of the upsetting situation that faced her, now that she'd read every word of her contract. She stood in line at the made-to-order salad bar in hopes that eating something light would settle her stomach.

"Next?" called out a short, dark-haired young man wearing a nameplate that identified him as "Tony Perez, Salad Associate."

"I'll take the Arugula Carpaccio, please, with the raspberry balsamic dressing on the side."

The cafeteria worker gazed curiously across the counter. "Best choice we offer," he complimented her, adding, "You just got here, right? You're the new food blogger we just bought?"

Kerry gave a short laugh. "Well, yes…I do sort of feel as if I've been bought and sold. How'd you guess?"

He pointed at the ID around her neck.

"*And* you ordered the arugula with thin-sliced beef. Half the people who work here claim they're vegetarians or vegans, and besides, it's a new item and nobody wants to take a chance until I can tell them it's a favorite with some of the bigwigs." Tony Perez grinned as he began to assemble her order. "Also, I saw the announcement on the company website last week. Only a foodie would know what a killer salad this is," he said, his smile growing even wider. "I only added it to the menu on Monday."

Kerry smiled back, cheered by Tony's enthusiasm for his work as she took the plate piled high with fresh greens, topped with paper-thin slices of grass-fed beef—or so the menu card on the glass case asserted

"I'll let you know how I like it, but it looks wonderful."

"And tell me what you think of the salad dressing. It's made with locally-produced olive oil and raspberries from an organic farm just north of here."

Kerry was immediately intrigued.

"You sound very knowledgeable about what's going on in this neck of the woods. Can you give me the contact info for the local olive oil producer you mentioned?"

Tony shrugged. "Sure...I'll come over to your table before you leave. I'm just getting off my shift." He glanced at the clock that registered two p.m. "In fact, I was thinking about going over to Berkeley later this afternoon to pick up a case of Montisi Olive Oil at Amphora Nueva. Rumors are, they're just delivering their latest press."

"Really? It's just been released?"

"Yeah. The Montisi ranch is up north, near Petaluma, forty minutes from here in Sonoma." Tony hesitated and then blurted, "Wanna come with me to Berkeley? The olive oil store is fantastic! You won't believe how much stuff they stock from all over the world!"

The brash young man was obviously eager to make friends with his company's latest acquisition, despite his lowly status as "salad associate." Kerry admired his moxie. And besides, it appeared as if he might be well connected to the food scene in the Bay Area. She was already worried about keeping up with the crazy deadlines stipulated by the sweatshop contract she'd unwittingly signed.

She smiled at Tony. "The olive oil store sounds like it might make for a good first blog post, but you'd better let me see how I like the salad. Talk to you in a bit."

Kerry headed for a small table-for-two positioned away from the other diners. She was not in the mood to meet or talk to any of her fellow slaves. However, her spirits perked up the instant she sampled Tony Perez's leafy concoction. The fresh, peppery arugula was complemented by the full-flavored slices of delicious *carpaccio*, and the entire assemblage was wrapped in a smooth slurry of rich, fragrant olive oil with an after-burner hit of raspberry-flavored balsamic vinegar.

It was *brilliant*!

She was just rising from her chair to find Tony when the young man came bounding over.

"Well?" he demanded.

"It's absolutely wonderful!" she declared. "The blending of flavors and textures is first rate, and the *freshness* of all the ingredients—"

"Then you wanna go over to Berkeley with me? The people at Amphora Nueva are kinda friends of mine. They sell only the best stuff—and can tell you all about the scams in the olive oil biz!"

Tony's enthusiasm was infectious, but first she had to have it out with Charlie about the Addendum that he'd signed in her stead without telling her.

"What's your cell number?" she asked. "I just checked into my cube and I have a few things I need to take care of. Can I call you and let you know if I can make it? If not today, then I'd love to go there with you another time."

Tony whipped out his cell, got her email address and phone number, and sent her his contact information as well.

"I need to leave by no later than three-fifteen," he warned, "otherwise the traffic across the Bay Bridge is killer."

Kerry nodded, her thoughts careening between several story ideas based on what Tony had told her and her burning desire to tell Charlie Miller exactly what she thought of him for the second time in a single day.

"I'll call you either way," she promised. "And thanks! You've been the nicest thing that's happened since I got here."

Kerry figured that the quickest route to finding Charlie in the huge office complex was to ask for directions to Vice President Beverly Silverstein's office. Once there, however, another junior assistant type leapt up from a chair inside the glass-fronted conference room where Kerry spotted Charlie, along with their mutual boss and several other jeans-clad whiz kids, as well as a man who *might* have been approaching fifty.

Kerry wondered if the adult supervisor-looking guy was LifeStyleXer's CEO, Harry Chapman, gathered with his inner circle around the polished, oval glass table where one of their number was giving a Power Point presentation with a display of brightly colored pie charts.

Kerry heard a whoosh of air as a painfully thin young guard dog pushed open the conference room's glass door and rushed toward her before Kerry could rap her knuckles on the transparent wall and embarrass Charlie so he'd come out in the hall.

"I'm sorry, but you can't go in there...they're in a meeting," the twig of a woman added, stating the obvious. She swiftly handed Kerry an envelope as if she somehow knew the visitor was due to arrive. "Beverly said to give you this."

Startled, Kerry stared at the missive the young woman had practically shoved into her hands.

"What *is* this?"

"Your housing voucher for the W Hotel down the street. You have two weeks free lodging until you find a place to live," she said with a bright smile.

"*Two weeks?*" Kerry protested. "In a city with a zero vacancy rate and eleven blog deadlines from hell? That's ridiculous! Where will Charlie Miller and I keep our furniture when it arrives from New York?" she demanded.

Glancing worriedly over her shoulder, Beverly Silverstein's messenger grabbed Kerry by the arm and with surprising force for an anorexic, guided her a few feet down the hall toward the elevator.

"Shhh…there are some high-level discussions going on in there about the IPO!" she admonished. "I was told that Charlie would help you sort out your belongings when they came and—"

"*Charlie!*" she echoed, shocked that an underling would be on a first-name basis with an employee who had arrived less than two hours earlier. "How the hell do *you* know what that rat man Charlie Miller would or wouldn't do?"

She glared over her shoulder at the man himself who, by this time, had turned in his chair and was staring nervously back at her.

Kerry held his glance for a long moment as a warm, pulsing sensation flooded up her arm. She glanced down at the Claddagh ring whose center had turned pearly white.

Smile sweetly and make a dignified retreat!

The voice in her head was adamant and she chose, at that moment, to believe it was her own good sense that advised her to get away from the conference room as fast as her legs would carry her before she decked the young woman now clutching her other arm.

"Ah…okay, then," she said, tugging free.

For some reason she had a moment's sympathy for the messenger who had been tasked to give her such an ignominious brush-off. At a mere twenty-something, the poor, skinny excuse for a human being had already sold her soul.

Kerry somehow summoned a smile.

"You try to have a nice day, won't you?" she addressed her latest minder. "And when you get something to eat after the meeting—and I hope that you *will*—try the arugula and *carpaccio* salad in the cafeteria. It's fabulous!"

***

Kerry made fast work of checking into her assigned room at the W Hotel on Third and Howard streets where a reservation had been made in her name—only—by "LifeStyleXer's Vice President, Beverly Silverstein, *herself,*" the desk clerk admiringly informed the new guest. "I hear that's a cool company to work for," she added, noting, "I'm just finishing up my degree in computer science at SF State. Could I get in touch with you, Ms.—" she glanced down at the registration, "...Ms. Hannigan, when I graduate? Maybe you could put in a good word?"

Still steaming that Charlie's latest girlfriend had plotted every aspect of their arrival in San Francisco, Kerry grabbed her key card off the front desk and snapped, "Contact Beverly Silverstein directly and see how much she helps *you!*"

By three o'clock, she had unpacked her belongings, reached Tony Perez by mobile phone, and was standing curbside when a battered VW Jetta drew up to the hotel's entrance.

"Hop in...we gotta get over the bridge before it's bumper to bumper," he directed.

Traffic was sluggish, but moving, as they crossed the four-and-a-half mile expanse of water separating San Francisco from the East Bay communities of Oakland—and a few miles further north—Berkeley, the university community nestled into hillsides with spectacular views back to the city. Then a thought struck her.

"Isn't the Bay Bridge the one that collapsed in the earthquake?" she asked, suddenly apprehensive as she gazed out the car window at the enormous body of water whizzing by below.

"Way back in 1989," he assured her cheerfully, "but they've done a retrofit."

"Oh. Great. So…Tony," she asked, wanting not to think about either the bridge, incipient earthquakes, or the impossible situation that had so suddenly been thrust upon her today, "tell me, how did you became Salad Man at LifestyleXer?"

Tony, his eyes on the road, gave a short laugh.

"My parents were field workers, you know? From Mexico. I was the eldest, so I grew up making the meals for everyone in my family when they crawled home at the end of the day, down in Castroville." Tony paused, adding with a big grin, "You know Castroville, dontcha? 'Artichoke Capitol of the World?'"

Kerry nodded. She'd done her research about the agricultural bounty in California.

"Well, even as a little kid, I always liked to cook," he said with a shrug, "and when I flunked out of community college because I hated it—and I couldn't afford culinary school—I decided two years ago to get hands-on experience, here in the city, and learn as much as I can while I keep an ear out for a job at one of the top restaurants." He looked across the passenger seat and grimaced. "I know that sounds pretty cocky…that I could go from a cafeteria to a name restaurant…but I think I'm really good."

Kerry thought with a stab of guilt how Angelica had cheerfully spent more than fifty thousand dollars on Kerry's tuition at the CIA, and here was a guy willing to slave in a cafeteria to be able to do what he loved.

"Well…based on that salad of yours I ate today, I don't think you're too cocky at all. I'm guessing that you have everything it takes to become a great chef."

Tony's tanned complexion took on a glow, his pleasure at hearing her words obvious.

"Wow! And coming from *you*…double wow! Thanks!

And *I* guess this is the time I should admit I am a huge fan of your CookChic blog...and have been ever since you began posting."

Kerry was pleased by the fact that her blogs might be educating the next generation of great chefs and his kind words assuaged her guilt, somewhat, about not directly putting to use what she'd learned at the CIA.

Tony wound his car up Ashby Avenue, climbing successively higher into the Berkeley Hills with each turn in the road. At length, he made a right on Domingo and parked in the shadow of the massive Claremont Hotel, a shingled extravaganza from another era, he explained, that still hosted weddings and temporarily housed well-heeled out-of-towners visiting the UC Berkeley campus.

They parked and entered the cool confines of the "Amphora Nueva Olive Oil Works," as it said on the business card Kerry grabbed from the counter. In the next moment, she heard a man's voice call out at the rear of the shop to someone entering from the service door.

"Hey, Ren! Great to see ya! That's your latest? Well then, just wheel that dolly right in here, my friend. I can't wait to taste that first press of yours! We've all been waiting with bated breath."

"We are *so* in luck!" Tony whispered loudly. "The rumors were true! That's Renato Montisi *himself* back there," he added excitedly, nodding in the direction of the rear of the large room that had rows of two-foot-high stainless steel olive oil dispensers lined along the wall. "Montisi Ranch usually presses their olives in mid-to-late November, and then delivers soon after, and I guess today's the *day!*"

The store's proprietor walked up to the tall, good-looking figure he had hailed as "Ren" who had wheeled in his dolly loaded with a large, stainless steel drum. Printed on its circumference was an olive branch logo and the words MONTISI RANCH OLIVE OIL.

From across the store, Kerry absorbed the view of the six-foot, broad-shouldered man delivering his wares and felt an unexpected flutter in her chest at the sight of his full head of dark blond, wind-blown hair that was barely tamed by a pair of pricey Ray Ban sunglasses perched just above his tanned forehead. About her age—or perhaps a few years older—his high cheekbones and square jaw, along with trim arms that were also tanned despite its being early December, made him appear more like a sought-after ski instructor than a rancher. She could also easily imagine him in an expensive suit and tie, addressing an audience in the LifestyleXer boardroom. Yet, here he was, wearing jeans, work boots, and a brown T-shirt with the same Montisi Ranch logo stamped in khaki green across a muscular chest that couldn't help but capture a bystander's attention.

"Hey, how's everybody doing?" Ren asked of store owner Michael Bradley and his staff that had gathered in a circle around the dolly. "Yep, this is our latest press. Do you have some bread to give it a taste?"

"C'mon!" exhorted Tony in a harsh whisper. "Let's get in line!" He grabbed her arm and hustled toward the small crowd in the back. "Hi," he boldly addressed the group. "I'm Tony Perez and this is Kerry Hannigan, who just moved to San Francisco from New York. She's the CookChic food blogger and I brought her here because maybe she'll do a post about your latest product, Mr. Montisi...and also about the store," he added hastily to the owner of Amphora Nueva.

Both men turned to stare at the interlopers while Kerry could feel her pale complexion flush with color. She was embarrassed by Tony's brashness and a promise she'd write a blog about a new product she hadn't even tasted yet.

"Oh, please," she protested. "We don't mean to interrupt..."

The man who had just delivered his latest harvest met her glance and a moment later was smiling broadly.

"You're not interrupting," he said, extending his hand in greeting. As soon as Kerry felt his palm wrapped around hers, she sensed a curious vibration traveling from the ring finger of her right hand, straight to her chest. "I'm Ren Montisi, and—as a matter of fact—I subscribe to your blog, so I'm very aware that you know your stuff." He cast her a confident smile, releasing her hand. "You're just in time to give me your opinion of this year's first press."

"I-I love olive oil, but I'm certainly no tasting expert—"

"All I want is your unvarnished reaction as a consumer. We bottled this only last week."

Their eyes met and Kerry realized she was actually holding her breath. A strange current of...*what*? Excitement? Anticipation? Whatever the sensation was, Kerry had felt a second tremor pass from Ren's hand to her solar plexus.

"S-sure..." she managed to stammer. "I'll tell you what I think...honestly," she added in the name of journalism.

He took a few small cubes from a basket of bread cut from a French baguette that the store owner had handed him and offered one to her and another to Tony. Then he put a small porcelain saucer beneath the spigot on the steel drum and allowed a stream of green-golden olive oil to fill halfway to the rim.

"Everybody ready?" he asked, his gaze making a sweep of his audience. Despite his smile, Kerry thought she noticed tension gathering at the corners of his generous mouth.

By this time, several other customers had joined the small throng, each holding a cube of bread between forefinger and thumb. Kerry leaned forward, followed eagerly by Tony

Perez, and dipped her bread into the pool of oil, watching the bread quickly absorb the liquid like a miniature sponge.

She turned away from the group, popped the small square into her mouth, and allowed the bread and dripping oil to slide over her tongue. At first, there was a fresh, familiar taste of olives, soon followed by a sparkling, peppery finish she found utterly delicious. Like Tony's raspberry salad dressing, it was one of the most wonderful flavors she'd ever tasted!

She turned back and again locked glances with the creator of this liquid gold. Eyes wide with astonishment at the complex flavors flooding her taste buds, she continued to slowly chew the bread and finally swallowed it.

"Oh…wow," she pronounced on a long breath. "Oh, *really* wow! I have never tasted anything like this in my life!" She laughed and pointed to the big stainless steel drum, addressing the owner of Amphora Nueva. "Can you please decant about ten bottles of that for me?" she asked. "No, make that an even dozen."

Ren Montisi was blatantly staring, eyes crinkling with relief he couldn't disguise.

"No!" she assured him quickly, "I really mean it. I want to send this amazing stuff to friends as this year's Christmas presents, instead of wine." She took a step forward and gazed into amber eyes of variegated shades that reminded her of the colors in Central Park each autumn. With those amazing eyes and Ren's dark blond hair, she speculated that the original Montisis must hail from the north of Italy. She held his glance and said, "I truly think this may be the best olive oil on the planet."

"Have you been to Tuscany?" Ren asked.

"Yes, but I never tasted anything like this."

"Sometime, go to the little village of Montisi—not far

from Montepulciano—about forty miles south of Siena," he said, flashing a dazzling grin as he confirmed her conjecture about his family's origins. "The oil from the original Montisi groves rivals this...almost," he added, continuing to look at her with unnerving interest, which prompted her to glance down at the Claddagh ring, rather than drown in his steady gaze. Its stone was pure white and pulsing.

Ask for an interview. Go see the ranch where the oil is produced!

Kerry was about to open her mouth to repeat these thoughts aloud when Ren said, "Why don't you come see where we make this? We're hosting a bunch of food writers like yourself at the ranch tomorrow, which means you'll probably feel right at home. I'm sure Chef Jeremy can make room for one more place setting."

She glanced over her shoulder at Tony. "Tony Perez and I work for the same company now. He's in charge of salads at the LifestyleXer dot com cafeteria and is a big fan of your oil."

Ren's smile faded and he said, "Oh...well...perhaps since it's two of you—"

Tony shook his head sorrowfully. "I gotta work tomorrow, but Kerry can tell me all about it. It's her very first day in California, Mr. Montisi, and she can't miss out on something like this."

Kerry observed another of Ren Montisi's faintly devastating grins spread across his handsome features as he turned to the owner of Amphora Nueva.

"Well, now, why don't we decant thirteen bottles of Montisi's finest for these nice folks?"

***

Ten minutes later, Ren fished into his back jean's pocket

and brought out a business card imprinted with his ranch's logo that he handed to the young woman with the shoulder-length, jet black hair and totally arresting sapphire eyes. He couldn't believe his luck running into one of the major food bloggers in the country. And what a stunner! What was she doing in *this* store on *this* day, he marveled?

"Here's where you come tomorrow," he explained. "Do you think you can find your way to us? On a Saturday, it should take you about forty-fifty minutes up Highway 101 from the city. We'll be serving wine and iced tea and a few things to nibble on at twelve and we'll sit down to lunch at about quarter to one."

He'd never wanted anyone to accept an invitation to see the ranch as much in his life as he did Kerry Hannigan. Jeremy had been the first to talk about her blog and her philosophy about how America should eat food grown close to its source. "The Hundred-Mile Diet" had become a cliché in Northern California, at least, but the woman standing only a few feet from him had a way of telling stories within her blog posts that won his rapt attention and admiration from the first time he'd read her work.

He would never admit to anyone that he'd studied her picture on her website late one evening, but it was nothing compared to seeing first hand that lovely pale skin with cheeks that blushed when she was excited, as he'd observed earlier when she'd tasted the oil-infused cube of bread. And despite all the food she must consume for her job, she had a slender figure, but one with curves right where they should be. She couldn't be more than five-feet-four, which was so different from—

He didn't want to make comparisons. Studying Kerry Hannigan's every gesture, he had the strangest inclination to take her in his arms to see if she'd fit snugly under his chin…

She was talking to him now, he realized with a start.

"Would it be possible to show up at your ranch...say, at ten-thirty," she inquired politely, "so I could do a quick interview and you could show me the olive groves and your production facility before the hordes arrive? And may I take some photos for my blog?"

"Absolutely, but can you make that eight-thirty?" Ren countered and then grimaced. "I know that's ridiculously early, but I've got to be on tap for my staff getting ready for that big busload of your fellow writers due to arrive sometime before noon. That way, we can walk the groves and see the vegetable garden and the lavender fields, and then sit down in my office with some coffee to talk before things get too hectic."

"Perfect!" she exclaimed, and he was exhilarated to see by the color staining her cheeks, evidence that she was clearly excited at the prospect of visiting the ranch.

"And if you have a tight deadline tomorrow," he ventured, "while we wait for the other food writers to arrive—or after they depart—you can use my computer, if you want or need to. I'll be busy being the genial host."

He was determined to offer the woman every courtesy to smooth the way for a possible mention in her influential blog. If she used his office, he thought with a sudden sense of pleasure that raised his flagging spirits, she'd hang around the ranch a little longer and that would be great on its own merits.

Ren struggled to bring his thoughts back to the business at hand. A relieved expression lit up her lovely features.

"Borrowing your computer would be a huge help," she said. "I've just been assigned an extra blog post every Saturday, so I'll definitely take you up on your offer after everyone leaves, if I may."

"It'll be all yours," he said with a laugh. "By then I'll be on cleanup duty."

It seemed like some sort of miracle that this amazingly talented star of the food world wanted to tour his family's domestic olive oil operation and taste Jeremy's wonderful food made from ingredients grown within steps of their commercial kitchen.

Finally, he thought, the Montisi Olive Ranch and its manager might be getting a few breaks, as a spreadsheet flashed through his mind with some discouraging profit-and-loss totals at the bottom.

For Kerry's part, Renato Montisi would have been amazed to know what was whirling in her head as the clerk assembled the bottles of olive oil on the desk and began to wrap each one for transport to her friends and relatives on the East Coast.

Her mind was filled with a sense of what she could only describe as unbridled euphoria. Thanks to this astounding meet-up, not only would she get to interview the personable producer of a wonderful artisanal product, she'd also meet a raft of fellow food writers in *person,* instead of merely online. Even better, she already knew she'd get at least three or four blog posts out of seeing the olive groves, the bottling facility, and dining with nationally known culinary critics. Maybe she could even *recruit* some of them to do what she did, but in their own cities?

Relief swept over her at the thought that in one fell swoop, she could make her first week's crushing deadlines and suggest some viable names with whom to launch the LifestyleXer/CookChic brand in ten major markets, as she was contractually obligated.

And it had all happened on her first day in California! She glanced at her right hand. Surely the Claddagh ring couldn't take credit for *everything*?

Tony broke into her jumble of thoughts.

"You can borrow my car tomorrow," he offered, almost worshipfully, his attention glued—not on her—but on the bottles of olive oil that Amphora Nueva's proprietor had already decanted and had handed to him, corks firmly in place.

"Thanks," Kerry replied, turning to offer her new friend her heartfelt appreciation. "That's very sweet of you, but I'll just lease a rental." To Ren Montisi she added, "This is *so* nice of you to make time for me, given all that you have to do tomorrow. I'm really grateful—and I absolutely love your olive oil!"

She lowered her eyes with embarrassment in reaction to Ren's look of mild amazement. Was he so unaccustomed to such high praise for his wonderful product, she wondered?

He's intrigued with you, *you ninny!*

Startled, she glanced down again at her right hand in time to see the ring wink in a flash of white. She moved closer to the counter where she gave the clerk a credit card for the twelve bottles that had been filled for her at the back of the store, and then insisted on paying for Tony's as well.

"You told me about this place and drove us here," she announced firmly.

She seized the pen to sign the purchase slip and couldn't help but notice that the ring's emerald gemstone had once again turned opalescent. The next thing she knew, the voice in her head rang out for the third time since entering the shop.

Good going, my girl! Today's events will prove excellent for more than just your blog...

***

On Saturday morning, Kerry was thankful for her rental car's GPS that easily guided her through the empty streets at seven-thirty a.m. in downtown San Francisco to the Golden Gate Bridge that led north to Marin and Sonoma counties. She felt a thrill as the two orange-colored steel towers rose up, reassuring beacons that she was on the right road. She gave a quick glance to her left and took in the wide expanse of the Pacific Ocean where the morning sun spread a layer of gold stretching all the way to China, it seemed. On her right side, the enormous oval that was San Francisco Bay was dotted with a few large and small craft making ivory trails in the churning waters around Alcatraz and Angel islands.

Less than forty minutes later, just as Renato Montisi had directed, she took the exit before Petaluma Boulevard and followed successively narrower roads through gently rolling hills dotted with oak trees and cattle, until she spotted a wooden sign carved with bas-relief olives on a branch of a tree. She made a left turn down a tarmac road that wound into its own eight-hundred-acre valley with groves of sage green olive trees marching up and down the hills on either side of her car.

Kerry inhaled deeply of air scented faintly with lavender and rosemary and thought she'd landed squarely in some uncharted corner of heaven. At the next bend in the road she noted that an entire field was planted, not with olive trees, but with rows and rows of lavender bushes, devoid of blooms in December, but stately in the way their sage stalks blew gently in the morning breeze.

She passed through a pair of stone stanchions, drove another quarter mile on hard-packed dirt, rolled to a stop on a wide, gravel turn-round and spotted Ren, once again clad in jeans and work boots. Today, he looked handsomer than ever in a collared, dark green polo shirt, no doubt worn in honor of the impending arrival of the nation's top food writers.

He advanced toward her across the parking area in front of a low-slung, corrugated steel building she assumed housed the olive pressing facility. Two Labradors—one black, one chocolate-colored—danced excitedly around their master.

"Meet Scusi and Prego," he announced as she emerged from her car's driver side. He pointed to his left. "Ciao, the barn cat, is in the lavender bushes over there. C'mon, hop into my truck for the Grand Tour. The dogs will follow us and get some exercise as I show you the ranch."

Kerry gingerly climbed into his truck's cab, happy she'd decided against wearing a sundress and sling-back heels in favor of a tapered pair of navy trousers, rubber-soled red flats, and a navy-and-white striped sweater with a red cardigan slung across her shoulders.

"It's really great you're willing to spend some time with me at such an early hour and before that gaggle of food critics descends on you for lunch."

"Best part of the day," he said, briefly glancing across the truck's passenger seat and offering her a mildly rueful grimace. "Actually, I was worried because my chef was a bit under the weather this week, but everything seems well in hand this morning." He piloted his khaki colored pickup truck along a road flanked by an expanse of olive trees in all directions. "Ah..." he said, pointing through the windshield, "here's the view I wanted you to see."

The pair exited the truck and stood on a rise that offered a panoramic vista of gentle hills intersected by even more rows of mature olive trees. The groves were bordered by another collection of waist-high lavender bushes.

"The flowers make their appearance in May and June, as do swarms of bees which, as you probably know, are essential to propagating all sorts of things we grow here."

Kerry concluded that the plants' mere presence accounted for the faint scent in the air she had detected earlier and that she loved so much. In the distance were several more lavender fields, "to encourage as many bees as possible to visit us," he elaborated.

She cast a sweeping gaze at the entire landscape and said softly, "We could be in Tuscany right now. It's...just gorgeous." She glanced sideways and was struck by the faintly Roman cast to Ren's profile. "I bet your family couldn't believe this scenery when they first saw it."

"Exactly right," he answered, indicating they should continue down the dirt road on foot. "The story goes that the minute that my great-grandfather, Renato Montisi, Senior, arrived from Italy and saw this land just before the turn of the twentieth century, he and his wife had just enough money to buy ten acres. Every cent he earned thereafter went into purchasing the other seven hundred and ninety."

"So your grandparents and parents chose to raise olives, too, instead of grapes?" asked Kerry. "Isn't it pretty rare that a family business survives more than three generations?"

"Well, in our case, it didn't," Ren replied, staring off into the distance. "Except for naming me after *his* grandfather, my father was the rebel. Went to law school at Cal and wanted nothing much to do with ranching after that." He paused and then continued. "Both my parents died in a private plane crash flying out of Palm Springs in bad weather. I came to live here with Nona Concetta when I was twelve. My grandfather, Renato, Junior, died three years ago, so I chucked Silicon Valley—which, trust me—I was only too happy to do," he added with a grim smile, "and took on the management of the ranch from my grandmother, who will be ninety-two next year."

Kerry thought of Angelica and how much she missed her already, wondering what Ren's grandmother was like, a woman a decade older?

By this time, Prego and Scusi had caught up with them and followed in their wake down a steep section of the road that ended in a small creek bed at the bottom of the ravine.

Kerry stole a quick look at her host's left hand and asked, "And so...you are the third Renato Montisi, yes? Is there a Renato Quattro you'll be training to take over here someday?"

After all, not every man wore a wedding ring.

Ren shot her a puzzled look. "You're asking am I married, and do I have children?"

Kerry flushed, embarrassed by her obvious probe. She expected some sort of scolding jolt to shoot up her arm from the Claddagh ring, but felt no such sensation. Before she could apologize, however, Ren turned to meet her glance.

"Yes, I was married, but no children. My wife died several years ago as a result of a skiing accident."

"Oh," she said on a swift intake of breath. "Oh, I am *so* sorry, Ren. You've lost your parents *and* your wife, and your grandfather, too. That's awful...and I apologize for bringing it up. I was just being a nosy reporter."

She was startled when he placed his hand on her arm and gave a slight shake of the head.

"You don't need to apologize. You wanted to know about the ranch and my role here. It's fine. Really."

Once again, at his touch, a strange tingling spread up her arm and the moment seemed suspended in space as if they'd slipped off the time wheel and were simply *there* together with clear, crystalline space surrounding them.

Ren turned and pointed. The tree-filled hills came back into focus.

"Would you like to see how honest olive oil is made?" he asked.

All Kerry could manage was to offer a slight nod and follow him back uphill to where he'd parked his pickup truck.

Chapter Four

Kerry's breathing had almost returned to normal by the time they'd driven back to the gravel parking lot. Once inside the low-slung bottling facility, Ren gave her a quick rundown about the process of the mill turning olives into Montisi Extra Virgin Olive Oil.

"These large stainless steel troughs are where the olives are separated from the leaves and branches, washed, and eventually pressed by that large, revolving stone disk over there that crushes the fruit and extracts the liquid," he explained.

"Olives are fruits?"

"Yep. They grow on trees and have pits, so they qualify," he said with a laugh. "This first pressing—done 'cold' without heat or chemicals and hence, the term 'Extra Virgin'—eventually ends up in large vats before being decanted into bottles like the ones you purchased at Amphora Nueva, or the oil is stored in stainless steel drums."

"Like the one I saw you deliver to them yesterday, yes?"

Ren nodded, continuing, "Unlike wine, olive oil is best when used as soon after it's harvested as possible." He pointed to a bottle sitting on a nearby counter. "See...we stamp the *harvest* date, not the bottling date—which, with some outfits, can be a couple of *years* after the olives are picked and pressed." He pointed to a back shelf. "There are a few dusty bottles sitting there from last year that are probably rancid by now."

"Is it true there is a certain amount of fraud and misleading advertising in your business?" she asked, suddenly putting on her reporter's hat.

"Just read Tom Mueller's book *Extra Virginity* and you'll learn all you need to know about that subject."

Kerry nodded. "I read the original piece Mueller did for *The New Yorker*, which got him the book contract, I heard. So you agree with his analysis?"

Ren grimaced. "Not only do I agree, I'm living with the consequences of my product being undercut by mislabeled olive oil posing as Extra Virgin...but that's a longer conversation." He stole a glance at his wristwatch. "Want to have a quick tour of the ranch's kitchen garden? Then, I've really got to check in with our chef and staff about today's lunch."

"Are you sure you have time to show it to me? You could just point me in the right direction and then direct me to your office. I promise I'll stay out of your way until my fellow foodies arrive." She was grateful that he had been willing to spend so much time with her, given the imminent arrival of some serious VIPs.

"We've just got time. I want you to see every carrot and herb plant, 'cause I'm hoping you get at least five blogs out of what you've seen today," he teased, pointing toward a screen door and guiding her outside the olive mill and into the parking lot again.

All during their tour she had been snapping photos on her iPhone and paused to take a picture of Scuzi, Prego, and the barn cat named Ciao. The three animals were outside the building waiting patiently for Ren to reappear.

"If these cute guys have any specific jobs around the ranch, I can even do a blog about *them*," she proposed, a giddy feeling of sheer happiness bubbling in her chest at the sight of Ren's faithful companions. She adored animals, but had never been allowed to have a pet as a child in Manhattan. And Charlie had been allergic to anything with four feet—or so he said.

"Scuzi and Prego are actually very effective watchdogs and chase off their fair share of coyotes and raccoons, and Ciao is in charge of catching mice wherever she finds them."

Kerry quickly snapped a series of pet portraits. "I'll post their story next Saturday," she said, chuckling, "but today's blog will definitely be about the food writers lunch."

That'll take care of that pesky extra blog they expect you to do!

Kerry didn't have time to speculate whose pronouncement had just sailed through her mind as she concentrated on keeping up with Ren's long strides leading toward the magnificent vegetable and fruit garden laid out at the back of a cluster of one-story buildings that served the various activities at the ranch.

"We planted half an acre of mostly vegetables a few steps from the door to our big kitchen where the food for the ranch's special events is prepared," he explained.

They had only walked twenty feet along the path that cut between the herb beds and pole bean plots when Kerry heard Ren's cellphone emit an insistent sound. He fished the device out of his jeans pocket and stared at a text.

"Oh boy...this is *not* good."

"What?" Kerry said.

Ren's voice conveyed his alarm. He showed her his text message.

Major emergency. Chef sick.

"Oh, no! Do you have a sous chef?" Kerry asked,

knowing precisely how dire this situation could be, given that a busload of national food writers were due at the ranch within a few hours.

He punched in a text message.

"Yes, I've just told Jeremy's assistant, Sara Lang, to call for an ambulance."

"How far along is your prep?"

"Let's go see," Ren said, heading toward the kitchen door some fifty feet from where they were standing. "Jeremy Garafola is a terrific chef and a great guy and he'd never—"

By this time, they had both burst into the main room of the separate building that housed the kitchen, only to see a large bald-headed man in white chef's attire doubled over on a bench next to the farmhouse dining table. At the sink stood a stocky young Mexican-American who was washing dishes. As they entered, he cast his employer a worried glance.

Meanwhile, a woman about Kerry's age with long blond pigtails draped down the back of her white chef's jacket like a cast member from *Little House on the Prairie* was yelling into the phone attached to a nearby wall.

"Well, how *long* before you can get here?" she demanded shrilly. "We need *help* with this Goddamned luncheon, Tommy! I can't do this all by myself. Jeremy is toast! We're waiting for an ambulance, you jerk! Well, screw *you!*" And she slammed down the receiver.

"Take it easy, Sara," Ren admonished sharply, and then leaned over to bring his face even with Jeremy who was clutching his midsection and gasping with pain.

"God, I'm sorry, boss. This came on so suddenly. One minute I was fine, and the next—"

"It's going to be all right, buddy," Ren reassured him. "Just hold on. The Sonoma County cavalry is on its way, right, Sara?"

"Well, I hope so!" she snapped. "I called them right after you texted back." She turned her attention toward Kerry. "Who are *you*?" she demanded. "I want this kitchen clear of visitors, Ren! We have enough problems without—"

"This is Kerry Hannigan," Ren cut in. "She's a graduate of the CIA and a well-known food blogger. And she's *my* guest today at the food writers luncheon, so cool your jets, will you, Sara?"

"Well, how do you expect there to *be* a food writers lunch with this mess, Renato!" she shouted, and Kerry sensed the woman was on her way to a complete meltdown.

An amateur in the kitchen...

Kerry surveyed the counters. A big bundle wrapped in white butcher paper and marked SALMON FILETS had yet to be opened. Piles of winter root vegetables, including carrots, turnips and beets, along with Brussels sprouts, were draining on a sideboard—uncut. On the marbled pastry counter it appeared that Sara, her cheeks smudged with flour, had been working on making Parker House rolls. Close by, a big bag of sugar stood, unopened, probably waiting for someone to prepare the dessert.

Just then, sirens could be heard as a county fire truck and an ambulance pulled up outside. Ren dashed through the screen door.

"In here, fellas..." he shouted and within minutes, the groaning chef was strapped on a gurney and wheeled toward the door. "Sara, you go with him!" Ren ordered. "Make sure he has his wallet with his insurance information."

"But—"

"I mean it," barked Ren. "You ride in the ambulance with him and text me when the hospital can confirm what's wrong. José and I will handle the lunch. Now, get *going!*"

"Are you crazy!" she screeched. "You can't even fry eggs

and José is nothing but a glorified bus boy! Send *him* in the ambulance—"

"We're going to *need* a bus boy today, and a sous chef, and a hard worker, and José is all three. Now do what I say!" he insisted.

"Or *what?*" she hissed, her eyes shifting over to Kerry. "You'll recruit Ms. CIA to replace me...after all I've done around here!"

"Will you just do what I'm asking?" Ren said measuring out his words equally.

Sara shot both Kerry and the hapless José equally poisonous glares and stormed out behind the EMT brigade. Kerry was relieved to see the woman sprint into a nearby building that looked as if it might have been a former bunkhouse and quickly emerge with a wallet in her hand. Soon, the sirens began to wail once more, and the two red vehicles disappeared up the ranch road in a cloud of dust.

Kerry glanced at her watch. It was ten o'clock in the morning.

"Well...Mr. Montisi...José," she said with a sense of excitement she hadn't felt since the meal she'd produced for her "finals" at the Culinary Institute of America, "it's two hours to Show Time. Let me lend you a hand."

For Kerry, the next hours were a complete blur as José readied the outdoor grill—located just steps from the kitchen door—and prepared the root vegetables for roasting, after which they'd be finished on the open fire, along with the salmon which would be cooked, al fresco, at the last minute.

Kerry donned a long white chef's apron that hung to her ankles and immediately went to work creating a dill aioli sauce for the salmon from a giant jar of mayonnaise, lemon, fresh garlic, Ren's olive oil, along with fresh herbs she cut from the kitchen garden when she raced out to gather a huge basket of greens for the salad.

"Be sure to mention to the tour guide that we made both the dressing and salmon sauce with Montisi Extra Virgin Olive Oil," she urged Ren with an encouraging smile, hoping to calm the near-panic atmosphere in the kitchen. For her part, she'd felt nothing but a soaring sense of exhilaration, up to her elbows in fresh ingredients.

The heart knows, doesn't it, Kerry?

Ignoring the Claddagh's latest little message, Kerry thrust a small lettuce leaf into the dressing, sampled it, and added another large dollop of Napa Valley Mustard, an additional plump garlic clove, and several more grinds of cracked pepper.

"Here...taste this," she urged. She dipped another piece of lettuce into the dressing, popped it into Ren's open mouth, and experienced a strange sense of intimacy in that simple gesture. "What do you think?"

Ren chewed slowly, his eyes closed. Then he opened them.

"I think it's genius." Their glances locked. "I think *you're* genius."

"Let's wait till this meal is served before you say that," she cautioned, busying herself with tidying up the cutting board so Ren wouldn't see the damnable color she could feel flooding her cheeks.

I met this man yesterday! Cool it!

She shifted her gaze to the ring on her right finger. The heart-shaped emerald remained green as green could be.

While the rolls were baking, the "Three Musketeers," as Kerry dubbed the efficient team of Ren, José, and herself, raced outdoors to set individual tables positioned around an open-air pavilion—designed and built to Grandmother Concetta's exact specifications, Ren explained.

"Thank God there's no wind today. We have outdoor heaters in the barn but they'd be a bitch to haul over here."

"No time, anyway," Kerry agreed. "But no worries…it's going to be a fine California day." She pointed to the thick beams supporting the building's tile roof. "How in the world did you find someone to build something so authentic? It's absolutely beautiful and completely in keeping with everything else on the ranch."

"Concetta tracked down the son of a craftsman her father-in-law knew in Tuscany and had it built in Montisi, shipped in pieces to the ranch, and reassembled here. She planted every one of the wisteria vines you see winding around each pillar."

The terracotta Italian floor tiles beneath the roof had been installed on a broad promontory overlooking olive groves that marched up and down several hills barely a football field from where they stood. A heavy basket of cutlery in her arms, Kerry paused to stare at the panorama surrounding them.

"Good heavens, this is *another* gorgeous view! And to think you grew up here." Then, she turned and abruptly asked Ren, "What did you plan for centerpieces?"

His expression went blank and he asked the question of José in Spanish, who timidly stammered, "Señorita Sara…non…"

"No worries," Kerry repeated swiftly. "You expect thirty-two guests, plus the driver and tour guide, right? Which means we should set seven tables with about five guests each, don't you think? Didn't I see some small pots of succulents on the back patio? José could wipe the pots clean, wrap them in those colorful tea towels I saw piled up in the pantry, and put them on the tables, along with pitchers of ice water with thinly-sliced lemons, and we're good to go."

"Brilliant!" Ren agreed, and translated Kerry's idea to José, who sprinted off to collect terracotta pots of local cacti, while Ren and Kerry doled out the silverware and linen napkins.

They were just putting the final touches to the table settings when Kerry suddenly exclaimed, "What was Jeremy serving for dessert?"

Ren's expression of alarm showed the anxiety he had managed, thus far, to keep under control.

"Some fruit tart thing, I think," Ren said. "Sara was up to her elbows in flour yesterday, but I didn't see anything stored in the big cooler, did you?"

By this time, José had returned with a wheelbarrow full of clay pots, so Ren inquired about the dessert course. José grimaced and answered in rapid Spanish, with doleful looks in Kerry's direction.

"José says Sara's efforts didn't quite work out so Jeremy decided this morning that he'd make pumpkin *crème brûlée*," he announced with a groan.

Kerry fanned her right hand through the air. "Piece of cake...or I should say, piece of 'custard!' Canned or fresh pumpkin?" In response to Ren's apologetic shrug, she turned on her heel and sped toward the kitchen, shouting over her shoulder, "Never mind. This is an emergency...and I'm betting your chef said he could substitute this dessert because he knew he had ten tins of pumpkin on reserve in his pantry!"

Amazingly, all was in readiness when the sleek black

Sonoma Tours buses, fresh from several stops at nearby wineries, rolled up, spilling out their occupants who were obviously feeling no pain.

"Lucky for us they're already three sheets to the wind," mumbled Ren out of the corner of his mouth as the two of them stood by to greet the arriving guests.

"Everything will be *fine*," Kerry whispered. "You play host and get them seated and their drinks filled, and I'll send out José with our *very* simple vegetable hors d'oeuvres and more wine. Then come back as soon as you can and we can get you grilling the salmon, which only will take a few minutes to cook and can be served at room temperature. Meanwhile, I'll toss the salad and start plating everything else."

Ren shot her a look of pure gratitude as he took several steps forward to extend his hand in greeting to the food writers.

"Well, hello," he addressed a large-boned woman first out of the bus and wearing an outsized floppy straw hat. "Welcome to the Montisi Olive Ranch. We're *so* delighted you can join us today…"

The Three Musketeers did double duty as wait staff with Kerry instructing them in her "swarm technique" whereby each guest at a table was given a plate of food before the next table was served.

"There's nothing worse than waiting for the last person to have a plate put down in front of them," she said under her breath, and then smiled prettily at the woman Ren had first greeted off the bus whom Kerry recognized as the food critic for a major newspaper back East.

Blog material alert!

She almost laughed out loud when she glanced down at the Claddagh ring glowing a shade paler than its normal emerald green.

"All right...yes, I hear you!" she muttered, sprinting back to the kitchen to line up on a serving tray three dozen ramekins of perfectly-baked pumpkin *crème brûlées* that had been cooked while their guests were having their lunch.

She picked up the device all serious chefs, including Jeremy Garafola, had in their kitchen arsenals: a mini blowtorch to perform the final touch on the desserts. She had just finished caramelizing the last crust of melted sugar when Ren burst into the kitchen, slightly breathless, with José padding into the room behind him.

"What are you, some kind of witch woman?" Ren marveled with an approving glance at the array of desserts. "José's bussed the luncheon plates into bins we hid behind the pillars and this wild bunch are happily asking about the final course." He watched admiringly as Kerry put a dollop of freshly whipped organic cream on the top of each dessert, plus a thin sliver of mandarin orange and a sprinkle of candied ginger she'd discovered in the larder. "These are absolutely stellar," he proclaimed.

"And you can say every scrap of what we served came from the ranch or Sonoma County, yes?"

"Well, at least from Northern California. The fresh salmon were caught further north of here. The vegetables and salad came from the ranch, and the pumpkins are grown and canned in the Central Valley. So, I guess we *can* say it's all grown or produced in our state."

"Close enough for government work," Kerry replied, and handed the first heavy tray of desserts to José. "Let's rock n' roll!"

Ren picked up the second tray while Kerry led them out the kitchen door, down the brick path, and into the pavilion, her heart soaring with a sense of accomplishment.

As soon as the threesome appeared bearing the desserts, the entire assembly of food writers began to clap.

The diners were soon dipping into their *crème brûlées*. One by one, they rose from their seats and began to shout "Chef! Chef! Chef!"

From the sidelines where the Musketeers deposited their trays after serving dessert, Ren stepped forward and gave a nod of acknowledgment to Kerry, whereby Kerry nodded emphatically back at Ren—then they burst out laughing. Impulsively, she seized both Ren and José's hands, and together, she urged the three of them a few steps forward nearer their applauding guests and the trio took an impromptu bow.

The food writers' approval swelled and the kitchen staff found themselves surrounded by smiling, appreciative diners. Kerry felt her hand vibrating and was not at all surprised to hear a now familiar voice resonate in her head.

Brava! This is what it feels *like to follow your heart, Kerry, m'girl...*

The sun was beginning to sink behind one of the western hills when the last of the black wine tour busses slowly rolled across the gravel parking lot with its load of food writers and headed for San Francisco and another "dining experience" at one of the city's top restaurants. Before they'd left, Ren had given the visitors his "Grand Tour," along with bottled sample miniatures of his celebrated olive oil.

Kerry glanced at her watch and gave a little yelp.

"Oh, Jeez! I have less than an hour before my next blog

deadline! Could I sit in your office and write my piece on your computer? I had no idea what time it has gotten to be."

"Of course," Ren promptly agreed. "Let me get you set up in that building over there while José and I start the cleanup. I also want to call Sara and find out what's happened with Jeremy."

"Yes, the poor guy was in the back of my mind all day," she said. "You haven't gotten a text from Sara?"

Ren pulled his cellphone out of his pocket and shook his head. "Nothing. And that's not a good sign."

"No," Kerry agreed worriedly, "it's probably not."

No sooner had Ren turned on his computer in a building next to the kitchen then they saw a taxi making its way down the ranch's entrance road. They heard the passenger door slam and Sara Lang emerged. Ren went to the screen door and called out.

"Hey, Sara! In here! I was just about to give you a call. What's the latest?"

Sara, looking weary and out-of-sorts, marched through the door and threw herself onto a leather easy chair in the corner of Ren's Spanish-tiled office.

"God, what a day!" Then she noticed Kerry sitting at Ren's desk. "*You're* still here?"

"Kerry saved our bacon, actually," Ren intervened with annoyance. "She pitched in and we managed to pull off the lunch...quite nicely, as it turned out."

"Well, bully for both of you," Sara responded, closing her eyes and heaving a groan. "You had a lot more fun than I did, I can tell you that."

"How's Jeremy?" Ren pressed. "Did they find out what's wrong with him?"

"Gallstones. He might have to have an operation." Sara opened her eyes and looked briefly at Kerry and then back at

Ren. "He said to tell you that he'd be on the phone to you tomorrow and will let me know what I need to do to keep things going. Apparently, there are a few tours of nobodies scheduled next week. Nothing I can't handle," she added with another pointed glance in Kerry's direction.

"Let's talk about this in the kitchen," Ren said. "Kerry's on deadline for her blog and needs some peace and quiet."

"Does she, now?" Sara snapped. "Well, I need a drink and then it's bedtime, don't you think? I'm completely whacked after that miserable mission you sent me on today. You owe me, big time, darling Renato."

Startled by this statement, Kerry quickly looked down at the computer keyboard and began typing the slug line that identified the name of her blog, the sequence number, and date it was due to post.

Bedtime? 'Darling Renato?' What's with that?

Jeremy's medical escort asked no details about how the luncheon went, nor offered anymore particulars about the chef's condition, but rather, stomped on ahead of the ranch manager in apparent high dungeon.

Drama queen!

As Sara and Ren left the office, Kerry turned back to the blank computer screen and forced herself by sheer habit to concentrate. Soon, she began typing furiously, relating the tale of the cooking emergency at the Montisi Olive Ranch, along with pictures she'd snapped of the plated fare she'd helped serve. She included a wide shot of the seven round tables with diners holding up their wine glasses in an impromptu salute. It had been a thrilling day, one during which she felt alive and at the top of her game. The entire experience was marred only by the heavy presence of the woman who had just arrived and made it clear she wished Ren's visitor would go away.

Kerry contemplated the blog post she'd just produced, and as an afterthought, she decided to include her recipe for the dill aioli sauce served on the salmon that had earned her kudos even before the standing ovation for the pumpkin *brûlée*. After rereading her prose to catch any typos, she pushed the Publish button and sank back in the expanse of Ren Montisi's desk chair.

She was aware of a warm, comforting sensation of being embraced by a half circle of well-worn leather that, daily, surrounded the very nice man with whom she had worked side-by-side this amazing Saturday.

Then she thought of Sara and her obvious possessiveness when it came to her employer. The situation had all the hallmarks of being quite dicey and one—given Kerry's own recent troubles as a third wheel—she wanted no part of. She wondered if she shouldn't just leave a note of thanks on Ren's desk, retreat to her rental car, and head back to San Francisco? She was bone weary herself after the day's momentous events, and, like Sara, wanted nothing more than to collapse on her 600 thread count sheets at the W Hotel.

Say goodbye in person! It's merely good manners...

With a sigh, Kerry saved her work in her Dropbox account, shut down Ren's computer, turned out the office lights, and walked up the brick path to the lighted kitchen.

Through the screen, she saw that Ren was seated in a chair next to the long wooden farmhouse table, while Sara was stretched out on the small sofa adjacent. Each had a glass of wine and appeared deep in conversation in the otherwise deserted room. The tableau looked comfortable—and familiar—as if the pair might actually be more to each other than merely employee and boss. Kerry hesitated, and then gave a light rap on the screen door.

"I'm taking off," she announced, "and just wanted to say

thanks again, Ren, for the tour and our interview today."

"Weren't we going to continue the interview in my office?" he asked, swiftly rising from his straight-backed chair.

"I can email you any additional questions I have for the other blogs I'll do this week."

"You made your deadline?"

"Yep." She took a step into the room and nodded at Sara. "I hope Jeremy is better tomorrow and can avoid surgery. Please tell him I said hello." She turned to Ren. "He bought beautiful salmon. I can tell that guy is definitely an ace in the kitchen. 'Night, all."

"At least let me walk you to your car," Ren proposed quickly. "Or better yet, stay for a bit and have a glass of pinot with us."

This time, the voice in her head gave her a real start.

Say yes to the wine!

Kerry gave a small shake of her head. She was already trying to extricate herself from the gnarly threesome of Charlie, Beverly, and herself, and did not need another similar situation in her life, especially sensing the sulk that Sara had sunk into as soon as Kerry—whom she clearly considered an unwanted interloper—walked through the kitchen door.

"It's getting late, so no wine for me, thanks," she said, trying to sound casual, "but I'd say yes to walking me to the car. I'm a city girl and—"

"Remember, the dogs and the cat keep the critters away," he said with a smile as he took her arm and escorted her out of the kitchen.

Kerry sensed hostile eyes boring into their backs as they trod the path with Prego and Scuzi following along behind. They strolled down the slight incline to the big parking lot where Kerry's economy rental had nearly disappeared in the gloom. When they reached the vehicle parked under the canopy of a palm tree sitting in an enormous planter box, Ren took the keys from her hand and clicked open the lock.

"I can never thank you adequately for what you did today," he began. "It was nothing short of a miracle that we pulled off that luncheon with such quality—and style— and it was entirely due to you."

He leaned against the car's roof, his face only inches from hers.

"No...it wasn't just me. We were the Three Musketeers, remember?"

The night sky was now studded with a million stars, thanks to the Montisi Ranch being folded into a valley far from city lights. Ren pointed out the Big and Little Dipper and the North Star as she heard the dogs patrolling along the lavender hedges nearby.

"It's so *quiet*," she whispered.

"Listen, though, and you'll begin to hear the night sounds...birds rustling...the wind through the olive trees..."

They remained absolutely still and Kerry felt Ren's tall frame radiating a heat that made her want to draw closer to stay warm against the dropping temperature. She wondered if she were imagining, too, the spark of an electric current that seemed steadily to grow stronger, compelling this near-stranger to lean down...and maybe even take her in his arms...

Startled by this thought, she turned and reached for the car door.

"What an amazing day," she said, pulling it open, an action that required Ren to take a step backward. "I loved every minute of my visit, and I really appreciated the tour of the ranch and all the good material I have for future blog posts." She cast him a sideways glance. "The one I just wrote about today went 'live' a few minutes ago. Any sharing on the Montisi Facebook page would be most welcome, especially since this will be my first blog written in California and all eyes will be watching at LifeStyleXer."

"Done!" he pronounced. "Or at least, done as soon as I get back to my office tonight." Then he added, "Where can I be in touch with you in case I have anything else to add?"

Kerry had trouble suppressing a grin while she fished out her cellphone and zapped him her contact information.

"It's probably best to text me, though," she explained. "I'll be pretty busy cranking out eleven blogs this week and following up on getting some of your guests I met today to sign on to blog about food and restaurants in their various cities." She smiled at Ren with heartfelt gratitude. "You were really great to let me recruit a few of them before they all got back on the bus. It was my only chance and—"

"Glad to be of assistance and I hope some of them pan out." He looked at her somberly. "Your new bosses have piled a lot on your plate, haven't they?"

Kerry nodded and gave a short laugh.

"They also expect me to find my own place to live within two weeks, can you believe it? After that, my room at the W Hotel is on my nickel. I've *got* to spend some time tomorrow looking for a place to rent." She found herself staring into eyes full of sympathy, a shade darker than she remembered, now that night had fallen. Flustered, she quickly murmured, "Well...never mind. It'll all work out, I guess. 'Night, now."

"Goodnight, Ms. Kerry Hannigan." He held the car door open while she settled into the driver's seat. "You'll hear from me soon," he added, and closed the door firmly.

Yes, you will...

She put the car in gear and saw that the ring offered a

single wink in the murky confines of the driver's compartment. In her rear view mirror, Ren remained standing in the parking lot, his two dogs at his side, as she nosed her rented vehicle down the dirt road away from the ranch buildings. A sliver of a new moon in the December sky rose above Sonoma County's rolling hills as she cautiously found her way down the country road to Highway 101 and headed south, traveling the 39 miles toward San Francisco.

And despite the triumph of this day and the sense of wonder at the beauty of the Montisi Olive Ranch—to say nothing of the warmth in her host's manner just now—her main memory of the last ten minutes was the malevolent force of Sara Lang's parting glance.

Chapter Five

By Sunday noon, Kerry could see that her first blog, illustrated with a few of the photos she'd taken between tossing the salad and helping Ren and José serve the tables of food writers, was an instant hit. The analytics told her that the story of the near-disaster was being tweeted and re-tweeted by some of the attending food writers themselves, and shared all over the blogosphere's top food sites. And before she could even finish her coffee and eggs benedict that she'd had sent up from room service, the CEO of LifeStyleXer, Harry Chapman—Beverly Silverstein's boss—had sent her a priority email.

Welcome aboard, Kerry, and great first post! Just the right "You are there" tone we're looking for.

She was even more gratified to note that Chapman had copied Beverly, Charlie, and even the HR head, along with the little czarina, Tiffany Gergus, who had assigned her to her cubicle and treated her like dirt.

Kerry swiftly hit "Reply All" and responded.

Thanks. More to come!

A cascade of complimentary me-too atta-girls followed from each of Chapman's addressees, to which Kerry responded aloud in her hotel room, "Yeah...*right*. I bet you're all deliriously happy for me!"

As soon as room service removed her breakfast cart, she got down to writing two more blogs based on her journey to Amphora Nueva and reminded her readers to look for the harvest date on olive oil, rather than the bottling or 'use by' date. Within another hour, she'd also produced an 800-word riff on the best winter vegetables for soup making and ideas for planting, come spring, an all-organic kitchen garden—including pictures she'd snapped with the excellent lens on her cellphone.

Just as she'd embedded the last image, scheduled the day and time for the next post—12:01 a.m. and 12:01 p.m.—and pushed Publish, her cellphone rang.

"Kerry? Good morning! Just checking up on you to see if you survived your baptism by fire yesterday. It's Ren. Renato Montisi."

As if she hadn't instantly recognized his deep voice.

"H-hey there," she stammered. "Have you heard any more news about your chef?"

"I went and picked him up from Marin General this morning. He definitely has a problem with his gallbladder and it looks as if he's scheduled for surgery in a couple of weeks...or sooner, if he has another attack."

"Oh, poor guy," she sympathized. "That's certainly nothing to look forward to."

"Look, Kerry...I'm driving into the city this afternoon to visit my grandmother at the San Francisco Towers where she's living now. Can I take you to an early dinner afterward?"

Kerry glanced at the few apartment vacancy ads she'd pulled up on her laptop computer and sighed.

"How early? I've managed to get my blog posts done for

tomorrow, but I absolutely *have* to go see some apartments for rent before I find myself homeless in two weeks. I can't believe how expensive it is to rent even studios around here!"

"It's the digital explosion," Ren commiserated. "The world is moving to San Francisco to be part of this revolution and we're a small, cramped city. Why don't you text me where you'll be around five and I'll come collect you. We can eat after that."

Kerry agreed to Ren's proposal with a profound sense of gratitude that she had something to look forward to after undoubtedly chasing all over town in search of a hovel that probably would cost three thousand dollars a month to rent.

"That sounds great. I'd love to."

Then she suddenly wondered what Sara Lang would think of this plan?

It's none of her business!

Startled, Kerry didn't even try to guess where *that* thought came from. She confirmed her supposition by looking down at the glowing gemstone on her right ring finger. Meanwhile, Ren reminded her of his cellphone number and Kerry was soon in the hotel elevator, on her way to seek a new home.

Just before five o'clock, Kerry wearily leaned against a run-down wooden building on the edge of San Francisco's Chinatown district, wondering if she could face looking at yet another doghouse for which its owners were asking the moon. She texted Ren the address of her final day's attempt to put a roof over her head, and got a reply that he'd be there in less than ten minutes.

The "studio with a view" was three flights up and might have actually been a butler's pantry or very large broom closet in another incarnation. The kitchen consisted of a shelf, half-refrigerator, toaster oven, miniature microwave, and tiny sink. The "view" was of the tops of trees planted in the minuscule backyard of the neighboring dilapidated four-story building across the way.

She was just about to bid a hurried farewell to the bored real estate agent glued to his cellphone when she heard steps on the outside stairs.

"Ah…there you are!"

Ren, appearing in the open doorway far more refreshed than she felt, was dressed in gray slacks and a cream and black Harris Tweed sports jacket.

"Perfect timing," she said, trying to hide the discouragement that had, after such a demoralizing afternoon, invaded her very bones.

Ren gave the cramped living space the once-over and said with a straight face, "Not quite right for you, is it?" He seized her by the hand and headed for the one and only door.

Kerry waved at the real estate agent, who didn't even bother to look up.

"Thanks for showing this," she called to him, "but I work at home and I'll need—"

"No worries," the agent cut in, clicking off his cellphone. "I think I rented it already." He patted a file folder. "I got five applications this afternoon. The owner is bound to accept one of 'em."

Kerry remained silent until she climbed into the passenger seat of what Ren quickly disclosed was his "city car from another life," a late-model Mercedes. He soon was headed down California Street toward the Bay Bridge side of town.

"The money around here puts New York City to shame," she groused, and then shot Ren an apologetic look. "I don't mean *you*...I could see how hard you work at that ranch. I just mean..."

"I understand what you're saying," he sympathized. "All the millionaires manufactured every time a Facebook or Twitter or LinkedIn sells its stock to the public means that twenty-two-year-olds will be outbidding you at just about every turn. It's why I jumped at the chance to bail out of being a venture capital guy and moved back to the ranch to help out my grandmother. It was all getting a bit much for my taste."

"Speaking of your grandmother," Kerry asked, "how was she? I take it she lives in a retirement home here in the city?"

Ren nodded. "A very *nice* retirement home. The San Francisco Towers is a stone's throw from the Opera House and City Hall. It looks more like a Four Seasons Hotel than an old folks home. Last month, Concetta had her ninety-first birthday, and today she was her usual peppery self, always complaining that they rarely serve real Italian food...but we had a nice lunch there together."

"Oh, you've just eaten?" Kerry asked. "Well, then, don't feel you have to—"

"I had a small salad, which is why Concetta was giving me grief. Actually, I'm starving," he said as he pulled up to the curb and gave his keys to the parking valet. "Come...I'm taking you to one of my favorite restaurants."

By this time, they had arrived on Mission Street, near the waterfront. Ren took her arm and guided her in the direction of a brass and glass revolving door. To its left was an equally shiny brass plaque that declared they had arrived at "Boulevard."

Kerry had read volumes about this eatery of renown, housed in a landmark building on the historic Embarcadero that faced the Bay Bridge whose massive silver struts soared above their heads. She smiled at Ren as they entered, delighted this had been his choice.

"Boulevard was practically Number One on my list to try as soon as I got here."

After giving their waiter their wine order, perusing the extensive menu, and then ordering their selections, Ren gazed across the small table at his diner partner.

"So tell me," he asked. "You said you were a city girl. How do you feel about living in *this* one, now that you're here?"

Unable to conceal her discouragement, given all the events of the past seventy-two hours, Kerry responded with a small shrug and suppressed a sigh.

"It's too soon to judge, I guess," she temporized. "It's just all the *pressure,* you know? The move three thousand miles across the country. The extra blogs I stupidly agreed to produce, along with all those writers I'm supposed to recruit. And then there's finding a place to live in a no-vacancy town. All that, plus a few other things I'd rather not think about."

"Tell me," Ren urged.

"Tell you about the things I'd rather not think about?"

"The reason I'm prying is that Jeremy is on strict bed rest until all the tests come back and they know whether he'll need surgery. He can only get up to go to the bathroom."

"Oh, lord…that's not good. Do you have a lot scheduled at the ranch next week?"

Her mind had started to race. She suspected Ren had an ulterior motive in mind when he asked her to dinner—other than merely wanting to connect with her winning personality, she thought wryly.

"We have a couple of no-sweat events scheduled in the next few days," he said with a shrug. "Nothing like what we faced yesterday." Then he raised his wine glass.

"Here's to you and the incredible job you did, not only saving the Montisi Olive Ranch from a complete disaster, but pulling together a meal that was truly incredible."

"Your chef had already planned it and laid in all the food—"

"Yes, but everything would have fallen apart if you hadn't picked the right stuff from the kitchen garden for the salad and made that killer dressing, to say nothing of that amazing dill sauce for the salmon, *and* produced thirty-six incredible pumpkin *crème brûlées* out of the back of our pantry. Not only *that*," he added, setting his wine glass on the table and gently seizing her hand, "you whipped out a wonderful blog that brought the entire culinary emergency to vibrant life. You are one talented lady, Kerry Hannigan."

Ren was staring directly into her eyes as waves of palpitations in the hand he was holding out-vibrated her other hand wearing the Claddagh ring.

Perhaps there was more to his dinner invitation than pure business, she thought hopefully.

"Thank you for such kind words, but really—"

"*Really*, Kerry," he came back at her, "why do you underestimate yourself so much?"

Yes, why do *you?*

Kerry felt like slapping her right hand with her left, but couldn't because Ren still encased her palm in his own.

She affected a shrug. "I'm sure Sara could have managed just as—"

"Sara would have made an entire mess of everything," he cut in, not letting go of her hand. "In fact, she was well on her way to doing just that when Jeremy doubled over Saturday morning."

"Then why does she work in the kitchen?" Kerry asked

bluntly.

Ren broke their glance and released her hand.

"That's something *I'd* rather not think about...at least not at the moment."

"Ren! C'mon! You've asked *me* to tell all. I want to know why such a disagreeable woman is in your employ...or is it something personal?" she added, and then instantly regretted such inquisitiveness on her part.

Just at that moment, the waiter arrived with their entrees and the diversion appeared a welcome delay to Ren's having to answer her question.

When at length they were alone again, Kerry's dinner companion would only say, "Sara was given work at the ranch as a result of a tragic circumstance in her family. It seemed a temporary solution that's now dragged on far too long. After her behavior these past weeks, even before you witnessed her rudeness for yourself, I've been wracking my brains for how to...how to—"

"Tell her it's time to move on?" Kerry interrupted. "It's actually probably kinder to let her know sooner, rather than later, if that's what you want," she declared, wondering why men so often withdrew their affections long *before* they leveled with the women in their lives as to how they really felt about them?

What was Ren's relationship with Sara, anyway, she wondered, recalling the sense of familiarity that appeared to exist between them when she'd entered the kitchen the previous evening. Was this a "Charlie Move?" Was Ren trying to solve two problems at the same time: unloading *his* girlfriend while acquiring a temporary chef? Because that's what all his praise appeared to be leading up to.

In the space of an instant, the atmosphere between them had grown heavy and uncomfortable. For the next half hour while they ate their meal, she strove to keep her end of the conversation light and impersonal with comments about the food and questions as to the probable source of various local ingredients. As soon as the coffee was served, Kerry pointedly looked at her watch.

"Well, this has been lovely," she said, "but I'd better get back to the hotel. Cube-land awaits tomorrow, bright and early."

Ren swiftly caught the attention of their waiter and signaled for the check.

"Kerry..." he began. "Something happened just now, and I want you to tell me what it is."

She hesitated and then blurted, "Look, you have things you must be dealing with that I know nothing about, and the same is true with me."

Ren paused. Then he nodded agreement. "That's a fair assessment, I'd say...but even so, a chill just wafted through here. What happened?"

"Since you asked, you should probably know there's a lot about my move to San Francisco that—"

The waiter interrupted with the check just then and Ren paused to sign the credit card receipt. Kerry took that as a signal to rise from her seat, threading her way through the restaurant with her escort following along behind. Once in Ren's car, she turned and offered a tight smile.

"Thanks again for dinner. It was delicious."

"We discussed the food, but didn't particularly savor it," Ren countered. "You haven't answered my question. Why did you shut down on me?"

Kerry was caught off guard by Ren's refusal to pretend their dinner date was a casual affair that had simply fizzled between two people who barely knew each other. Feeling the heat of his steady glance, she hesitated for a moment and felt a pulse of energy shoot up her arm.

"Here's the deal: on the flight coming out here Friday, I broke up with my live-in boyfriend and business partner of over a year because I found out he was having a Facebook—and now a real life—affair with his former high school girlfriend who just happens to be our *new* boss at LifeStyleXer. I'm afraid I have a lot on my mind right now."

"Good God!"

Kerry said crossly, "Well, *you* appear to have a tangled situation of your own, so…"

She couldn't think how to finish her sentence. After all, she'd just *met* the man who was now piloting his Mercedes up California Street, away from the downtown W Hotel.

Ren stared straight ahead, driving in silence a few minutes more until, at length, he said, "I am not involved with Sara Lang on any level that I think you're assuming I might be."

Why did Kerry get the sense that—as with President Clinton's denial of his relationship with Monica Lewinsky—Ren had parsed his last sentence *very* carefully?

She was about to respond when he continued, "I'd still like to discuss one of the other reasons I asked you to dinner, besides wanting to thank you for yesterday. Will you have a quick nightcap with me at the Top of the Mark? I wouldn't be a good ambassador to San Francisco if I didn't show you the view." She could feel him studying her profile when he added, "Please, Kerry."

Ren continued to drive the car up California Street's steep incline, past Powell. She gave a brief nod of assent, then saw that right beside them, an iconic San Francisco cable car was creaking up the hill.

"It's amazing those old things are still running," she commented, hoping to lighten the heavy atmosphere in the car.

"Those bables are more than a hundred and forty years old, but they draw a lot of tourists to this town, so somehow the city engineers keep them going."

Wisps of fog had begun to swirl around the hood of their car as it crested Nob Hill, a summit that featured a square park surrounded by a group of magnificent buildings. On Kerry's right stood the six-story "wedding cake" beaux-arts Fairmont Hotel.

"It was restored after the disastrous earthquake and firestorm of 1906," Ren explained, his tone acquiring the *politesse* of a tour guide. On the north side of the park he pointed out the former Flood mansion—a brownstone that now served as the exclusive Pacific Union Club.

"Still only male members, I read somewhere," Kerry said.

"Right. Some of us have been trying to change that, but so far...no go."

On their left was the much taller Mark Hopkins Hotel. Below, Ren pointed to the Stanford Court, and in the other direction, near the towering Grace Cathedral, the Huntington Hotel.

"Some of these hotels on Nob Hill replaced the mansions destroyed in the quake that had belonged to the four railroad barons that built the western section of the transcontinental route...and so these post-quake buildings were named in their honor."

Ren wheeled the car into the gated and bricked courtyard of the Mark Hopkins and immediately liveried doormen on both sides assisted them out of their vehicle.

Kerry began to shiver in the damp, cold air. She wrapped her arms around her upper body, hurrying toward the hotel's entrance. Ren quickly caught up with her and put a protective arm around her shoulders clad in a thin sweater.

"First lesson in San Francisco. Whatever the season, always carry a fleece jacket," he joked, and Kerry could feel herself smiling in spite of the dark mood that had overtaken her at dinner.

Ren guided her up the red-carpeted steps, through the revolving glass door, and into the warmth of the plush lobby. Kerry was surprised when he kept his arm around her, even as they waited for the elevator which, when it arrived, whisked them nineteen floors to the hotel's former penthouse, now a bar with reputedly the best view of both bridges in the entire city.

Stepping out onto the top floor, Kerry halted in her tracks.

"What a shame. Look at how thick the fog is up here. There's absolutely *no* view."

"Good," Ren declared. "We have to talk. You'll see the view another day. Come...shall we take that table in the corner?"

A waiter across the empty room gestured they could sit anywhere they liked.

"A stinger?" Ren asked her when a member of the staff came swiftly to their side, since they were virtually the only customers.

"Fine," she said with a nod, wondering why Ren couldn't have said whatever he had to say to her in the car on the way back to her hotel.

"Two stingers," he repeated to their waiter who left to fetch drinks made of brandy and *crème de menthe*. Ren fingered the corner of his cocktail napkin and then abruptly declared, "I still wish you'd tell me why things went sideways with us back there at Boulevard, but since you don't seem to want to talk any more about it, I might as well just say what's on *my* mind: I want you to come work at the ranch. Starting tomorrow."

"*What?*"

Kerry seriously doubted she'd actually heard Renato Montisi correctly. Had he just offered her the job of her dreams?

"Come work for me. *With* me," he amended

"But I only started my new job out here on Friday!"

"I know that," he said with a laugh. "But *my* job offer includes full-time housing," he added with a sly smile, watching her reaction. "A cottage of your own on the property…and a few other nice perks like healthcare. Bonuses, too, if we do well."

And any other additions you had in mind?

Kerry knew that thought had *not* come from the Claddagh and felt heat flood her cheeks.

"But if Jeremy is sick, you need a full-time chef, won't you, and I just signed this iron-clad contract and—"

"The Montisi Olive Ranch needs a lot more than a cook," he replied tersely. "I need an ace director of marketing and public relations, to say nothing of better content and digital management on our website and—most importantly—a product development person if we're to survive as a small, artisanal producer. I saw from your old website, you didn't just write a blog. I need someone to do a lot of the kind of work you did for the company you sold to LifeStyleXer."

"That's only because we were a four-person start-up! All of us did *everything*, including making the coffee."

"Well, we're a small enterprise as well, and your experience in your start-up, along with all the other things you can do, makes you the perfect person for the job."

"But I've lived in a city all my life! I know nothing about ranching."

"We have to make *more* than just olive oil, Kerry, or the

Montisi Ranch can't continue. We need to develop other products using the remnants left after the olives' first pressing and market and distribute them, just as you would with any item made in New York or New Jersey," he declared. "We also have to figure out ways to get more people to *pay* to visit the ranch. I think a compelling Internet presence like you developed for your own website is how we could do that."

"But Ren—"

"You are one of those rare people that knows tech stuff *and* the specialty food world *and* how to drive traffic to our Internet business selling whatever the heck we figure out to do besides just making olive oil." He flashed her his killer grin. "*And* you're a great cook."

"And you think *I* can do all that?"

"There you go...underestimating yourself, again. Absolutely I think you can do it...and *more*. Even more to the point, I think it's work you would *love!*"

Kerry frowned as she allowed Ren's words to sink in. When she didn't answer him, he ran his fingers distractedly through his dark blond mane.

"Besides all your knowledge of the food world, you have style. You can turn on a dime. You're flexible...a team player...fun to be around...considerate of your underlings—"

Kerry felt a wash of pleasure hearing such kind words. Except for her godmother, it had been a long time since she'd been offered praise like this. She suddenly thought of Angelica with a pang of longing. If only she could hop a cab and spend some time in her wise, comforting presence discussing what happened with Charlie and, now, these new complications in her life....

Just then, their waiter appeared with their drinks and she paused until he had departed. Then she shook her head.

"Look, Ren, I can't tell you how flattered I am by your proposal, but I signed a deal with the company I moved out here to work for, and they think my blog is part of their value now, especially as they tee up their public offering. They'll *never* let me out of my contract so quickly."

Now it was Ren's turn to remain silent. Kerry wondered what else he could possibly come up with that could surmount the many impediments confronting the possibility of her becoming part of the team at the ranch.

At length he said, "Maybe there's a compromise here. Maybe you can keep up the blogging part of your current job—which is your principal value to them, right? In fact, doing that would probably only *benefit* us at the ranch, too. You could work mostly from Petaluma, and persuade the CEO to assign someone else the management of the other bloggers recruited for the ten cities." He paused and his smile was faintly calculating. "Your old boyfriend might be just the candidate for that job. Make him work for those stock options, for God's sake."

Kerry couldn't help but laugh. Then she grew somber.

"But there's one big problem with your scheme. The HR witch says no WAH."

"HR?" Ren said, his tone communicating his disdain. "Those people would be prison guards if they hadn't gotten jobs in the digital industry. You've only been dealing with the bean counters. You're *good*," he said urgently. "*More* than good. You're spectacular in all that you do. Top brass really don't care anymore *where* you do your work as long it's as first-rate as yours is. I can speak from experience on this. Ask for what you *want* from them and you might be surprised what the CEO will say. Meanwhile, what I'm offering is a job where *all* your many talents would be put to good use!"

"You sound like an executive recruiter, not a rancher."

Ren's intense scrutiny felt as if she was suddenly minus every stitch of clothing.

"I know what I want and I'll do everything I can to get it."

"And you've decided you want me? On your payroll, I mean," she amended, "after seeing me work at your ranch only one day?"

"In a word, yes. I can't believe I've just met the one person exactly suited to help me figure out other events and activities at the ranch that people would pay for to keep this hundred-year-old place afloat."

"But, Ren—"

He didn't even let her finish her sentence.

"Look, Kerry...let me say to you what I told my grandmother today: if we can't figure out how to make this ranch pay its way, we'll have to consider selling most of the land before she passes—or she'll have to move out of the San Francisco Towers within the year."

Kerry considered what it would be like for Angelica to have to leave her home in New York at her age. "That's terrible! Are you certain it's as dire as that?"

"After this year's harvest, I did a thorough audit," Ren said, grim-faced. "The ranch is in a cutthroat, competitive business where some of the giant olive oil producers and distributors in this country and Europe sell fraudulently labeled, unregulated products that have sat in vats for *years*. Their rock-bottom prices sold to unsuspecting customers are driving us right out of business. The expenses involved in running an honest operation *and* paying Concetta's costs in that luxurious retirement home don't add up anymore," he explained soberly. "If I can't turn the ranch into a viable enterprise—I'll have to go back to the VC business and sell the place so Concetta can remain where she is."

"Would selling the ranch to keep her at the Towers be okay with her?"

A shadow of deep sorrow invaded Ren's features. It was an expression she'd witnessed when she'd rushed to Angelica's apartment in the late afternoon on 9/11.

"The last thing that should happen is for my grandmother to be forced to move—*or* sell the ranch," Ren replied. "Either choice would probably kill her in a week."

Chapter Six

Ren's somber mood signaled to Kerry that his efforts to recruit her services had been a sort of Hail Mary pass aimed at remedying a situation that was a lot more dismal than she could have imagined yesterday when everything seemed utterly idyllic in Renato Montisi's world.

Meanwhile, her mind was spinning. On one hand, she was utterly drawn to the life she'd glimpsed at the ranch, to say nothing of the sense that a magnetic force neither she nor Ren could explain was pulling them closer by the second. Still, the sensible, *logical* part of her brain told her that the notion of forsaking LifeStyleXer, and all its potential "upside," as Charlie would surely term it, to come work for an enterprise teetering on the brink of apparent insolvency might prove to be the worst of both worlds.

No guts, no glory, Kerry m'girl!

Kerry refused to glance down at her ring. *Why* was life always so complicated, she mourned silently? So many things had piled on top of her and suddenly, it was all too *much*: Charlie's betrayal...the sheer self-interest and meanness of Beverly Silverstein and the HR trolls she'd had to confront...her stupidity to have signed a contract she hadn't read carefully...the loss of familiar surroundings and...most of all, the absence of Angelica's calm presence. As Maggie Doyle once said: she just didn't have the bandwidth to deal with it all! She grasped for a way to let Ren down gently.

"Your proposal is amazing and totally unexpected, but it would definitely cause an uproar where I work." She took a large sip of her stinger to buy time to *think,* acutely conscious that Ren was gazing at her with unsettling intensity.

"Is what I'm proposing something you'd *want* to do if you weren't in the situation you find yourself in at your company—and with your boyfriend?"

"Charlie Miller? *Ex* boyfriend!"

"Ex," he repeated. "And glad to hear it. But on its own merits, Kerry," he pressed, "what do you think of the idea of us working together to make the ranch self-sustaining and maybe even *profitable*?"

I would so love to do that…

There was no concealing the pure joy she'd felt cooking in that wonderful kitchen for people who cared about food as much as she did, or the satisfaction of being part of a team in a beautiful place like the Montisi Olive Ranch. But there were so many obstacles standing in the way, she thought, and they came rushing at her, one by one.

"Your offer is—in a word—wonderful," she told him frankly, "but how can it work? Don't you see, Ren? You're asking me somehow to wiggle out of a binding contract I recently signed, forfeit my big pay day after LifeStyleXer goes public, and come to work for you at an admittedly shaky enterprise—just like that?"

"Yup. Just like that." His demeanor had shifted and Kerry knew she was catching a glimpse of Renato Montisi, the hard-nosed executive. "We're grown ups now, Kerry. We get to choose what we want. We also sometimes have to make hard choices."

"Hard doesn't begin to describe what's happened to me in the last week."

Refusing to offer sympathy, Ren asked baldly, "How much will they pay you for those carrot-and-stick stock options?"

"I get half a million bucks if I hang in two years past the IPO that's scheduled immediately after New Year's. After that, I'd get more stock, the longer I stayed...that is, if they still like what I do," she amended, thinking of the contract's clause stipulating that her supervisor could can her at any point.

"Well..." Ren considered slowly, "I didn't think recruiting you would be easy, but...wow...five hundred K, plus. They must *really* think you're one of their gold-plated assets—and they're right."

"Thank you. I never quite believed it myself."

"I can see that." Ren remained silent for a moment and Kerry could tell he was carefully considering his next words. "What if you *didn't* quit your job, but simply came to live on the ranch and helped us out as much as you could until two years are up, when you could decide if life at the ranch suits a city girl like you?"

"You'd wait that long and risk my not giving you as much of my time as you need *now* to help fix things with the business?"

"Yes, I would," he said. "I know you wouldn't stint on what you committed to do for the ranch. That's how much of a difference I think you could make in our enterprise."

"Wow," was all Kerry could manage to reply.

"I'll give you the Mercedes so you can drive back and forth to the city." At her look of astonishment, he shrugged. "I like driving the truck. You'd continue your routine as a food blogger and your other duties for LifeStyleXer...and given that you won't be paying for rent or food at the ranch—and they're paying you at least some salary to boot—

I bet your company could get the W Hotel to make you a deal booking a room there two days a week. That way, you can be at the ranch Wednesdays through Sundays and only be locked up in your cubicle Mondays and Tuesdays!" he finished triumphantly.

Kerry wondered if Ren had stayed up all the previous night plotting strategy to convince her to take the job.

By this time, his signature grin had spread across his handsome features. "And here's another bonus: I promise I won't work you to death the first two years and we'd share the workload on new projects at the ranch, fifty-fifty."

"Better make it more like eighty-twenty, with you doing most of the heavy lifting for a long while," she cautioned. Then, recalling Angelica's penetrating questions before she left New York, she asked Ren, "Oh. And if I said yes to this crazy scheme of yours, what's my salary down the road?"

"Well, when we know this is going to work for both of us, I'll grant you the same amount I'll be paying myself, plus a participation position in the ranch's overall business."

"You obviously learned at the knee of *The Godfather*. You're pretty much making me an offer I can't refuse."

"That's my plan."

Kerry's excitement had gone from mere bubbles in her solar plexus to a rolling boil. It *was*, in fact, her dream job—or would be, eventually, if she and Ren could make all the moving parts work properly.

A studied risk is what this is...

Working at the Montisi Olive Ranch could certainly prove a failure, but Ren's plan had all the ingredients that—if the two of them worked hard and had some luck—could result in sublime success.

"And this agreement between us will all be in writing?" she pressed.

"Every word." He seized her hand once more, and a wave of adrenaline shot up her arm. "I witnessed you operating with tremendous grace and goodwill under terrible pressure. That was all I needed to *know* you're the kind of person I've been praying would come along."

Kerry suddenly recalled her godmother Angelica's words about her husband Brian and their getting engaged in a week. "We just *knew*!" she'd exclaimed.

*He's just speaking professionally...*Kerry scolded herself, and immediately she felt another jolt skitter up her arm.

No, he's not!

When she glanced down at her hand, the heart-shaped stone was pulsing pure white. Meanwhile, Ren was pointing out the window beside them.

"Well! Will you look over there? See how fast the fog lifted. There must be strong winds out there on the Bay." He smiled at her confidently. "Before you give me your final answer, I want to show you something."

He pulled her from her chair and led her to another window facing north, swinging his right arm under her chin and around her shoulders as if they'd known each other forever. The next thing she knew, her back was pressing against his chest.

"Just look at the Golden Gate Bridge, lit up, over there," he murmured. His breath near her ear was pleasantly laced with brandy in the stinger he'd sipped. With his free left hand, he pointed at the bridge aglow against the night sky. "To me, it's one of the most beautiful sights in the world...and the road across it leads toward everything I love." Ren turned her around to face him. "Please, Kerry...I know we've known each other exactly three days and you're probably still licking your wounds about what happened to the partnership that brought you to San Francisco—"

"I'm well out of that, believe me," she murmured, feeling as if she might faint from the sensation of the two of them standing so close. "I'm still pretty stunned by everything that's happened this week."

"So am I, in a way," he confessed, pulling her against him so that her hips brushed his pelvis, sending shock waves clear through her. "After you left, yesterday, it came to me, all of a sudden, in a way I can't explain. It just seemed like our talents and sensibilities would be a perfect match for everything that's important in my life." He nodded in the direction of the glowing bridge. "Please say you'll take that road out there."

Kerry sensed that any second now, he would lean down and kiss her.

"And here I thought you were just going to offer me a job as a temporary cook," she teased, tilting her face toward his.

Ren wrapped his arms around her waist so she had nowhere to look except into his eyes that had turned the color of dark amber shaded by the blackness of the night outside. No one except her godparents had ever given her a sense of being protected like she felt in his arms. Ren cocked his head to one angle, their lips nearly touching.

"Those blue eyes of yours...your hair," he whispered. "Hannigan, you're something else, you know that?"

Kerry raised her hand to brush the backs of her fingers along the side of his cheek when a sudden, alarming thought brought her up short.

"But what about Sara?" she blurted. "How will...adding me to the crew at the ranch sit with *her*?"

Renato took a step back and remained silent for nearly the count of ten. Then, he turned away from her and stared out the window at the crystal lights twinkling in the distance.

"She won't like it," he stated flatly. "Just like she didn't like it when I married her sister."

"Sara Lang is your *sister-in-law*?" Kerry exclaimed. "Well, *that's* a little factlette you neglected to disclose!"

A mental file folder spilled out all the instances when Sara-of-the-blond-pigtails had been rude and possessive, and behaving like a jealous lover, not a grieving sister of Ren's late wife. Without so much as a glance at the Claddagh ring, she turned abruptly, marched over to their abandoned table, and grabbed her purse.

Ren was right behind her.

"Wait, Kerry! Where are you going?"

"To get a cab." She turned. "Don't you get it? I don't want any more *drama* like this in my life!"

"I told you before, my wife died! She was killed in a skiing accident."

"Really? So one sister passes away and you road-test another?" Kerry snapped, turning away to head in the direction of the elevator.

Ren seized her arm to keep her from leaving. Instead of the furious expression she expected to see, he merely looked exasperated.

"You *are* still licking those wounds over that Charlie guy, aren't you?" he said, releasing her from his grip when she turned to face him.

"Not really," she retorted. "And don't tell me you didn't notice," she added sarcastically, "that your sister-in-law has the hots for you."

"Just to be clear," Ren countered, "and in case you were still wondering, Sara and I have *never* had an intimate relationship before, during or after I married her sister."

"Well, she sure acts as if you have! Trust me, Ren, I don't need another hairball like the one I'm already dealing with, and Sara's rotten attitude toward just about *everything* has all the makings of one!"

"At least let me explain why she's on the ranch."

Kerry took a deep breath.

Hear him out, silly girl!

She sighed with resignation. "Okay. Shoot."

For a long moment, Ren gazed out the big, plate-glass window that faced the Golden Gate Bridge, its blinking red tower beacons warning off low-flying aircraft. Kerry could tell he was watching a movie she couldn't see.

"After Sandra died three...almost four years ago now, her sister, Sara, went into an emotional tailspin. To put it bluntly, she had a nervous breakdown—or close to it. Her family couldn't deal with her, so I said my sister-in-law could come live at the ranch until she got back on her feet. She's been a total pain in the ass since the day I met her in college, but I felt sorry for her. We all did."

Kerry froze. Her experience with Charlie *had* prompted her to jump to conclusions. Sara's presence on the Montisi Ranch was an act of charity on Ren's part. She could feel color rising in her cheeks.

"Oh. Oh hell!" Kerry said, turning to face him. "Ren, I am so sorry—"

"As I said, it's been over three years since Sandra's accident. Sara's a lot more stable now, and I'm the first one who wants her to move on with her life, but—"

"How did the accident happen?"

Ren remained silent for a long moment. Then he answered, "If you come across the street with me, I'll tell you the whole sorry tale."

"Across the street?" she echoed. "Why across the street?"

"Because the bar's closing and I booked a room at the Fairmont for tonight."

Kerry frowned.

Ren quickly added, "I have a meeting with my banker first thing tomorrow. I didn't feel like driving back to the ranch tonight and turning right around to come to the city tomorrow morning. And besides, the manager is a friend. He gives me a friends and family discount."

"Oh," was all she could manage, her mind skittering toward thoughts she knew she shouldn't be having.

Ren 's expression had relaxed, and a ghost of a smile appeared. He lightly placed a hand on each of her shoulders.

"If I promise to be a very good boy—which won't be easy, I might add—would you consider having a cup of coffee with me where we can talk privately? Since you may be *considering* doing business with me," he said with a wry expression, "I want to give you a brief history of the last ten years."

By the time they were midway in the crosswalk that separated the Mark Hopkins Hotel from the Fairmont crowning Nob Hill, she took his arm.

"Look...I really need to apologize for judging you as I just did a few minutes ago. All situations are not necessarily the same," she added, upset with herself that she had ever equated Ren's behavior to that of Charlie Miller's.

Ren steered her in the direction of the hotel's *porte-cochère* where a series of luxury vehicles were rolling up to the Fairmont's carpeted entrance.

"Well, thank you for that. I can certainly understand why you may be a little gun shy after what happened to you lately."

"I'll tell you the gory details about that...sometime," she offered as the two of them reached the top step. "But first, it's your turn."

"Good. I want to know everything, so I can punch the guy in the nose for you. And that Beverly woman, too."

"Another perk I get if I come to work at the ranch?"

Ren laughed and nodded at the doorman who ushered them inside. Kerry walked in first and then halted her forward progress in order to say something that had continued to weigh heavily.

"If I join your staff, you're going to have an even *bigger* problem with Sara Lang, so before you tell me whatever you plan to tell me here, I need to let you know that the unresolved situation with her makes me very leery of getting involved at your ranch professionally…or personally." She was amazed at her own frank admission that she felt the same zing between them that he obviously did. "But!" she continued, holding up one finger before Ren could protest. "I'll definitely hear you out if you promise to put me in a cab afterwards."

Ren appeared to consider the bargain and said, finally, "Fair enough."

Kerry waited discreetly in the Fairmont's magnificent cream-and-gold lobby while Ren checked himself into the hotel. A brochure on a side table revealed that the soaring gold-leaf pillars and impressive gilded plasterwork spoke volumes about California's first licensed woman architect, Julia Morgan, who, at a mere thirty-four-years-old, restored the burnt-out hulk in the wake of the 1906 earthquake and firestorm.

She looked up from reading just as Ren turned away from the front desk and inclined his head toward a bank of elevators several yards further on.

"This place is spectacular," she exclaimed as they rode to the fourth floor.

She felt a faintly unnerving flutter of excitement when the two of them walked down the carpeted hall to his assigned room. Within moments of entering a small, elegant suite consisting of a sitting room, with a bedroom visible through a half-opened door, he had ordered room service to bring up a *cappuccino,* a pot of tea with milk on the side, "and a plate of *biscotti,*" he finished, and replaced the phone receiver in its cradle.

Ren indicated that she should sit on the brocaded love seat upholstered in a subtle gray to match the gray, silk bedspread Kerry had glimpsed through the door. He settled into an upholstered club chair nearby. He inhaled a deep breath before he began to speak.

"Twelve years ago, I met both Sara and Sandra Lang at Stanford when they were undergraduates, a year apart, and I was at the business school. I met Sara first, but was more drawn to her younger sister, Sandra, because of her athleticism and...well...a more outgoing personality."

"You mean, in contrast to Sara's gloomy-gus approach?" she couldn't resist commenting.

Ren raised an eyebrow and nodded.

"Sandra was an amazing athlete...a top tennis player in college and a fanatic skier, ready for any adventure. Looking back, I think I simply got married in 2007, a few years after Sandra graduated, because the choice seemed to be either do that, or break up. During my twenties, our close circle of friends were getting married in rapid succession and everybody we knew just expected us to make our relationship official."

"But the trouble is, you don't really know who you are, or what you truly want in life till at least after thirty, don't you think?" Kerry said fervently. "I know *I* didn't."

"I totally agree. In my case, I had my shiny new business school degree and was about to move to Mountain View in the heart of Silicon Valley, ten miles up the road from the university, and join a VC firm—"

"Venture Capitalist, right?" she confirmed.

"Yeah...we had the heady job of investing in new companies we thought might be the next Google or Facebook. Sandra's future plans after graduating centered around playing tennis and skiing wherever there was snow, and — well — *me*."

Just then, there was a discreet knock on the door and a voice called out, "Room service!"

The waiter swiftly brought their order in on a tray and departed. Kerry stirred milk from a small pitcher into her cup of tea while Ren settled back against the chair holding his coffee.

"In those first years after grad school and my marriage, I was basically going along with everybody else's program," Ren continued his narrative. "I was working nights and weekends on the deals we were doing, while Sandra and her sister spent most weekends at the Lang's family house in Squaw Valley on Lake Tahoe."

Ren fell silent and stared into the surface of his coffee. At length he said, "Sandra and I were drifting apart, mostly due to my allowing my work to be the central focus of my life, along with her obsession in the early days of our marriage to try out for the USA Olympic Ski Team."

"Did Sara ski, too?"

"Yes, but never on the level of her younger sister. In fact, that's pretty much Sara's problem. Sandra got what Sandra wanted with ease and grace, and Sara always came in second."

"Was Sara training to try out for the Olympic Team as well?"

"They both gave it their all, but it was pretty clear that Sandra was the one that had the best shot. Sara finally gave up and got a job as a glorified administrative assistant at

Lehman Brothers in San Francisco and drove up to Tahoe from the Bay Area on the weekends with me, while Sandra stayed at Squaw, training seven days a week." Ren took a sip of his coffee, swallowed, and continued.

"One winter, about four years into our marriage, I got a call that Sandra had been hurt on the slopes. Turns out that Sara had goaded her sister to ski off the cornice at the top of the mountain just as bad weather was closing in. Everything had iced over and Sandra crashed into a tree, breaking her thighbone, and had to be brought out by the ski patrol. A lot of things happened after that, and my wife ended up in a coma."

"She went into a coma as a result of a broken leg?" Kerry asked, bewildered.

"After the surgery to repair her leg, she caught one of those terrible infections in the hospital. It came on fast and galloped through her system. As her husband, I had to make the decision to pull the plug. It was pretty devastating…for Sara, especially."

"Survivor's guilt?"

Ren nodded. "In spades. After all, she'd dared Sandra to go down that run and then chickened out."

"Oh, my God…"

"Yeah, it was pretty gothic. For my grandmother and me, it felt like a rerun of my parents dying so unexpectedly in the plane crash. Sara, though, was basically a basket case and in those first weeks after Sandra's funeral, Concetta and I both worried she might…do something really terrible."

"Where were the sisters' *parents* in all this?" Kerry demanded.

"Wendell and Doris?" Ren shook his head in disgust. "The Langs are the quintessential Baby Boomers, if you know what I mean. Very 'do your own thing and don't bother us.'

After Sandra died, essentially they just told Sara to suck it up and not be such a pain in the ass."

Kerry heaved a sigh. "You must think I'm a total jerk...and maybe I am, but it just looked to me as if you and Sara might be—"

"I know how it looked," Ren interrupted. "Jeremy hinted to me just the other day that he also thought Sara and I had become an item in recent months because that's the way Sara *wants* everybody to think."

"That's pretty weird..." ventured Kerry, "and must have been tough to deal with."

Ren nodded. "Sara's been problematic from day one. She apparently had set her sights on me at Stanford, and when I chose her sister, she began to invent a story in her own mind that she and I had *always* been destined to be together, which was pretty weird as time went on, given Sara was partially responsible for what happened to Sandra."

"Then, why in the world did you ever bring Sara to the *ranch*—even if you felt sorry for her?" Kerry asked, exasperated.

"She'd lost her job in the crash of 2008 when Lehman Brothers collapsed and then got laid off again right after Sandra died in 2011. Her roommates kicked her out of their apartment for not paying her share of the rent and her parents were living in France. She called one day, literally begging me to please give her a job—*any* job."

"But she's been on your ranch a couple of *years*, Ren."

There had to be more to this than he was revealing, she thought. Maybe Ren had some survivor's guilt of his own?

"To my surprise, Sara made a big effort, when she first came to the ranch, to make herself useful when we hosted events, especially in the kitchen. Jeremy was kind enough to teach her the rudiments of being a sous chef." Ren put his coffee cup down abruptly and caught Kerry's gaze. "I needed the help, frankly. The ranch's finances were a mess when I took things over, and until recently, I had no idea Sara had always had this *fantasy* in her mind about the two of us. She wants what she has always wanted: the life that Sandra had. Her psychiatrist recently called me to explain."

"Really?" Kerry asked, startled. "That shrink must have felt he had a duty to warn you. Otherwise, wouldn't patient-confidentiality prevent him from saying anything?"

Ren nodded. "Right after I talked to him—the day before I met you, incidentally—I told her parents I'd done my duty and now it was their turn to deal with their daughter."

"And?"

Ren cocked an eyebrow. "I'm waiting to hear their plan."

Kerry gazed across the narrow space that separated them. "That sounds pretty open-ended, Ren."

Frustration clouded his features. "Honestly, I've done my best to treat her as a sister, but she..." His sentence drifted off.

Kerry, recalling Sara's expression of instant dislike the minute Ren had escorted her into the ranch kitchen to meet Jeremy, asked quietly, "So...basically you're in limbo with Ms. Sara Lang?"

"I've let it ride because we're so short-handed, and now, with Jeremy down for the count..."

Kerry could sense the weight of the world pressing down on him and without warning, the ring on her right hand began vibrating.

Think, Kerry m'girl! What would make you happy?

Before she could weigh her next words, she heard herself saying, "Look, Ren, I'd love to work with you as a profit-sharing partner in your olive oil adventures."

A look of both relief and joy spread across his face. "You

would?"

"Yes!" she said firmly.

"That's wonderful!"

She raised her hand in warning.

"But for this to work for me, I couldn't move to the ranch or accept any money from you until I renegotiate my deal with LifestyleXer."

"I have no problem with that."

"Let's hope LifestyleXer doesn't have a problem, either." She smiled, hoping to reassure Ren that she was willing to go out on a limb to try to find a way to come to the ranch. "I'm excited about the idea of devising whatever else we can to sell with the Montisi brand, *plus*," she said with deliberate emphasis, "I'd absolutely *love* to be Chef Jeremy's Number 2 as soon as Sara leaves."

"Great!" Ren said with an affirmative nod. "It's *all* great."

She fixed Ren with a steady glance. "And when do you expect that will be? Sara's leaving, I mean?

Ren sobered. "I can't tell you that yet, but as soon as possible. You'll have to trust that if she creates any problems in the meantime, tell me right away and I'll take care of it."

Kerry was suddenly filled with doubt. *Could* she trust this man? What if he'd made these promises merely to solve his own problems at the ranch and wouldn't actually do what he said he would?

Studied risk, remember Kerry? This is one of them...

After a long pause, she said, "Well, thanks for explaining everything." She gave him a measured look. "I have to be straight with the people at work that I want to change my deal, so I'll make an appointment with my CEO tomorrow and let you know how it goes."

"I know this probably feels as if you're making a very big leap of faith like the one when you decided to come to San

Francisco—" he began.

"Oh, no," she assured him. "This feels very, very different." She glanced at her watch. "But, it's getting late. I'd better go." She rose and picked up her handbag off the sofa. "I'll try to get in to see the big boss at work and hope I can negotiate an exit strategy where I won't lose everything I've worked for the last two years."

Ren rose to his feet, his eyes alight. "But you've just given me a definite 'yes'—yes? You're committed to come work with me at the ranch?"

"I've given you a definite 'maybe,'" she corrected him.

Kerry could sense a subtle shift in Ren's demeanor.

"Ah...the money, is it? The stock options *carrot*? I can practically hear that conversation in your head. I've heard it often enough in my own. You'd like to keep the bird in the hand and capture the one that's just fluttering within reach."

His expression had become unreadable and Kerry knew instinctively that she'd disappointed him somehow.

"It's not *just* the money, Ren! I worked my ass off to get to where someone is offering me a half million bucks, and I have every right to try to see it through, if I can. And besides, I don't want to work at the ranch behind the back of my current employer. You wouldn't like it if I did that to *you*. I need to have a conversation with the big boss and see if I can renegotiate my deal and, by the way, *you* need to get Sara Lang off the ranchero, right, *señor*?"

Without reply, he rose and walked with her toward the door.

"How about you give me your answer tomorrow night, Kerry, after you've met with the CEO? I've got to get someone teed up right away to give the ranch its best chance for survival, and if it's not going to be you..."

Kerry rested her hand on the hotel suite's doorknob,

wondering if the electricity she'd felt flowing between them earlier was merely wishful thinking on her part. In a flash of insight she could see that Ren Montisi did not like to get *left*. And, he was also a tough businessman, and likely skilled at playing both Good Cop/Bad Cop to secure what he was after. Right now, it felt as if he were suddenly playing Bad Cop to pressure her to help solve his problems at the ranch.

Was this just another Charlie Miller move, she wondered bleakly? Worse yet, was this really her dream job, or would the presence of Sara Lang in her life turn it into another nightmare?

Kerry glanced down at the Claddagh, wishing for the first time that it would offer clear guidance. The emerald retained its normal color without a hint of iridescence.

For once in your life, just do what you *want!*

Startled, she continued to stare at her hand, expecting the ring's gemstone to change color—which it did not. Those were *her* thoughts, she marveled. With absolute clarity, she *knew* she wanted to do the kind of life's work represented by the Montisi Olive Ranch, whether Renato Montisi and she were an "item" or not. It felt so liberating to finally know what her path should be! She squared her shoulders and in her most professional manner, bid Ren farewell.

"I'll do my best to get in to see the CEO first thing tomorrow. Meanwhile, let me know if you've gotten a commitment from Sara to leave by the end of the month."

And with that, Kerry allowed Ren to say a circumspect "Good night," and put her in a cab downstairs, noting that another invasion of fog off the wide Pacific Ocean now cloaked the night sky atop Nob Hill.

Chapter Seven

Monday morning, Kerry took the elevator at LifeStyleXer directly to the floor where Harry Chapman's office was located next to the glass-enclosed conference room. It wasn't even eight a.m. yet, but instinct told her that with an IPO deadline looming, the company's CEO would be at his desk when the markets in New York opened three hours ahead of California time. She knocked at his open door, apologized for interrupting, and was bidden to take a seat.

Chapman, a trim man who looked to be in his early fifties, listened without interruption as she swiftly explained her sudden and unexpected offer to live on the Montisi Olive Ranch and—in exchange for a roof over her head—lend her talents as a part-time chef and food consultant to this enterprise.

She did her best not to lose her nerve when she saw that the CEO's features had grown grave.

Before he could respond, she hastened to add, "Finding somewhere decent to live in San Francisco in my price range is practically impossible. And, actually, I think my *not* sitting in an office cubicle all day and being part of the world of everything I'll be writing about—as I did with the first few posts you seem to like so much—will greatly enhance the quality of my blog and keep driving traffic to the parent website. I'm happy to work in the city two days a week if you'll cover a room at the W on Mondays and Tuesdays."

She nearly winced when he raised an eyebrow at that suggestion, but plunged ahead with the proposed arrangement she hoped he'd agree to.

"Honestly, Mr. Chapman," she rushed to assure him, "working among the artisanal California food producers can only be good for *this* company. I think my living in Petaluma two-thirds of the week will be good for *both* our causes."

She held her breath, watching Chapman mull over her long speech. She wondered if she had just made the stupidest move in her life.

The CEO began to tap one end of his pen on his desk.

"Okay," he said with a final flick. "Here's what I'll agree to do: The company will cover two days a week at the W Hotel and we'll keep our arrangement with you—*minus* fifty percent of that weekly salary Ms. Silverstein agreed to pay you. I'll keep two-thirds of your stock options intact—*if* the number of page views on your blog remains as high as it is today until LifeStyleXer goes public in a few weeks and, after that time, restore them to the full five-hundred thousand dollars *if* the page views *remain* at least eighty percent of that figure, on average, for the next two years."

After only a few seconds' hesitation she said, "Fair enough," and then added with a *frisson* of trepidation, "And can this new agreement be drawn up as a separate contract from Charlie Miller's? He's really much more suited than I am to managing those ten new food bloggers I'm recruiting…and, by the way," she told Chapman parenthetically, "I already lined up four good ones at the food writers' dinner I attended at Montisi Ranch over the weekend."

"Well, that's excellent news," Chapman said, appearing pleased. "Good idea. I'll make a note to have Ms. Silverstein tell him he'll manage the national food blog team once you've recruited the remaining six."

Kerry could barely keep from grinning. "Also, Mr. Chapman, I believe that Ms. Silverstein has assigned Mr. Miller some tech projects, as well. His job, now, has very little relation to what you've hired me for, which is why I'd like my contract to be separate."

Harry Chapman paused and appeared to be considering her words carefully.

"Yes," he agreed, nodding his assent. "You and Mr. Miller are fulfilling different roles now that you're here working for us. I'll let HR know what we've decided today, and have Legal draw up your new agreement."

"That's terrific."

Chapman pointed to his computer's screen. "By the way, Ms. Hannigan, my wife is a huge fan of your blog, and has been ever since you started writing it. She made that marvelous dill sauce recipe of yours for the salmon we served Sunday night and she loved the second blog you posted this morning about what to plant in an edible, organic backyard kitchen garden." He laughed. "It's a good thing I like vegetables."

"T-that's wonderful!" Kerry stammered. "Thank you so much for telling me."

He leaned forward and tapped his pen once more on the desk. "What you've been writing about is exactly what we needed to add to the mix of what we're doing around here. In fact, it's very important to the overall approach we're taking with the company leading up to the IPO. So, good job!"

Kerry felt color infuse her cheeks at hearing such high praise and rose from her chair, anxious to depart Chapman's office before he had any second thoughts.

"Thank you so much for seeing me this morning without an appointment," she said, reaching across his desk to shake his hand. "And you have my absolute promise to work harder than ever to merit your wife's and this company's support."

Harry Chapman nodded absently and began typing notes into his computer that Kerry could only assume were the details of the new bargain they'd just struck.

"Check your email later today," he confirmed, not looking up. "You can print out, sign, and deliver the new contract directly back to me."

"Will do," Kerry said over her shoulder, exiting his office as quickly as she could before she ran into any vice presidents who might be wandering the halls.

Kerry slipped into her Aeron chair inside her cubicle, pulled out her cellphone, and texted Ren the news that her negotiations with LifeStyleXer had concluded, resulting in everything she wanted in order to be able to move to the ranch as a Montisi Olive Ranch food and marketing consultant—and "Jeremy's sous chef," she added, for good measure.

Within seconds, an electronic message popped on her screen.

Totally delighted. Pick you and luggage up at seven and take you to dinner at Poggio's in Sausalito to celebrate on the way home?

She felt a fluttering and glanced at her right hand, only to realize that the feeling of butterflies was vibrating inside her own chest.

Perfect, she texted him back. Then she realized Ren hadn't mentioned the situation with Sara. She'd ask him when he picked her up at the W later.

By close of business later that same day, Kerry received her new contract and delivered it—signed—back to Harry Chapman's desk. Just as she was leaving, she nearly groaned out loud at the sight of Beverly Silverstein briskly walking down the hall in her direction. Kerry glanced at Harry Chapman's door that she'd left ajar at his request.

"You've been meeting with Harry?" Beverly demanded with a sharp edge to her tone. "What about?"

"Just summoned for a little meet-and-greet," Kerry said with a deliberate shrug. For some reason, she was no longer intimidated by the woman and continued to walk past her. Over her shoulder she added, "Turns out, Mr. Chapman's wife is a big fan of my blog. Isn't that great?"

Before Beverly could say anything else, Kerry stepped into the elevator that would take her down to the floor where she could write a couple more blogs in her despised cubicle with the knowledge she would only be sitting in it two days a week.

At ten minutes before seven p.m., she checked out of the W Hotel and made a reservation for a single room there, every Monday and Tuesday night "for the foreseeable future," as she informed the desk clerk. Ren was waiting in the Mercedes at the entrance when she wheeled her suitcase through the doors and halted at the curb.

"Is this all you have?" he marveled.

"This is it, at least until my stuff from New York arrives," she replied. "I guess I'll have to put most of it in storage until we see how everything works out."

Ren grabbed a hold of her wheelie to store it in the trunk of his car and grinned.

"It's going to work out just fine."

"What's the latest about Sara?" she said, hesitating to get

into his car.

"Tell you at dinner."

Once again, Kerry wondered if she weren't about to trade the problems of dealing with one difficult female for another. As they headed across downtown San Francisco towards the Golden Gate Bridge, she longed to ask Ren exactly what, if anything, had been decided. Then, she resolutely pushed all thoughts of the yawning unknown from her mind and gazed at the dark expanse of water on both sides of the bridge. She'd made her decision, and come what may, she'd power through it.

Once on the Marin County side, Ren took the first exit off Highway 1 and wound his way down a steep incline and into the maritime village of Sausalito. Lights winked at her from the cluster of dwellings that climbed the hills above the Bay as if they were part of a landscape in Portofino, Italy.

Ren left his car with the valet, took Kerry's arm, and guided her into Poggio's Trattoria on Bridgeway, Sausalito's principal thoroughfare. Close by was a series of piers where several luxury yachts and the ferries to San Francisco docked, along with more modest sailing craft.

"What a pretty place!" she exclaimed, pointing to several art galleries and shops they passed whose windows displayed chic clothing and all manner of handicrafts.

"It's a town of about seven thousand, full of artists and serious sailors," he explained. "Sausalito is fighting to hold on to its uniqueness against an onslaught of digital millionaires who are buying up houses here, right and left."

"I can certainly understand why they might want to live here. What an amazing waterfront town, and yet so close to the city."

Once inside Poggio's, they were led immediately to an intimate leather-clad booth whose high sides bookended a table with starched linen and a forest of stemmed glasses and handsome cutlery.

Ren ordered a plate of bruschetta and a bottle of *Veuve Clicquot*.

"Shouldn't it be *Prosecco*?" she teased, referring to an Italian sparkling wine.

"This calls for busting the budget one last time," he replied and then fell oddly silent as their waiter poured the French champagne into slender, crystal flutes.

When they were alone again, Ren raised his glass.

"To you and our new venture," he toasted her, "and I can't wait to hear how you pulled this off!"

With some pride, Kerry described her session with CEO Harry Chapman and the fact he'd agreed to a renegotiated employment package.

"Chapman seems to be a very decent guy, and he actually *listened* when I explained what I wanted to do and why. Luckily," she said with a laugh, lifting a piece of toast with tomato, basil and drizzled olive oil from the plate that sat on the table between them, "his *wife* is a fan of my blog and he appears to listen to her, as well!"

"Sounds like you convinced him to let you keep your stock options."

"Two-thirds of them to begin with, and half my current salary, which seemed fair, since I'm not available to do much else but my blogs for them." She briefly recounted the rest of the CEO's changes to her employment package, concluding, "If I hang around past the two year period, I get more stock." She smiled, and added, "But I fully expect to be working full time at the ranch by then, so *that* won't happen."

"You are the *best*, Kerry Hannigan," Ren said, smiling back. "Not bitten by the Big Bucks Bug, are you? What a gal..."

With a shrug, she popped the bruschetta into her mouth, slowly began to chew, and closed her eyes, savouring the explosion of flavors. Then her lids flew open.

"Poggio uses your olive oil, doesn't it? This is one fabulous concoction they've just served us!"

Ren inclined his head modestly. Kerry took a deep breath. Despite her brave words about her future at the ranch, she couldn't seem to stop worrying about Sara Lang. The truth was, the woman *was* a problem for her as well as for Ren, and she wanted an idea what she would be facing by living in Petaluma.

"So tell me," she asked. "What's the latest about Sara? Did you two have a chance to talk since yesterday?"

"We did," Ren confirmed. "It wasn't a very pleasant conversation, but I got her to agree to move on within the month, whether or not she's found a new job."

Kerry supposed that was progress, if not perfection.

"One problem, though," he added.

"What?" she asked, wondering what trick Sara might be concealing up her sleeve.

"We added a dinner on Tuesday for visiting experts from the UC Davis Olive Oil Center."

"That's where they test products for purity and grade and publish their findings—to the dismay of the cheaters," Kerry confirmed, "the ones claiming extra virginity for products that are actually of a lower grade?"

"Exactly. It's a big deal, and with Jeremy forced to stay off his feet most of the day, would you be willing to take charge, with José and Sara assisting? I'll help, too," he assured her.

"And protect me if Sara suddenly decides to find a new use for the kitchen knives?" she asked, only half in jest.

"I won't leave you two alone for an instant," he assured

her.

"Well, if Jeremy can give us both directions from the couch, she'll probably behave, don't you think?"

"Let us hope. You and I will just have to work on marketing and product development issues later in the week."

Kerry groaned inwardly at the thought of dealing with the quarrelsome woman under the pressured circumstances of producing a stellar meal for such an important group, but then she reminded herself that Sara would be gone in a month.

"Despite my concerns about your sister-in-law," she mused, "I might as well admit to you that hanging out in the kitchen is the part of the job I most look forward to."

"Slaving over a hot stove?" he asked skeptically. "Some kind of feminist writer *you* are."

"It's pure heaven to me!" she assured him, laughing. "I'm excited about the other things you want me to do, and I don't want Jeremy to think I'm trying to replace him, but I just love that commercial kitchen of yours, and the vegetable garden right outside, to say nothing of the wonderful outdoor oven you've built. It's just that—" She paused, gathering her thoughts. "It's just that it's the perfect *combination* of everything I've dreamed I wanted in my life."

Ren and Kerry locked glances and once again since meeting this man, their surroundings seemed to blur around the edges and all she could manage to do was gaze across the table as currents of unexpected elation filled her chest.

Just then, the waiter arrived with steaming plates of perfectly cooked *al dente* pasta coated with a rich lamb Ragu sauce for Ren, and another that was laden with freshly steamed mussels in a garlic-laced broth for Kerry.

The moment of intimacy was broken, but thoughts of

Ren's nearness and the emotion that appeared to have passed between them lingered as she studiously focused on twirling her fork into the long threads of linguine placed before her.

Later, in the half hour it took to drive from Sausalito to the ranch, Ren outlined his strategy for the next business quarter. Before Kerry knew it, his car was turning left, past the ranch gate and down the hard-packed dirt road. Prego and Scusi bounded down the path, tails wagging wildly, as Ren collected her luggage from the trunk and led her up a gentle hill, past the large greenhouse situated twenty yards beyond the kitchen.

They approached a whitewashed, batten-board bungalow perched on the low rise, its two front windows anchored by dark green wooden flower boxes planted with squat holly bushes. Their bright red berries reminded Kerry that Christmas was a mere two weeks away. Could she sneak back to New York for two or three days and surprise Angelica, she wondered, as she noticed that lights glowed from the inside of the cottage, warm and welcoming.

"Here we are," Ren announced, as he put a key in the lower portion of a forest green double Dutch door and pushed it open. Kerry heard the pride in his voice as he pointed out the stone fireplace, updated kitchenette, single bedroom, and a bathroom sporting a claw-and-ball tub.

"My grandmother used to come out here to paint in this little cottage." He gestured toward the windows. "She said it has the kind of daylight that inspires creativity…so I thought it might be just the place for a writer. José spent all day getting it ready, and I got the tech guy out to install a router so you can have Wi-Fi up here."

"Oh…that's fantastic!" Kerry replied, clapping her hands.

She followed him further into the living room where she

noted the stacked logs awaiting a match to light a cozy fire. A small, round table for two took up one corner, and a hand-woven rug graced the hearth.

"What a little jewel box of a place!" she exclaimed. "And that's the perfect spot for my laptop computer," she said excitedly, pointing to the little table. "I can crank out eight-hundred words at a shot within view of gorgeous olive groves climbing up the hill!"

"So, it's not too small?"

"Oh, no..." she said on a long breath, turning in a circle. "It's perfect! This is a dream cottage for someone like me." She turned toward Ren and added gratefully, "I can't quite believe I get to live here!" As she spoke, Ren's steady gaze made her pulse speed up in dizzying fashion. "Thank you so much, Ren. I feel as if I'm in some dream..."

For a long moment, they simply stared at each other. Kerry felt in that instant that there was a strange force field drawing them inexorably closer to one another.

Finally Ren said, "I'd better go see how Jeremy is doing." He turned away and strode toward the Dutch door whose top section was open, offering a glimpse of the greenhouse below. "He supervised José and Sara's putting together a farm-to-table dinner tonight that we served to a small group of local restaurateurs and I want to hear how he thinks it went."

He paused at the door and although the distance between them had widened, Kerry continued to sense the same magnetic pull as before. Somehow, it seemed the most natural thing in the world when he asked, "Want to come with me?"

Kerry nodded as a little ripple of happiness skittered down her spine.

When Ren pushed open the screen door to the

commercial kitchen, Jeremy was sprawled on the leather couch. José stood at the sink, rinsing the last of the dishes and putting them in the heat sterilizer, while Sara was sitting at the table with a large glass of cabernet at her side.

"Hi, all. How'd it go tonight?" Ren asked.

Jeremy looked up and greeted them wearily, "Hey there...and welcome, Kerry. We sure could have used *you* tonight. It's going to be so great having you here."

Sara was staring sullenly into her glass.

"Oh? What happened?" Ren inquired.

Jeremy darted a glance at Sara and shrugged.

"I'm obviously not operating on all cylinders right now, and it just felt as if our timing was off. José was great following my instructions on making most of the food, but..." He paused and addressed Kerry. "You probably know what I'm talking about. It was one of those nights when we just weren't in the zone, you know what I mean?"

Before Kerry could respond, Sara spoke up with an unpleasant edge to her voice.

"You mean *I* wasn't in the *zone*," she mimicked. "Well, what do you expect, Jeremy? I had to do the desserts *and* make the salad *and* serve and clear—which is usually José's job!" She shot a sharp look in Kerry's direction. "Of course, you probably think that everything will magically be peachy keen, now that *you've* ridden to the rescue."

"Kerry's work the day Jeremy got sick speaks for itself," Ren said, his exasperation evident, "and you could probably learn something if you'd drop the attitude and just pay attention."

"Oh, really? *I'm* the problem? Just wait a while," Sara predicted darkly. "I googled the words 'Kerry Hannigan, chef.'" Her eyes narrowing, she pointed her index finger toward Kerry but addressed her employer. "The only paid cooking job this fraud's ever had that came up in the search results was at a sleazy pub in New York that her parents owned prior to her getting her high-and-mighty degree from the CIA." She affected an innocent shrug. "I don't get it...why is she here, Ren, unless you've got something else going on you'd like me to break to my parents who still think you're in mourning over their *other* daughter."

Ren's expression was a study in neutrality, although there was no mistaking the anger in his tone.

"Sara," he said, "I hate to *sound* like one of your parents, but you'd better just say goodnight. Then, I'd like to see you in the office at nine o'clock, sharp, *capisce*?"

Adding to the acute discomfort of everyone in the room, Sara stonily remained sitting where she was. Kerry wanted nothing more than to grab her suitcases out of the cottage on the hill and head straight back to San Francisco.

What in the world had she gotten herself into?

Uncomfortable silence continued to poison the air. At length, it was Kerry, herself, who ended it.

"Well, on that happy note, I think I'll leave you all." She addressed the exhausted-looking chef. "I've been hired here to help on the business side, but call on me, Jeremy, whenever you need a hand. I am more than happy to offer it, including tomorrow night's dinner for the UC Davis Olive Oil folks." She turned to face Sara. "I can understand how my being hired has upset you, but I am not the enemy, and you're only hurting yourself by behaving like this."

And before anyone in the kitchen could say another word, Kerry was out the door and sprinting toward her little bungalow, its two windows glowing a warm welcome in the absolute stillness of the surrounding hills.

***

By the time Kerry reached her new front step, she heard the kitchen door down the hill open and slam shut and two angry, but indistinguishable voices floated on the evening air. She turned around in time to see Ren and Sara gesticulating at each other and walking swiftly along the lower path in the direction of the ranch office.

Ren had probably reached his limit and Kerry wondered what he would—or could—do to resolve the situation any sooner than scheduled. She could only pray that eventually things would settle down and she could begin what she hoped was a completely new chapter in a wonderful lifestyle that had somehow fallen into her lap.

She turned her back on the drama unfolding in Ren's office and entered her new living quarters. Within minutes, she had unzipped her suitcase and hung her clothes in the bedroom closet. Her next task was to crank out two more blog assignments, which she did over the next hour and a half, despite her thoughts occasionally wandering down the hill. She'd brushed her teeth and was about to get ready for bed when she heard a knock on the door. Ren, himself, stood on the cement front step with a grim expression, his hands in his jeans pockets.

"That was bad," he said without preamble. "I told her after you left that she has two weeks to find herself another place to live. Then I called her parents in her presence and asked them to alert Sara's shrink and make arrangements to house their daughter as soon as they can. I've had it."

"But what about poor Jeremy? José's been great, but—"

"Plan B," Ren cut in. "Like you said, you'll be Jeremy's backup, if that's okay with you, and the marketing side of things will definitely have to wait, because I fully understand that your first priority is pumping out those blogs and there won't be time—"

"As of today," she interrupted him, "my first priority is *all* of it." She was buoyed by the fact that Ren hadn't hesitated to make such a tough decision. "And we wouldn't be able to make progress with *any* of the things you want to do around here unless you ordered Sara Lang to go her merry way, as you just did." She reached out and briefly touched his arm. "I realize that there are probably many layers to all of this that I can't possibly know about, but I truly appreciate what you just did. Keep the faith, Ren," she added, echoing the Claddagh's earlier message. "We'll figure all this out."

"Well, all I can say to that is, thank God I made that delivery to Amphora Nueva in Berkeley last Friday." Without warning, he reached across the threshold and took her into his arms, pulling her close. "Otherwise," he whispered against her ear, "I might never have met you, and then where would I be?"

Kerry marveled at how natural it felt to be enveloped in Ren's embrace and she leaned into his torso, luxuriating in the mere feel of her cheek resting against his broad chest. At length, she pulled away and tilted her head to be able to look at him.

"If we *hadn't* met last week, you'd be in a lot less complicated situation than you're in right now," she chided. "But since we can't turn back the clock, how about you step into my parlor and we close the door so that every ranch hand on the place doesn't have such a grandstand view?"

Ren didn't break his hold of her, but simply moved the two of them a few feet past the front door and pushed it closed with his foot. His hands then framed her face, his fingers threading through her hair, sending cascading warmth up and down her neck.

"I have wanted to kiss you from that first day I watched

you close your eyes and run your tongue over that cube of French bread soaked in my olive oil."

"Good food is a sensual experience, don't you think," she whispered, "just like—"

"Oh...yes..." he murmured, stopping their exchange as he settled his mouth on hers.

His lips were soft, then insistent, then demanding, and Kerry suddenly wondered if she'd crossed some desert landscape in the past week to find a cool, comforting oasis where she could drink her fill. His arousal pressed against her midsection, signaling that the magnetic pull she was certain they'd both been sensing since the day they met had finally culminated in electrifying sensations coursing through every cell in her body.

When, at length, they allowed an inch of space between them, Kerry inhaled a shaky breath.

"This is pretty insane, don't you think? I haven't even slept one night on your ranch and look at us!"

"It's crazy good," he said, his voice ragged. "I've never felt this...this *need* to be so close...wanting another person to be part of my life...being with someone who makes me feel as if I *have* a life..."

"I feel it too," she replied, barely above a whisper, "but really, Ren, it hasn't even been a week since I found out about Charlie and—"

"Who *cares* about them?" He seized her by her two shoulders and looked as if he was almost angry.

"I don't care about them, either," she insisted, "but I care about what's happening to *us*. How can we know this is real? Talk about crazy!" she added with a rueful smile. "We need to slow down. We're supposed to be boss and employee, remember—"

"We're partners! I felt it that first day when Jeremy got

sick and you—"

It was Kerry's turn to cup Ren's face between her hands.

"I felt it that day, too," she acknowledged, and stood on her tiptoes to kiss him briefly on the lips. "But we've only worked together *one* day. Let's take this partner business...and everything, really...in steps, or you'll scare me to death."

"Well, we can't have that..." he mumbled, pulling her toward him again and nibbling her ear. "Okay then...so...since I'm still the boss, I say—let's go in *there*," he declared, nodding his head in the direction of the bedroom.

"Ren! I'm serious! I want to savor what seems to be happening here..."

"You mean this?" he said, gently cupping one breast and strafing her stiffened nipple with his thumb through her clothing. "Or, do you mean plain old falling in love? Because I think that's definitely what's going on here."

"You do?" she whispered, wondering if she could keep her balance should he touch her other breast.

"It's happened," he stated flatly. "At least to me, it has, and if I don't get out of here in the next five seconds, I might just drag you into Nona Concetta's spare bedroom and have my way with you on top of that quilt in there she stitched...which *would* feel pretty insane."

He leaned forward and kissed her again with a ferocity that left Kerry feeling as if she were a marked woman. Then he abruptly turned and left the cottage.

She stood at the open door, watching him stride down the hill toward the low-slung farmhouse where he worked and slept. The instant his tall figure disappeared into the gloom, she felt her ring finger pulse with warmth.

Know thy heart, indeed, Kerry m'girl...

Chapter Eight

The following morning, Kerry awoke at six with birds chattering outside her window, as if scolding the universe for the low-lying fog that enveloped the rows of olive trees outside her window. She forced herself to fire up her laptop and wrote another two blogs, one about the work of the UC Davis Olive Oil panel of experts whose mission it was to determine which oils they deemed of highest quality. The second post was about preparing a dinner for the same distinguished group later that night with ingredients that would come within a ten-mile radius.

By eight-thirty, a damp chill continued to linger in the air when she walked down the hill, her mind focused on sipping a strong cup of coffee that she hoped José had made by the time she arrived at the building housing the ranch's commercial kitchen.

She pushed open the door to an empty room and flipped the light switch to search the well-organized pantry for the coffeemaker, filters, and grinder, happy to discover a bag of San Francisco Fog coffee beans in the big walk-in freezer.

She'd scrambled a dozen eggs for whoever would eat them and perused Tuesday night's menu that Jeremy had posted on the cork bulletin board. José soon appeared, followed five minutes later by Chef Jeremy, himself. After a congenial consultation, all three got busy doing the prep for the UC Davis dinner. When Sara hadn't made an appearance by eleven o'clock, Kerry called Tony, "the Salad Associate at LifeStyleXer," she explained with a grin to Jeremy. Tony instantly said he was delighted to lend a hand as soon as he got off work at the company cafeteria.

"If we can't depend on her," Jeremy agreed, "a cook's gotta do what a cook's gotta do."

Around one o'clock Sara flounced into the kitchen with Ren—who'd been informed of her tardiness by Jeremy—following close behind. She announced pointedly to the chef that she would make the dessert and salad dressing.

Jeremy and his second-in-command exchanged looks, but Kerry kept to the task she was currently assigned without comment. Ren assumed the job of peeling a pile of root vegetables José had pulled from the garden that morning.

Out of the corner of her eye, Kerry noticed that Sara had quickly proceeded to measure out oil for the cake batter she was making. While the round pans were baking in the oven, the young woman silently poured oil from the same bottle into a bowl containing the ingredients for mustard vinaigrette.

Fifteen minutes later, Kerry smelled something burning.

"Your cakes!" she cried, and raced over to the large stainless steel commercial oven on the far side of the room. She glanced at the temperature gauge. "You set it at *five hundred degrees*, Sara!" she shouted. "What the—"

Sara merely smiled and said, "Oh. Really? Gee. Sorry. My mistake," and continued to whisk the oil into the salad dressing.

Jeremy pulled himself off the couch and moved with obvious discomfort to Kerry's side, glancing worriedly at the clock.

"Shit, Sara!"

Kerry opened the oven just as one of the cakes burst into

flame. The others were already blackened and useless. She flicked off the oven, grabbed a quilted mitt, and tossed the cake and its pan into the stainless steel sink where José turned the water on to put out the flames. Alarming hissing sounds and smoke filled the kitchen while Sara remained where she was, calmly whisking the salad dressing.

"You did this on purpose," Kerry accused her, racing to open the door and windows to prevent the smoke alarm from sounding. "You're either just a jealous idiot or a very sick puppy. You could have burned down the place!"

By this time, Jeremy and Ren had joined the two women who were less than a foot apart, glaring at each other through the smoky interior.

"I don't actually care which it is," Jeremy shouted at his erstwhile sous chef. "Just get *out* of here, Sara. Go sit in your room until your two weeks are up!" Kerry could tell that Jeremy already appeared to regret he'd jumped off the couch so quickly when the cakes caught fire.

Sara whirled to face the chef. "So Ren told you I have to leave in two weeks, instead of a month?" She was red-faced and Kerry wondered if she would, indeed, seize a butcher knife and go after anyone within reach.

"Yes," Ren confirmed. "I told him this morning."

Ignoring her employer, she shouted at the chef, "And did he tell you he's already shacking up with Ms. Perfect here?"

"It's none of my business who he's shacking up with!" Jeremy replied, his complexion drained of color. Kerry thought she saw him wince with pain.

Kerry banged her fist on the counter near the bowl of vinaigrette.

"I am *not* sleeping with the boss, though I imagine I will one of these days, Sara, so I think you have a choice: make an utter mess of everything in the time you have left here on the ranch where your brother-in-law offered you shelter and amazing kindness—or pull yourself together and grow up! But one thing is certain...you can't have your late sister, Sandra's life, and you sure as hell can't have *mine!*"

The look that passed over Sara's features was a blend of shock and pure hatred. Meanwhile, Kerry detected a highly unpleasant odor wafting from the bowl of salad dressing Sara had been making. On impulse, she grabbed a spoon and stuck it into the emulsified liquid to sample it.

"Good God!" she exploded, squeezing her eyes shut. "This salad dressing is *rancid!*" She opened her eyes to stare at Sara, the full extent of the woman's efforts to sabotage them becoming all too clear. "You deliberately used discarded oil from that back shelf in the mill that would *ruin* the Montisi Ranch's reputation with the UC Davis olive oil experts tonight when we served them a salad that would taste absolutely disgusting!"

Sara ignored Kerry's accusations and turned on Ren, instead.

"You haven't even known this woman a *week* and she swans in here and practically takes over the place."

"Sara, just stop it!" ordered Ren.

"I won't stop it!" Sara's voice had gone up an octave and she seemed on the edge of hysteria. She shook a finger at Ren, her eyes narrowing. "I know what you've got planned, installing her in your grandmother's cottage that Sandra always wanted for her workout studio! You're just waiting for Concetta to kick off and until she does, you'll keep this Hannigan woman around until her stock options reach 'bingo' in a couple of years. That should tide you over and solve your current cash-flow problems, won't it?"

"How do you know about *my* stock options?" Kerry demanded, glaring at both Sara and Ren.

Sara continued, unfazed by Kerry's outburst.

"You'll be sitting pretty, won't you, Ren? She's got a better payout potential than the Lang family, you think? Traded us in for that little bitch, have you, you bastard!"

Ren ignored Sara, urgently saying to Kerry, "I have *never* discussed your financial situation with anyone!"

It was Sara's turn to bang her fist on the counter. "You think it's beneath my dignity to listen at office doors when our future is at stake, Renato Montisi?"

"*Our* future? For God's sake, Sara, we don't *have* a future!" Ren exploded. "We've never had one—before, during, or after I met your sister. And as sorry as I am that Sandra died at such a young age—and in such a terrible way—neither of you, nor your parents, ever seemed to grasp what was important to anyone but yourselves!"

Sara was shaking with fury. "Well, I can see, now, that the only thing really important to you is this ranch...and that you'll do virtually anything to keep it afloat! Even latch on to Ms. Moneybags Hannigan, here, whom you've known about ten minutes! And you think *I'm* crazy? *You're* crazy—like a fox!"

Kerry's gaze swept the kitchen. Ren and Sara looked as if they were about to come to blows. Jeremy had collapsed on the couch and was massaging his stomach. José's face had a pinched expression, no doubt straining to better understand the heated English being shouted by his co-workers.

Oh, Lord, thought Kerry, was Ren Machiavellian enough to be waiting for his grandmother to die, meanwhile latching onto some potential 'venture capital' to keep the business going? Was all the heat generated last night manufactured because of a couple hundred thousand dollars' worth of stock options?

Her brain felt as if it were about to explode. Then a voice

in her head brought her up short.

Kerry! Don't be daft. Get the facts!

Kerry shook her head as if refusing to listen to the thoughts flying through her mind and made a beeline for the door, slamming it shut with tremendous force and sprinting up the hill to the safety of her little cottage. All the way along the path she blotted out the Claddagh's cautioning voice, wondering—even if Sara was a "borderline personality" and her accusations about Ren were false—how she, Kerry, could ever achieve any sort of serenity in her life with Ren's past with the Lang family permeating everything?

What *was* this? *Fatal Attraction—Part 2?*

Exhausted by her warring thoughts, Kerry shut the Dutch door with a bang and turned the lock, her eyes filling with tears. Had she been so vulnerable last week that she had blindly walked into a situation that was either Charlie Miller all over again—or something worse?

She lowered her gaze to her right hand. The ring's clear emerald stone stared back at her coldly. Maybe she should have just toughed it out in her cubicle at LifestyleXer. At least, in two years she'd have half a million bucks coming her way and not have to deal with lunatics like Sara Lang.

So, you're going to believe the one person on this ranch who wishes you ill?

"Oh, shut up, will you?" Kerry exclaimed, shocked to see that the ring was glowing as if it were a white rose in full bloom.

Renato Montisi loves this land and its bounty in the same way you do!

Kerry clapped her hands over her ears. If she couldn't stomach Life With Sara, or the cubicle on Howard Street, or the techie creeps in all of Silicon Land—she could just chuck it all! She could simply hand over her blog's rights to Harry

Chapman, go back to New York, and work at her parents' restaurant until she figured out the rest of her life.

But even if you did slink back to Manhattan, you'd never know how it might have turned out with you and Renato Montisi!

The Claddagh ring had suddenly begun to pulse like a mixed-up stoplight, alternating between an emerald gemstone and an opal. Obviously, her thoughts and the ring's were clashing and it was slowly driving her crazy.

"Will you please *stop!*" she begged aloud. "Leave me alone!"

Unbidden, a memory of Ren flashed in her head, outrageously handsome in his well-worn jeans and work shirt, leaning forward in the kitchen as she slid a lettuce leaf, dripping in the mustard dressing she'd made with the ranch's olive oil, between his lips and the intimate look of pure pleasure that had passed between them.

Remember those moments...remember what makes you happy...

"It's going to make me happy if my blogs keep driving traffic to LifestyleXer dot com and I earn half a million bucks!" she yelled into an empty cottage.

Oh, really?

Steeling herself, she sat down at her tiny kitchen table, the early afternoon sun flooding through the front windows. She knew what to do! She'd write about as many subjects as she could think of in order to bank pieces if she should decide, in fact, to throw in the towel at the ranch and move back to San Francisco to live in some hideous apartment that doubled as a dog house.

She might as well face it, she though morosely. She and the ring on her finger had painted themselves right into a corner.

***

Hunched over her laptop for the next hour, Kerry's back was aching. Before she shut down her computer, she made a quick check of the online metrics in the last twenty-four hours to confirm that her blog posts were still were gaining page views as they had been since the very beginning of CookChic. Then, as was her habit, she scanned the comments posted below her last several blogs, and reared back in her chair, staring in disbelief. A series of nasty remarks from visitors whose names were unfamiliar and did not include any of her usual fans formed a column of negativity the likes of which she'd never seen from the first day she began posting. Even while she was looking at the screen, four or five more popped in between a few of her stalwart supporters that had begun to reply in her defense.

"What the—?"

Every time she refreshed the page, a few more ugly comments winged in, all of them slamming either her writing or her opinions.

There could only be one answer to what was going on: Sara Lang.

That woman is a devil!

Kerry felt the ring grow warm on her finger.

That woman has a big hole in her heart that you didn't cause and you can't cure. Just do your job!

Her job? She *was* doing her job! She was writing the best material of her life and look what was happening!

Then she suddenly remembered: tonight's dinner for the visiting olive oil experts! She'd abandoned ship and it was just after four. Out her window, Tony's battered Jetta had just wheeled into the gravel parking lot and screeched to a halt.

Two hours to Show Time!

Whatever was going on in her personal life had to be put on hold. She couldn't let poor Jeremy down.

***

By some miracle, Jeremy, José, Tony, Ren, and Kerry produced an excellent dinner of roasted Petaluma organic chicken, marinated in this year's Montisi olive oil, garlic, fig-laced balsamic vinegar, and crushed, fresh rosemary. The poultry was plated on a bed of perfectly steamed root vegetables, fresh from the garden, along with Tony's *carpaccio* salad as a starter. Dessert consisted of tarts made with fruit from a neighboring orchard. Kerry had folded puff pastry over halved pears, along with caramelized sugar, in several of chef's large frying pans and baked them—pan, fruit, and all—in the oven.

"Wow!" said Tony admiringly as he watched Kerry invert the contents of the pans onto large, round platters, fruit-side-up and surrounded by a golden, flakey crust. "That's amazing!"

"It's a great thing to do when you're really pushed," she replied, "and fortunately, Jeremy keeps a well-stocked pantry for just such emergencies. The puff pastry is from a box, but of course, it's the *best* brand."

Kerry and Ren had exchanged barely ten words during the frenzy that preceded the dinner, and Kerry helped with the cleanup in the kitchen while he entertained his guests following the meal.

Sara was nowhere to be seen. When Tony and José went out to the pavilion to bring in the last of the dishes, Kerry asked Jeremy what had transpired after she escaped to the cottage earlier that afternoon.

"She just stormed out of the kitchen as soon as you left. Ren followed her, trying to talk some sense into the woman. No doubt our very own drama diva's still sulking in her room," Jeremy said wearily, sinking onto the couch. "And

Kerry…I just wanted to say…I hope you didn't take anything she said about Ren seriously."

"Hey…" she replied, trying to keep a light tone, "this whole deal with me here on the ranch is just a shakedown cruise," wondering how many more revolting comments had been posted to her blog by now?

"Not as far as I'm concerned," Jeremy replied. "I've decided to have my gall bladder taken out next week. I hope we can count on you to keep this boat on course."

Kerry hesitated, and then said, "Of course. I'll stay here at least until you're back on your feet. After that, frankly…it's anybody's guess."

Within the half hour, the kitchen was restored to its usual, pristine condition and Kerry walked Tony out to his car, relating to him the cascade of negative comments that had suddenly appeared in relation to her latest blog posts. She briefly described recent events at the ranch and outlined her suspicions that Sara Lang might be the cause.

"Well, let's find out if it is her," Tony said.

"Can you do that?"

"We can try. I've got a few geek buddies at work who can run a check on the names and Internet addresses of the people posting that crap." He grinned. "The NSA's got nothing on these guys. I'll text you later."

"Tonight?" Kerry asked, startled to think that she might quickly get to the bottom of what was going on.

"Tonight, or first thing tomorrow. These are the weird nerds at LifeStyleXer who sleep under their desks." He gave her a buss on the cheek. "And thanks for asking me to work tonight." He waved an envelope containing the cash she'd given him. "This ranch is da bomb!"

***

That night, Kerry slept fitfully, hoping to hear a ping on her cellphone that Tony had sent her a text message identifying who was piling in with so many damaging comments that could bring her page views down and—if the negative spiral continued—cause her to miss the goals the CEO had set in order for her stock ultimately to vest.

By six-thirty, dawn was just filtering through the olive groves outside her window, and still there was no word from Tony—or any text from Ren, for that matter. She decided to dress, bundling up in a turtleneck sweater and a puffy down vest and knee-length coat to ward off the early morning chill. To pass time until Tony contacted her with news, she ventured out of the cottage and along the lavender hedges that would be blooming in June, Ren had told her.

You don't want to miss that, *do you?*

She glanced down at her ring, glowing eerily white in the gloom and uttered her favorite French curse. *"Merde!"*

She snapped off a lavender stock and sniffed it, detecting the faintest essence of the familiar scent, even without a bloom. She had always adored this particular aroma, especially in those bars of lovely French soap or in body lotion…

Staring at the sage green plant held between her fingers, a jumble of thoughts began to crowd her brain.

I love this place…I love this life! *I want to learn to be a steward of land like this…to grow and make wonderful food! To find new uses for what's currently discarded. No grasping, manipulative, crazy—okay,* wounded*—woman is going to drive me off without a fight! Ren and I are exactly the same: this sort of life…this* path*…is the path we choose to walk.*

By this time, not only was her hand vibrating wildly, but her entire body was shaking, whether due to the morning chill or something Kerry found quite frightening to contemplate: she was either as off her gourd as Sara Lang, or the Claddagh ring knew her far better than she knew herself...

Then, she actually heard her stomach rumble.

She needed a cup of good, strong tea, and she needed it *now*!

Kerry once again found the kitchen deserted at this early hour and immediately flipped on the electric kettle. Then she set up the coffeemaker for the others she knew would soon be streaming in, and cracked a dozen eggs into a bowl, certain that "if she scrambled them, they will come."

Sure enough, Jeremy was the first to pad through the back door in jeans and a ranch T-shirt. He gratefully accepted a cup of proffered coffee while she sipped her tea.

"How's your midsection feeling this morning?" she asked.

"Holding its own...for the moment." He nodded at the pan of beaten eggs she was slowly stirring. "Nice simple food for this boy until I have the operation."

Next, Ralph Larimore, the head gardener, walked in, followed by José, each dishing up the eggs she'd concocted, laced with fresh thyme, along with toast and jam Jeremy had made from ranch strawberries grown the previous season.

Kerry had almost finished her breakfast when Ren strode through the screen door and served himself the last scoop of scrambled eggs.

Still standing, plate in hand, he asked Kerry to follow him to his office before reminding Jeremy that some cosmetic moguls were scheduled to arrive for heavy hors d'oeuvres and wine pairings from four to six, later that day.

"They're going on to have dinner up in Healdsburg and

spend the night there," he explained. "We should have them here for drinks and the hors d'oeuvres only about two or three hours."

"No problem, boss," said Jeremy as Kerry followed Ren out the kitchen door.

"Cosmetic moguls?" Kerry repeated. "You must be kidding! They want to visit an olive ranch instead of a winery?"

"They're doing both," he replied, his features continuing to reflect tension from the drama with Sara the previous night. "They're part of some trade group from New York and LA—here mostly for a tour of the Sonoma vineyards—but our agent booked them for a drop-by here, too. Ka-ching, ka-ching…though not very much."

By this time they'd entered Ren's office, his desk littered with spreadsheets.

"Looks like you've been working all night," she commented.

"Nearly. I wanted you to know exactly where we stand financially, and to try to convince you that everything Sara claimed was false about my waiting to pounce on your incipient millions."

"Oh, Ren…" she began.

"The trouble is," he cut her off, "as I told you before, we *are* on shaky ground, but that is *not* why I felt like hauling you off to a cave somewhere yesterday."

Kerry offered a bleak, apologetic smile before she replied. "I gave what happened in the kitchen yesterday some serious thought and concluded that Sara was just projecting what *she* would do if she thought she could get her hands on someone else's money. She reminds me a lot of Charlie Miller."

"I told her last night to clear out. Today. Even if you weren't in the picture, her last little number—using rancid olive oil in a meal for the very people who are trying to expose the crooks in our business—crosses a line that can never be erased. She's toxic and there's nothing I can do to fix her. I honestly hope she'll be okay wherever she ultimately lands, but I'm counting the minutes until she leaves."

Kerry could see that Ren was upset in a way he couldn't disguise and her heart went out to him. With everything he was dealing with, and *had* dealt with since his wife's death, Sara's betrayal had obviously struck deep. She was tempted to tell him of her suspicions regarding the vicious comments on her blog, but decided not to add to his woes until she had confirmation from Tony and his cyber-sleuths.

Instead, she said, "Well, I've got something that may cheer you up."

"What?"

"You're not going to believe this, but I have an idea you could suggest to your guests tonight—or at some point in the future."

"You do? *What?*" he repeated.

"What if *we* started a line of natural products like soap and body lotion made from the second press of the olives, *plus* our own lavender essence harvested from all those lavender plants around here? And if we can't produce enough, we can contract with other olive ranches and lavender farms in California, but brand it as our own special formula."

Ren gazed across his desk with a look of amazement.

"Now, why couldn't *I* have thought of private label cosmetics/beauty products? I've been staring at those rows of lavender since I was a toddler!"

Kerry laughed and settled back in the chair opposite.

"Yeah...but I'm female and I *love* all that lavender-scented stuff like body lotion, bath oil, and bubble bath!" She smiled encouragingly. "Promise we can have bubble bath as one of our products?"

Ren leered at her across the desk. "What an arresting thought. You. Naked in a bathtub filled with Montisi's lavender bath gel."

"Not so fast, big guy! There are a few other things we need to discuss."

Ren regarded her for a moment, a distant, guarded look invading his eyes.

"Just tell me, Kerry. Are you going to stay...or go?"

She hesitated less than an instant before she answered. "Stay."

"Even after what happened yesterday?"

"Just let me know when Sara Lang has left the building, will you?"

Ren's expression revealed he didn't know if she was kidding or not.

"What if I offer you a fifty-fifty deal on this cosmetic idea—if we can make it work?"

Kerry sat straighter in her chair. "Renato Montisi, if you are suggesting that I am merely withholding my favors, just to strike a good deal—"

"Absolutely *not!*" he cut in. "I'm saying I need a partner like you...in my work...and in my *life*. If that scares you, I'm sorry...but you'll just have to accept that's how I feel."

"It does scare me a little. It's only a week on Friday since I put on—"

Ren looked puzzled at her non sequitur. "Put on what?"

She hesitated to provide an answer. Did she really know Ren well enough, yet, to talk about the ring on her finger?

"It's nearly a week since I left New York," she amended, "and met you the very same day. I can't believe I'm living here...in such a beautiful place. I can't believe...*any* of it. But here I am," she said smiling at him with a rush of happiness she couldn't deny to either of them. "It's all been pretty amazing, don't you think?"

Ren leaned forward and seized both her hands in his, a look of relief spreading across his face.

"What's even more amazing is that I feel as if I've known you, always."

Kerry nodded. "It was if we *recognized* each other the moment we met. It's absolutely crazy, isn't it? No wonder it drove Sara bonkers. She sensed our connection, right from the first."

Just at that moment, she glanced out of Ren's office window and spied his sister-in-law hauling a big suitcase across the gravel parking area. Sara yanked opened the trunk of her car and heaved in the piece of luggage, along with several other cases sitting nearby. Without a pause, she retraced her steps toward the building Kerry assumed was where she slept—and disappeared through its door.

Clearly, she was leaving the ranch.

Kerry's mobile phone pinged. It was a text message from Tony.

Call me asap

Meanwhile, Sara had reappeared with another suitcase.

"So she *is* actually leaving," Kerry said, pointing out the window. "What about her family? Has she some place to go?"

"Tahoe. Her parents grudgingly said she could stay in the house up there for a while and look for work at one of the hotels. I told her if she behaved herself for six months, I *might* write her a reference about her work here."

"You are a very decent man, Renato Montisi," Kerry said

quietly. "I actually feel very sad for her, but I'm glad you're not giving her your recommendation right away."

Sara Lang was a totally confounding person, and before Kerry could detail for him what had been happening overnight on her blog, Ren said, "And, just for the record, I don't give a flying fig about your stock options. Who knows, if in two years, they'll even be worth the paper they're printed on. I've seen a few IPOs get bad press right before they've gone on sale and then tank, big time. I hope you get that dough, but a lot can happen in the tech world in that time."

Kerry's stomach clenched. What if Sara's backhanded efforts not only screwed up *her* potential payday, but also diminished or sabotaged LifestyleXer's IPO, itself?

Ren seized her hand once more, forcing her thoughts back to the present.

"Look, Kerry...who can tell what's ahead for us after only knowing each other such a short time, but I want to say here and now that I will *never, ever* ask you for a penny of your money. You and I and the rest of the crew on this ranch are going to get this place onto solid ground by dint of our joint efforts, doing projects like your brilliant idea, just now, of using the second pressing to make olive oil and lavender-based cosmetics and beauty products."

"But what if that idea is a bust? There might be too much competition, or we can't get the distribution, or—"

"Look! You're the one who said 'Keep the faith.' If we don't succeed at this or some other idea we think up, I can go back to being a VC and *you* can run the ranch."

Kerry had a sudden thought. "But if Concetta gets wind you've gone back to Silicon Valley...she might decide to sell this place."

"She can't."

"Of course she can!"

"She's already deeded the ranch to me. The week before last."

"She *has*?"

"Concetta's turning ninety-two this year. She and I had talked about how to arrange her affairs in her final years so she'd want for nothing. She insisted before the end of the tax year on putting me on the deed as co-owner with the right of survivorship. I told her to do it *only* on the condition I could make it pay enough to sustain her at the Towers. If I can't, then we sell the place and put the proceeds to fund her living where she is."

"Ah, yes..." Kerry said with a smile, "you told me how she's queen of the San Francisco Towers. But it's super deluxe, right?"

"Very. The Towers is practically next door to the Opera House, and she couldn't be happier—and neither could I. I have her power-of-attorney and I decided last night that I won't even tell her if I have to sell."

"You are truly a stand-up guy, Renato Montisi...especially given how hard it is to make a living as a rancher."

"Well, she raised me, remember. It's the least I could do for her at this stage of her life. If everything goes south here, I can always carve out ten acres of the eight-hundred for ourselves, build a little house on them, and suit up as a Vulture Capitalist again."

Ren paused and pointed out his office window as the two of them watched Sara prepare to get into her car. Kerry hesitated for only a moment and then told Ren about the bizarre raft of negative postings that had suddenly plagued her blog.

"Do you think I should confront Sara before she drives

away?" Kerry said, rising from her chair and preparing to sprint out the door.

Both Ren and a voice echoed in her head. "No...we need to get the facts before we make a serious accusation like that."

Kerry glanced down at the phone in her lap.

"Oh, my God! I forgot! Tony just texted me. Maybe he has some news."

The cellphone only rang once before her call was answered.

"Kerry? You won't believe this." She swiftly put her phone on speaker mode so Ren could hear Tony. "My tech buddies had a hell of a time last night, but guess who they finally think were responsible for those nasty-grams?"

"Sara Lang," Kerry pronounced with a sinking heart, watching Sara's car roll across the parking lot and head down the drive.

"No!" Tony lowered his voice to a hoarse whisper. "We think it has to be Charlie Miller and Beverly Silverstein!"

Kerry could only stare, open-mouthed, at Ren whose expression told her he wasn't particularly surprised to hear this.

Tony continued, "My guys traced the IP addresses all back to LifeStyleXer, though the names of the supposed commentators are all bogus."

"Then how can we prove it's Charlie and Beverly?"

"Well here's the weird thing. Both of them posted some *positive* comments from their own email addresses at the company...probably to cover their tracks. With Beverly's supposedly *nice* posts, she used the Safari browser to access the Internet...but Miller apparently posted *both* his real and bogus comments using an obscure browser called 'Bark.'"

"You mean he didn't use Chrome or Safari?" Ren cut in.

"Right. The nice comments he made under his own name, *and* the nasty ones you saw on your site, *both* were posted via the *same*, weird browser, Bark," he reiterated.

Kerry turned to Ren. "Bark was founded by a fellow tech pal of Charlie's. It's never really caught on. He's the only person I know who still uses it."

Tony chimed in, "It's just circumstantial evidence, but it's pretty strong."

"As they say in the crime shows," Ren commented dryly, "both those two had 'motive, means, and opportunity,' plus—apparently—Bark."

Tony said, "I had the guys make printouts of what they'd tracked back to Bark, but get your fanny back to town. This is pretty explosive stuff, and I don't want any of us to get nicked by the shrapnel."

"We'll be there within the hour," Ren announced. To Kerry he said, "C'mon…let's go! I'll ride shotgun."

Kerry nodded, jumping up from her chair. To Tony on her cellphone she said, "You are way more than Salad Man, Mr. Perez…and trust me, I won't forget this."

"How about someday making me a sous chef to your sous chef, as long as it's not working with that nut job I met yesterday."

Kerry glanced out of the window just as Sara Lang's car disappeared from view.

"No worries on that score," she said, pointing silently out the window for Ren's benefit. "In fact, we need to bring you back with us to help with a bunch of cosmetic tycoons visiting the ranch late this afternoon. See you soon, and *please*…put those printouts somewhere safe, will you? Meet you in the cafeteria."

Chapter Nine

Forty-five minutes later, Ren nosed the Mercedes into a parking spot in the subterranean garage of LifestyleXer's office building on Howard Street. He and Kerry sprinted toward the elevators that would take them to the company cafeteria. They froze at the door. Beverly and Charlie were sitting together in front of a laptop at a table for two at the far side of the large room.

"Looks like they're still at it," Ren said in a low, angry voice. He whipped out his cellphone and snapped a picture of them huddled over the portable computer, instant messaging the image to Kerry's phone.

"Yeah, busy trying to torpedo yours truly, her blog posts, and—ultimately—her payday," she whispered back.

Fortunately, the pair was so absorbed in what they were doing that they never looked up. Behind his salad-making station, Tony glanced in both directions before he handed Kerry a file folder.

"It's all in there," he said in a hoarse whisper, handing her the evidence which Kerry clutched to her bosom.

"Let's get out of here before they see us!" Ren urged, and soon the two were back in the elevator riding up to the CEO's floor.

When they arrived at Harry Chapman's office, his administrative assistant's chair was empty but, fortunately, Kerry's boss was at his desk, a plate with a sandwich and potato chips sitting beside his computer screen. Ren waited just outside the door as Kerry gave a quick knock and apologized for the interruption. As succinctly as she could, she described what had been happening to her blog posts.

Chapman's expression grew grave as he studied the printout detailing the raft of negative, damaging comments on her site, along with the circumstantial evidence tracing them back to the company's email server. Kerry explained Charlie's connection to the founder of the obscure browser called Bark.

"Mr. Chapman, you can bet not many people here use that browser to access the Internet or LifeStyleXer email accounts," she pointed out, handing him her cellphone. "Here's a picture taken of them huddled over Charlie's laptop in the cafeteria less than ten minutes ago. Since both the complimentary posts Charlie made—as well as the derogatory comments I *think* he and Beverly conspired together to make—used Bark to access the Internet, we can check the time codes on this picture of Beverly and Charlie and compare it to the time codes of the latest nasty-grams sent ten minutes ago and see if they match up. It's *got* to be them!"

Kerry could tell LifeStyleXer's CEO had begun to do a slow burn.

"This pre-IPO period is a highly sensitive time. If it got out that company insiders were sabotaging your success as one of our most popular bloggers, the media blow-back could possibly diminish our chances for having a successful public offering—to say nothing of damaging you professionally and financially."

Kerry merely nodded, wondering what he would—or could—do about it. Chapman once again flipped through the pages that Tony's team of techies had provided.

"Isn't this at least some sort of professional malfeasance?" she asked. "I agree...it would be terrible if your board or the public knew that one of your vice presidents was doing something like this."

"What I don't understand is why would two of our own employees stoop to this?"

The previous, sleepless night, Kerry had closely compared her previous contract with her revised version Chapman had approved.

"My new contract with you merely changed the terms of *my* service, but all other paragraphs regarding Charlie's redefined deal remained the same, *except* for the fact Charlie was to assume responsibility for managing the team of bloggers you plan to hire." She gave a shrug. "I hate to say it, Mr. Chapman...but keeping track of ten bloggers, their twice-daily posts, and the paperwork involved in shepherding and paying so many independent contractors was going to be a lot of *work*—-and from my experience, actual daily assignments are not for our Charlie Boy. I think he was totally pissed off that I renegotiated my deal and he got stuck with more work than he bargained for...and I think wanted to punish me." She hesitated and then added, "And since my contract still says if my supervisor—who, right now, is Beverly Silverstein—doesn't find my work up to par, I can be fired at any time." She pointed to herself. "I was the old girlfriend, so why *wouldn't* she want to be in on this, too?"

It was plain from the scowl on Harry Chapman's face that he agreed that the circumstantial evidence against the two was convincing. "Neither Ms. Silverstein nor Mr. Miller apparently bothered to consider that hurting the CookChic blog could impact the overall health of our company," he fumed.

"So what happens next?"

"Well, I won't even ask how you came by these persuasive printouts, Ms. Hannigan, but the deal between you and me still stands. I will order the site administrator to remove all spurious comments from your blog site immediately and post a disclosure that those entries were bogus and apologize to you publicly. As long as you keep up your fine work, I'm certain that you'll meet the requirements of our recent arrangement."

"And what about Charlie and—?"

"They're history." He gathered the paper evidence into a neat stack. "HR will let them know they have to be out of the building within the hour."

"But even if you fire them," Kerry protested, "they can still try more dirty cyber tricks from outside the company if they have the right tech connections."

The CEO slowly shook his head.

"I think that reminding them I will *personally* set up an electronic watch system over your blog from here on out will greatly discourage them from making any more mischief for the rest of their miserable lives!"

"I hope so," Kerry replied, doubtfully.

Harry Chapman chuckled. "I'll also tell them that one more wrong move might open them to federal prosecution for playing nasty little games like this on the World Wide Web. Maybe they'll believe it."

Ren and Kerry—with Tony due to arrive after his shift at the cafeteria—returned to the ranch later than they'd hoped, by which time Jeremy looked as if he were about to keel over.

"Rest right there!" Ren commanded, pointing to the leather couch.

Kerry apologized for their tardy arrival, especially

considering the fact that the cosmetic contingent was due in less than an hour.

"Jeremy, you've done the lion's share of the prep, so why don't you just supervise from right there and tell me what to do next," she urged.

The chef nodded gratefully and stretched out, sipping water with a slice of lemon floating in it. After a half hour, he admitted he still wasn't feeling particularly well, and Ren insisted he retire to his room.

Between those assembled in the kitchen, including the faithful José, along with Tony Perez, the four worked together as a well-coordinated team. Fortunately, the visitors were fifteen minutes late in arriving and Kerry was relieved that the spread of tapas-like hors d'oeuvres—where every dish made use of Montisi olive oil in some fashion—was both simple to make and a tremendous success. Ren served both as wait staff and the gracious host, insisting that Kerry accompany him to receive kudos from their guests.

After the group had departed for their dinner in Healdsburg, Tony returned to the city and José tackled the few cleanup chores left. Ren untied Kerry's chef's apron from behind her back and hung it on a hook next to several others. He took her by the hand and opened the screen door, leading her into the chilly December air, his arm firmly slung around her shoulders as they made their way up the slope to her cottage.

When they reached the front step, Ren turned and pulled her hard against him. The temperatures were dropping and Kerry burrowed into his chest.

"Mmmm...you feel wonderful," she murmured.

Ren's arms tightened around her. "I like this: pleasure *and* business! You'll be pleased to know that the president of the Organic Cosmetic and Beauty Products Association was intrigued by what he saw here and told me tonight that he'd make introductions, once we have our prototype products ready."

"That's wonderful…" Kerry murmured, reveling in the feel of Ren's chin resting on the top of her head. She heard him chuckle.

"All day long, I couldn't get the vision out of my mind of you in a bathtub full of Montisi lavender bubble bath." He began to kiss a path from her ear down to her neck, whispering, "When we make some of this stuff, I hope you'll let me rub—"

Kerry glanced at her right hand, her palms flat against Ren's chest. The ring's stone glowed like a strong and steady beacon. Then she wrapped her arms around Ren's torso and snuggled, again, against his shoulder. An amazing sense of the *rightness* in every single aspect of her life settled over her.

Ren seized her hands from behind his back.

"Let's go inside or the staff will be gossiping, big time, if they see us making out like this on your front porch."

"Oh, I expect it's far too late to worry about that."

He turned and opened the front door, pulling her gently inside. "Even so…this is better," he said, replacing her arms where they'd been around his waist.

"Oh, yes…"

The cottage's front room was in shadow, with the drapes only half open and to Kerry, it felt as if they were wrapped in their own private cocoon. His hands roamed her back, pressing the length of her body against his, offering clear evidence of his rising ardor. Then he bent down and seized her lips as Kerry felt her ring finger begin to throb, along with other parts of her anatomy.

Yet, in the far recesses of her mind, a familiar fear began to edge into her consciousness as Ren's kisses traced a delicate path down her neck. How could the miracle that had happened to her in the space of a week possibly be *real*? And how could she trust her own judgment after making such a terrible mistake with Charlie? She waited for her own thoughts to caution her against the direction she knew these embraces would lead if she truly allowed her heart to have its way.

But instead, all she heard resounding in her head were five whispered words.

Yes...this is *the one!*

Relief and a sense of utter peace enveloped her as real and reassuring as the warmth of Ren's body next to hers. Kerry raised her arms to thread her fingers through his hair, a rich, dark gold in the rays of the porch light filtering through the cottage window. Then she leaned back in his arms.

"I can't wait for you to meet my godmother, Angelica Fabrini Doyle. Do you think we have the budget to fly back to New York for Christmas?"

"Well, I already like the sound of her Irish-Italian name. Let me take it up with the Finance Committee." He paused. "Great! They said 'yes.' Economy class."

"She's going to be just wild about you, Signore Montisi."

Ren pulled her close again.

"Ah....Kerry Hannigan," he murmured. "You're magic...*this is* magic..."

Kerry smiled against his seeking lips.

"Faith and Begorrah, I do believe it *is...*"

It suddenly occurred to Kerry that it was just past midnight. Today marked a week since Angelica had bestowed on her the heart-shaped gemstone, held between two metal hands and framed by its tiny gold crown. In just a few more hours it would be seven full days since she had placed it on her finger, which meant that soon, the Claddagh would be nothing more than a pretty piece of jewelry...but no matter. Her godmother's gift had worked its enchantment.

And then, the sounds in Kerry's world were that of a breeze blowing gently through the olive trees on the hills that surrounded the cottage. The sage-colored leaves and dormant stalks of lavender sighed in the wind, an echo of other soft exclamations of pleasure and delight.

The first night Ren stayed with her in the cottage, Kerry pointed to the Claddagh ring and explained its symbolism: friendship, loyalty and love.

"My godmother gave this to me the day before I moved to California and urged me to know my own heart, just as the inscription says." She slipped off the ring and pointed to the words incised in the metal. "I honestly believe that accepting its message led me to you...but I want to earn my way at the ranch as *myself*, and by my own contributions and talents—and not as your girlfriend." She searched Ren's face for his reaction as she restored the ring to her finger. "That's why I want to wait a year to make our engagement official. Just know, though, that the Claddagh ring will always symbolize what we have together."

She wasn't quite ready to tell him of the still, small voice that she was certain had come from the emerald heart during that first week. Ren seized her hand and admired the ring before replying with the grin that had won her heart from the first.

"I totally understand your wanting to prove yourself here, but trust me," he teased. "We're not fooling anyone."

"Maybe so," she'd replied, "but I like the idea of being

secretly engaged. One day, if the ranch is in the black, I'll let you buy me another ring…or I'll take off the Claddagh now, and we can use it as our engagement ring then, if our budget is still tight."

Ren smiled at her with a tenderness that brought tears to her eyes.

"I love that ring," he assured her. "Keep it on, but turn the heart toward your own so it tells the world you've made your choice."

Kerry promptly did as instructed. Ren held her right hand in his.

"Every time we look at it during the year," he said, "we'll *both* know what it means." He kissed her on her nose in quick succession to emphasize each word. "Friendship, loyalty…and love." Then he kissed her properly, murmuring, "Especially, love."

And so it was that Kerry Hannigan and Renato Montisi walked out of Tiffany's in downtown San Francisco one December afternoon—a year to the very day of their first meeting. Ms. Hannigan had a brand new square-cut diamond surrounded by smaller stones on the ring finger of her left hand. In the store, she had slipped the Claddagh into its burgundy leather box and stowed it in her purse with the intention of telling Ren, later this glorious day, how the Ring of Truth had worked magic in their lives.

They were due to pay a visit to Ren's grandmother at the San Francisco Towers, not only to announce their official engagement, but to report on the success of their beauty products line based on the year's olive oil and lavender harvests.

"The fact we didn't lose money the first year is amazing," Ren declared as he parked the car in the garage beneath the Civic Center, "to say nothing of making a modest profit, thanks to all the other things we're doing at the ranch."

"And then you blew most of it on this ring," Kerry said, admiring her left hand for the thousandth time as she got out of the car.

"The last of my VC money," he admitted, "which I am only too happy to spend on the woman I love." Then, he very carefully leaned her against the Mercedes and kissed her senseless.

Before visiting Concetta after her evening meal, they had decided to have an early supper themselves at five o'clock at one of their favorite spots in Opera Plaza, across from San Francisco's magnificent, gold-domed City Hall. Afterwards, Ren proposed a stroll along Van Ness to admire the opera house itself, along with the Herbst Theater, home of the San Francisco Ballet.

They had just finished sharing a salad and a shepherd's pie when Kerry pointed out a noisy group wearing heavy stage makeup entering Max's and crowding into a large booth across from theirs.

"Looks like they're from the opera or ballet," Ren noted. "Probably grabbing a bite after the matinee."

One young woman, Kerry noticed, was silent among her boisterous companions. Her lovely features grew grave, and then tears suddenly began to spill down her heavily painted face. A soft sob escaped her lips and she swiftly rose from her seat at the end of the banquette and dashed outside into the soon she brought her two hands to cover her face in an expression of anguish that Kerry found difficult to watch. The contrast between the joy that she had been feeling all afternoon, and the abject misery radiating through the pane glass separating the two women, spurred her to action.

"Ren…I'll be right back!"

Her fiancé looked up from signing the credit card slip and his brows furrowed.

"Are you all right?"

"I'm fine," she assured him, jumping up from their booth. "Give me a minute, will you? I'll meet you here in just a sec."

Before Ren could answer, Kerry disappeared from his view and bolted out the front of the restaurant. Digging into her handbag, she wrapped her fingers around the small ring box and walked hurriedly toward the woman laid low by such sorrow.

"Look," she said, breathlessly, "I know you don't know me. I am so sorry for whatever has happened…"

The woman's expression of surprise became one of acute embarrassment and she turned her back on the intruder.

"This may seem kind of crazy," Kerry said in a rush, "but I want you to have something that's very precious to me." She circled the woman and reached for her hand. "Please take this," she urged and thrust the ring box into her palm. "When you feel a bit calmer, take out the ring and read its inscription. There are instructions that came with it when my godmother gave it to me a year ago at a time I was feeling pretty much the way I imagine you feel right now."

by its small, golden crown.

"It's called a Claddagh ring," Kerry said explained. "It came from Ireland. It survived the nine-eleven tragedy in New York and who knows what else? I don't totally understand it either, but *read* the instructions folded into the top of the box," she urged, closing the lid and handing it back. "You'll just have to trust me when I say this ring could change your life."

Just then, Ren emerged from the restaurant's front door with a worried expression that brightened as soon as he caught sight of Kerry.

"*There* you are," he called to her. "I thought you'd vanished into thin air."

Kerry turned to the stranger. "Keep the faith that all will be well," she urged softly, and then walked the fifty feet to Ren's side.

As she hooked her arm in his, he asked curiously, "Do you know that woman? She looks absolutely stricken. What's wrong?"

"I could see through the window that she was terribly upset about something, so I ran out to see if I could help."

Ren inclined his head over his shoulder and asked, "Did you find out what had happened?"

Kerry gave a slight shrug.

"Actually, I have no idea...I just wished her a bit of Irish luck, trusting that eventually, everything will be just fine."

****

A Diva Wears the Ring

Diana Dempsey

Chapter One

Veronica Ballard stood on the sidewalk outside the restaurant clutching the ring box, passersby throwing quizzical glances in her direction as they pushed past her en route to their evening's entertainment. She didn't need a mirror to know she looked a fright, tears and stage makeup funneling down her face to stain the neckline of her cream-colored sweater. At least she wasn't ruining her costume. But she'd had to leave that purple taffeta extravaganza behind at the Opera House for the next time the company mounted *Don Giovanni*. Chances were good that next time, too, she would be singing a minor soprano's role.

Then again…perhaps at last her life was changing.

As the chilly San Francisco night swirled around her, Veronica glanced at the ring box and considered the airmail letter inside her handbag, which had shown up in her mailbox that very morning.

It couldn't be coincidence that she received those two extraordinary items just hours apart. It had to be a sign of *something*. No one who believed in destiny as fiercely as she did could think anything else.

Again Veronica opened the box that cradled the ring; again she touched the green-colored gemstone in the shape of a heart set between golden hands and capped by a crown. It can't be a genuine emerald, she concluded, no one would give that to a stranger; though just as that idea settled in her mind a sort of shimmer seemed to course through the gemstone, as if daring her to deny its authenticity.

"Veronica?" a male voice called behind her.

She spun around. It was Dominik, the bad-boy tenor from Budapest with the carefully disheveled blond hair, famous for cutting a swath through the ranks of the sopranos in every production in which he appeared.

"Are you all right?" he asked in his lightly accented voice. "We're all worried about you."

Even among opera singers, who embraced drama every chance they got, Veronica's bursting into tears, fleeing a restaurant table, and nearly toppling two busboys on her way out the door was histrionic behavior.

Veronica stuffed the ring box in her handbag, not wanting to have to explain that, too. "I'm sorry. Here we all are to celebrate our final performance, and I have a meltdown."

"Forget about the celebration." Dominik edged still closer. "It's you I'm worried about."

Veronica watched Dominik switch on his legendary charm. This time he didn't bother to say *we're worried*, and she could guess why. No doubt he was thinking there was still time to make her one of his conquests. Dominik was far from boyfriend material, though her boyfriends were always other opera singers or musicians. (And once a conductor, though that had earned her some grief.) Who else would they be? Those were the men she spent time with, the men she got to know. More than that, they were as unmoored and peripatetic as she was. They understood her life because they lived it, too.

"Are you worried about Florence?" Dominik went on. "You shouldn't be, you know. You'll be wonderful."

Indeed she was petrified about the new role in Italy but

not for the reasons Dominik assumed. "It's all happening so fast," she told him.

Dominik was only inches away. It had to be said: Those hazel eyes of his were mesmerizing. Maybe she'd been wrong to keep him at arm's length. How odd that for once she'd been cautious.

Now she let herself speak freely. "The thing is, I received a letter from my birth mother. This morning." Even though she heard the words come out of her mouth she still couldn't quite believe them. "The first one ever."

Dominik frowned. "Birth mother?" he repeated, and Veronica realized she'd reached the limits of his excellent English.

"I'm adopted. From Russia."

His brows flew up in shock. "You're Russian?"

"Sort of. My parents adopted me and brought me here to the Bay Area when I was only a few months old."

Understanding dawned. "Oh, I see. Birth mother. I see." He nodded. "I see how you could be Russian," he added, and Veronica knew what he meant. The blond hair, the fair skin, the blue eyes: She was a facsimile of Julie Christie's Lara in *Dr. Zhivago*, though nowhere near so beautiful.

"I've been writing to my birth mother for years," Veronica went on. "Well, I write a letter and a contact in Moscow translates it and sends it on to her."

And every time Veronica's contact forwarded her the return receipt, proving the letter had reached its intended recipient.

"But after all these years," she added, "this is the first time she's ever written to me."

"Wow! Amazing. After all this time."

Veronica's parents would be seriously distraught to hear that this time their precious daughter got a response. Which was why so far she'd kept this stunning development to herself.

From the first, her parents had been forthcoming about her adoption. Even as a small child she remembered fingering the yellowing documents from the orphanage that told the melancholy tale of how her birth father was largely absent and her birth mother couldn't afford to feed yet another mouth. So many times during her childhood Veronica had pored over the photos of her parents' epic trip to Moscow, separated into Before and After they claimed their infant treasure. The Before photos were a travelogue: St. Basil's Cathedral, with its whimsical bonnet of crayon-colored onion domes; the neoclassical majesty of the Bolshoi Theatre; the brooding hulk of the Kremlin. Baby Veronica was the star of the After photos: sitting in a borrowed high chair in a nondescript hotel room, baby food everywhere but in her mouth; in a sink awaiting a bath, naked and howling; swaddled in blankets to sleep in a suitcase, no crib for a bed. She grew up hearing that her parents, well past the bloom of youth when she came into their lives, had "picked her out special." Russia hardly provided a beacon of hope for Americans in those days—or now—but it had for Georgette and Ed Ballard, whose adored Veronica was the only child they would ever call their own.

It was with exquisite guilt that Veronica first inquired how they would feel if she tried to contact her birth mother. By then she was out of college and taking her first steps toward a career in opera. Something in her had to know where she came from. With her past a virtual blank she'd spun so many wild scenarios in her mind; she longed to know if any of them were close to true. So often she fantasized that her birth parents were the source of her wondrous voice. Maybe one of them was even an opera singer. By that point she understood that such a gift rarely translated into riches—not even in the U.S. or Europe, so she wouldn't expect it in Russia.

To this day she cringed recalling her parents' shocked silence when she first brought up the topic. Bad as it was, their silence was easier to take than their pained acquiescence, and infinitely preferable to the muffled sobs she heard that night through the thin wall that separated their bedroom from her own.

Now Dominik peered at her closely. "I understand why it would make you cry to hear from your birth mother."

"It's not just that she wrote me. I mean, yes, that's part of it, but that's not all of it." Veronica's voice caught. "It's what she wrote me." This part she wished she didn't have to say. "She wrote that she's dying."

"Oh my God," Dominik breathed.

Veronica burst into fresh tears. Dominik took that as an opportunity to bundle her into his arms.

Every time she thought about the letter, she could scarcely believe it. All these years—How many now? Ten? Twelve?—she'd hoped against hope that someday something more than a return receipt would show up in her mailbox. Finally it did and it said this. Maybe it was true what people said, to be careful what you wish for.

Even though she was sobbing, Veronica kept going. "She wants me to come to Moscow to meet her. And it has to be soon because she could die any time."

"Really? She wrote that?"

Dominik didn't say anything more but she knew what he was thinking. She was thinking it herself. All of this was so surreal it seemed almost staged, like an opera. A tragic opera. Complete with ticking clock.

Veronica banished those thoughts. She pulled back. "I've

made you a mess now, too." She found a tissue in her handbag and dabbed ineffectually at his black sweater, stained not only with her tears but also a splotchy mess of mascara and stage makeup. "Thanks to me you don't look ready for a cast party, either."

"Maybe you'd feel better if we did something quiet at my apartment, just the two of us." Dominik eyed her steadily. "And then we wouldn't have to say goodbye quite so soon."

Even without the pangs of lost romance, there were so many goodbyes in what they did. Nothing lasted. The curtain went down on relationships just the way it did on productions. And love them or hate them, you never knew when you would see these people again, these people you had worked with, sometimes lived with, for months. It might be the next opera or it might be never again in your life.

Thinking about nothing lasting nearly launched Veronica on another crying jag. But she managed to stave it off. "I better just go. My flight to Italy is tonight and I don't have much time to get ready. But I should go back inside to say my goodbyes."

"Let me at least drive you to the airport."

He wouldn't take no for an answer, not that she fought him very hard. So it was that a few hours later she sat in Dominik's rented car, showered and changed, passport and boarding pass in hand, luggage in his trunk, and mystery ring in her handbag. She wouldn't examine that further until she was alone.

"Thank you so much for driving me," she told Dominik, wondering if there was any chance he was more considerate than she'd given him credit for.

"No problem. I can practice the route for tomorrow. And maybe I'll drive to Florence to see you," he added.

"You can't do that! It's too far."

"It's less than a thousand kilometers from Budapest."

"That's still a nine hour drive. At least." She'd sung in enough operas in Europe to understand that.

"What do they say in English? You're worth it."

She had to laugh. "I bet you say that to all the sopranos."

"No! With you I really mean it."

He probably owned a lovely bridge she should consider buying, too. She hadn't misjudged Dominik after all, Veronica decided. His seduction scheme had failed in San Francisco but clearly he was ready to give it another whirl in Tuscany.

He spoke again. "You better be careful with your birth mother, Veronica."

She stiffened.

He went on. "I mean, she writes you that she's dying so you have to fly to Russia right away? It makes me think of those fake emails from Nigeria."

"It's not like that at all." Veronica heard the defiance in her tone. It was not for Dominik to say these things, a man who had never met her birth mother and never would. "It's perfectly natural for her to want to meet the child she was forced to give away before she dies."

He waited a bit before he spoke again. And when he did, his tone was much milder. "What does she know about you?"

By now, quite a bit. Veronica had been cagey in her early letters, as she'd been counseled. But her words flowed more freely with every letter she wrote. She'd sent photos, too. And once a CD recording of what she considered her best performance.

Now Dominik's little rented car was speeding south on the freeway. It wouldn't be long before they reached the airport. "Does she know you're an opera singer?" he pressed.

"You and I both know that doesn't mean I'm rich."

He laughed. "*We* know that, yes."

Many opera singers flirted with the poverty line. Not Dominik, because of his looks; and not Veronica, who was hardly a star but had been fortunate. She even made enough money to rent an apartment in the heart of San Francisco, though only because she shared it with two other women.

Again Dominik laughed. "Does your birth mother know you're not fat?"

"That must mean I'm a failure as an opera singer. So she can't want money."

Dominik dropped the topic after that, no doubt sensing she'd had enough. They chatted about trivialities as he drove the last few miles to the airport, where the international terminal was abuzz.

The moment came to say goodbye. "You'll be able to sleep on the flight," he told her.

She doubted that. Not after everything that had happened that day.

Dominik made a move to embrace her but she outmaneuvered him and kissed both his cheeks in that European way. She watched him step back with disappointed eyes and bet he wouldn't be making that nine-hour drive after all.

As Veronica went in search of her check-in area, she thought again of the ring in her handbag. Judging from what the dark-haired woman had told her, it had something to do with Ireland. How ironic that the Florentine opera company had booked her to fly Aer Lingus to Dublin, of all bizarre routings, before they had her continue on to London and then Rome.

It wasn't because the Irish national airline was cheaper, Veronica decided, and opera companies always chose the cheapest routings for their Not Quite Stars. It was Fate sending her yet another sign.

Chapter Two

Veronica was still in U.S. airspace when she pulled the ring box out of her handbag, emboldened by the cheap but chilled chardonnay she'd procured during the happy visit of the beverage cart to her row in the boonies of coach class.

She suspected the female passenger in the middle seat might have commented on the ring's beauty if Veronica hadn't come off as so neurotic. That's the view your fellow travelers tend to take when you obsessively smother your hands with sanitizer. Then again, while a cold would be inconvenient for any traveler, for Veronica, who needed her throat and nasal passages in perfect working order, it would be catastrophic.

The cabin lights dimmed. All around her people settled in to sleep. Veronica settled in with her thoughts, which careened tirelessly across her mind like so many crazed pinballs.

She gazed at the ring, which apparently she was supposed to place on the fourth finger of her right hand with the crown facing out, as befit a wearer "whose heart was yet to be won"—at least according to the article she'd read online. A few minutes trolling the Web and already Veronica was well versed on the Claddagh—on an ordinary Claddagh, anyway. The diva in her doubted there was anything ordinary about the ring she was now examining. This ring was truly Diva Worthy. There was nothing ordinary about its heft, or its mesmerizing heart-shaped gemstone, or the singular way it had come into her possession.

And while the love, friendship, and fidelity that were symbolized by the Claddagh were all well and good, what compelled Veronica's mind were the phrases written on the aged slip of paper inside the box that held the ring.

Be brave!—for the ring of truth will test you. Once on your finger, its power to speak endures but seven days. Listen and learn, lest you lose its wisdom and your heart's desire…

Seven days. One week. Long enough to do what her heart demanded.

Veronica fixed her eyes on the ring's tiny inscription. *Know Thy Heart.* "I already do," she whispered.

For ancient as the phrases on the ring and the note might be, to Veronica they might as well read: *Catch the next flight to Moscow.* At this moment she had one and only one heart's desire, and that was to meet the woman who had given her life. She would have to be brave to accomplish that, because she would have to stand up to her director and conductor in Florence and make them understand.

Veronica had no patience for the doubt in her mind. She shoved it aside like a piece of rotten fruit. No, she decided, this couldn't be a scam. No mother could be so cynical that she would tell her daughter she was on her deathbed if it weren't true. And no, it wasn't too much to ask a child to drop everything to fly across one ocean and two continents to come to her dying mother's side. Probably the diagnosis was sudden, or her mother had taken a sharp turn for the worse, or she had only now accepted what the doctors had been telling her for months.

Veronica didn't know how she could live with herself if

she didn't honor this summons. How could she pass up the chance to see this woman's face, to hear her voice and feel her touch? How could she forego the opportunity to ask the questions she'd for so long harbored in her heart? And what would it say about her if she put her operatic career above her dying birth mother?

As Veronica's jet shot eastward through the inky night sky, she had the odd sensation that indeed her life was about to change—as the dark-haired woman had warned her it might. Very slowly she lifted the ring from the box and slipped it on her finger. It emboldened her from that very first second, though maybe all women who wore magnificent rings believed they could achieve anything if only they tried.

"Whatever I have to do, I will go to Moscow," she murmured, and just as the last syllable left her lips the gemstone glowed with an odd milky opalescence, as if sealing her plan with its official approval.

Eighteen hours, two layovers, one bus ride and one train journey later, Veronica arrived in Florence. It was evening. She made her way through rain-slick streets to the massive Palazzo Vecchio, the crenellated Romanesque palace with soaring clock tower that to this day served as the city hall, and behind which her guesthouse awaited. She dragged her body and her luggage up four dim flights of stairs to the room the opera company had rented for her.

It was small, lovely, and spotless, with peach-colored walls, a hardwood floor, all white furniture, and diaphanous curtains behind which Florence throbbed. She had her own tiny bathroom and a kitchen she would share, quite possibly with another singer and certainly with two black cats, which greeted her with a level of enthusiasm one did not expect from felines. The proprietress had left her a note, a bottle of red wine, bread and soup, and a chocolate. That last immediately went down Veronica's throat while the cats watched her with inscrutable eyes.

Her clothes she tossed on the floor of her room but the ring went carefully back into its box. She placed it on the nightstand, ran a bath, ate and drank, and fell into bed. No urban cacophony four stories below her window would keep her from sleeping that night.

She woke to leaden skies and a ball of dread in her stomach. It was one thing to ponder asking for time off before her rehearsals even started; it was quite another actually to do it. It didn't help that indeed there was another singer in the adjoining bedroom. In a twist Machiavelli might have crafted, the singer turned out to be Veronica's understudy. She had the nerve to be a strikingly attractive brunette at least five years Veronica's junior.

Even worse: She was Italian, just in from Bologna. That was fairly alarming for an American soprano who was about to tackle an Italian opera—Verdi's *Il Trovatore*—in Italy in front of Italian audiences and critics.

And to do so after a truncated rehearsal schedule, if Veronica had her way.

The understudy opened her lovely mouth to loose her outrageously melodious speaking voice. "Hello, I am called Carina," she cooed. Of course she had a pretty name, too, which meant "little darling." "I will be so happy to hear your Leonora," she added. "I am sure I will learn so much from your interpretation."

Suddenly Veronica wished she'd spent more of the journey reviewing her notes on the libretto.

They spent some time gossiping about the staging, always a minefield in *Il Trovatore* because the plot was so complex. Of course Veronica's character died in the end but it wouldn't be her first time trying to hit the high notes from a supine position on the stage floor.

She kept the conversation short because even though she wasn't required at the opera house for hours, she was desperate to get there to make her case to the director and conductor. If she ignored the high price of the airline tickets, it would be possible to fly to Moscow that night, via Rome. Given the timing of the return flights, she would miss two days of rehearsals. She had hoped she might miss only one. She had so few to begin with.

With the ring returned to her finger and a scarf bundled protectively about her throat, Veronica cut her way through chilly December streets to the opera house. Its exterior was surprisingly simple as these things go, all white stone fashioned in a neoclassical style. Inside Veronica found the usual magic.

She made her way to the stage and walked onto the floorboards, her heels echoing in the emptiness. Somewhere her new colleagues were bustling about—she'd heard them as she wound her way through the backstage maze—but she didn't have to deal with them yet. For now it was just her and the opera house.

She moved downstage and stood perfectly still. Beyond the thick walls, the world and all its troubles were at bay. Inside it was only silence...and anticipation. Sometimes she thought this was what she lived for more than performing itself, this anticipating the performance, knowing it would soon transport her to the place she loved most, where she was giving voice to the music she adored and where she knew with all her soul that she was doing the thing she was born to do.

It bemused her when people asked why she was an

opera singer, as if it were something she had chosen to do. That didn't even approach the truth. She didn't choose opera. Opera chose her. Opera chose her as a channel through which it would flow. Once opera had taken her prisoner, which it had done while she was still a child, she was powerless to escape. She didn't care that she didn't create what she sang; she didn't care that she was no more than a vessel for the music. She would do whatever the music asked her to do, to the best of her ability, for as long as she was able.

Last year her friend Lizbeth had quit opera. She had married her boyfriend and gotten pregnant and quit. Veronica had been stunned. Though she never admitted it, privately Veronica judged Lizbeth a better soprano than she was herself. Lizbeth's arpeggios were dazzling; her nuances could make Veronica weep.

Yet Lizbeth had had enough of singing minor roles. One too many people had asked why she continued to slog along opera's tortuous, uncertain path. Of course no one ever asked Renée Fleming or Kiri Te Kanawa that question. They were Divas with a capital D. They were stars, superstars, richly rewarded for their efforts.

But what about those soloists who failed to become superstars? Who, like Veronica, spent their careers singing tiny roles in large productions or large roles in tiny productions? Who were best friends with the heartache but strangers to the glory? Traipsing from opera house to opera house, sleeping so many nights in strange beds, struggling to rub more than a few coins together, suffering the unspoken derision of everyone who believed they weren't quite good enough to achieve stardom. Veronica had quietly despaired that a large role in a large production would ever be hers. For her, too, the magical age of thirty had come and gone. That was the age at which the voice "ripens" — or so everyone said.

Well, Veronica was thirty-four. Her voice was as ripe as it was going to get.

Yet some might say she had at last arrived, at least in a fashion. She had a principal role in a fairly large production. It wasn't terribly high-profile but it just might prove to be the break she'd long been looking for.

Which rendered the request she was about to make all the more foolhardy.

Veronica heard heavy footfalls behind her in the wings. A male voice called out. "Can it be? Can it be my Leonora?"

She turned to see her director, the almost-famous Rinaldo Nardovino. "*Bellissima!*" he cried, clapping his hands and beaming as he strode toward her. He wore his customary charcoal-colored turtleneck, his wild black hair blown back from his face as if he'd arrived at the theatre in a windstorm. He clasped Veronica's arms and drew her close to kiss her flamboyantly on both cheeks.

"Your flight was good?" he bellowed. "You sleep like a baby last night?"

Rinaldo liked posing questions to which you could only answer yes.

"You like how you are close to the Palazzo Vecchio? Is perfect location?"

He allowed her only a few syllables for a response.

"You are ready to sing for me?" he finished, and without even pausing for a reply took Veronica's arm to lead her backstage.

She managed to forestall him. "Rinaldo, I have to talk to you about something. Is Julian here?" She half hoped the Austrian conductor wasn't in the house. He had a reputation as the hot-tempered type.

A look of concern creased Rinaldo's face. "What is it,

bella?"

She tried not to worry that already she'd been downgraded from *bellissima*.

"Tell me," he demanded, "what it is you need from me."

Veronica twisted the ring on her finger and found she didn't even need to take a deep breath to find the temerity to speak. "I need you to allow me to meet my mother for the very first time."

Rinaldo's dark eyes flew open. It was a dramatic opening to be sure but Veronica bet that was the surest route to an opera director's heart.

She explained, embellishing with all the pathos she could summon. She made sure to remind Rinaldo that she had understudied Leonora for him just eighteen months before. She'd dazzled him, which was why he'd hired her for this production. Moreover, he was so confident she knew the role that he hadn't even minded that she'd miss a week of rehearsals because she was finishing *Don Giovanni* in San Francisco. Still, it wasn't until the end of her monologue that, with the return of some trepidation, she uttered the alarming words *Moscow* and *fly tonight*.

That combination produced the reaction Veronica feared. Rinaldo reared back from her with an expression of such horror, you'd think she suggested that the company perform *Il Trovatore* in the nude or that he rewrite the ending so that instead of Leonora drinking the poison that leaves her stone cold dead as the curtain falls, she marches off-stage declaring she has a craving for pasta.

"But is impossible!" he thundered. "The preview is Friday! Today is Monday!"

"I will sing for you all day today. And tonight until I have to fly."

"But two days of rehearsals gone—"

"Leonora is in my blood, Rinaldo. I feel her in my bones. I know her as well as I know myself."

"But the fittings, the staging—"

"We can do the fittings this afternoon and you told me the staging is almost exactly the same as last time."

"I've made changes," Rinaldo declared. "It is not the same."

Silence fell. Rinaldo's scowl deepened. Then he spoke. "If you insist on this crazy thing, there is only one thing I can do. Carina must rehearse Leonora."

Of course that would be the outcome. Still Veronica cringed to hear Rinaldo say it in so many words.

Of course Veronica understood that she risked Rinaldo—indeed, everyone in the company—thinking she was certifiable to fly off to another country mere days before the biggest opening of her career, especially when rehearsal time was so limited. She could easily be deemed undependable, and not just here in Florence. Opera was a small world. The news of her abrupt decampment to Russia would spread to every house in Europe and America and could threaten her reputation from now until forever.

Then again...

Divas were supposed to be high-strung and emotional and impetuous. Sometimes the biggest stars were unbelievably histrionic, worse off the stage than on. It was even true that the bigger the tantrum a diva threw, the greater the awe she could inspire in directors and conductors, who seemed to believe that raging melodrama was the hallmark of only the most talented souls. More than once Veronica had been astounded at what directors and conductors put up with from their superstars. Yet they seemed to accept those tempests as the price they had to pay for working with artistic genius.

Again Veronica twisted the ring. *Be brave!—for the ring of truth will test you.*

She stepped back on her heels, imbued with an audacity she had never felt before in the presence of a director. "Fine!" She threw out her arms in a theatrical gesture. "Let Carina rehearse! She can sing Leonora from the moment the sun rises until the moment it sets but never will she sing Leonora like I sing Leonora!"

Veronica flung her words at Rinaldo as if they were daggers. He stepped away from her with astonishment on his face. Even though her heart was pounding, some part of her enjoyed his stunned expression.

"Let her sing Leonora!" Veronica repeated, her voice a shriek that bounced off the walls of the opera house. "While I hold vigil beside my dying Russian mother!"

Rinaldo recoiled, but this time, Veronica knew, it wasn't because he was shocked at what she was saying. He was shocked at himself for forgetting why it was that Veronica wanted to embark on this headstrong journey in the first place.

He bowed his head, closed his eyes, and put his hands together in front of his face as if he were praying. "*Bella*," he murmured, "*tua mamma.*"

At that mention of her birth mother, Veronica burst into tears. And not even by design.

This time it was Rinaldo who bundled her into his arms; this time it was his turtleneck she mussed with mascara and lipstick. "Of course you must go. It is your mother. My God. Forgive me."

He had caved. She had won. If this was the ring in action, she'd take it. "I will still be your Leonora," she insisted through her tears.

"Of course you will. There will be no other." He paused.

"Carina will rehearse, because I must have her rehearse, but you will be my Leonora."

Veronica could only hope that Carina was not some modern-day Maria Callas who would take Leonora to heights no one had ever dreamed of before.

"I'll be back Wednesday night," she told Rinaldo. "As soon as I'm off the plane I'll sing for you again."

"*Bella*, you will sing for me today only a little. Then you will rest. You will need all your strength for your journey."

Chapter Three

Veronica had known it would be cold in Moscow in December but she had never guessed the snow would be so very deep.

It lay unbelievably thick upon the ground, and in such high drifts she feared she would suffocate if she lost her footing and fell. Above her head the sky wasn't blue but gray, heavy with clouds that sagged so low she believed she might actually touch them if only she reached up an arm. The light was milky, too, milky and wan, and already fading.

That thought made her heart thump in her chest. She had to keep searching. She had to find the grave before it got dark.

Up ahead, in front of a stand of leafless trees, was a church. It was almost entirely white, like the rest of this all-white world of snow and sky and gravestones, but its onion dome was a gentle blue, the color of a robin's egg.

Maybe someone there could help her.

She tried to move her legs faster but the snow did its best to hinder her. With every step it became more difficult to make progress. By now her heart was pounding, and despite the iciness of the air a trickle of sweat shivered down the back of her neck and disappeared beneath the collar of her fur coat.

For a moment she was surprised she was wearing fur. Then she remembered. Her name was Veronika and she was Russian. Russian women wore fur, fur coats and fur hats. It was the only way to keep warm in this frigid land.

She halted to listen to the bell-like tinkle of a wind chime. She *wanted to reach out to steady herself by grabbing onto a headstone but that seemed disrespectful. She allowed only her gaze to settle on a nearby grave but that made her even more confused. If she was Russian, why didn't she understand the names on these grave markers? They were inscribed in an alphabet she recognized but couldn't read.*

And the crosses atop the graves were strange as well. They had a low horizontal bar that angled down from right to left. She thought she'd seen such crosses before but didn't understand why that bar was there. What did it mean?

Nothing she saw made any sense. Which meant it would be impossible for her to find the grave in time...

"Miss? Miss?"

Veronica jolted awake. The female flight attendant was shaking her by the shoulder.

"You must put your seat in the upright position," the attendant ordered, then pressed the button to do it herself when Veronica, groggy from sleep, was too slow to react. "We're about to land in Moscow," she added before bustling away.

Indeed, there came the noise and the shudder of the landing gear deploying.

The dream fled Veronica's mind, replaced by a realization that hit her as sharply as a slap. She, born in Russia but quickly whisked away, was about to set foot on her native soil for the first time since she was a baby.

She'd imagined this scene so many times but now it was actually happening.

In her spun scenarios, she was never alone as she made this journey. She was with her parents, or her mother at least, conspirators as they retraced steps taken almost thirty-five years before. Yet now she felt like a traitor to her parents. For the first time in her life, she hadn't told them she was leaving one country for another. Not only that, the previous night she had lied in reply to an email from her father, writing that they had done this and that in rehearsal that day and would do this and that tomorrow. She had even concocted what she'd eaten for dinner, creating a sumptuous Italian meal that bore no relation to the fast food she'd scarfed at the airport in Rome during her stopover. She'd had a nightmarish fantasy that the plane to Moscow would crash and her parents would be informed that their daughter had perished on a flight they hadn't even known she was taking, a flight that was meant to land in a country from which they'd delivered her years before.

They would never understand. They would die not understanding.

The wheels of the plane touched down, lifted, touched down again for good. Veronica's torso strained against the seat belt as the pilot applied the brakes. She had arrived safely. She was in Russia.

Outside the plane's windows, the sky was so black it might as well have been the middle of the night. Yet it was morning, getting on toward six a.m. local time.

It wasn't until Veronica was standing in the interminable line for foreign arrivals that she remembered the dream. She closed her eyes against the sterile, fluorescent surroundings and allowed different images to fill her mind.

Snow. Sky. Odd white crosses.

Yes. Russian Orthodox crosses. She'd learned about those in her girlhood, when she'd steeped herself in Russian culture.

She knew whose grave she'd been searching for.

Behind her eyelids tears pricked. Maybe, as fast as she'd gotten here, she hadn't been fast enough. Maybe she should have come straight to Moscow from San Francisco, not bothered to go to Florence. She could have saved so much time. But instead she had put her opera career ahead of her birth mother.

Behind her someone coughed. Someone nudged their suitcase forward so that it collided with her legs. She snapped her eyes open and closed the distance that had opened between her and the traveler ahead of her.

She glanced at her right hand, adorned with the ring. She was wearing it for a crazy brew of reasons. For one, she had come to enjoy its magnificence on her finger. If she obeyed its rules, she would have to give it up soon enough. Better to enjoy it while she could. And it was far too extraordinary to leave behind in her random Florentine guesthouse, where it might not be safe (from Carina or anyone else). Then there was the bizarre courage the ring seemed to give her, which might or might not be imaginary. Still, she would grab courage wherever she could find it in the coming days.

Now it troubled her, though, that according to the note in the box the ring was supposedly the "ring of truth." Was it trying to share its so-called "wisdom" when she'd fallen asleep on the flight? That was the first time she had slept wearing the ring. Had it taken that opportunity to send her a message via a dream?

Yet Veronica had no doubt the ring had helped catapult her to Moscow. Why do that if her birth mother would die while Veronica made the trip?

Or had Veronica missed her chance by making a selfish stop in Florence?

Finally it was her turn to face the stern immigration clerk, who was displeased by her hastily organized visa. He grudgingly allowed her through, thanks to the arrangements previously made by her agent, who knew how to pull a string or two in every country where there stood an opera house. He had made abundantly clear to Veronica that he wasn't happy to grease the wheels of this trip. But still he did it, and here she was.

As her agent instructed her, she took an express train, then the metro to reach the place he had booked for her to stay. She couldn't miss it, he'd told her, and he hadn't lied.

The Kudrinskaya Building proved to be a massive Stalinist pile with a Gothic flair, complete with forbidding sculptures topping its five towers and a spire crowned by an enormous gold star. It turned out that Russia had its own "Seven Sisters," built after World War Two when Stalin lamented the absence of skyscrapers in Moscow compared to "capitalist cities" and so ordered seven of these monoliths to be constructed. This one was centrally located, with embassies nearby, she was told, and bars and restaurants. In its own formidable way the building was quite beautiful, its lobby ornamented by high arched ceilings, Corinthian columns sculpted of marble, and gorgeous mosaic floors.

Veronica's apartment was on the eighth floor, with white walls, a parquet floor, and sweeping views of the river and numerous landmarks. Not that she could see any of them, as the sun still hadn't risen. She had read that at this time of year the sun would put in an appearance after nine and disappear by three.

No wonder the Russian spirit was different from that of, say, the Italians.

At that moment, though, Veronica didn't need sunlight or bars or restaurants. What she needed was sleep. It wouldn't do to exhaust herself and it was still several hours until she was to meet her longtime contact at the orphanage. From there they would continue on to the home of her birth mother.

How she was to sleep with that agenda for the day, Veronica had no idea.

Yet sleep she did, a few hours at least, after which she showered and went in search of coffee and something to eat. Here, with no kind proprietress to anticipate her needs, she had to venture boldly forth.

Now the sun was up, though it managed only a meek display, and the ice-cold streets were busy. Given her opera career Veronica was a world traveler, used to unfamiliar places, so it was easy to find what she needed, especially in this neighborhood, which did seem to cater to an embassy crowd. A tiny part of her was irrationally disappointed that Moscow seemed so strange and foreign. Yes, it was a majestic European city like others she had known, but she didn't feel a kinship with the people around her, bundled against the biting wind; nor did her rudimentary understanding of the Cyrillic alphabet help her much when it came to reading the offerings in the coffee shop. And she had to stare for a long time before she understood what was being sold at the standing-room-only kiosk on the street: vodka, apparently for a late-morning pick-me-up. She had hoped that being here in Moscow she might feel a primal echo deep in her soul assuring her that *yes, yes, this is where you come from. You're one of us.* But even in these hours before she was to meet her birth mother, Veronica felt even more adrift than usual in a foreign land.

In the end she had to force herself back on the metro to make the trip to the orphanage. And every time the train stopped at a station, bringing her that much closer to her destination, she felt a wild impulse to bolt from her seat and get on the train across the platform, the one headed in the direction she had just come.

Veronica didn't think of herself as weak or timid. Yet her

mouth was dry and her heart beat a staccato rhythm in her chest. It wasn't really that she feared her birth mother had just died. More, it was that Veronica feared she was still alive.

Soon, so soon, would come the moment when she would meet her birth mother for the first time. She would no longer be a mirage, a fantasy, but flesh and blood, maybe not beautiful, maybe not talented, maybe not particularly loving. It occurred to Veronica that over the years her birth mother might not have thought about her much. Maybe she'd been too busy caring for the babies she had kept. Maybe there *was* something cynical and grasping about her desire to meet Veronica now at the end of her life, as Dominik had warned and Veronica herself had feared.

The train slowed as it approached Veronica's destination. People gathered at each set of doors, preparing to exit. Veronica remained in her seat, acutely conscious of the ring on her right ring finger. It felt oddly weighty.

Even though she'd come so far, she wondered what to do. *Stay on or get off?*

The train screeched to a stop. The doors slid open.

Get off.

Veronica obeyed, though she wasn't even sure from where the instruction had come, her own mind or the ring's will or her innate refusal to be a coward. She rose and leaped out onto the platform a second before the train's doors swished shut, almost but not quite nabbing the flying wool fabric of her coat.

She glanced down at the ring. It was having one of its opalescent moments.

Did this ring just give an order? Did I just obey?

All Veronica knew was that the ring was certain she had done the right thing.

Chapter Four

From afar Veronica recognized the so-called "baby home" where she had been dropped off days after her birth. She had seen its photo so many times. It didn't seem to have changed one iota in thirty-five years. It was built of red brick, three stories tall, and unremarkable in every way except that she had lived the first few months of her life there. Less fortunate children resided there for five years before being transferred to another, no doubt equally bleak location.

Staring at it from half a block away, snowflakes whipping in the relentless wind, Veronica was saddened that this structure housed children. It seemed far too grim for that cheerful purpose. Surrounded by uneven concrete, bordered by a chain-link fence, it had no trees or shrubs and too few windows, and none of those boasted the bright cutout daisies and sailboats you would see on the windows of a grade school back home.

It was only when she stood a few yards away that she heard the first signs of young life. Giggles. Shrieking. Laughter. Rolling in waves from behind the building. A child, a boy, maybe four years old, darted out front chortling with glee, his cheeks cherry red from the cold. In navy jacket and trousers, knit cap on his head, he bent, gathered snow for a ball and spun around to fling it wildly through the air where, Veronica gathered from his howl of joy, it hit its mark.

She watched as a dark-haired man whose sleek black overcoat was dusted with snow raced forward to scoop up the boy and hoist him playfully in the air. The boy unleashed a yowl of protest that instantly morphed into a cry of joy. A few swings later the man carefully returned the child to the pavement, where the little fellow scampered back toward the rear of the orphanage as fast as his legs would carry him. Then the man straightened and looked at Veronica, who stood on the opposite side of the chain-link fence.

She froze. Transfixed by the man and his gaze, she couldn't move or look away. One thought filled her mind: The Almighty certainly did the women of the world a favor when He created this particular man. He was very handsome, with broad shoulders and dark tousled hair. There was an elegance both to his wool overcoat and his bearing, and the burgundy scarf around his neck had the luxurious look of cashmere. Somehow he managed not to appear too perfect, though; there was a crookedness to his smile, a mischievous glint in his eye, and the hint of a five o'clock shadow.

He cocked his head, assumed a puzzled expression, and opened the gate in the fence to usher her inside the inner sanctum. "You're not from around here. And we don't get too many strangers." Lo and behold, not only did he speak English, but his accent was as American as her own.

Veronica was both pleased and disappointed. She'd hoped this might be Viktor, her contact and translator, who would accompany her to her birth mother's house. But now that she had heard him speak, she knew he couldn't be, which was a real shame because she wouldn't mind spending some time in this man's company. Apart from his good looks, he had a solid, reassuring air about him, as if he were the sort of man who could take care of business.

"You're American, too," she said as five children gathered around them, one more adorable than the next. All their little faces gazed up at her with curious, assessing eyes. The boy who'd thrown the snowball said something to the man, who replied in what sounded like fluent Russian. He then switched to English for Veronica's benefit.

"My friend Sergei here would like to know your name. I would as well." He smiled, which was a fairly devastating thing to witness.

"Veronica." She cleared her throat. "Veronica Ballard."

"Nicholas Laver." He extended his gloved hand. "And this is Sergei, Tatyana, Yulia, Aleksandr, and Marina."

"Very pleased to meet all of you," Veronica said. *"Oichen prijatno,"* she managed, one of the few phrases she remembered from her childhood Russian lessons, which produced a round of claps and giggles. *"Oichen prijatno,"* the children echoed, after which the little girl named Yulia sidled closer and took bashful possession of Veronica's hand.

Veronica smiled down at her sweet heart-shaped face then raised her gaze to Nicholas. "Do you work here?"

He shook his head. "I'm with the embassy. In the economic section."

It was true that Veronica could more easily believe the dashing Nicholas Laver to be a diplomat rather than an orphanage employee. But she was supposed to buy that he toiled away in the economic section? That seemed far too dry and dusty a specialty for a male specimen like this one. Then again, maybe he was actually a spy and the whole "economic section" thing was just a cover. She wanted to believe that even though she knew the diva in her dramatized everything.

Yulia tugged at Veronica's hand to pull her toward the rear of the orphanage. Nicholas halted the forward progress.

"Are they expecting you inside?"

"They should be. And my friend Viktor is supposed to meet me here."

"All right, then," and he waved his hand to redirect Yulia to the orphanage's front entrance. She began pulling Veronica more forcefully.

There was no stopping it now. Veronica hoped the courage the ring seemed to give her wasn't imaginary, for ready or not, she was about to enter the orphanage she'd wondered about her entire life, pushed and pulled by a mini posse of four-year-olds.

It was here in this redbrick building in a workaday corner of Moscow that her whole life had changed. It was here that her birth mother made the final decision to give her up, here that her parents made the final decision to claim her, here that the film of her life had gone from black and white to crayon-bright Technicolor.

In the orphanage's front room, she had to catch her breath. It was overwhelming to be inside this mythical location after so many years of imagining it. Fortunately, she had a moment to gather herself as Yulia let go of her hand and led the other children screeching down a corridor, presumably in search of an adult to deal with the new arrival.

Veronica shed her coat, trying to take in everything around her. It all looked remarkably the same as the photos fixed in her memory, as if time had stopped the day she'd escaped this place in her new parents' arms. There was the lumpy sofa with the striped green fabric and too-white antimacassars, evidence this room was mostly off-limits to the wee inmates. There was the pine table with the arrangement of seven brightly painted nesting dolls, the smallest the size of a thimble: the Matryoshka, perhaps the friendliest symbol of Russian culture. Hanging on the wall was the same bland landscape that had hung there decades before. Only the calendar was different, but it occupied the exact same spot it had in 1980.

She felt Nicholas's eyes on her face.

"Have you been here before?" he asked quietly.

She nodded. She couldn't speak.

He filled the silence. "I know the feeling."

Before she could ask what he meant, a short, plump woman with thinning gray hair and old-lady eyeglasses bustled into the room, wearing what Veronica's mother would call a housedress. The same five children, now unburdened by their coats and hats, followed in her wake. The woman's hands flew to her face before they reached out to grasp Veronica's arms. "It is Miss Veronica?" Her English was heavily accented.

"Yes." Veronica felt tears prick her eyes. Already. That was the problem with being a diva, even a pale version of one; your emotions were always so close to the surface. You could never tamp them down.

"The last time I see you, you are a little baby. And now—" The woman's voice broke off. She shook her head as if amazed by what time had wrought.

"You were here when I was here?" Veronica managed.

"I hand you to your mother. I read your name and then I remember. Mrs. Georgette." Now the woman also had tears in her eyes.

Veronica choked on a sob. The woman grabbed her in a hug. The children were mute throughout this display, Veronica noted through her tears; they could do no more than watch in apparent wonderment. Out of the corner of her eye Veronica saw the girl named Marina silently take Nicholas's hand.

Eventually the liquid moment ended, and she and the

woman pulled apart. Nicholas handed Veronica a handkerchief while the woman whose name was Masha, she now knew—mopped her own face with a tissue she pulled from a pocket. Another older woman scurried into the room bearing a teapot, cups, and a plate of cookies. This got the children quite interested, but they were shooed away.

Nicholas was about to join them for tea when his cell phone rang. He disappeared down a corridor, to Veronica's disappointment. She was curious what could possibly tie an American diplomat, who was probably a spy, to this obscure orphanage, officially Baby Home Number 36.

And now she'd never know.

"I'm afraid duty calls," he returned to say. He bent to shake Veronica's hand. "It was very good to meet you. I hope your visit goes well." He and Masha exchanged a few words in Russian before he exited the orphanage.

Masha looked after Nicholas with adulation written on her face. "I hand Nicholas to his mother, too."

Veronica was stupefied. "*He* was here?"

"Then he go to Chicago." Masha beamed. "From baby I know he is special. But he surprise me how special."

Veronica accepted a teacup and a cookie. "What was he doing here today?"

"He come to play with the children. In winter he play in snow with them. In summer he play with ball."

"That's"—Veronica was so astonished that a man like that would spend his free time in this way that she suffered a momentary loss for words—"extraordinary," she finally finished.

"You are special, too," Masha assured her. "Famous opera singer. Viktor tell me."

"I wouldn't say *famous*," Veronica began.

Masha clapped her hands. "You sing for the children!"

Veronica hesitated. "If you don't mind I'd rather not today." It wasn't that she lacked a go-to aria for these occasions, but she was getting impatient. And a trifle worried. She set down her cup. "Do you know if Viktor has arrived yet?"

That question produced dead silence. For quite a while the older woman did nothing but stir her tea and bite her lip. Finally: "Viktor cannot come today."

"What?"

"He call me. His car have trouble." Masha raised pleading eyes to Veronica as if she didn't want to be blamed for this snafu.

Though it registered as far more serious than that to Veronica. "But we had this all arranged!"

"Do not blame Viktor," Masha said. "Please. His car is old."

Veronica wasn't surprised to hear Masha make excuses for Viktor. He had ties to the orphanage. In fact, that's how Veronica had hooked up with him in the first place, when she began her search for her birth mother. "Well, can he do it tomorrow? Can he get his car fixed this afternoon?"

Masha twisted her hands in her lap. "To get car fix is not so easy—"

"So you're telling me Viktor can't do it tomorrow either."

Masha was silent.

"Okay." Clearly it was time to regroup. Veronica realized she should have expected some kind of hiccup. She was in Russia pretty much on a wing and a prayer. "Well, there must be *somebody* who could take me. How about somebody from here at the orphanage? Of course I would be happy to pay."

Masha screwed up her face. "Only a few ladies here."

"I would be happy to pay," Veronica repeated, trying

hard not to dwell on how little time she had to spare. Her flight out of Moscow left the following night. She had to be on that plane or her role as Leonora would be gone, and most likely her career along with it.

"No lady can go," Masha said. "We here for children. Nobody have car."

"Well, is there somebody else like Viktor?"

Masha shook her head. "Nobody like Viktor. Can you wait till end of week?"

Veronica couldn't even wait until the day after tomorrow. "Not really, no."

Masha lay her hand on Veronica's knee, her expression regretful. "I'm sorry, Miss Veronica."

It hit Veronica then. Here she was all alone in Russia, where she knew no one and spoke only a few words of the language, and she'd been foolish enough to rely on an oh-so-fragile plan that she should have known would fall apart. "Oh my God," she murmured, and rose to her feet.

She turned away from Masha to stare out the nearest window. All this might have been for nothing. She might have made this entire trip for nothing, jeopardized her career for nothing. And it seemed so much worse to come so far and not meet her birth mother than never to have come at all.

She began to pace, her mind whirling. Yes, she'd been able to get to the orphanage, but she had no clue how to find her birth mother's house, which was outside Moscow. Of course she'd searched for the town on a map, and she could probably get Masha to help her figure out how to take a train there, but then what? Was it even possible to hire a taxi in a Russian town as small as that one? And even if it were, she didn't know her birth mother's address. She hadn't bothered to get it from Viktor because she'd expected him to be by her side the entire time.

She glanced at the ring, whose gemstone had lost its opalescence. Apparently it wasn't pleased with this turn of events, either. Maybe this was another one of those tests of bravery.

If so, it was a big one. Because even if Veronica did succeed in getting to her birth mother's house, she couldn't talk to her without a translator. The two of them could stare at each other and hug and hold hands, but Veronica wanted to communicate more profoundly than that.

Damn that Viktor! Why hadn't he taken the metro to the orphanage as she had? Even if his car wasn't working he could still accompany her by train. He could still be her guide and translator. And Viktor knew it was now or never. He knew Veronica's birth mother was dying. He'd translated the letter she'd written to Veronica, and he understood that was why Veronica was making this hell-bent trip.

"Oh my God." Veronica's knees gave out when a new idea swam into her mind. She sank back onto the lumpy couch with the green stripes.

It had been hours since she'd had the dream of the graveyard, and she'd allowed herself to discount its message, but now she had to wonder if maybe, after all, the dream had been right. Maybe this morning when Viktor had called her birth mother to make the final arrangements, he'd found out she was dead. And so he had made himself unavailable. He didn't want to face Veronica's heartbreak and so concocted the lame "my car broke down" excuse. He might as well have said his dog ate his homework.

Masha appeared in her field of vision, holding up her cell phone. "I have idea, Miss Veronica. Call Nicholas. Maybe he take you to your mother."

Chapter Five

Veronica didn't wait for a second invitation to place that call. And to her immense relief, Nicholas immediately agreed to drive her to her birth mother's home—which was a full hour out of town—to translate for her, and then to return her to the Kudrinskaya Building afterward.

There was only one hitch: Work would tie him up for three hours at least. So her birth mother would have to make herself available for a nighttime visit.

"I'll call Viktor," Nicholas said, "get the particulars from him, and then call your birth mother."

Veronica hadn't known that men like Nicholas existed anymore. "I don't know how to thank you."

"I understand how important this is," he told her.

Yes, he would understand that. He'd been an orphan, too. Veronica resisted sharing her concern that her birth mother had died. For one thing, there was no rational way to frame it. *I dreamed I was searching for her grave. And when I had the dream I was wearing a ring that speaks the truth. So when Viktor pulled his disappearing act, what else could I conclude?*

It was an agony waiting for Nicholas to call back. When finally he did, he delivered the news Veronica longed to hear. "Your birth mother very much wants to see you, regardless of the hour."

Veronica clutched Masha's phone. *She's still alive.*

"You understand," Nicholas went on, "that she's quite ill?"

"She wrote me that she's dying."

"I'll get to the orphanage as soon as I can."

Veronica shivered. The way he said it, she worried they might not make it in time.

She glanced at the ring. Now the emerald gemstone was nearly as white as the snowflakes drifting lazily toward earth outside the window, like sighs from the heavens. The ring had come through for her yet again. Nonsensical as it seemed, it was as if the ring had contrived to put Nicholas at the orphanage to make up for Viktor's lapse and take her to her birth mother.

Still, she had to suffer through another agony of waiting. But the clock ticked faster than it might have when Masha allowed her to help care for the children. She learned that this baby home housed ninety children up to age five, with only four caregivers present at any given time. It broke her heart to see infants who were nearly a year old barely able to sit up in their cribs. Had they enjoyed the devoted care of loving parents, they would be crawling or taking their first steps or even walking by that age.

At last Nicholas arrived. He hurried inside the orphanage's front room accompanied by a blast of frigid night air. Little Marina, now in her nightgown, somehow managed to escape her bed and grab him around the knees. Finally he had to pry her little body off his own and leave her, red-faced and wailing, inside.

The door closed on the orphanage. It was past seven now, dark save for a line of streetlights that stretched far into the night. The sidewalks were nearly empty, but cars still lined both sides of the road. They set off, walking past a row of buildings as institutional in style as the orphanage. Almost immediately Veronica slipped on a patch of ice.

"Careful." Nicholas offered her his arm. "My car is just up the street."

They fell into step. "Those children hate seeing you go," she said after a time.

"It's the same for me. Every time."

"Your attention must mean so much to them."

"They get so little of it. I mean, the staff are great, but they're woefully shorthanded."

"I learned just how much today. It boggles the mind."

"Every time I visit I think there but for the grace of God go I."

Veronica knew the feeling. If it hadn't been for her parents, who nearly bankrupted themselves to adopt her, she would have been one of the thousands of abandoned children for whom a knock on the door never came. She squeezed Nicholas's arm. "Masha told me."

He glanced down at her and returned the squeeze. He said nothing, but nothing needed to be said. Both of them understood how fortunate they were.

A few minutes later he was settling her in his small black Renault. "I can't thank you enough for doing this," she told him.

"Honestly, I'm happy to help." He turned the ignition and the engine responded. No car problems here. That meant it would be only one hour more until she arrived at her birth mother's house, after she'd been waiting a lifetime. It was hard to fathom.

Veronica fell silent. In short order they encountered a fair amount of traffic, not surprising in a city of ten million people. Moscow drivers seemed as aggressive as their California counterparts, but she soon discovered that Nicholas could hustle with the best of them.

When they were tooling along a four-lane highway, she spoke again. "Did you try to get posted to Moscow so you could be close to the orphanage?"

"I wouldn't say that, but I had a focus on Russia from early on. I knew someday I'd land here."

"Where else have you been posted?"

"Angola, to start. Then Egypt, Uzbekistan, and now here."

A little different from the overseas travel she'd done thanks to her opera career, which was all Western Europe with one expedition to Singapore. With U.S. opera companies in such poor straits, American singers often found more opportunities abroad—for paid work, at least. "So you must speak several languages," she said to Nicholas.

"Three well and a smattering of others. English and Russian, of course, French, and enough Arabic to get by, though I can't read or write." He glanced at her. "What do you do?"

"I'm an opera singer. A soprano."

"Really?" Nicholas didn't mask the astonishment in his voice. "That is very impressive."

"Not so much. It's not like I'm famous or anything."

"Maybe not yet. You must speak several languages, too, in that line of work."

"I wish. All opera singers have to know some Italian, French, and German, but for most of us, our vocabulary is truly bizarre. I know how to tell you that my lover ran off with my sister or that I stabbed my father's courtesan in the heart, but I couldn't have a normal conversation if my life depended on it."

Nicholas threw back his head and laughed. In that moment Veronica could imagine him as an imp of a boy.

She'd known him only a few hours, but already she liked

him a lot. He was so good-looking, and so considerate. He just had a wonderful way about him. He seemed almost too good to be true.

She glanced at his left hand to see if it sported a telltale gold band and was pleased to note it did not. Still, that didn't prove anything. She tried to sound only casually interested. "Do you have family here in Moscow with you?"

"No. My parents, cousins, everybody are all back in Chicago."

Right answer. "Yes, I remember now, Masha did mention Chicago." She hesitated. "If you don't mind my asking, how old are you? I'm wondering if we were at the orphanage at the same time."

"Wouldn't that be incredible? But I doubt it. I'm older than you. Thirty-six."

"Yes, you are older than me." She said nothing more.

Out of the corner of her eye she saw him glance her way and chuckle. She kept her gaze straight ahead and smiled. She hadn't flirted with a man in a long time. And with a man like Nicholas—never.

Veronica looked down at the ring, wondering if it had an opinion of her traveling companion. She found herself caring quite a bit what it thought. Happily, not only was the emerald gemstone back to being a milky cream color, now it even glowed in the dark as if going opalescent weren't endorsement enough. Then again, Veronica was about to complete the journey on which the ring had helped dispatch her, so she would expect it to be satisfied.

It was more than a little nerve-wracking when Nicholas exited the highway for the town where her birth mother lived. "This is bigger than I thought it would be," she told him, peering through the black night at the numerous high-rise apartment blocks that rose from the wintry landscape.

Thousands of windows, it seemed, shone with the glow of lamplight. "It's really a city, not a town."

"I bet there are a hundred thousand people living here." Nicholas drove the Renault over a river lined with trees on both banks. "And more in the summer when people come to their *dachas* to escape Moscow."

Veronica knew about those second homes, required by law to be small, owned by ordinary city dwellers as well as the wealthy and powerful. Back when Russians were severely restricted in owning property, the tradition of the *dacha* allowed them to call a plot of land their very own.

Old and new were cheek by jowl here: a glass office building next to a Russian Orthodox church built of white stone, with multiple spires and an onion dome painted a brilliant gold. They also came upon a low-slung mint-green train station that had the look of having stood in that exact spot for a century.

"This must be a stop on the Trans-Siberian railroad," Nicholas said. "Hold on a minute. I have to check the directions."

The Renault rolled to a stop on the side of the road. Veronica remained fascinated with the scenery even though it had stopped changing. "Isn't this place big enough to have an orphanage? Why did my mother take me to Moscow?"

Nicholas looked up from his cell phone, glowing in the dark. "I can think of any number of reasons. Maybe she thought she'd go back and get you the next day if she left you at an orphanage nearby. Maybe she was embarrassed to leave you where she lived, where she knew people. Or maybe she thought you had a better chance of being adopted if she took you to Moscow." He turned his dark eyes to hers. "That's one thing you could ask her," he added gently.

It struck Veronica then. *My birth mother must be as nervous as I am.* Maybe even more so. She might think her daughter was angry with her for giving her up.

There certainly had been times when it pained Veronica that *she* was the baby her birth mother had relinquished. Why her and not another? What was wrong with *her*? But eventually she came to think of her birth mother as a tragic figure who was forced to make an impossible choice, a sort of Russian Fantine who had to allow another to raise her beloved Cosette, never a day passing that she didn't wish life had dealt her a different hand.

Veronica shut her eyes. *I can tell her I know she loved me. I can tell her I'm not angry and never really was.* Now, at the end of her birth mother's life, all that mattered was giving her the peace that would come from seeing the child she had been forced to abandon. By coming all this way, Veronica could help heal the last open wound of her birth mother's life.

Nicholas broke into her thoughts. "It's not far from here. Shall I keep going?"

"I wish I'd brought something. I didn't think to bring something."

Nicholas smiled. "You're bringing all you need, Veronica."

She nodded, hoping he was right, and motioned for him to drive on. He made a turn and rolled the Renault up a commercial strip, identical concrete apartment towers rising above small storefronts, banks, and restaurants. Leafless trees lined both sides of the street, along with cars that had seen better days. Scattered neon signs made a feeble attempt to light the glacial night. A few pedestrians hastened along the sidewalks, so bundled against the cold that Veronica could see almost nothing of their features.

Then Nicholas stopped at an intersection, and Veronica found herself staring at a young woman who couldn't seem to decide whether to cross the street. She hesitated at the corner and gazed beyond the Renault at something well behind it. Unlike everyone else, this woman's head was bare. She had long straight hair, dyed so platinum blond it was nearly white, and her eyes were heavily made up with liner and mascara. She'd gone overboard with the makeup, but she was dressed all in black and stylish in her own way. Now Veronica saw she held a cell phone to her ear. She might have been standing at Union Square in San Francisco.

That might have been me if I'd grown up here. Veronica would be living one life instead of another. No one could know if it would be better or worse. But she would have grown into that confident young woman only if she'd found a way to triumph over her birth mother's poverty. That would have been no mean trick in any country, let alone this one.

And you would never have known your parents. You would never have become an opera singer.

It was her destiny to have parents who could make her dreams come true. Yes, they'd had to scrabble hard. It had been a never-ending struggle to afford singing lessons, piano, all the training required to hone the gift of their daughter's voice. But Veronica knew they believed it had been worth it, as did she. Veronica wouldn't be who she was if she couldn't sing. She would be a pale shadow of herself.

Nicholas continued through the intersection and made a few more turns. Then he slid the car into a parking space and cut the engine. He gestured to the concrete apartment tower across the street.

"Is that it? We should go in," she added, stating the obvious. Still, something kept her from exiting the car. "Did you ever try to find your birth mother?"

"I never did."

"Did you think about it?"

He seemed to weigh his words. "I considered it. But when it came down to it, I just didn't care to unwrap the past."

His words hung in the air.

"I know I may be disappointed," Veronica said into the silence. "I have a mental image of my birth mother, and I know it may turn out not to be true."

Nicholas said nothing.

She went on. "My parents would be crushed if they knew I was doing this. They've been so wonderful to me all my life. All they've ever done is love me." She had to stop speaking.

Nicholas leaned closer. "Veronica, you're not doing anything wrong by trying to meet your—"

"That's another thing. My parents named me Veronica." A rogue tear escaped. "They had another name picked out, but in the end they kept the name my birth mother gave me. Veronika. Do you know how much that means to me?" Now she was on the verge of sobbing.

"Tell me." He handed her a fresh handkerchief. Apparently he had quite the supply on hand.

"It's a sign of respect, to my birth mother and to where I come from." She blew her nose and wiped her face. She must look such a fright, and just when she wanted to look her best. "They didn't try to rub out my past. They embraced it."

"That was a very generous thing for them to do."

"It was."

"It's also a beautiful name, Veronica. It suits you."

She was not so distraught that she missed the compliment. She glanced at Nicholas, who—she didn't think she imagined it—was eyeing her with some appreciation. She swiped at her nose one more time. "How did your parents come to name you Nicholas?"

"Well, they didn't keep the name my birth mother gave me, which was Oleg."

She smiled. "You don't seem like an Oleg."

"The name means holy, which actually suits my parents pretty well."

"They're religious?"

"They're both ardent Catholics. But once they knew they were adopting from Russia, they went into a major Nicholas and Alexandra phase. Nothing could keep them from naming me Nicholas."

Not even that the last czar came to a pretty nasty end. "What do your parents do?" She found herself wanting to prolong the conversation, even though they were sitting in a cold car in the dark, even though the birth mother she'd long dreamed of meeting was awaiting her.

"My dad's a doctor. My mom's a potter. She makes gorgeous pieces. She's extremely talented."

Veronica remembered her mother telling her years before that you could learn a great deal about a man from the way he treated his mother. Now, watching Nicholas's eyes shine with admiration for his mother's achievements, Veronica had the idea he treated her very well indeed.

"She did have one big disappointment in life, though," he went on.

"Surely not *you*." She hoped Nicholas would catch that now she was complimenting him.

"No. But she was never able to conceive. My parents took that as a sign from above, but I know it hurt them."

"My mother conceived a few times, but she was never able to bring a baby to term." That was an intimate revelation, but somehow in this place she'd never been, with this man she barely knew, Veronica felt comfortable making it. "But I tell you, when I was with those children today—"

"I know what you're going to say. Sometimes I think I'd feel guilty fathoring a child of my own. When there are so many children out there who need homes."

"You could always do both. Have a child and adopt a child."

"Yes—"

"Or have a child and adopt *two* children."

Nicholas chuckled. "That would be perfect."

Yes. Veronica had long thought that would be perfect, too.

She and Nicholas stared at each other across the small expanse of his car. Outside a pedestrian hurried past, reminding Veronica of the rush she should be in. She forced herself to look away from Nicholas's dark eyes. "I think I'm ready now."

"You're sure?"

She loosed a nervous chuckle. "I'm such a diva. I've been worried my birth mother would disappoint me. Now I'm worried I'll disappoint her."

Very gently, Nicholas turned her chin toward him. "There's no chance of that, Veronica."

Chapter Six

If Veronica had grown up in this building, she would have lived on the eleventh floor. She took that as a good sign. Eleven was her lucky number. She was eleven when she started voice lessons and that was also the year that her father brought home her beloved orange tabby cat Pumpkin.

Good omens were what she focused on as she and Nicholas pulled open the heavy metal door of her birth mother's apartment building, a relic of the Soviet era. As they made their way through the dimly lit ground level, Veronica knew she had entered a tenement by another name. It was dank, rundown, and oppressive—the smell of urine hung in the air; a sullen huddle of men smoked cigarettes in a corner, pausing to regard her and Nicholas with suspicious eyes; yellow and rust-colored paint peeled off walls pockmarked by graffiti.

The Cold War-era elevator began grudgingly to lift her and Nicholas to their destination, protesting every foot of the climb. Nicholas spoke into the silence. "Just so you know, this building is typical. It's not unusually bad."

"They're all like this?"

"The Soviets provided housing for their citizens, but they made a point of making all the buildings alike. So life would be the same on every block, in every city, all across the country."

Veronica supposed that was the revolutionary way.

"They're all in bad shape like this?"

"They're poorly maintained as a rule."

"It doesn't seem like the fall of communism has helped people much."

"It's been very uneven. Some people it's helped a lot."

Veronica knew about the oligarchs who'd pocketed outrageous sums when Russia privatized its state-owned businesses. But it was clear her birth mother and many others like her had been left out in the cold.

The eleventh floor lacked the smell of urine but was otherwise morosely similar to the ground level. The heels of Veronica's boots echoed on the concrete floor as they walked past one metal door after the next.

She halted abruptly. "I just thought of something. I could have brothers and sisters waiting for me, too. I know they exist. I can't believe I didn't think of that."

It was another astounding possibility.

Veronica continued on, finally locating her birth mother's unit. She paused before knocking, Nicholas a reassuring bulwark behind her. It was amazing to know that from this moment on, she would know her birth mother. She would understand what kind of people she came from. She would become like everybody else who could recite those basic facts from their life story and take them entirely for granted.

She steeled herself for whatever might follow and rapped on the door.

It was pulled open by a woman of Masha's age, with curly hair, dyed copper red, and small dark eyes. She was plump and wore a no-nonsense gray skirt and sweater. She looked Veronica over with frank curiosity then gave a small smile and ushered the arrivals inside.

Veronica understood this woman was not her birth mother. As hushed words passed between the woman and

Nicholas, Veronica took in the apartment. *This is where my mother has lived her life. This is where I would have grown up.*

It was clean but—she had to admit—bleak. The floor was brown linoleum; the walls were covered with faded floral wallpaper. At least it was intact. Yellow draperies hung at the windows, which were cheery, and area rugs did add warmth, as did a quietly whistling radiator. The furnishings were basic and the worse for wear. Veronica told herself it was madness to be disappointed that she saw nothing in her favorite color of blue.

Beyond, in a room she couldn't quite see, she heard a cough. Her heart skipped a beat or two. *That must be my mother.*

Nicholas spoke in her ear. "This is your mother's friend Fedosia."

"Is anyone else here?"

"I don't think so. Fedosia wants to make tea."

"That's fine. But I want to meet my mother."

Fedosia might not speak English, but she understood that. She gestured to Veronica to move deeper into the apartment. Her heart now galloping a crazy rhythm, Veronica led the way into one of the two main rooms. And there, beneath a thin blanket on a pull-out bed, propped up against a stack of pillows, lay her mother.

Tears filled Veronica's eyes. She scuttled forward, dropping her handbag en route, and clasped her mother's hands in her own. She stared into the older woman's eyes—a greenish blue, like her own—and struggled with what to say in this moment. Somehow she couldn't find it within herself to say "mother" so she choked out an almost unintelligible *SDRAS-vui-tye*—a rather formal way to say "hello" in Russian.

Her mother smiled, nodded, and said hello more

informally, then patted the blanket by her side to signal Voronica to oit. Veronica threw off her coat and obliged, twisting her body so again she could hold her mother's hands in her own.

"Veronika," her mother said, pronouncing the name in the Russian style.

"Yes. It's really me." *And this is really her. This is really her.*

Her mother squeezed Veronica's hands. She remained dry-eyed, but again she smiled.

They stared into each other's eyes, Veronica blinking back tears and succeeding only to a point. Of course Nicholas stepped forward to produce a handkerchief. Her mother glanced at him and said something, to which Nicholas replied. Veronica looked at him with a question in her eyes.

"She wants to thank me for bringing you here," he explained.

Veronica nodded mutely. No language contained the words to thank Nicholas sufficiently for that. She studied her mother's face. "I do see myself in you." That was a phrase she'd never before been able to say, and never would again until she had a child of her own. "Especially," she added, "in your eyes." Their shape was the same, as was their distinctive aqua hue.

Sitting on a folding chair that Fedosia brought into the room, Nicholas translated. Her mother nodded, smiled. Fedosia piped up with something. "Fedosia says the shape of your faces is the same as well," Nicholas said, "and that it's clear you're mother and daughter."

Again her mother squeezed her hands. Veronica could only shake her head in wonderment. She had never before seen her features mirrored in another human being. It was surreal to know that this woman's blood flowed in her veins; this woman's DNA was a match with her own.

She did note, with dismay, that her mother looked shockingly older than would a 60-year-old American woman, and not just because she was ill. That was the unfortunate byproduct of a hard life in a harsh location.

Still, gray-haired and lined as she was, and even as again she turned her head away to cough, Veronica's mother did not look to be on her deathbed. Her frame was far from skeletal and her skin, while pale, was healthy in tone.

Veronica kept her voice gentle. "How are you feeling?"

Her mother shook her head as if that were a topic she didn't care to delve into. And indeed Nicholas translated that she did not feel well but did not want to discuss it. "She says there will be time to talk about that later," Nicholas finished.

Fedosia spoke. "And today is a good day," Nicholas translated. "Of course it would be, because you are here, Veronica."

That called for another round of hand-squeezing, and more tears on Veronica's part. "There are so many things to talk about." Veronica swiped at her nose. "I don't know where to start."

"I would love to hear about your mother's life," Nicholas said, then began a back-and-forth with Veronica's mother that he summed up when Fedosia returned from the kitchen bearing black tea and cookies, the same repast served to guests that Veronica had enjoyed at the orphanage.

Nicholas leaned forward with his forearms on his thighs. "Your family has lived in this town for generations, Veronica. The men have worked in construction for the most part. Your mother worked as a baker until she retired."

"Did you enjoy your work?" Veronica asked. "Do you like baking? I don't get much chance but I love to bake."

It turned out that her mother had labored in an industrial setting and chronic injuries she sustained over the years forced her to retire early.

Veronica was embarrassed to pose the next question but so curious to know. "I don't suppose there are any singers in the family?"

"No singers," Nicholas reported a moment later. "But one of your aunts painted."

Veronica's mother gestured to an oil painting hanging across the room above a small television. Veronica rose to inspect it more closely. Now here was something lovely—a blonde girl in a lacy white dress kneeling on a beach, so engrossed in building a sand castle that she was unaware she was being watched. Beyond her an orange sun sank into an ocean that stretched into forever. Finally Veronica saw something blue: the endless ocean.

"That's beautiful," Veronica said. "It's impressionistic in style, isn't it? With those little dabs of color that disappear into the whole and the wonderful way the artist depicted the light of the sun on the sea." She turned back around toward her mother. "I have an aunt who did this? She's very talented."

Again her mother patted the spot at her side. Veronica rushed to rejoin her. "I know I have brothers and sisters. I'd love to know more about them."

She had three brothers and a sister, she learned, all married with children of their own. That meant, Veronica realized, she not only had siblings but nieces and nephews, too. She should have realized she was likely to be an aunt, given the ages of her siblings.

"Yes," Nicholas said, "your brothers are thirty-eight, thirty-six, and thirty-five, and you have a sister who's"—he hesitated—"thirty-two."

Veronica looked down into her teacup, nearly empty now. She set it down.

Veronica was thirty-four. That meant her mother had given birth to another child after her, another girl, whom she had kept. For a moment the childhood agony came back. *Why me? Why was I the baby my mother gave away?*

Nicholas leaned closer. "Are you all right?"

Beside her, her mother sat up straighter and said something. Nicholas did not immediately translate.

"I'm all right," she told him.

"I'm sure there's an explanation," Nicholas said.

Her mother was speaking more forcefully now.

"She says she understands why you're upset," Nicholas said.

Her mother clutched at her arm until Veronica pivoted to face her.

"The problem was your father," Nicholas translated. "He would come and go. After you were conceived, and when you were born, he was gone. That was why your mother was unable to raise you. She had three sons already, she had to work, and she had no one to ask for help."

Veronica had always known her biological father was a deadbeat. It said as much in the adoption papers. Still, here where most people didn't stray far from where they were born, you'd think some family members could have helped.

"Then a year or so later," Nicholas went on, "your father came back into the picture. And for several years he stayed."

Which must be why her younger sister did not also land in Moscow's Baby Home Number 36.

Her mother's eyes, so like her own, were pleading. "She wants you to try to understand," Nicholas said. "Life is a struggle in Russia, not like in the United States. There, families don't have to separate. Here sometimes they do."

Veronica knew she was a stranger to adversity. She didn't understand what it meant to be beset by difficulties every day of your life, to know you would always be working a back-breaking job, living in a soul-crushing apartment building, raising children alone because the man you loved would come and go on a whim.

Again she took her mother's hands.

"And when it came to your father," Nicholas went on, "your mother says he was not a bad man. But he was unreliable. In some ways he just never grew up. But she loved him."

"Where is he now?"

Her mother looked away, shook her head, and began speaking in a low voice. This time Veronica understood one of the words she uttered.

"It's been years since your mother has seen him." Nicholas leaned close. "Veronica, she thinks that since he hasn't come back again, he's probably dead."

Yes, that was the word Veronica had understood. *MERT-vye*, the Russian word for dead.

Since there was so little mention of her biological father in her adoption papers—and what there was, was negative—Veronica had never spent much time spinning fantasies about him. Still, there was a certain grim finality to learning he was most likely deceased.

"May I see a picture of him? In fact, I'd love to see any pictures you could show me."

Nicholas said something and Fedosia bustled off to another room, returning with a couple of photos and a stack of airmail letters tied with string. "Your mother kept every letter you ever sent her," Nicholas said.

That Veronica could plainly see. "Yes, and Viktor's translations, too."

"These are your brothers," Nicholas said as her mother held out a faded photograph of three brown-haired boys posed stiffly in front of what looked like a school. They were all dressed alike in short-sleeved white shirts—"school uniforms," Nicholas explained.

Veronica peered at the photo, then pointed to one of the boys. "He kind of looks like me." As with her mother, there was something in the shape of the face.

"And here is your sister." Her mother held out the other photograph. It depicted a bride, beaming as she strolled through a summertime park arm in arm with a strapping young man, holding up her voluminous skirt to keep it from sweeping the grass.

"She's wearing the kind of gown she would wear in the United States," Veronica observed.

Her mother said something. "You're not married, right?" Nicholas asked.

"That's right."

Nicholas chuckled at her mother's next remark. "She wants to know what you're waiting for."

Veronica raised her eyes from the photograph to Nicholas's face. "You may tell her I haven't found the right man yet. And my career doesn't make it easy."

"Why not?" Nicholas wanted to know. "What is it about being an opera singer that would make it tough to be married?"

"I don't hear you translating, Nicholas."

"Sorry." He cleared his throat and said something to her mother. Then followed an extensive conversation, involving Fedosia, which Nicholas didn't bother to translate. Finally he spoke again to Veronica. "I asked if there were more photos you could see, but apparently there aren't."

"Really? Not even one of my father?"

"Your mother says they have almost no good photos and she's embarrassed to show you poor ones."

"I don't care about that."

"She says photos are a luxury this family can't afford."

Veronica quashed her disappointment. "That's a shame." Though she shouldn't be surprised. The family might live hand to mouth. Again she regretted that she hadn't brought something. "Do my sister or any of my brothers live close by?"

"Your sister and two of your brothers do," Nicholas reported. "One of your brothers moved to Moscow."

"Is it rude to say that I had hoped at least one of them might be here today?"

There was another barrage of conversation among Veronica's mother, Nicholas, and Fedosia. Finally Nicholas spoke again to Veronica. "Your mother says she couldn't be sure you would come today. You and Viktor were supposed to arrive in the afternoon but then you were delayed. And your siblings all have jobs, they have families—"

"But when you called earlier, Nicholas, didn't you say for sure I'd be coming today?"

"I did." He met her gaze. "I don't know how to explain it. Maybe something got lost in translation."

Chapter Seven

Again Veronica's mother grabbed her arm. Veronica twisted to face her and give her hands another squeeze.

Though they exchanged smiles, and Veronica's mother freed one of her hands to smooth back a lock of Veronica's hair, Veronica couldn't deny a certain sinking of the heart. Though she tried very hard to fight the feeling, she found this, all of this, a bit of a letdown.

She hadn't known what to expect from meeting her birth mother, not really, but it wasn't this. There was a tepid quality to the evening that flew in the face of all her fevered imaginings. She had expected these moments of first acquaintance to be more epic, more momentous. She had anticipated a warm connection, if not immediately, then in short order. She had longed for a meeting of the minds with her birth mother, a resonance in both hearts—and fully expected both. After all, she and this woman shared the profoundest of bonds. But try though she might, she couldn't shake a certain awkwardness. She sensed a distance between herself and her birth mother she didn't know how to bridge.

It was exactly what adoptees warned of. It was why so many did not try to find their birth parents. Parents and children who spent all their lives together sometimes failed to find a deep connection; why should parents and children who'd been separated be spared that fate?

Veronica, ever the diva, had been sure she'd be one of the lucky ones. Even when she knew her birth mother was dying, she'd still been convinced that she would enjoy the rapturous, tear-filled, Hollywood-perfect reunion of mother and child. She would be a mini me of her mother: the same in look, build, and style. They would share many of the same gestures. They would laugh at the same silly things—even though they spoke different languages. They would like the same foods—even though they lived in different culinary cultures. The fact that this scenario played out for no mother and daughter pairing that Veronica had ever known did not impinge on her fantasy.

Her mother raised Veronica's right hand to examine the ring, then motioned to Fedosia to come closer to scrutinize it as well. Far from the lamp's glow, the emerald gemstone appeared almost black. Veronica was surprised: She had expected it to gleam with pearliness here in her mother's presence. The two women twisted the ring this way and that, cooing with an admiration that embarrassed Veronica. She couldn't take credit for the ring's magnificence; she was its keeper for a short time only; but though she couldn't pinpoint why, she had the idea her mother wouldn't believe that. She considered regaling everyone with how it had come into her possession but bit back the impulse.

"Your mother says your ring is very beautiful," Nicholas said.

"Please thank her. It was a gift." From whom, she would never know.

"Nevertheless, your mother says, you're a fortunate woman because you could afford to buy a ring like this for yourself."

Veronica didn't know what to say to that. Her mother went on speaking.

"Your mother wants to know if you sing all over the world?" Nicholas said.

"Europe and the U.S., mostly."

"San Francisco," her mother said, her accent making the words hard to understand.

"I live in San Francisco, yes."

"In Victorian," her mother added.

"Not in a *whole* Victorian. I live on just one floor, in a flat." She almost added: *Sharing with two other women so I can pay the rent.*

Her mother continued speaking. "You stay in hotels all over the world when you sing," Nicholas translated. "Like Pavarotti."

At that, Veronica had to laugh. "Not at all like Pavarotti!" It had been decades since the world-famous tenor had stayed in a fourth-floor walk-up guesthouse, if he ever had. "I was lucky enough to work with him once, though."

Nicholas leaned forward. "That must've been an amazing experience."

"It was. I did an apprentice program with the Santa Fe Opera, and Luciano Pavarotti taught a master class." She smiled at the memory. "He helped me learn to pronounce the 'O' sound in Italian, which can be tricky for non-native speakers. I think if it hadn't been for him I never would've gotten my current role." Which she dearly hoped she still had. "Leonora in *Il Trovatore*. In Florence."

"One of my all-time favorite cities. Where are you staying?"

"In a guesthouse behind the Palazzo Vecchio."

"I envy you." They smiled at each other until Nicholas switched to Russian to translate what Veronica had said. He stopped, though, when her mother spoke over him. "Your mother says you must have had very expensive training to become an opera singer. Your parents must be wealthy people, otherwise it wouldn't have been possible."

Veronica shook her head vigorously. "No. It wasn't like that at all. My parents had to struggle to make my training possible. A lot of the time my father had two jobs."

Nicholas translated, but Veronica could see that her mother wasn't listening. Instead she was resettling herself on her pillows, grimacing slightly.

When her mother uttered a low moan, Veronica flushed from shame. Here she was jabbering on about Italy while her mother was in obvious distress. She rose to plump the pillows herself, a lump growing in her throat. She had feared the specter of death would hang over this reunion, and though it had not, now she was reminded that her time with her birth mother would be precious and short. "Nicholas," she murmured, "my mother may not want to talk about it, but I have to ask again about her health."

Nicholas began to speak but Veronica's mother shushed him with a wave of the hand. "She says we can talk about that tomorrow." His voice registered the surprise Veronica herself felt. "She apologizes," he went on, "but she's very tired."

"I can certainly understand that but"—Veronica struggled for what to say—"I would love to see her again tomorrow, but I can't impose on you like that, Nicholas."

"It wouldn't be an imposition if I offer." He regarded her steadily. "And so I hereby offer."

"Are you serious?"

"Absolutely." He rose to his feet. "If you're sure you'd like to come again, then I'll bring you."

"Of course I'm sure." This time Veronica hugged her mother, and kissed her cheek. The older woman managed a feeble smile.

Veronica and Nicholas stood in the tiny entry to make what turned out to be prolonged arrangements with Fedosia, who referred to a morning visit by a doctor.

Nicholas's expression was thoughtful. "Fedosia says there's a slim chance there may be a special treatment for your mother. Her doctor will come here in the morning to discuss it with her."

"Really?" Veronica grasped Fedosia's arm. "Is that why my mother didn't want to discuss her health, because she didn't want to raise my hopes? If that were true, that would change everything."

If it weren't hopeless for her birth mother, Veronica might be able to develop a relationship with her. That's what they needed to dispel this stiffness between them: time. They could write letters and, when she was working in Europe, Veronica could visit. Eventually mother and daughter would find their natural familiarity.

Nicholas and Fedosia spoke at length. Finally: "I asked if we might be here for the doctor visit," Nicholas said. "Fedosia keeps saying she's not sure exactly when it's going to happen, but now she's named a time."

Veronica frowned. "I would like to be here but don't you think it's kind of presumptuous? I am her daughter but we've just met."

"If I knew more about her condition, I might be able to help. Fedosia hasn't even been able to tell me what your mother is suffering from."

No doubt Nicholas had connections and so could help. "We could hover in the background," she said, "and you could talk to the doctor before he or she leaves."

A plan was set. Beneath a night sky obscured by a forbidding mantle of clouds, Veronica and Nicholas walked back to his Renault. "It'll snow tonight," he said as he held open the car door while Veronica settled in.

"That may make it harder to get back here tomorrow, if there's a big storm."

They didn't speak again until they were once more on the nearly empty highway leading to Moscow. "You're being so generous with your time, Nicholas," she said into the silence. "Really, I don't know how I'm ever going to thank you."

"I just want you to be careful, Veronica."

It was a different man in a different car on a different highway, but he was speaking almost exactly the same words Dominik had spoken three nights before. "What are you talking about?" she asked, though of course she knew.

Nicholas appeared to choose his words carefully. "I'm a little concerned about all this."

So am I. She banished the thought. "I'm concerned about my mother's health, absolutely."

"How do you feel now that you've met her?"

It was hard to put into words. "I think I'm in shock. I know for most people it's totally normal, but it's the first time in my life I've been around someone who's blood."

"Is that how she feels to you?"

"I feel a connection to her," Veronica lied.

Nicholas said nothing. A snazzy German car rocketed past on their left, maybe driven by an oligarch hastening back to Moscow.

"You might as well get it off your chest," she said a few minutes later. "When you said you were concerned, what did you mean?"

It took him a while to speak. Then: "Even before the conversation with Fedosia, which I will tell you was pretty bizarre, a few things troubled me."

Veronica fiddled with the ring. A few things troubled

her, too, but she was trying to ignore them. "What did Fedosia say that was so bizarre?"

"I didn't translate all of it because she would say one thing, and then she would say something else that contradicted it. But I promise you that when we get back there tomorrow, the doctor will have come and gone."

Snow started to fall. Veronica watched flakes dance in the black sky above their speeding Renault. "I wouldn't be at all surprised if my mother didn't want us there while the doctor is examining her. It's an invasion of her privacy."

He ignored that. "The way Fedosia was talking about the quote unquote special treatment—"

"Why do you say it that way? You don't believe it exists?"

Again he seemed to be picking and choosing his words. "I'm just concerned they'll ask you to pay for this treatment, which, I'll be honest with you, Veronica, I am not sure exists."

"First of all, not *they*. Fedosia. My mother didn't breathe a word about any of this. And you know what? Even if my mother did ask me to pay for it, what would be so wrong with that? I'm her daughter, and even though I'm far from rich, clearly I have more money than she does."

"Veronica, I'm on your side here."

She knew that was true. She didn't need the ring pulsating with white light to clue her in on that. For what seemed like the millionth time that day, and for who knew what reason now, tears again stung her eyes.

"I don't want you taken advantage of," he went on.

The tears were so close to the surface that she had to choke out the words. "Nicholas, you are being incredibly kind to me, but I am not some idiot you have to protect."

"You just have to remember that corruption is ingrained in— "

"Yes, there's a lot of corruption in Russia. That is not news to me. But do not try to tell me that all Russian people are corrupt."

"You know I'm not saying that."

"Maybe you've gotten cynical from living here so long. Maybe you've seen too much. And besides, all I really hear you saying is that you don't trust Fedosia."

Nicholas didn't speak for a time while he maneuvered around a few slow-moving vehicles. It seemed to Veronica that he was using the interruption to gear up for an even touchier subject.

She turned out to be right.

"I wasn't comfortable," he started, "with everything your mother said."

She bit back her agreement. "Do you mean when she was asking about my opera career?"

"She was mostly asking how much money you make."

"That's got to be high in the minds of people who don't have much money."

"She barely listened when you talked about your master class with Pavarotti. She didn't ask a thing about the production you're in now, or about any of the productions you've ever been in. And the only thing she wanted to know about your training was how much it cost."

And she didn't ask me to sing. It was the one constant of Veronica's life: People she just met were always asking her to sing. Masha had earlier that day. Strangers did all the time. But the woman who had given her life didn't request a single note.

"I thought she would ask you to sing," Nicholas said, unsettling her even further by echoing her thoughts. "Hell, I wanted her to. *I want to hear you sing, Veronica. But I wanted her to be the one to ask.*"

Veronica said another thing she didn't really believe. "You can't expect a woman on her deathbed to be demanding an aria."

Nicholas was silent. All the same Veronica knew what he was thinking. *Yes, you can. Because if she doesn't hear an aria from her daughter now, she never will.*

Veronica's tears had receded. Now she was feeling combative. "I bet you're going to tell me you don't think she's really sick."

He hesitated. "I heard that cough. I don't think she's well."

"Well, I'm glad you don't think the entire thing is a pretext to get the rich American opera-singing daughter she gave away to give her money."

He was quiet for a long time before he spoke again. "It will anger you to hear me say this, Veronica, but that is a possibility I want you to consider."

I beat you to it, her mind screamed. *I've already started considering it …*

"You know what?" She wrenched the ring off her finger and flung it in her handbag. Her mind was already telling her things she didn't care to hear, and she was not eager for the ring to chime in. "I really appreciate everything you're doing for me, Nicholas, you are truly going above and beyond. But I don't want to talk about this anymore."

She twisted her body away from him to put an exclamation point on her dismissal and stared resolutely out the window. None of the scenery was clear, though, not with the impenetrable darkness, the swirling snow, or the tears blurring her vision. She was left to her thoughts, which were no comfort at all, even with the ring banished from her finger.

She didn't shed one tear on meeting me. I was a sniveling mess, but she was as unemotional as could be. She didn't ask a single thing about the parents who raised me. She didn't want to know if I have brothers or sisters in California. She didn't care what my favorite subject was in school or did I play any sports or did I have a dog or a cat or a fish. Do I have a favorite holiday? Was I ever in love? Am I in love now? Maybe with the mysterious somebody who gave me this damn ring?

Maybe a few days ago the ring had given Veronica clarity and courage, but now it was just irritating her.

Know thy heart.

Her reply to that directive was to kick her handbag deeper into the footwell.

As promised, Nicholas deposited her at the Kudrinskaya Building. She was retrieving her handbag from the depths of the footwell when he forestalled her by laying a hand on her leg. "I'm going to send some dinner to your apartment, because you have to eat and I bet you don't have any food up there. What unit are you in?"

She told him.

"I'll call one of my favorite places. They're still open and they're fast. They service the embassy all the time. I'll have them include a bottle of wine."

She wouldn't protest that most nights. She certainly wouldn't tonight.

She forced herself to look Nicholas's way. "Please forgive me for being an ungrateful snot." He shook his head. She continued without letting him speak. "You've already done so much for me but I want to ask you for one thing more."

"Name it."

"I want to arrive early tomorrow at my mother's. Maybe even a full hour earlier than we said we'd show up."

"Fine. We'll miss more of the traffic that way."

"I'm forcing a really short night on you."

"The ambassador does that all the time. No problem."

He smiled, but she refused to be charmed. At the moment Nicholas seemed in league with the supposedly truth-telling ring, which meant he was on the outs with her.

He went on. "May I ask why you want to get there so early?"

She told her final untruth of the night. "I want to have as much time as possible with my mother."

Nicholas nodded. She had the idea he didn't believe her but that didn't come as a surprise. She already understood he would be a hard man to fool.

Chapter Eight

The next morning Veronica found out that Nicholas was a soothsayer. As he had predicted, they entered her birth mother's apartment to have Fedosia greet them with the news that the doctor had already made his house call.

Veronica wordlessly shed her coat, scarf, and gloves. So. She was to believe the doctor had come and gone. Even though she was standing in this apartment before eight a.m. and Fedosia had said the doctor wouldn't appear until nine at the earliest. And that was not even getting into the dubious assertion that doctors in Russia's less than world-class healthcare system made house calls on impoverished patients.

Earlier that morning Veronica had established a guiding principle for what she knew would be a difficult day, the last day she would see her birth mother alive. It was this: She would not be upset or disappointed or disillusioned if her birth mother asked for money for medical treatment.

It was not a crime to be poor. It was not a crime to request help from someone more fortunate than you. And if ever there were an understandable reason to ask, saving one's own life was it.

In fact, Veronica thought as she dressed for the day, asking for help requires that you swallow your pride and risk humiliation. It takes guts. And Veronica would admire her birth mother for having guts.

With this guideline in mind, Veronica felt confident returning the ring to her finger. She had left it on the bedside table while she slept, not wanting to risk another nightmarish dream. But after her shower, she slipped the ring back on and reminded it, with some asperity, that she *did* know her heart. After all, that's how she had gotten to Moscow in the first place. And now her heart's desire was to help her mother financially any way she could.

Now Veronica stood in the minuscule entry of her birth mother's apartment and handed Fedosia the box of *pastila*, pastries made with sweet apple paste, that she had purchased en route. Nicholas had recommended them as a delicacy, and she had wanted to bring something special. "How did the appointment with the doctor go?" she asked Fedosia.

Fedosia replied with atypical animation. She was wearing the same clothes she'd had on the night before, but this morning everything about her was amped up.

"They've had good news," Nicholas translated. "The doctor said that indeed your mother is a candidate for a special treatment that might save her life."

Nicholas relayed this information as if he were a newsman under the strictest injunction to appear impartial. It was only because of the prior night's conversation that Veronica knew he didn't believe a word Fedosia was saying.

There would be no *I told you so's* from him, Veronica realized. And he would leave it entirely up to her to judge the veracity of what she was hearing.

Veronica found her birth mother in the same bubbly mood as Fedosia. Mother and daughter exchanged kisses and smiles before Veronica settled on the pull-out bed, clasping her mother's hands. "This is pretty incredible news from the doctor! Tell me everything he said."

Nicholas duly translated. Despite the momentousness of this new treatment option, it soon became clear the doctor had offered remarkably few details about it. The treatment would have to be done in Moscow, in a cutting-edge facility. For that reason it was expensive. But there was an excellent chance it would prolong her mother's life by years, and really, it was nothing short of miraculous.

Veronica pivoted to face Nicholas, who was once again in the fold-out chair Fedosia had carried from the adjacent room. "Do you understand exactly what it is my mother is suffering from?"

"I haven't been able to pin that down. Both Fedosia and your mother keep saying it's complicated and has to do with why she retired early."

"And this treatment is available now because—"

"Apparently it's new. I asked if it was experimental, and your mother said yes. But the doctor is very confident about it, especially in her case. She says," he finished, "that it's the only thing that's given her any hope."

Extraordinary timing, it had to be said. The miracle cure raises its head just as Veronica touches down in Russia. She turned back around to face her mother. "When does the doctor want to start this treatment?"

At that, her mother looked away and shook her head, as Veronica had an inkling she would. Perhaps Veronica, too, was a soothsayer. Or perhaps she had merely heard the word "expensive" in Nicholas's translation.

Eventually her mother spoke, and Nicholas translated. "The problem is that the treatment is expensive," he repeated. "Since it's experimental, it's not covered by the basic healthcare program. Only people who can afford it can get it."

"What do your children say about it?" Her children who

were not around today, either, who, like the grandchildren, were never around, no matter that the matriarch was on her deathbed getting word of an astounding last-minute reprieve or that their long-lost sister from America had suddenly materialized in Moscow.

"Of course her children are desperate for her to live," Nicholas translated. "They would do anything they possibly could."

Except be by their mother's side.

"But they can't help," Nicholas went on. "None of them has any money."

Veronica's mother chose this moment to grip her hands and squeeze. Hard.

Veronica wanted to help—she'd come here with that intention—but how in the world could she afford to pay for an expensive medical treatment? True, she did have some savings. And maybe she could take out a loan.

She looked into her birth mother's aqua eyes, boring into her own, asking a question that needed no words to be understood.

Veronica answered. "Do you want me to pay for this treatment?"

The moment Nicholas translated, and even though Veronica hadn't yet agreed to pay for anything, her mother burst into tears. *Now* her tears flowed. She pulled Veronica into a bear of a hug—revealing a grasp that was astonishingly strong for a dying woman—and wept copiously. A wail even escaped her lips and ascended to the heavens.

As Veronica held her mother, she struggled to understand how it could be that her wishes were coming true and still she felt nothing, nothing at all. Now, there was a real chance her birth mother would live. Now, her birth mother was overcome with emotion, thanks to her beloved Veronika saving the day.

Fedosia, by now also a fountain of tears, came over to give Veronica's birth mother a hug. Veronica rose to walk across the room. She exchanged a glance with Nicholas, whose steady gaze neither accused nor endorsed. He was leaving it all up to her, as she had known he would.

Veronica watched the tableau of her mother and Fedosia hugging. This wasn't like last night anymore. The discussion of the miracle treatment and the expense involved wasn't coming from Fedosia alone. It was coming from her mother, too. It was coming from both of them.

Nicholas made a restless move and rose to his feet. He spun away as if he'd had enough.

Veronica watched him pull his cell phone from his trouser pocket. "Nicholas," she said to his back, "will you please ask my mother if I should get in touch with the doctor to find out how to pay for the treatment?"

He turned back around and nodded without enthusiasm. His question broke the hug between Veronica's mother and Fedosia, who shook their heads in unison. "They're telling me the doctor doesn't want to be bothered with that kind of detail." Again his voice betrayed no reaction. "It's better if you do a wire transfer straight into your mother's account."

Veronica nodded slowly. Fedosia stood to allow her to resume her rightful place at her beaming mother's side. As she sat, Veronica understood why it was that she felt so hollow. Later she wondered if that was what gave her the strength to speak her next words. That, or the ring, that damn ring, that kept pushing her off the highest branch whether or not she felt ready to fly.

"I wish," she told her mother, holding her hands, holding her gaze, "that you had been honest with me."

She waited for Nicholas to translate. She sensed his surprise as he stepped closer to do so. She felt him behind her as she watched her mother's eyes go from joyful to disbelieving.

"If you asked for money just to live," she went on, "I would give it to you. Despite what you think, I don't have that much to give. But I would give it to you. After all, I am your daughter. And you are the woman who gave me life."

Veronica had to pause as her throat constricted and her eyes filled with tears. Her birth mother remained dry-eyed.

"But I won't be tricked into it. Which is what's happening, because you're not being honest with me."

Veronica had to force the words out. Then she had to listen to them hang in the air as she waited for Nicholas to translate. She felt her mother withdraw her hands and watched her eyes narrow. She had known she would anger her mother, but she told herself that's what happened in families. Family members got angry at each other from time to time. Then they forgave and they forgot. That was as long a thread in the tapestry of family life as love and devotion.

She glanced at the ring, whose gemstone sparkled with white light. No surprise there: Veronica understood by now it sanctioned everything that required courage. Funny how often courage was required to get at the truth.

Veronica swallowed hard and spoke again. "I'm sorry but I don't believe any of this about the so-called special treatment. It doesn't add up, none of it does, and I just don't believe it. I think you made it up so you would have an excuse to ask me for money."

Her mother began to blubber in protest, but Veronica stilled her.

"Stop, please stop. Just be honest with me. Tell me once and for all. Is there really a special treatment?" Taking in her mother's sturdy build and rosy cheeks, she heard herself go one step further. "And are you really so sick that you're dying?"

Nicholas finished his translation. Veronica's mother said nothing. Veronica kept her gaze on her mother's flushed face, saw, though she wished she didn't, the calculation in her eyes, the weighing of what to say and what not to say. In the silent room she listened to the relentless tick tock of the wall clock in the kitchen, counting off the seconds while her mother put Truth on the scales of her mind. All four of them, it seemed, were suspended in a breathless moment, anticipating something, no one knew what, like those few seconds before the curtains part and the first notes of the opera ring out.

Finally her mother spoke, her voice firm and her eyes hard. "I'm shocked you're asking me this," Nicholas translated. "Every word I told you is true. What kind of woman are you who believes a mother would tell her daughter she's dying when she's not?"

"I don't want to believe it—" Veronica began but her mother cut her off with a comment she could tell was biting though she didn't understand a single word.

Nicholas didn't immediately translate.

"What did she say?" Veronica asked him without turning around. She had to ask a second time before finally he responded.

"She said she can tell you don't have children because no woman who bore a child could ever suspect such a thing."

That propelled Veronica to her feet. She knew, she *knew*, her mother was lying. And she was in no mood to get a lecture on maternal love from the woman who had given her away. "I get that you know more about bearing children than I do. So maybe you can explain something to me. Why exactly did you give me away? I keep hearing that you would've had a hell of a time raising a fourth child on your own. But you and I both know what was very likely to become of me if you left me at an orphanage."

In Russia the stigma attached to orphans was horrible. People seemed to blame the children, innocent as they were, for being abandoned by their parents. The vast majority of orphans were never adopted, and at age eighteen they were unceremoniously released into the streets where chances were excellent that they would become thieves, prostitutes, drug addicts, or a tragic combination of all three.

Her mother sputtered. Nicholas translated. "I wanted a better life for you," he said. "And I knew you'd be adopted."

"How? How could you possibly know that?"

As she watched her mother struggle to frame an answer, and as Fedosia raised her voice to Veronica, saying who knew what, Veronica suddenly felt herself filled with the same reckless abandon she'd felt when she told Rinaldo he could take his rehearsals and shove them because she was flying to Moscow to meet her dying birth mother.

"Is that why you took me to Moscow?" she asked her mother. "Is that why you carried your newborn all the way to Baby Home Number 30 at Kudrinskaya Plaza?" She prayed Nicholas would translate verbatim without questioning her, and apparently he did.

Her mother replied with vigor. "Yes," Nicholas translated. "I carried you all the way there so you would be adopted."

"Because I'm sure this town is big enough to have its own orphanage. But instead you carried your four-day-old baby all the way to the middle of Moscow, where the embassies and the foreigners and the rich Russians are, because chances were much better there that a wealthy family or maybe a family from overseas would adopt me and give me a better life. Is that right?"

"*Da! Da!*" her mother cried after Nicholas translated. *Yes! Yes!*

"Do you think about me every April? When the flowers start to bloom? Do you think about carrying me to the orphanage then? Because that time of year I always think about you."

"Yes, always in spring," Nicholas translated, and though for a few minutes now Veronica had had little doubt, at that moment she knew for sure.

"Just so you know, Nicholas?" She spun around to face him, turning her back on the impostor beneath the fraying blanket. "My birthday is in October."

Nicholas already knew what orphanage Veronica had been adopted from, because it was the same as his own. Baby Home Number 36, quite a lengthy metro ride from Kudrinskaya Plaza, one of the few locations in Moscow Veronica could name. She might not have borne a child, but she knew with all her heart that this was something no mother could ever forget, not even as she lay dying.

She must have swayed because Nicholas grabbed her to steady her. He said something to her, but she couldn't quite catch it. Her mother—or whoever she was—said something as well, loud as could be, but to that fraud Veronica had stopped paying attention.

Though she had a thing or two she wanted to say, she realized. She turned back around to face the impostor, who still had faithful lap dog Fedosia at her side. Probably they had a deal to share the plunder they stole from the gullible American.

"You said one thing that was true," Veronica told her. "No mother would tell her daughter she's dying when she's not." She stepped closer. "But now we both know you're no mother to me. So why don't you tell me one more true thing. Who the hell are you?"

A lot of time was wasted as Veronica's so-called mother loosed a river of crocodile tears and wailed to the heavens over her unhappy lot in life, having an ungrateful daughter who didn't recognize all that her mother had tried to do for her. Fedosia pitched in with harmonic flourishes of her own. Watching it impassively, Veronica thought it was exactly the sort of melodrama that operagoers love.

Finally the falsity ran its course. Against the barrage of Nicholas's shouting and Veronica's refusal to be moved, the charlatan caved. She admitted that no, she was not Veronica's birth mother. She was Veronica's aunt, the younger sister of the woman who had given Veronica life.

"Where is she then?" Veronica demanded. "Where is my birth mother?"

The conniver waved a dismissive hand, as if she barely cared enough to reply. "*MERT-vye.*"

Veronica felt a punch in her soul when she heard that word again. Dead.

Her birth mother was dead.

Chapter Nine

She didn't know how she made it to the door of the apartment, but it was there that Nicholas stopped her by grabbing hold of her arm. He spun her around and pulled her to his chest.

She let herself be held against him. She felt the steady drumbeat of his heart against her cheek and his hand in her hair. "She didn't just lie about being sick," Veronica whispered, needlessly, because Nicholas knew the twisted tale as well as she did. "She lied about being my mother."

"I am so sorry."

"I would've forgiven her if she'd only been lying about being on her deathbed. I mean, that's a monstrous thing to lie about, but I would've forgiven her. I can imagine her getting that desperate. If she'd admitted that, Nicholas, I'd be asking you to drive me to the bank right now so I could give her money."

"I know you would."

"But to lie about being my mother—"

Nicholas hushed her and held her and caressed her hair as if they had all the time in the world. It calmed her a bit, though still she felt oddly breathless. It was as if she'd run a race. Maybe she had. She'd been chasing a dream only to have it explode right in front of her eyes.

"I wanted to know what kind of people I come from."

From the other room she could hear Fedosia and her scoundrel of an aunt shouting at each other, no doubt one blaming the other for their scheme unraveling. "And now I do. Monsters who pervert the most precious things in life to get what they want."

"That may be what your aunt is like but—"

"You were right, Nicholas. About everything." She pulled away from him. "I didn't see it, I guess because I didn't want to."

He forced her to look into his eyes, black with intensity. "Veronica, she gave you all kinds of reasons to believe her. She's living in your mother's apartment, for God's sake. Then there's the family resemblance. Plus she has every letter you ever sent your mother. And she knows a lot about you."

"Now I understand why I didn't feel connected to her." Veronica didn't care that she was contradicting what she'd said before. Nicholas would think she was a crackpot, but he probably already did. "Not only is she not my mother, but she's a lying, scheming witch."

"You'll get no argument from me."

"I have to get out of here."

"We need our coats. And you have a scarf and a purse, too." He backed away from her. "Stay here. I'll get them."

When he returned bearing everything they'd brought with them, yelling something back over his shoulder, Veronica saw her trickster aunt in his wake, on her feet, walking steadily, yelling back, right as rain.

She's alive. That liar is living and breathing and walking the earth and my birth mother is dead.

The dream had been right. Her birth mother did lie in a graveyard buried beneath drifts of snow.

The pretender, her features twisted with fury, opened her mouth to spew something.

"Don't you say another word to me!" Veronica shrieked. She pulled open the apartment door with such force it slammed hard against the interior wall, rattling everything in sight. She flew into the corridor to escape the rant, other doors to other apartments opening and people peeking out to witness the commotion.

Veronica didn't wait for the elevator, which she knew would take an eon to arrive on the eleventh floor. She ran down the twenty-two flights of stairs, her heart and heels pounding, the smell of urine in her nostrils, Nicholas behind her following step by step.

Icy air smacked her face when she emerged from the building. She continued to run, her boots crunching on the hard-packed snow, her eyes squinting against the glare of the winter sun, as blinding as a surgical light.

She threw herself in Nicholas's car the second he unlocked the doors. All she wanted was to flee. Get away. Begin to try to forget.

How she would manage that trick she had no idea.

Nicholas tossed their belongings in the trunk. He joined her in the Renault and they sped away. Apparently his desire to be gone was as powerful as hers.

Another thought occurred to her. "Do you think Viktor was in on this? Or Masha?"

"No way. I've known Masha for years and she's a sweetheart through and through. I can't believe it of Viktor, either."

"I keep thinking somehow he must've known my birth mother was dead."

"I don't see how. He's a translator. He lives in Moscow. He wouldn't have been in contact with your birth mother unless she got in touch with the orphanage to try to find you and so needed a letter translated into English."

"It was the other way around for me. He translated my letters to her and forwarded them on. He got only one letter back from her to me." Which, as it turned out, was crafted by her malevolent aunt.

Veronica's head throbbed. She lay her hand on Nicholas's leg. "Please pull over."

He obliged. "Are you okay? What is it?"

"You're going to think I'm nuts. I want you to take me to the train station."

"What? Why in the world would you want to go there?"

She looked down at the ring, all pearliness gone. It was then that she started to cry. She hadn't when she'd been up in that wretched apartment but now she feared she might never stop. *I want to put all this behind me. Everything that has to do with Russia. And that includes you.* She heard a shrieking in her aching head but forced herself to keep speaking. "I have to be by myself, Nicholas."

"Veronica"—he handed her a handkerchief from his bottomless supply—"we don't have to talk if you don't want to but it makes zero sense for you to take the train."

"Please try to understand."

She had to stop speaking. Why was her head in such agony? She blamed it on the good-for-nothing ring that had sent her on this pointless journey. It was no doubt trying to make amends for this fiasco by bombarding her mind with yet another ludicrous scheme. She attempted to wrench it off her finger, but of course it wouldn't cooperate. It was wedged on as if her finger were swollen from heat when in fact it was ice-cold to the touch.

She gave up. "All I can tell you, Nicholas, is that I can clear my head better if I'm not with you, if I'm surrounded by strangers who don't know what a fool I am."

"Listen to me." He twisted towards her. "Don't blame

yourself for trusting that woman. I certainly don't blame you. The fact that you wanted to so much only goes to show what kind of woman *you* are. And when her story got too far out there, you spoke up. That had to be hard, but you did it. You should be proud of yourself for that."

She was. At least she'd proved she wasn't so weak that she'd believe a preposterous tale just to fuel her illusions about her birth mother.

"Something else occurred to me," Nicholas went on. "I don't want to raise false hopes, but we don't know for sure that your birth mother is dead. We only have your aunt's word for it and that doesn't count for much."

"She is dead, though, Nicholas, I know it." *I had a dream that told me so. I just didn't want to believe it.* More tears flowed as Veronica recalled that lonely frozen graveyard her mind had conjured. Nicholas began to protest but she stilled him with a shake of the head. "Please." She swiped the tears from her cheeks. "Please just leave it be."

Clearly he didn't want to do that. "It's just that since your birth mother did live in that building, we could ask around, find out where your siblings are—"

"I can't take another disappointment, Nicholas. And I've already taken up too much of your time. The truth is I just want to get away from here. I do have a flight to catch. I just want to get back to Italy. When I'm back in Florence, everything can be normal again."

Eventually it would be, anyway. She would get back into the rhythm of rehearsing and performing and be able to push this nightmare to the back of her mind where she could lock it away.

"And in Italy I can sing." She grabbed his hand and choked out the words. "I want so much to sing, Nicholas. When I sing I forget everything else."

He laid his free hand on top of hers. "Are you really, truly sure you want to take the train?"

No, her heart said. "Yes," she told him.

He sighed. No one could mistake the sadness on his face, not even an idiot like her. "I don't want this to be goodbye, Veronica."

How could it be anything but? He worked in Russia. She worked in the U.S. and Europe, and before this ill-fated trip had never been in Russia in her life. And at the moment she was hardly aching to return.

"You've been amazingly good to me, Nicholas. But we have no choice but to say goodbye." She forced a chuckle. "Besides, you've got better things to do than ferry around some delusional diva."

He made his voice light, too. "But you're *my* delusional diva."

She couldn't let herself imagine that. She knew Nicholas was a truly rare find. But she'd chased enough fantasies for one lifetime.

She let go of his hand. He turned on the Renault and duly pointed it toward the mint-colored train station she had admired on the drive into town. He helped her buy her ticket, but she wouldn't allow him to wait with her for the train.

They said their goodbyes in the terminal, buffeted by hordes of bundled-up travelers rolling suitcases and rushing toward platforms.

"I wish it had worked out differently," Nicholas told her.

Veronica had the idea he wasn't referring only to her so-called birth mother. She took his hands and raised herself on her toes to kiss him on both cheeks. "*Ciao,*" she said, and then she forced herself to walk away from him, not to look back, not to run back to his side, not to imagine what might have been.

What was that verse in the Bible about putting away childish things? She stood on the platform in the piercing wind and looked it up on her phone. It was from First Corinthians, Chapter Thirteen, Verse Eleven: *When I was a child, I spake as a child, I understood as a child, I thought as a child; but when I became a man, I put away childish things.*

That was what she must do. Renounce all childish fantasies, whether about her birth mother or a handsome stranger. Those were dangerous. They led to heartbreak. If nothing else, surely she should understand that by now.

On the train, her headache remained agonizing despite aspirin washed down with coffee, the caffeine cure that usually worked miracles. She couldn't let herself doze off to ease the pain because she couldn't get the ring off her finger and wouldn't risk another subconscious message couched as a dream. She had no desire to find out what else the ring wanted to tell her that she didn't care to know.

And she had an idea who and what another dream would feature. Not a graveyard this time, but an embassy. A man who worked there, a man who had been an orphan like her—in the very same orphanage, in fact. A man who worked all around the world, as she did, and who might be able to understand her like no other man ever could.

Instead of wallowing in that romantic illusion, she tried to lose herself in the scenery flashing past the train windows. A carpet of snow that stretched as far as the eye could see. Endless groves of leafless birch trees, their white bark splashed with splotches of black. Then, unmistakably, more hustle and bustle, indicating that the train was cutting its way through the outskirts of the metropolis.

When Veronica reached her station and exited the train and transferred to the metro line, she, who believed everything happened for a reason, recalled the grand cosmic reason why she had met Nicholas Laver. It had nothing to do with romance and everything to do with her birth mother. Without him the mystery of her birth mother would still overhang her life. Now she knew her birth mother was gone. Whether she'd been good or bad, Veronica would never know. Over time, maybe she'd come to believe it didn't matter. Regardless, Nicholas would always be a critical part of her reaching that understanding and she would always be grateful.

In her apartment in the Kudrinskaya Building, Veronica cleared out her belongings for her departure. Then she stripped down until she was naked as the day she was born. Of course now the ring slid off her finger, mocking her for the trouble she'd had with it earlier. She showered and washed her hair under the hottest water she could bear, as if scalding herself would purge the day's miseries.

In short order Veronica was back in the metro, this time burdened by her luggage and heading for the airport. She would arrive in plenty of time. Maybe she'd even be able to kiss Mother Russia goodbye sooner than expected, if she could land a seat on an earlier flight.

It wasn't until she was a few stops shy of the airport that she realized she wasn't wearing the ring. She dove into her handbag. There was the ring box. Empty.

She got off at the next stop, ignoring the man who kept trying to tell her that the airport was still two stops away and surely the blonde with the luggage wanted to go all the way to the airport? She waved him off and dumped the contents of her handbag onto a bench. She searched it thoroughly. No ring.

Then she set her rolling suitcase on the bench and conducted a second methodical search, even though she had no memory of packing the ring in her suitcase and had no idea why she would do such a stupid thing because surely she wouldn't risk that such an exquisite, even if maddening, ring would be snatched from an unlocked bag?

Veronica soon realized she hadn't done that stupid thing. Apparently she'd done something even stupider: She'd left the ring at the Kudrinskaya Building.

She straightened and put her hands on her hips. Of course she could just continue on and forget it. She was under no obligation to retrieve the ring. A dark-haired woman had handed it to her and now it would find a new home. Someone new would claim it.

Of course that new someone would not be handpicked. Nor would they have the little paper that explained everything, which was in the ring box and so hopelessly separated from the ring. Again Veronica opened the box, half expecting to see the ring magically restored. Maybe it would even cackle at her. No such luck.

She glanced at her watch. She had time to race back and forth and still make her flight. And, it couldn't be denied, something in her didn't want to leave the ring in Russia, about which she didn't have the highest opinion at the moment.

Of course the ring might already be gone. Perhaps her room had already been cleaned and someone had made off with it. Or soon would.

In any event, she needed to hurry.

Veronica rushed to the opposite platform. The wait for the next train seemed interminable. All the way back to central Moscow she wondered how she could possibly have left the ring in the apartment. She had certain ingrained habits from her years of travel, and one of them was to do a thorough inspection of wherever she was staying before she departed, to make absolutely sure she left nothing behind. She had conducted just such an inspection this afternoon.

Eventually she made it back to the Kudrinskaya Building and succeeded in convincing the surly gatekeeper at the front desk to allow her once again into the apartment she had so recently vacated.

And there in her bedroom, to her immense relief, she found the ring, in plain sight, on the very nightstand where she had set it before showering. At the time, she remembered well, it had taunted her by slipping off her finger with exquisite ease. She had set it on the nightstand next to her watch, earrings, and necklace, all of which she put back on when she dressed. How she had managed not to see the ring to put it back on as well was beyond her. How she could have missed the ring on the nightstand—which she was certain, *certain*, she had checked before she left—was beyond her as well.

She was down in the lobby preparing once again to depart for the metro when who should appear like an apparition before her but Nicholas.

He was out of breath. He grabbed her by the arms. "I am so glad I caught you, Veronica. I had no way to reach you. When we talked on the phone before, you were using Masha's mobile."

Yes, she had been. It was at the orphanage when she was importuning Nicholas to take her to meet her birth mother in Viktor's stead.

"I can't believe I caught you," Nicholas repeated, and Veronica would not have been able to believe it either were it not for one thing.

She glanced down at the ring, restored to her finger. Its gemstone winked up at her, blinking with white light.

"You have got to come back with me to that apartment

building," Nicholas told her. "I met a really lovely woman who was best friends with your birth mother."

Chapter Ten

There are moments in life when you stand at a major crossroads. Two paths diverge, and you can choose but one.

Veronica Ballard's moment came in the grand high-ceilinged lobby of Moscow's Kudrinskaya Building as a winter afternoon's darkness fell across the land. If she went with Nicholas, she would miss her night flight to Italy. She would have to persuade Rinaldo that even though she was once again pissing all over his production, he should allow her to go on stage as his Leonora after a scant few hours of rehearsal, her first performance the all-important preview.

If she did not go with Nicholas, she would pass up the only chance she would ever have to learn the truth about her birth mother. At long last, Nicholas assured her, her questions would be answered. This neighbor was her birth mother's closest friend. She had lived near her for decades. She had watched Veronica's siblings grow up. She had details about Veronica's mother that Nicholas knew Veronica would want to hear.

To her dying day, Veronica could not know which path she would have chosen if she did not have the ring on her finger. It was hardly lost on her that the ring had pulled a disappearing act that succeeded brilliantly in drawing her back to the Kudrinskaya Building at the very moment Nicholas arrived there with news of this neighbor. The ring was practically shaking her by the shoulders and screaming in her car.

Know thy heart, it implored.

She supposed there had been a time when she had doubted the ring. But that time had surely passed. "Where's your car?" she asked Nicholas.

Minutes later, once more on the highway she was getting to know so well, Veronica listened to Nicholas relay how he had ferreted out this neighbor by knocking on the other doors of the corridor where Veronica's mother had lived. "The neighbor's name is Anya. She and your mother were friends for years."

" 'Were.' " Veronica looked out the window as Moscow receded in the distance. "So I was right that my birth mother is dead."

Nicholas spoke softly. "Anya said she died a few months ago." He was speeding down the highway but lay a soft touch on Veronica's leg. "Let her tell you."

What Nicholas knew but did not reveal at that moment was that Anya wanted to do more than tell Veronica. She wanted to show her.

He drove to the outskirts of the city where Veronica's birth mother had lived, to a spot where urban life gave way to a pine forest. On a narrow curving road, he slid the Renault behind a parked car and cut the engine.

"What are we doing here?" Veronica wanted to know.

Nicholas gestured to the forest, midnight dark, though it was early evening. Veronica saw a small light bobbing in the distance. "This is where Anya wanted to meet you. That's her out there, with a lantern."

"What's she doing in the middle of a—" Veronica began to ask until she looked more closely and realized this wasn't merely a pine forest.

It was a cemetery.

"Russians sometimes set graves among the trees," Nicholas murmured. "They don't always clear the land."

Veronica saw that now. Low spindly iron fences demarcated family plots, with headstones at one end shaped like the crosses she had seen in her mind's eye, with an additional low bar that tilted down from right to left.

Russian Orthodox crosses, just like she had seen in her dream.

Veronica's heart hammered in her chest. The scene wasn't precisely the same, but still it seemed as if her dream were about to play out before her eyes. "My mother is buried here," she whispered.

She got out of the Renault and headed toward the lantern.

Anya did not move as Veronica approached her across the uneven snow-covered ground, keenly aware that Anya was standing beside her mother's grave. As in her dream, her ears caught the tinkling of a wind chime. This time, though, she was not in a hurry and she was not alone. Anya came forward a few steps, set her lantern on the snow, held out her gloved hands, and uttered a small cry.

The two women pitched together in a hug. Anya, a thin woman in a bulky coat, kept repeating something through her tears. Veronica couldn't speak for her own sobs. Anya, who was not her blood, cried and rocked and cradled Veronica the way she had longed all her life to be held by her birth mother. She knew now she would never feel that incomparable embrace. But Anya, who clearly had loved Veronica's mother, was giving her solace in her mother's stead.

At last they pulled apart. Nicholas spoke from behind Veronica. "Anya is saying you are very beautiful, Veronica.

Your mother would be so proud."

Veronica didn't want to let go of Anya's hands. "You were friends for a long time?"

"She was my best friend all of my life," Nicholas translated, now holding the lantern and casting a circle of light around their huddled trio. "I miss her every day."

Pulling Veronica by the hand, Anya led her toward a headstone. It looked like every other, but yet there was none other like it, for her birth mother lay beneath.

"Rada Grigorevna Kozlovskaya." Anya pointed in turn to the names inscribed on a silver medallion in the center of the cross.

So many times Veronica had rolled the syllables of that name on her tongue. "She died in September?"

"She had a heart attack," Nicholas translated.

Veronica stared at the date of her mother's death. September 28th. What had she been doing that day? How could she have lived through that entire day with no idea that something so monumental had occurred?

Anya squeezed Veronica's hand and spoke again. "She never stopped thinking about you," Nicholas said. "She loved you all her life."

"Why didn't she respond to any of my letters?"

"She didn't want you to feel any pull back here," Nicholas translated. "She said life could be cruel in Russia, and she didn't want you dragged into that."

Anya kept speaking. "Your mother felt terrible guilt about taking you to the orphanage," Nicholas went on. "So much so that she went back a few months later. But you were already gone. Your mother was told you'd been adopted by a couple from California."

Why had Masha not mentioned this? Maybe she felt guilty that she had not been able to reunite Veronica with her birth mother. Though she shouldn't. If the chance came for a baby in her care to be adopted, Masha was right to grab it with both hands.

"Years later," Nicholas went on, "your mother started receiving your letters from California so she knew what she had been told was true. She also knew you had a good life, which is what she wanted for you above everything else."

"Do I have brothers and sisters?" Veronica asked.

"Two brothers and a sister"—he hesitated—"who survived."

Anya tugged Veronica toward the headstone that rose from the earth beside her mother's. "That is your brother buried there," Nicholas said.

"One of my brothers died?" Veronica peered at the headstone. Her poor brother: She could see in the lantern's glow that he had lived only ten years.

"Cancer," Nicholas reported. "Which was why it was impossible for your mother to take care of you. She was overwhelmed taking care of such a sick child while raising three others."

Anya added something else. "Anya believes it was losing two of her children, your brother and you, that weakened your mother's health. Her death was sudden, but on some level it wasn't a surprise."

What a huge load she had carried. And, given what Veronica knew from her adoption papers, with virtually no help from her children's father.

"He is dead as well," Nicholas reported. "Your mother loved him, but she couldn't count on him. Your mother was a dreamer," he went on as Anya spoke. "She trusted people she shouldn't. Including her younger sister, who came to live with her in the last few years. She knew what you'd written in your letters and apparently saw an opportunity after your mother died to profit from your success."

"Did my mother ever play the CD I sent her? Did she like my singing?"

Anya cried something out as she threw back her head and clapped her hands. Nicholas laughed. "Your mother loved it, Veronica. She listened to it all the time. In fact she played it so loud she drove the neighbors crazy, even Anya sometimes."

Then Anya again grew serious. She grasped Veronica's hands before gesturing behind her toward her mother's grave.

"Veronica, your CD is buried with your mother," Nicholas murmured. "Her children knew she would want something of each of them with her for all time." His voice cracked and tears ran down Anya's cheeks. "Anya says it makes her very happy to think that your mother is hearing your voice in heaven."

Veronica couldn't keep her control after that. What a gift dear Anya had given her. The next time she sang, and every time thereafter, she would imagine her birth mother hearing her and smiling, her pain extinguished at last.

In the cold, in the dark, with Anya's story told, they didn't linger. Veronica touched her birth mother's headstone, and her brother's, and slowly walked with Nicholas and Anya over the snow-covered earth back to their cars.

"Anya understands you have to get back to Italy," Nicholas told her, exchanging what looked like a conspiratorial glance with the older woman as he helped her into her car. "But she wants to have a party for you the next time you're in Moscow. You could meet your siblings and Anya's husband and children as well."

"That would be incredible," Veronica told Anya. "I would love to see you again, and to meet your family." The prospect of returning to Russia felt very different now. To meet her brothers and sister Veronica would fly back in a heartbeat. And next time she could sing for the children at the orphanage, too.

Veronica and Nicholas bid Anya goodbye. Back in the Renault, he turned the ignition and raised the heat. "How do you feel?"

"Worlds better." She felt a warmth deep inside, even in the frigid car. "Anya has a heart of gold and that makes me believe my birth mother did, too. You can tell a lot about a person from their friends."

"I agree."

"And what she told me about my mother, and my brother, too, it explains things. I understand now why she gave me up. She had such a hard life, Nicholas. I just wish she would've let me do something to help her."

"It sounds to me like you did. From what Anya said, your singing gave her a lot of joy."

"Now I have to get used to the idea that she's gone."

They sat for a moment before Veronica spoke again. "You made all this happen, Nicholas. I don't know how to thank you. If you hadn't—"

He reached across the gearshift and took her hand. "That's the last time you're allowed to mention it, Veronica."

"But I—"

"Did you ever think I might have an ulterior motive?"

That silenced her. She gazed into his dark eyes. Outside in the endless night the wind gusted, rattling the car. Inside with Nicholas she felt warm and safe.

"I just want to be with you, Veronica," he said softly. "It's that simple. I don't know how to explain it but whatever you've got I'm buying."

This time the diva was lost for words. Nicholas released

her hand to brush her cheek.

"So if you really want to thank me," he went on in that same spellbinding tone, "you can tell me tonight isn't goodbye."

She found her voice. "I don't want it to be goodbye but" — she shook her head — "we only met yesterday. How can you feel that way about me so fast?"

"Oh, I don't know that it's so mysterious." He looked away. "Maybe I've been around the block a few times, and so I know a gem when I see one. Maybe I have friends who give me grief for spending so much time at the orphanage and I want to tell them my dating plan only needed time to work." He gave her another of his dazzling smiles. "Because look what showed up on the doorstep."

She had to smile back. It wasn't accidental that she'd shown up, either. She'd been propelled there, by her destiny, by the ring, by an otherworldly mix of the two. "It's been an intense couple of days," she allowed.

"You're telling me. I know more about you than some women I've dated for months. And what I see I like, Veronica." Again his voice dropped. She sank into its lower register like a baby into warm bath water. "I like how soft your heart is, and how passionate you are, and how much you want to trust. But you've got a backbone, too. I also get where you come from, and I suspect it makes you look at the world the same way I do." Again his hand reached up to caress her cheek. "Last but not least, you're stunningly beautiful. And even though I haven't heard any evidence yet I hear tell you're a fantastic opera singer."

"I'm not bad," she murmured.

They stared into each other's eyes. Snowflakes gathered on the windshield as if trying to buffer them from all the madness of the world outside. Veronica held still as she watched Nicholas's eyes drop to her lips. A moment later he leaned close, and his mouth found hers.

He left her breathless, as somewhere deep in her heart she had known he would. He pulled back the tiniest bit, but even that was too much. "Indulge your romantic side, Veronica," he whispered. "Be my Leonora."

"You remember what role I'm singing?"

"I remember everything you ever told me."

They kissed again. Veronica knew what she wanted to do to him, what she wanted him to do to her. Imagining all that wonder left her mouth dry and her knees weak.

"We should go back to my apartment," he murmured a moment later.

"Yes."

"I wish it weren't an hour away. But maybe while I drive you can sort out your flight."

"Yes." There were practical matters to attend to. One was to call Rinaldo. Maybe it would be easier to do that in a lust-induced haze. She was petrified what his reaction would be to her missing yet another day of rehearsals, the last full one.

Nicholas made good time back to Moscow. Veronica had seen him dodge traffic before, but tonight he seemed particularly adept. In the end she couldn't reach Rinaldo so she left a detailed voicemail. And she opted for the second departure of the morning, as she would miss rehearsals anyway and the first flight would require her to appear at the airport at the ungodly hour of five a.m. She had the idea she would have better things to do at that time than check in her baggage.

At one point as the Renault cut a swath through Moscow, Veronica remembered the ring. It felt very natural on her finger now, its gemstone a spectacle of glimmering green and white. Though she left it unchanged, for the first time she felt an urge to turn it around so that the heart would face inward, not the crown. She knew from what she'd read before that would signal that her heart had found its mate.

Her impressions of Nicholas's apartment, hastily gained, were favorable. It was on a quiet tree-lined street and backed onto a park. Small and charming, it had hardwood floors and clean white walls and pocket doors that hearkened back to an earlier era.

He poured them glasses of red wine, which they tasted between kisses. "I suppose I should feed you," he said.

She had breath enough for only one word. "Eventually."

Sometime in the delicious night, Veronica awoke. She lay still and listened to Nicholas's steady breathing. She reveled in his naked warmth beside her, and her lips curved in a knowing lover's smile. In the air hung a faint aroma of the eggs they'd scrambled when hunger of a different sort had driven them from his bed. They'd downed the meal with the red wine and yesterday's bread that did the job when it was toasted.

In the distance a siren wailed. A tree branch tickled the windowpane, making Veronica think the wind was still tumbling the snowflakes in a wintry dance.

Very carefully, so as not to wake Nicholas, she got out of bed. It had occurred to her she should charge her phone. She would need it in the morning.

In the living room, with its accent wall of striped wallpaper and bookshelves stocked with tomes in English, Russian, and French, she was attaching cord to phone when she noticed she'd received a voicemail hours earlier. She had been fully occupied, it was safe to say, and so had missed it. It was from Rinaldo.

Her heart thumped when she heard the message the first time. She had to play it a few more times because Rinaldo was so upset he lapsed into Italian occasionally and those parts were hard to understand. Though in truth she didn't need to grasp the words to ascertain their meaning.

This was too much. She had gone too far. What did she take him for? How little did she value his opera? Carina would be his Leonora, on Friday for the preview and on every other night. Veronica needn't bother herself to return to Florence from Moscow on Rinaldo's account. He was done with her. *Finito.*

The readout of the hour glowed ghostly white on her cell phone. If Veronica rushed, she could still make the earlier flight. The faster she got to Rinaldo, the more likely it was that she could change his mind. Her persuasive powers had never been stronger, she was sure of it. Especially armed as she was with the ring.

She threw her phone and its cord into her handbag and abandoned all efforts to be quiet. She raced around Nicholas's apartment grabbing articles of her clothing from all the places they'd been flung. She took special care to return the ring to her finger, knowing as she did its odd propensities when it came to international travel.

She was almost dressed when Nicholas appeared in the living room. He sported a robe and a dazed expression. "What in the world are you doing?"

"I have to catch the early flight. I got a call from Rinaldo. He"—she didn't want to say it out loud for fear that would set it in stone—"said he needs me back ASAP. I'll call you."

She tried to kiss him on the mouth but he moved his head slightly so her lips grazed his cheek instead. "I'm sorry, Nicholas. Please understand."

He shook his head as if he couldn't believe what he was

seeing. Veronica was unnerved to see a flash of the disillusionment he'd displayed in her aunt's apartment, when she'd asked the evil pair how they'd like her to pay for the so-called special treatment and Nicholas had assumed she'd fallen for their treachery. Now he started to speak. "Then at least let me—"

"I can't wait. I've got to go now. I'll take the metro."

She was out the door without looking back.

Chapter Eleven

Stunning scenery does not squelch your anguish when you've willfully demolished your career. Nor does it compensate for losing the love of your life.

Veronica was learning that lesson in Florence as she nursed an early evening cappuccino at an outdoor café at the Piazza della Signoria. Not even the Palazzo Vecchio or the replica of the David could salve her wounded soul. For Rinaldo would no longer have anything to do with her. And Nicholas wouldn't, either.

Rinaldo had told her *finito* in as many ways as it was possible to express it. And it was not because he didn't believe Veronica could sing the role of Leonora. It was because he could not forgive her disrespect. She had mocked his production. She had mocked him. *Finito*.

It was very possible her career would evaporate. Rinaldo could blackball her from Florence to San Francisco and back again. A major diva could survive such a firing. A lesser star could not.

With Nicholas, it was much worse. He wouldn't even respond. His mobile went to voicemail every time Veronica called. She was up to six calls, and each had produced the same result. She was pondering whether to make a seventh plea for forgiveness. Nicholas warranted a hundred tries.

She did not doubt she had behaved abominably. If a man had decamped from her bed the way she had decamped from his, she would never forgive him. She couldn't blame Nicholas for writing her off, which was the problem with placing a seventh call. She didn't have any more arguments to muster in her defense.

She was morosely counting the euros to pay for her cappuccino when something prompted her to raise her head to look across the *piazza*. And there right in front of her, as unexpected as a visitor from another world, stood Nicholas.

He wore a black trench coat and rolled a suitcase behind him. Under his arm was a rectangular parcel wrapped in brown paper and string. With people moving around him like guppies around a large fish, he stood on the paving stones worn smooth by centuries of booted feet and gazed at her.

She was thinking how he must not be angry with her— because why would he be in Florence if he were angry?— when his smile dispelled her last doubt. She leapt to her feet to catapult herself into his arms. "You're not mad at me. You don't hate me."

"I am a little mad at you. But I don't hate you."

"I called and called—"

"I was in the air. I got your messages when I landed."

She stated the obvious. "You followed me."

"I had to."

"How did you even know where to look for me?"

"You told me you were staying in a guesthouse behind the Palazzo Vecchio. I planned to check every guesthouse between here and the Duomo until I found you."

He stopped. She waited. The air in the *piazza* stilled, awaiting lovers' words it had heard before and would hear again.

"I love you, Veronica."

"Oh, Nicholas, I love you, too. So much." The words

spilled from her mouth before she could think to restrain them.

They kissed, two alone in a multitude, under a sky filled with stars and possibilities. The ring, Veronica had no doubt, had once again gone from emerald green to a pearliness as dazzling as the moon in its brightest hour.

She pulled back and pushed the dark hair from his forehead. "I just had the craziest thought." She stopped as suddenly as she had started.

"What?"

It was about the ring. All at once she didn't want to tell him. The ring was her little secret. And now, in the midst of the greatest happiness she had ever known, she understood what it had been up to all along.

The ring didn't send her to Moscow to meet her birth mother. It sent her to meet Nicholas. True, it gave her the gift of understanding where she came from, but really it was this man who solved the deepest riddle of her heart. And without the ring's intervention, she never would have found him.

The woman with the dark hair had said the ring was precious to her. Now it was precious to Veronica, too. For it had given her Nicholas.

She took his hands. "Let me tell you about Rinaldo. He fired me even though I flew right back. I was an idiot to walk out on you, Nicholas. I'll never make that mistake again."

Again that smile of his. "I think I deserve another 'I'm sorry' kiss."

She'd give this man whatever kind of kiss he wanted. When she was done, and only then, she posed another question. "What is that you've got with you?"

"For that, my dear Veronica, we should sit down."

They returned to the café table she had just abandoned and this time ordered Prosecco. The bubbles danced on

Veronica's tongue. "This feels like a painting," she told Nicholas when he handed her the parcel.

"Unwrap it."

It was a painting. It was the only lovely thing she had seen in her aunt's apartment, the oil of a blonde girl on a beach building a sand castle. Veronica raised questioning eyes to Nicholas, though she was beginning to understand.

"Your aunt said you had an aunt who painted that," Nicholas reminded her.

Veronica nodded. She found the artist's signature, partially hidden by the frame. Even in the fading light and with her poor grasp of the Cyrillic alphabet, she could read the first name. *Rada.* "My mother painted this," she murmured.

"That girl by the sea is you."

It was how her birth mother wanted to imagine her. In a beautiful place, happy, cared for, loved.

Veronica held the painting to her chest, tears welling in her eyes. "What a treasure, Nicholas."

"I suspected your birth mother painted it. Then Anya confirmed it. I wanted you to have something from your birth mother."

"And now I do." Tears spilled down her cheeks.

"Oh, good. You're crying. Now I know it's really you."

She gave him a light slap that ended in another kiss. "So my demon aunt was willing to part with this?"

"For the right price, she'd be willing to part with anything. Fedosia better watch out."

They got a good laugh out of that. They got another when again Veronica spoke, this time with a teasing lilt in her voice. "I have to thank you somehow for this, Nicholas."

She expected him to banter but instead his face grew serious. "Sing for me, Veronica. I want to hear you sing."

She had a moment's pause as she pondered making a spectacle of herself in this grand *piazza*. But for this man she would do anything. "There is a beautiful aria Leonora sings. It's called *'Tacea La Notte Placida.'* 'The Placid Night is Silent.'"

"What's it about?"

"A woman realizing that the man she loves is in love with her, too."

Nicholas lifted her hand to his mouth. "That sounds perfect."

Veronica rose and stepped away a few feet. She began to gather herself. It had been days since she'd sung, and the *piazza* was full of people. But tonight she cared only about pleasing one man. As she lifted her head, closed her eyes, and let the aria fill her soul, she realized there was someone else she was singing for, a woman who had left her earthly cares behind but who would never stop listening for her daughter's voice in the starry night.

Veronica opened her throat and loosed the aria's first notes across the *piazza*. She was vaguely aware of the surprise that reverberated around her. She sensed that surprise turn to pleasure, then entrancement. And as always, before long she lost herself in the music. The *piazza* and its ancient glories fell away. It was, more than it had ever been, as if she herself were Leonora, singing of a silvery moon, the chords of a lute, and the troubadour who called her name. For Veronica, too, love had made earth a paradise.

As the last note died away, applause thundered toward her. *Brava! Brava, bellissima!* Veronica bowed her head before lifting her eyes to heaven. She was quite sure that high above one star twinkled with very particular brightness.

Nicholas was on his feet, cheering and clapping and beaming. She was about to make her way toward him when a burly man with a dark beard waylaid her to hand her a business card. It bore a name Veronica recognized, of a well-known opera director. He was visiting Florence but was mounting a production in Berlin. What was Veronica's name? Who was her agent? Might she consider the soprano's role? For, he had to tell her, she had created an amazing moment. She had dazzled him. She had sung like an angel.

Veronica felt the splendid ring on her finger. She smiled at Nicholas and thought again of the twinkling star in the heavens.

No wonder. She'd had help.

It was foggy in San Francisco that January morning, a few weeks past the holiday rush. Veronica stepped out of the Buena Vista Café at Fisherman's Wharf. It was an appropriate breakfast spot for a diva with a Claddagh ring, as the café was famous for introducing Irish coffee to the American public. As it happened its breakfasts weren't bad, either.

She shivered as she gazed at the mist-covered bay, pondering whether to walk back to her flat or take the cable car. Her lilac-colored trench coat offered scant protection against the elements. She'd been silly to wear it, but she was in the mood for spring.

Spring meant Berlin, and her next opera, and Nicholas less than a three-hour nonstop away. His visit to San Francisco, during which he'd met her parents, had ended only a week ago, but the minute he left, she missed him desperately.

As she made the noble decision to walk off her eggs benedict, a brunette at the cable-car stop across Beach Street caught her attention. The young woman had the sort of creamy complexion that preferred fog to sun. She was attractive but seemed oddly flustered, and she was carrying the most unwieldy tote.

Veronica fingered the ring box in her pocket. The ring was nestled inside.

Once her face you see, you'll know the one who must the ring receive.

It could not have been more clear to Veronica if the brunette had had a target on the back of her trendy gray suit. The time for Veronica to cede the ring had come.

She couldn't deny a certain bittersweetness. It was as if the curtain were going down on a beloved production. When an opera closed, she was acutely aware of the great sopranos who had preceded her; she knew others would follow. She was one in an infinite line who had added to the opera's legacy.

So it was with the ring of truth.

Veronica approached the woman, who gave her a curious look as she neared. Veronica wondered if she herself bore the same joyous expression as the dark-haired woman who had given her the ring, if she glowed with the same inner light. What a wondrous thing to pass on.

Go do it again, Veronica silently urged the ring. *Go work your magic.*

****

Once Upon a Ring

Kate Moore

Chapter One

Tara Keegan had everything perfectly balanced, her muni card in her right hand, her workhorse monogram designer tote on her shoulder, and in her left hand a paper sack with a take out cup of morning dark roast and a pair of clean socks for her friend Eddie. The morning fog swirled up from the bay, pressing her gray suit slacks to her legs. The damp January streets gleamed with long streaks of red and green from the changing traffic lights, a reminder of the fading holiday season.

Tara's fellow commuters bent over their phones, caught up in their wired worlds. Only one person in the early morning crowd was looking about, a woman unfamiliar to Tara, a blonde in a trendy lilac-colored trench coat with the sort of looks that Hitchcock preferred in his heroines. The woman had no phone or purse or electronic device. She had an expectant manner, not wary, but on the lookout for something. It occurred to Tara that the woman was happy, not just good mood happy, but profoundly happy, inner peace kind of happy, reach the top of the mountain happy.

Tara stole another glance at her, trying to imagine what would bring out that happy glow in a woman. Some form of yoga or meditation? Endorphins from a dawn Boot Camp session? Of course, the woman might be in a relationship, but obviously not the usual sort of rent-and-space-sharing arrangement that passed for commitment in San Francisco.

And surely, she was not on her way to a six-figure, sixty-hour-a-week job in the bro-culture tech world. Perhaps she was an artist, although clearly not a starving one. Her hands were in her pockets, so Tara could not see whether the woman wore a ring.

Tara, of course, had the perfect job, as a concierge at the Hotel Belmont, a boutique hotel on the north side of Nob Hill. She had found her calling, welcoming tourists to her favorite city and making sure that they enjoyed its hills and views, its endless good restaurants, its history, and its mix of elegant sophistication and Bohemian zaniness. At work she had everything at her fingertips to solve visitors' problems and make their stay more enjoyable.

The inbound cable car came clattering up the hill, cresting Beach Street and rolling to a stop right on schedule. As Tara stepped forward, one of the regulars at her stop, a skinny, twenty-something man in designer tortoise-rim dark glasses, ear buds disappearing under his black hoodie, suddenly looked up from his phone and lunged for the car, cutting Tara off. She dodged to the right to avoid being sideswiped, and the heel of her pump went down in a gap in the pavement. Her ankle rolled. Her bag slipped off her shoulder. Nearly twenty pounds of essentials landed with bruising force on the crook of her arm. She felt herself toppling sideways, her left hand flying up, the paper sack with Eddie's steaming coffee swinging wildly. She pictured the full disaster, saw herself pitching forward under the wheels, the heavy car slipping back before the brakeman could stop it, the iron wheels rolling over her. She could see the headline—*Cable Car Amputates Hands of Woman Unbalanced by Handbag*. She would never again pet a dog, send a text, or bring Eddie his coffee.

As fast as the images came, a hand grabbed her left

elbow, arresting her fall. Straightening, she turned to see the calm blonde woman, holding her elbow, her grip surprisingly strong.

The woman smiled, her eyes alight with a gleam of satisfaction. She seemed to be having an "aha" moment, as if Tara were the solution to a puzzle, the missing clue to the *Times* Saturday crossword, the Higgs Boson particle. The genuine warmth of that smile was startling in a city known for people whose only means of connecting was a click on Tinder or a response to a Craig's List ad.

"Are you okay?" the woman asked.

Tara nodded. "Thank you." Usually, Tara was the giver of help, not the receiver, but she had her balance again, disaster avoided, and she hadn't spilled Eddie's coffee.

"Your bag must weigh twenty pounds." Again there was that sympathetic smile. The woman released Tara's arm as the others at the stop boarded.

"You planning to go to work today, girl?" the conductor called.

Tara put one foot on the wide running board.

"Wait!" The woman dipped a hand into the pocket of her trench coat. "I have something for you." Out came a ring box of scuffed burgundy leather. "Take this. Read everything. Trust me. It will change your life." She tucked the box in Tara's jacket pocket.

Tara just had time to crook her elbow around a pole before the car lurched into motion. She swung around to look back at the woman on the pavement, still standing there with that satisfied smile.

"My life is fine," she called over the clatter of the cable car.

"You'll see. Don't let your bag hold you back." The woman waved a friendly goodbye. Then she turned and slipped around the corner into the fog.

Tara leaned slightly, feet braced, adjusting to the slant of the car with its uphill angle. Two things puzzled her, about which she could not satisfy her curiosity while the cable car rattled along at its nine-mile-an-hour pace. She wanted to know what was in the box, and why the woman had picked her to receive it.

The woman hardly had the look of a terrorist, at least not the media's idea of a terrorist in a black ski mask and camo gear, and the box that rested against Tara's hip didn't tick or vibrate like an explosive device. Still, *life-changing* seemed a stretch. And as Tara was hardly in need of a life makeover, she found the woman's urgency and her words as curious as the box itself.

Her training kicked in as she reviewed the incident. As a concierge Tara made it a practice to listen between the lines, as it were, to figure out what clients were really asking. That's why the woman's comments about Tara's bag puzzled her. She had basically warned Tara that her bag, her favorite bag, was in her way. Tara had to disagree. Her bag made her better equipped for disaster than an astronaut headed for the space station, or explorers headed for the eight-thousand-foot depths of the Chevé cave system in Oaxaca. When disaster struck, Tara could always pull something out of her bag to save the day.

In Tara's experience one had to be prepared because disaster never came with plenty of warning, like an axe murderer in a slasher flick while the power was out, thunder rumbled, lightning flashed, and the heroine descended alone down the dark, creaking stairs of a deserted farmhouse toward the unexplained noise in the basement as the whole audience silently screamed, *Don't go there!*

Oh no, disaster came on sunny days, when things were

going well, and your guard was down. A smart person knew how to be ready. A smart person had a safety pin, a flashlight, a Band-Aid, spot cleaner, mace, or a pair of chopsticks that could be pressed into service to save the day. Tara always carried chopsticks in her bag. In fact, she had developed a system that was way ahead of airport security. Her bag was perfectly organized with what she liked to think of as her "kits," zippered clear plastic containers, ready for any and all emergencies.

Within minutes the cable car reached the top of its climb and turned east along Washington Street. At her stop Tara hopped off and headed for the hotel at her usual brisk pace, the mystery box bouncing against her hip with her stride. A few doors from the black and gold awning of the Hotel Belmont, where a narrow alley opened to the back entrances of several buildings, she knew she'd find Eddie cocooned in his drab green sleeping bag under a cardboard shelter.

San Francisco had an uneasy relationship with its street people. Churches sheltered them, non-profits fed and trained them, ER rooms treated them, the police periodically cleared them from the latest up-and-coming neighborhood, and tourists and business people tried *not* to see them. But Eddie wasn't some random homeless person; he was her friend.

Tara had met him her first day on the Belmont job. That day he'd been rolling up his sleeping bag and tucking it into a well-worn backpack, looking like an out-of-place mountain hiker, an urban Ansel Adams, with his wide-brimmed canvas hat. She put his age at pushing fifty with his lined and weathered face, his full graying beard and mustache, his bright eyes, and his squashed nose that hooked like a backwards J.

He had sized her up instantly. "Running away from home?"

The question had caught her off guard. "On my way to work." She had started to wish him a good day, not wanting to be rude, but inclined to move on without engaging, when he'd fallen into step with her, shouldering his pack.

"Then what's with the *suitcase* you're carrying? It looks like you have all your worldly belongings with you."

"Just a few items for emergencies."

He had glanced at her bag again. "What sort of emergency are you expecting? Earthquake? Terrorist attack? Alien invasion? You look like you're good to shelter in place for a month."

He made her laugh.

"I can definitely get through a rough day."

"You an EMT?"

She had laughed again. "A concierge at the Belmont." She had wanted to share her new job excitement with someone now that her grandmother was gone.

Their path brought them to the corner across from the Belmont. As they waited for the light, Tara could not help admiring the hotel, once the modest palace of an early twentieth century millionaire. It had been built after the devastating 1906 earthquake and restored by the Dorset Hotel Group in the '90s.

"You'll be fine if you roll with the punches."

Eddie's comment made her stop and look at him more carefully. He sounded like her grandmother. "What makes you so sure?" she'd asked him.

"Lots of punches." He pointed to his squashed nose. "Lots of rolling."

The light changed, and she started across the street, but Eddie didn't move.

"Just don't let that George scare you," he advised. He waved and turned away.

George, it turned out was the Hotel Belmont doorman, a figure of imposing grandeur. He and Eddie were opposites in appearance, if not in character. George, all polish and no nonsense from his top hat and overcoat with its gold shoulder bars to his white gloves and taxi whistle, ruled the pavement in front of the Belmont and indeed the whole block. Nothing disturbed the Belmont's guests as he greeted them or saw them off on excursions round the city.

Since that first morning, meeting Eddie had become a ritual. He had places to go during the day, but he liked to return to his North Beach haunts to sleep.

When Tara turned into the alley where Eddie was currently camping, she found him still under his damp cardboard roof, the end of his sleeping bag just visible behind a low iron gate at the foot of the back steps of a pale green Victorian townhouse wedged between a pair of newer brick condos. A string of foggy days, rare for January, had deepened the damp chill in the alley.

She set the bag of coffee and socks on the step below the gate and knocked on the wall. "Your wake-up call, sir."

Eddie liked to say that he needed just two things in the morning—good black coffee, and clean socks. "You've got to take care of your feet. You're on 'em all day."

When he didn't wake to her greeting, Tara lingered, wanting to be sure he was okay before she left him. She wasn't due at the hotel until the morning staff meeting.

She glanced up and down the alley, seeing only fog and damp. No one was about. Eddie liked to be up and gone before most people were stirring. He had a theory that he was repurposing San Francisco's only excess housing capacity by sleeping in doorways while homeowners were away.

"Hey, it's unused housing space, and it can house me for

a while and save a shelter bed for someone who really needs it."

What surprised Tara was that Eddie was pretty good at figuring out when people were away. On top of that he had dozens of survival strategies for using the city itself. In exchange for a shower, he did errands for a fellow vet who was wheelchair bound, and he had two luxuries, a PO box at a friendly postal annex site in the Embarcadero and a library card. He knew where to take a safe daytime nap, and where to store his few possessions, and he could sell the $1 *Street Sheet* to San Francisco's movers and shakers in their thousand dollar suits with Rolexes on their wrists.

She hesitated, unsure whether to wake him or not when he stirred and stretched. He gave her a hoarse croak of a good morning and reached for the coffee through the wrought iron gate.

"Are you okay?" She couldn't really judge in the gray gloom.

He took his first swig of coffee. "Sure. Did you break up with that absentee boyfriend of yours yet?"

"Nope."

Eddie asked about Tara's boyfriend nearly every time they met, and Tara had yet to confess that Justin Wright was the perfect boyfriend because he was pure fiction, an invention of Tara's own fertile imagination. She had invented Justin after her relationship with her college boyfriend Daniel flamed out in their late twenties, and a series of very bad Internet match-ups had left her feeling that she had no clue how to handle the post-college dating scene. Justin had been with her ever since. Or not *with* her, as she'd made him a consultant, always on the move to different client sites, usually foreign.

"Where's he off to this week?"

"He's got a consulting job in Sweden." That got Eddie's attention. Her remark caught him mid-sip, and he had a brief coughing fit before he could speak again.

"Sweden! Sweden! He can't take you anywhere while he's in Sweden. No *tapas* at Bocadillo's or drinks at the Top of the Mark looking out over the bay. What good is he?"

"Eddie, he's got to make a living."

"Dump him, Tara girl. The guy must have a suitcase for a heart. Go out with my guy. I'm telling you Jack is the one for you. Just say the word, and I'll connect you two."

"Thanks for thinking of me, Eddie, and I'll hold you to that promise about your Jack. He'll be my ace in the hole if things don't work out with Justin."

"How can things work out if the guy's in Sweden?"

"It's a global romance, Eddie." She pulled out her medical kit, extracted a couple of cough drops, and offered them through the gate. He shook his head and held up the coffee.

"I've got what I need. Watch out for that George, Tara girl."

"You watch out for that cold." She pocketed the cough drops he'd refused. Eddie was one independent man. "See you tomorrow."

George gave Tara a warm greeting and held the door for her. He might frown and bristle if Eddie crossed the hotel's invisible outer border, but he was a great ambassador for the hotel to all its guests. It was a shame that two of her favorite men had no use for one another. You couldn't meet George without thinking you could rely on him, but he was haughtier than *Downton Abbey's* butler, Carson, and regarded Eddie as a fenced dog regards a passing squirrel. At some time she knew they had had words. Eddie was a man who would have no patience with George's claim to own the public street.

George held the door for her, and she passed into the hotel. Few rooms in San Francisco matched the high-ceilinged lobby of the Hotel Belmont for quiet, old-fashioned elegance and the feeling that one had entered a well-managed private home. The tall gilt-framed antique mirrors and curated California oil paintings on the pale yellow walls, the fresh flower arrangements that spilled from blue and white vases on polished antique tables, the rich carpets, and fabrics that muted the sound of the city outside—all gave the room a feeling of old family wealth. Guests could gather in deep armchairs by the fireplace for coffee and pastries in the morning, or enjoy wine and cheese and bay views in the afternoon. And the place offered free Wi-Fi. Tara felt the Belmont offered visitors the best of old San Francisco's stateliness with a good dose of convenience as a bonus. As she crossed the lobby, she waved at Jennifer at the reception desk then shifted direction as Hadley Stewart signaled her from the concierge desk.

Hadley had the phone to her ear, her hand across the receiver. "What's the number of that 24-hour pharmacy you like? The guest in 403 left his meds behind."

Tara set down her bag, reached for a hotel notepad, and wrote the number.

Hadley mouthed a thank you as she punched the number into the phone. It was a small thing, but it was what Tara did, a hundred times a day, what she was good at. Helping Hadley help a guest made Tara feel her day was back on track. She crossed to the elevator alcove and the staff room door.

In the staff room she put her bag in her locker and clipped her Belmont badge to her jacket lapel. While the brand managers of the Dorset Hotel Group liked most of the employees in uniform, the dress code for the concierge staff specified business chic. For Tara that meant gray suits, dressy sweaters, heels, and pearls. Once she was ready for work, Tara reached for the *life-changing* mystery box. She had it in her hand when her boss, the general manager, Arturo Villanova, and her fellow staff members entered. She dropped the box back in her pocket and took her place at the table.

Arturo held a regular Thursday meeting to outline staff coverage for the weekend's events and to identify any special attention that particular clients required. The Belmont drew quite a few repeat guests, whose needs were well known. For the most part the staff who reported directly to Arturo made an experienced crew that worked well together. Jennifer managed the reception desk, Hadley headed housekeeping, Josephine Miles was the chef, and Noah Tibbs was in charge of valet parking and bellmen. Security was another matter. The Belmont relied on a group of four taciturn hulks, who had the social graces of San Francisco's own Dirty Harry. Everyone had been trained to call them for situations that required muscle rather than courtesy and graciousness, but they didn't attend staff meetings, and no one hung out with them. Tara had never called them.

"On your toes everyone." Arturo plugged in his tablet and flicked on the screen that laid out the weekend's staffing details. He turned, paused, and glanced around the room at his theatrical best. "Why do people come to San Francisco?"

In unison they groaned the expected answer to that very rhetorical question, "Romance."

"So at the Belmont we give them romance." There was the smallest hint of Arturo's native Spain in his raspy smoker's voice, and Tara thought he would make a good Gypsy King. Arturo had a following in the business because he set the highest standard of hospitality. He would spare no effort to improve a guest's stay. He instilled pride in everyone at the Belmont.

He rubbed his hands together gleefully. "Even though this is low season, at the Belmont we have a busy weekend ahead—two anniversaries, one honeymoon, one rehearsal dinner, and one—marriage proposal party." His tone implied that other, lesser hotels deserved to be empty. He turned to the screen with its calendar of room occupancy and staffing needs by date.

In spite of Arturo's obvious satisfaction with their success, Tara found herself fading in and out of attention. She knew just which junior suite he had set aside for the couple celebrating their fiftieth anniversary as well as the deluxe room where he would put the newlyweds. Her left hand in her suit jacket pocket encountered the worn little box, and its scuffed surface reminded her of the mystery woman's words. She was replaying those words in her mind when Arturo made a dramatic pause.

"Now, listen up children, timing is everything on Saturday. Our groom-to-be wants uninterrupted privacy for his evening marriage proposal moment." With his next breath, Arturo mentioned a name that got Tara's full attention. She nearly came out of her seat.

"Wait. Who's proposing to whom?"

Arturo frowned at Tara's interruption. Hadley gave her a nudge to suggest caution. One didn't interrupt Arturo.

"Daniel Lynch."

Noah chimed in. "The boy billionaire of Warp Speed Capital. He's proposing to the banking heiress, Nicola Solari, the one that looks like Scarlett Johansson."

Tara knew that her jaw had not literally dropped, but she could feel her slight double chin. She wouldn't catch stray insects, but she probably looked stunned. Her ex-boyfriend was coming to the Hotel Belmont to propose to a woman who appeared in the society pages of every publication in the city. No charity event happened without her fashionable presence. Tara was no hockey fan, but that her ex-boyfriend Daniel was bringing Nicola Solari to the Belmont to receive his proposal counted as a full-body check.

Stunned, unable to hear Arturo through the buzz in her mind, Tara felt the strongest urge to jump up from the table, grab her bag, and run. It made no sense. She ought not to care. She did not love Daniel, so what was this feeling of devastation about? She would figure it out later. Right now she needed to focus, stay in her chair, and behave like a professional. She pulled the little box from her pocket, folded her hands around it in her lap, and held on.

As Arturo went on filling in the details of Daniel's extravagant proposal plans, Tara's mind began to throw up explanations for her distress. Maybe it was simply that Daniel's plans emphasized her lack of plans. Somehow Daniel had moved on while Tara had become stuck.. She had not been paying attention, or she would have noticed Daniel appearing as Nicola's escort in the society pages. Now Daniel was proposing to a woman who was rich, thin, and beautiful, while she, Tara, was saving her pennies, dating an imaginary boyfriend, and dressing to minimize the effects of her love affair with salted chocolate gelato and a certain North Beach arugula-topped pizza. When was the last time she had gone running? She would have to start again.

Arturo explained how Daniel had arranged to take over the hotel on Saturday evening for the proposal and for a party of his friends and family. It seemed odd to her that Daniel would pick the Belmont for his proposal scene. Of course, he didn't know where she worked. They had not kept in touch. They had not even kept the friends they'd once shared, but if he wanted to impress Nicola Solari, there were more extravagant venues.

The next few minutes passed in a blur until Hadley nudged her again. "Tara, Arturo wants to know who you have lined up to do the flowers."

"Flowers?"

"For the proposal scene."

She had been imagining how Justin would propose to her at the base of Coit Tower, looking out over the bay. It took a moment for her brain to catch up.

Daniel had apparently requested the Tower Room for its view of the slender white tower on top of Telegraph Hill. He wanted the room strewn with red rose petals. He wanted champagne and chocolate-dipped strawberries and a photographer to capture every moment. He wanted a string quartet to play. In short he wanted a perfect cliché. Weeks earlier, before she had connected those requests with a specific client, she had ordered exactly what the client wanted. Now, however, something teased her memory. She had seen plenty of images of Nicola, and Daniel's generic romance choices did not seem right.

"Does Nicola have a favorite flower?"

Arturo nodded as if she were a bright pupil. "Thank you, Tara. Call Mr. Lynch, will you?"

Tara made a note. *Call ex.*

She could imagine how that conversation would go. She and Daniel had practically invented the IDO/NOWIDON'T romance. When they'd moved in together, she had started imagining Daniel's proposal, picking sites and times, always ready to look her most radiant. Daniel had focused on furnishing their apartment. He left the day the design store delivered the last piece they'd selected as a perfect fit for their odd-shaped living room. He left her with a huge rent, a camel-colored leather sectional, and a collection of matching all-clad cookware. In the end she had sublet the apartment and sold the furniture on Craig's List. She had dated persistently and unsuccessfully for eight months, and then one day, she just couldn't do it any more, and invented Justin. *Can't find the perfect boyfriend? Invent him.*

She had made Justin Daniel's opposite. He was indifferent to home furnishings, he preferred going out to cooking gourmet meals, and he would never break up with her.

When she looked back on her time with Daniel, she could see that she stuck with him out of her own fears rather than out of genuine admiration for his sterling qualities. When they'd met in those first days of college, she had been daunted by U C Berkeley's vast campus, endless course offerings, and hordes of students, and had appreciated Daniel's confidence in navigating the bewildering new experience. He was a planner and a tech whiz. He knew how to get a jump on housing or courses or events. He had strategies for the best place to sit in class, the best places to work on campus, the best ways to get across campus. She had envied his skill and worked to hone her own planning abilities. Only later did she understand that all Daniel's strategies were about Daniel needing to be first in whatever he tried.

As Arturo wrapped up the meeting, reviewing their assigned tasks, Jennifer pushed a note across the table in front of Tara. *Cough drop?*

Tara nodded. She realized she was still clutching the mystery box and put it back in her pocket. Under the table she passed Jennifer the cough drops Eddie had rejected. Jennifer mouthed a thank you, unwrapped a drop, and popped it in her mouth while Arturo looked the other way. She had been quick, but not quick enough. Arturo's ears caught the rustle of the wrapper, and he frowned at all of them. "Everyone's had a flu shot, right?" he asked.

They all nodded. Arturo had a horror of illness. No one came to work with even a sniffle at the Belmont. As they waited for his signal that the meeting was at an end, Arturo held them in place a moment longer with his stare.

"I don't need to tell you that we have a unique opportunity to begin a connection with two of the most prominent families in the city. If we want them to think of the Belmont as their home in the city, everything must be perfect this weekend."

He turned to Tara.

"One more thing. Ms. Keegan, I need you to tell me where your friend our neighborhood homeless man is camping out these days."

"You mean Eddie?" Tara was shocked. "But he never bothers the hotel's guests."

"Nevertheless, he needs to disappear, so to speak."

She met his gaze as squarely as she could. "You don't think I can tell you where he sleeps."

"Oh, I know you can, and the hotel expects you to recognize where your loyalty lies in this case. Just let security know, and they'll take care of it."

Tara didn't move. The last thing she would do was to put security onto Eddie. Even the cops would be kinder. The police did sweeps of certain neighborhoods, and San Francisco had special cleaning teams that rousted homeless people from the alleys around Market Street in the wee hours in order to clean up the ugly side of street life. She had never seen such a team in their neighborhood, nor did Eddie leave trash behind, but Eddie had a thing about authority, and there was no question that the hotel security team would be ruthless.

Tara resolved to avoid security, at least until she could warn Eddie.

The door closed behind Arturo, and she went straight for her bag. She didn't know what she was looking for. Her hands shook until she finally upended her bag. Her tidy kits came spilling out, but she could see nothing likely to help the your-ex-is-getting-engaged situation. She didn't need a Band-Aid or a phone charger or spot remover. She needed…What did she need?

She stood with her empty bag clutched to her chest, looking down at the items on the table—her kits for make up, and toiletries and hygiene needs, her wallet with IDs and credit cards, her business cards. Her water bottle, her dark chocolate, her grandmother's house keys, her music, an extra pair of flats, a zip drive, a phone charger, a pink jeweled LED flashlight, her chopsticks and measuring tape, and her pocket knife with all its tools. She had that feeling of an impending disaster for which the jumble on the table would be useless.

Against her hip she felt the bulge in her pocket and remembered the mystery box. She drew it out and looked at it closely for the first time.

The box had the look of something passed from hand to hand over a long time. She ran her fingers over the places where the burgundy leather was thin and scratched, exposing a soft dull brown under layer, like the toes of old shoes. A fleeting image of the sort of box she imagined Daniel giving his fiancée later in the weekend passed through her mind, black velvet with a Graff diamond the size of a fava bean.

When she flipped open the lid, she found a different ring from the engagement ring she'd been imagining. Nestled in a groove of the red silk lining was an old gold band made of two hands clasping a heart-shaped emerald wearing a little crown. She put the box down and removed the ring from its groove. In her palm it felt warm and alive. Immediately a familiar surge of longing for things long lost spiked in her. She felt as if she'd been hooked up to one of those hospital machines designed to record erratic heart rhythms, its needle swinging wildly up and down.

For a moment, with the ring in her palm, it was a September day, and she was eleven lying with her back against her shaggy black Bernese Mountain dog Sherlock, her bare legs stretched out on the warm boards of the porch of their Oakland hills house. She could smell her mother's oil paints, hear her father's endless rock music playing from his office, taste her grandmother's Sunday morning soda bread, and nothing would ever change. Her throat tightened. That had been the last day her father had been home with them.

She swallowed down the lump in her throat. Whoever had once owned the ring had lost things, she was sure. She lifted it up as if staring at it eye to ring would explain why it had the power to evoke such memories.

At eye level, the light caught an inscription on the inside. She turned the ring to read it. *Know Thy Heart.* The stranger's smile came back to her. Perhaps knowing her heart had given the woman that particular aura of happiness. Tara, however, was pretty sure she knew her heart, her unattached heart, and she couldn't claim to be floating on air. The woman's instructions came back to her. *Read everything. Trust me.*

She put the ring down and picked up the box again. Tucked against the red silk lining inside the box's lid was a small, folded square of yellowing paper. Tara unfolded the paper and read the message penned in a spidery script.

Be brave!—for the ring of truth will test you. Once on your finger, its power to speak endures but seven days. Listen and learn, lest you lose its wisdom and your heart's desire. When seven days pass, prepare to give the Claddagh as a gift. Once her face you see, you'll know the one who must the ring receive. On her bestow the ring of truth.

Tara looked from the paper to the ring. Its emerald stone seemed to glow, but the whole thing had to be a hoax. Though the paper looked authentic enough, and the script had the long, slanted letters of old documents like the *Declaration of Independence*, the idea of passing the ring along reminded her of the chain email letters that her college friend, Melissa, sent around, each promising extravagant life changes within the hour if she would just forward to five friends *Now!*

She refolded the message, returned it to its box, and picked up the ring again. So she was supposed to listen to it? She held it in her open palm again, waiting for it to speak, wondering whether it would sound like Johnny Depp or Morgan Freeman. *Please not Scarlett Johansson.*

Nothing. The ring sat in her palm without saying a word. No more memories came. A wise woman poet said there was an art to losing things and that it took practice, but Tara felt she had practiced enough. She glanced at the clock. She must have spaced out.

It's a ring, stupid, put it on.

Really, like wearing it would make a difference!

Tara's life did not need changing—perfect job, perfect boyfriend—and the ring was just a piece of metal and stone in spite of the greeting card sentiments attached.

What was she going to learn from a ring?

What harm could it do to test the thing?

She slipped it on her left hand ring finger, where she'd once imagined a very different ring would be. Oddly, it fit, and it looked surprisingly right on her hand. Tara stretched out her arm to admire the thing. Though it was nothing like the diamond she had imagined, the emerald stone seemed to glow again with a white inner light, and a voice that sounded suspiciously like Eddie's echoed in her head. *I know the man for you.*

She had plainly lost her mind.

The staff room door opened and Hadley poked her head in. "Tara, hello, time to work, you know."

"Oh, coming. I just..." She looked like a crazy person hugging her bag, with her hand stretched out over its contents littering the conference table.

Hadley's gaze zeroed in on the ring. "Ooh, is that a ring? I mean a *ring*? Did your guy Justin Whatsits finally propose? When was he in town?"

"Wright. His name is Justin Wright."

Hadley crossed the room and seized Tara's hand in both of hers. "Let me see. Oh, it's a Claddagh, how romantic? He's Irish, then, is he?"

Irish. The ring was Irish? Tara nodded. She couldn't say why. She wasn't ready to take the ring off her finger after it had just spoken to her, *if it had spoken*. She couldn't be sure, but she couldn't explain it to Hadley either. Better to let fictional Justin Wright save the day one more time. It came to her in a flash that she could wear the ring for the weekend, while Daniel courted his glamorous heiress. Her friends would not pity her. She wouldn't look like a loser. Then she would break up with her fictional fiancé. It would be the perfect ending to their story, and it would fit the rules of the ring. No reason she couldn't pass the thing on a few days early. She glanced at it again. It looked different in some way, dulled, less vibrant, but that didn't matter. She'd found a way to deal with Daniel's engagement party happening under her nose.

Chapter Two

Tara found herself needed as soon as she reached the concierge desk, a beautiful five-drawer mahogany Chippendale piece out of an English country house. Mrs. Alfred P. Woodford pushed her wheelchair bound husband across the lobby with energetic determination and a militant gleam in her eye that did not suggest satisfaction with the Belmont.

"Where's our driver, Ms. Keegan? We expected him at eight." The clock in the lobby began to strike the hour as she spoke, and a uniformed young man came striding in the front door.

"Ah," said her husband. "I believe Thomas is here."

"Yes, but, we should be pulling away from the curb already. Now we have to get you settled and wrestle with your chair and explain where we're going when we could have been underway."

"Of course, dear, but you'll manage. You always do." His eyes twinkled at Tara. For their anniversary each year the Woodfords made a pilgrimage to *Notre Dame des Victoires*, the French national church a few blocks away on Bush Street, where they had been married. In the past two years, with Alfred in a wheelchair, all the anxious fretful elements of Mrs. Woodford's nature had intensified. She would not be cheated out of her chance to complain.

"Yes, but, you know how traffic in the city makes it

impossible to get anywhere on time."

"The church will still be there."

"Let me help, Mrs. Woodford." Tara took over with Alfred's chair, while Thomas got the door. "Shall I call Father Pierre for you? Then he could meet you at the curb." With a little more fretting, a call to the church, and a great deal of patience from Thomas they were underway.

After the Woodfords left, Tara managed to get a much-coveted reservation for two foodie guests at the restaurant *Frances*, signed a younger guest up for the Uber phone app taxi service, and booked a spa day for a pair of sisters. It was just what she loved most about her job. When she handed a wine country tour packet to a visiting couple from Rhode Island, the green ring flashed on her finger. She smiled. She could deal with Daniel's proposal plans.

By any measure Jack Reeder could call himself a success even in San Francisco with its changing mix of fabled old fortunes and fabulous new ones. The medical practice he and his fellow physician Anne Campion had established in downtown San Francisco was thriving. The way they combined different kinds of expertise with new technologies for patient care felt right for a city of innovators and decidedly old-fashioned traditionalists. He could bike to work from his house in lower Pac Heights. He had a dog, lots of friends, male and female, and if he didn't have a CEO-sized yacht, he had a kayak to glide smoothly over the bay's waters or anchor in McCovey Cove to catch a splash home run from a Giants' game. Not bad for a farm boy from Eastern Washington who had made his way through school on student loans and odd jobs.

This morning Anne had reminded him that his success

required him to give back a little to the city. He sat at his desk, staring at the email she had forwarded to him from one of her former sorority sisters. The Charity Chicks and Benefit Babes Fundraiser was looking for bachelors to compete in a Mr. Single San Francisco contest. The money would go to the city's homeless shelters, and the publicity would boost Anne and Jack's medical practice. So he shouldn't hesitate. They had already written up a bio on him.

Who can resist a doctor with blue eyes and healing hands? Dr. Jack Reeder will win your vote and steal your heart. Trained as an ER doctor, a veteran of medical missions in Latin America, Jack studied at Washington State and did his residency here in the city, where he has his own medical practice, Whole Person Health. This hunky MD bikes to work, so he's as easy on the environment as he is on the eyes. No girlfriend—that we know of.

The write-up was technically true, except maybe the part about the healing hands. He had a curious brain and lots of good training from great physician teachers. He liked to listen to his patients, and he was willing to test more than one theory before he jumped to any diagnosis or prescribed a course of treatment. And he did like to *do* medicine, to see results, rather than simply refer his patients to specialists. That's what the ER had been all about, doing medicine on the spot, acting directly for the patient's benefit. And that was the thrill of a medical mission.

"Why are you balking at this contest?" Anne had asked him the day before. "I'm curious. I never see you hesitate."

He'd put her off, but the answer was simple. The write-up made him feel like a fraud. While most of his patients were pleased with his work, the words of one dissatisfied patient from his ER days stayed with him. More than anything he had wanted to fix that patient, so the man's words stuck, outweighing all the good comments on Internet rating sites since.

As that one homeless man had put it, jabbing Jack in the chest with a bony finger, "You may be smart, boy, but you try to fix people. You can't fix people like you fix cars. Fixing is not healing. To heal a person you've got to be in a relationship with the person. If you just see the disease or the broken body parts, you won't heal anyone. You heal by working with a whole person."

At the time, he had rejected the advice. He didn't appreciate anyone questioning his new skills, especially not someone whose lifestyle had landed him in the ER with a smashed nose and a concussion. Jack had been living in a small apartment with a crushing amount of student loans, but he had a degree and self-discipline and big plans. What did some homeless guy know anyway?

But the words had stuck. And when he heard the ideas of the homeless man echoed in the conversation of one of his more outspoken colleagues, he found himself thinking about whether he could practice medicine a bit differently from the way he had imagined doing it.

When he was ready to go out on his own, he'd sought out the fellow student who had been so outspoken in her views about what it meant to treat people. They'd hammered out a partnership, raised the start-up money, and begun their Whole Person Health practice, which they had located where even the homeless could find them. He owed Anne a favor, or two, or a hundred, so he should say yes to this request.

He deleted "healing hands" from the blurb, chose a picture of himself from the Whole Person Health website, and sent off an acceptance email to the Charity Chicks.

Since he and Anne had started Whole Person Health,

he'd been working on a relationship with his former critic. He knew he'd feel better about competing in the Mr. Single San Francisco contest, if he could get his favorite homeless vet to agree to get a flu shot before the flu season cranked into high gear. He logged off his computer and headed for the nearest food truck. With any luck he'd find his cranky critic today.

Just after noon, Tara found a moment to call Daniel. His executive assistant put her through to him, and she immediately offered her congratulations.

"Cut to the chase, Keegan. Is the hotel up to the job?"

"We are so on it. Does Nicola have a favorite flower? Peony, lilac, tuberose?"

"Red roses will work."

"So is red her favorite color?" Tara did not remember a photograph of Nicola Solari in red.

"Every woman likes red roses."

"Her favorite fragrance?"

"Expensive."

"Great, Daniel. You've been most helpful. Any other requests to make your stay more comfortable?"

"Buckwheat pillows."

"Does Nicola sleep with one?"

"I do."

"Okay. I'll look into it for you." Tara made a note.

"And I'd like an appointment at Goorin Bros. I need a new hat."

"Do you need an appointment with them?" The flagship store of the famous hat makers was just blocks from the Belmont.

"Timing matters. I hope you're up to this, Keegan. This

has got to be perfect."

For whom? The question popped into her head from nowhere, and she couldn't help pushing back a little. "Daniel, if you have any doubts, why this hotel?"

"The view of Coit Tower."

Daniel was right that the hotel had a perfect view of the iconic white tower at the top of Telegraph Hill overlooking the whole sweep of the bay.

"But does it make sense to host your engagement bash where an ex-girlfriend works? I can call one of our competitors if it seems awkward."

"Awkward?"

"For Nicola, because it's her moment."

"Oh. That's no problem. I never mentioned you to Nicola. You'll just be part of the staff and if the staff does their job right, Nicola will never notice them."

Ouch! "Okay, well then, thanks for the information about her preferences. If you think of anything else, please call. We'll do our best to make your weekend perfect."

Tara hung up and took a deep breath. Daniel's self-important, finger-snapping, bottom-line attitude had pushed her buttons. She had slipped as a concierge. Arturo wouldn't like her recommending a competitor to a client, especially not a client with important connections. She resolved to stay professional in her dealings with Daniel. Her ego might be in the ICU, but she'd survive. She'd make sure that Daniel and Nicola had their perfect weekend, even if Daniel's idea of perfect seemed to be about satisfying himself rather than his fiancée-to-be.

Daniel had obviously survived their break up, so maybe she could learn from him about cutting her losses. Maybe it was better to hit delete when the cursor hovered over files of early bad romances and move on, but didn't people open up to each other about their pasts, about their mistakes and their growth and the things that had happened to make them who they were? Something to think about after her break up with Justin to whom she was now engaged.

The thought made her glance at the ring on her finger, and she held up her hand to look at it again. *Hello, ring, I'm listening. Do you have anything to say?*

Predictably, the gold and green band was silent.

Jack found Eddie on a bench between the water's edge and the Ferry Building. He didn't try to fix Eddie any more. He just tried to keep the contact going, so he sat on the bench, prepared to shoot the breeze about the Warriors' prospects for the season or the economy, always Eddie's favorite topic. The fog had burned off, but the day was brisk, and the wind off the bay, sharp. Eddie had his hands wrapped around a tall, lidded paper cup. He looked warm enough in a worn, knee-length, navy wool jacket, and mostly he looked sober.

Jack didn't know when Eddie had decided get sober, some time after their disastrous experiment in living together. Living together seemed to bring out the worst in each of them. Jack kept trying to help. Eddie kept insisting that Jack's medical degree was worthless, that he knew nothing about helping a vet in Eddie's circumstances. The whole experiment exploded when Eddie tore the apartment apart in a drunken rage in front of Jack's then girlfriend Lisa. Both Lisa and Eddie had walked out on him, and he didn't see Eddie for more than a year, until he turned up in the ER that night beaten by a couple of thugs.

Jack had done a lot of work since then trying to understand guys like Eddie and trying to resist the impulse to "fix" the broken. Eddie had been right that *fixing* was not *healing*, but knowing Eddie was right did not make it easy to see him resisting services that could get him off the streets. The coldest, wettest days of San Francisco's brief winter lay ahead of them.

Jack unwrapped his turkey sandwich. He knew better than to offer any to Eddie. Pigeons strutted about at their feet, and a gull landed on the railing to watch Jack consume his sandwich. While Jack ate and Eddie sipped his hot beverage, they covered the usual concerns of local sports' fans, the Niners' playoff prospects, the Warriors' coaching woes, and the lead-up to spring training for the Giants. Then Eddie surprised him.

"You dating anyone these days?"

"No." Jack felt his old wariness immediately surface, and worked to quell it. He and Eddie had very different ideas about women. "Why?"

"I think it's time for you to meet this girl I know. I think you'd like her."

That was a new one. Jack tried to picture the sort of girl Eddie would pick for him. She would be someone Eddie had met in a recovering addicts' meeting or a veterans' group. Jack pictured tattoos and piercings. Or maybe she'd be a twenty-something barista, with whom Eddie had struck up a flirtation. He pictured tattoos and piercings. The old Eddie, before Iraq and alcoholism, had been a high school hero, Jack's hero, a popular football player who made diving catches and dazzling runs.

"Tell me about her."

"Tara's an Irish girl, descended from Irish people at any rate. She has that look—a smooth roses-and-cream complexion, hair like burnt caramel, big blue eyes."

"Figure?" Women in San Francisco tended to be model thin or athletically buff.

"She has a figure. You'll notice right away."

"So she's hot, but for some reason, she's available?" He tossed his sandwich wrapper in the trash, and the gull took flight.

"She's got this absentee boyfriend, Justin Wright, sort of like an absentee landlord. He neglects her, puts his work ahead of everything. She needs someone steady, reliable, like you."

"Did you just call me 'dull,' because I think you did?"

"You know what I mean. You're a regular guy. You're not one of these high-flying tech types. You've got a dog. Watson hasn't left you, right?"

"Now you're suggesting that I'd be good for this girl because Watson likes me. I feed Watson. What if she's romantic?"

"Oh, she's romantic. She just doesn't know it."

Jack realized that Eddie knew a lot about the girl, more than he imagined him knowing about most of the people he encountered in his life. Eddie, who was Mr. Self-Reliant, who would have found Walden Pond crowded, sounded almost fatherly toward this Tara.

"How do you know her?"

Eddie got up from his bench, moving stiffly and slowly. It could just be from the cold and from sitting so long, but Jack realized they hadn't gotten around to talking about a flu shot.

"She brings me my socks and coffee in the morning on her way to work."

"And where does she work?" Jack asked as casually as he could. He kept his gaze on a passing container ship. It would be unlike Eddie to reveal, even inadvertently, any detail that might let Jack know where he slept at night.

Eddie took his time shouldering his pack. "The Hotel

Belmont. She's a concierge there." He said it with obvious pride.

Jack got up, too, careful not to show that he'd picked up on what Eddie had revealed. It was stunning information. If Eddie accepted help from this girl regularly, he must be hanging out more or less permanently in North Beach, an area of the city that was marginally less dangerous for the homeless. Jack felt a certain tightness in his chest loosen a fraction at the idea.

"So, did I talk you into looking her up?"

Jack was due back for his afternoon round of appointments, and he had one stop to make on the way. He wasn't going to admit it, but he was curious about the woman who had won so much of Eddie's trust. "You did convince me that I've made a big mistake agreeing to compete in the Mr. Single San Francisco contest. What woman is going to be interested in a steady guy with great dog-feeding skills?"

"Well, listen, you take Tara out, and I'll get that flu shot you want me to have." Eddie turned and started to shuffle off. Squawking gulls swooped in over their abandoned bench.

"Did I say anything about a flu shot?" Jack shouted over the gulls' din.

"You can't stop being a doctor, you know. You've been checking my vitals mentally since you sat down. I'm going to give Tara your cell number."

Across the lobby Tara saw Jennifer approaching to fill in while Tara took her lunch break. She could use one. Mrs. Woodford had returned from lunch with another series of complaints, and a list of anticipated difficulties about their dinner plans.

Jennifer threw a quick glance around and unwrapped another cough drop. "Whew, it's a going to be a crazy weekend, isn't it? Just don't get in Arturo's way."

"I won't. Are you okay?"

"Just a dry throat."

"Listen, I've got to do an errand on my break. Can you keep the desk covered if I'm a little late?"

"No problem." Jennifer coughed. "But show me the ring. I heard from Hadley that your man proposed."

Tara held out her hand. Okay, the Justin Wright thing was getting a little out of hand. Now she was deliberately misleading her friends, and that felt weird. She promised herself she would make it up to them. George opened the door to usher in a young couple, and traffic noise briefly filled her ears. She couldn't be sure, but she thought she heard a voice. *You've been misleading your friends for years.*

Jennifer looked underwhelmed by the ring. "It must be an heirloom, huh? I mean it's not Tiffany's or anything, but it's sweet and traditional. It's Irish, too. I didn't know that your Justin could be so thoughtful."

Tara looked at the ring, which seemed to lose its luster as she wore it. Was she the only one who did not know her Irish rings? "That's Justin, so thoughtful."

"Oh. I didn't mean that he isn't. It's just that he always puts his work before you, you know, like when it's your birthday, or when you got promoted, and he was away."

"He does travel a lot." An unexpected thought popped into her head as if the words were spoken aloud, and she looked at the ring again.

Even your fictional boyfriend is a bad boyfriend. Why?

First the ring had sounded like Eddie, and now it

sounded like a therapist. Her imagination was clearly out of whack and inventing voices.

"Well, congratulations anyway." Jennifer took over Tara's position at the desk. "We should celebrate—pizza and gelato? And maybe the next time Justin's in town we'll meet him."

Tara nodded. "Sounds like a plan."

She collected her bag from the staff room and headed for the door. Since her grandmother's passing she made regular trips to her grandmother's attorneys' offices on Montgomery to handle matters relating to the estate. It was odd that the ring was Irish like her grandmother, whose people had come in the late nineteenth century to the foothills above Sacramento for the last of the gold in California's streams. She wasn't particularly familiar with Irish lore as her mother favored brioche over soda bread every time.

Tara ducked out of the hotel behind a pair of guests as George helped them into a cab. She wanted to avoid any awkward questions about Eddie until she had a chance to warn him. She had not yet seen any of the security men. Outside the hotel the fog had lifted on a sparkling, crisp day, sunlight glinting off gleaming skyscrapers and the bright bay. She grabbed a Muni bus down to the financial district.

The late lunch crowd of returning lawyers and legal assistants streamed back into the neo-deco building that housed the firm of Burke, Wright & Ross. Tara's heels clicked on the patterned floor. With the holiday decorations down, the grand foyer resumed its more understated elegance, not that anyone bunched in front of the elevators noticed. They all seemed intent on snagging a spot on the next car. Tara felt invisible in the mob. She glanced at her phone. No texts. She just had time to do her errand.

A bell rang, the doors opened, and the crowd surged

forward. Tara tried to press into the last available space before the doors closed, angling forward leading with her left shoulder. As she twisted to face the doors, she realized her bag was going to be caught. She tried to squish back and met a firm hand at her back.

"Whoa, lady, take that trunk of yours and get the next one," a male voice suggested.

Simultaneously, she felt her bag turned ninety degrees by unseen hands and looked up through the closing doors to catch the merest glimpse of a gorgeous man in a dark gray suit and blue tie. He had wind ruffled dark hair and a pair of steady blue eyes that made her heart catch. He had seen her need and acted. The doors closed on his grin, trapping her bag against her shins as the elevator rose in a quiet whoosh. Feeling that she'd violated the unwritten code of elevator etiquette, Tara hunched her shoulders, and tried to make herself as small as possible. She felt the ring on her finger where her hand clutched her bag and heard again in her head the stranger who'd warned her—*Don't let your bag get in your way.* At the first stop three people exited, jostling past her bag, making her tighten her hold on it.

She stepped out on the eleventh floor. Maybe she should retain Burke, Wright & Ross to defend her bag. *Really, her bag had never been a problem before today.* A tight squeeze in an elevator was just part of city living, and she'd reached her appointment on time. Her bag had hardly held her back. In fact, it had earned her a grin from a handsome stranger.

On her way back to the hotel, Tara looked for Eddie in two parks and one cafe. When she didn't find him, she turned back to the Belmont and reached her desk in time for a brief afternoon lull while most guests were out shopping or touring the city. As soon as she took care of dinner reservations for a foursome from Sydney, she started an

Internet search for Irish rings.

It wasn't hard to find them. They were called Claddagh rings and had a long history starting with a young Irishman captured by pirates in the seventeenth century and sold into slavery to a goldsmith in the Middle East where he learned jewelry making. Released after fourteen years, he had returned to Ireland to marry the girl who waited for him. *Talk about a global relationship*. The ring he fashioned for her represented love, loyalty, and friendship.

Since then the rings had been handed down in families and had accompanied the Irish wherever famine and troubles had driven them. The rich and famous had worn them as well as the humble and obscure. Over two hundred Claddagh rings had been recovered from the rubble of the twin towers after 9/11. That fact stopped her dead in her research tracks. A little *frisson* of awe passed over her.

She looked at the ring on her finger, wondering whether it had been lost on that day and found and passed on again because to bear the burden of such loss was hard work, and lighter for everyone if each bore it only a short time, sort of like the terrible burden of Tolkien's ring on poor unsuspecting hobbits.

She knew her own burden of loss was small compared to the losses of that day, but sometimes the memory of loss came back fresh and stingingly sharp. On a sunny October Sunday when she was eleven, a month into her parents' separation, before she had begun to use the word *divorce*, Tara had been reading in her favorite spot on the porch with her dog Sherlock when the first smell of smoke in the air alerted her to the fire. It was nothing like the smell of a barbeque.

She'd looked up as her neighbor's front door banged open, and the woman came running out to her car. Seeing

Tara, she shouted that there was a fire and they needed to evacuate the neighborhood now. Tara was still staring at her when a car careened wildly down their narrow street. The driver's panicked face had set her heart pounding, and she'd dashed inside to find her mother painting. Her mother insisted on confirming the news, but once she turned on the radio, she acted, instructing Tara to pack an overnight bag for each of them. While Tara put the bags and her rabbits' cage in the car, her mother went back to her studio. She gathered up several canvases, and as they rearranged things in the car to fit the paintings, Sherlock bounded away down the street. They took off, Tara with the car window down calling for Sherlock, while ash and embers blew around them in swirling eddies. The scale of that disaster was nothing like the attack on the Twin Towers, but people had perished that day, too, and at least one marriage.

Tara's grandmother liked to say that love was the enduring memorial that marked a person's passage through this life. But Tara's parents saw things differently. Each wanted to leave a body of work. For her father that meant his life-saving medical research; for her mother that meant her art. For them the fire had intensified that determination. Her father had disappeared into his research. Her mother had answered the old philosopher's riddle of what to save in a fire—the pet or the painting—by saving her paintings. Sherlock had not turned up among the lost pets recovered later.

There had been nothing left of their house but the foundation and the skeletons of appliances. The blackened twisted metal of Tara's eleventh birthday bicycle marked the end of the porch. Tara and her mother had moved in with her grandmother in the city. The rabbits had found a new home in Danville.

At her grandmother's house Tara collected the remnants of her childhood that had survived. The only toy left was Bingo Bear, a stuffed animal she'd wanted one Christmas because the TV ads had suggested that the bear could talk like a real friend. Her grandmother had given Bingo to her, but it had only taken Tara a few minutes to see through the illusion. Each time she pulled the string on Bingo Bear's back, he uttered a recorded message. She had abandoned him that day at her grandmother's, and so he'd been waiting there for her after the fire. As soon as her mother settled Tara in the city's French school—*so you can visit me later*—she had left for southern France.

Tara shook off the old memories and turned back to her research. There was no image that looked as old as her ring, nor anything in the information about a Claddagh with powers of speech. Now that she knew the ring was Irish, maybe she should listen for a voice like Bono's or her grandmother's.

A disturbance at the hotel entrance made her look up. George ushered in an elegant and obviously shaken woman, signaling to Tara with raised brows that he needed her help. Tara went immediately to the woman's other side to take her arm. She was tall and blonde, fortyish, with blunt girlish features and a perfect pouty red mouth, the lipstick flawlessly applied, the kind of mouth that invited male attention. A knee-length textured gray cashmere sweater over a white, collared shirt and jeans leggings flattered her slim figure, and jeweled open-toe heels revealed a great pedicure. She was a woman used to being noticed.

They guided her to a sofa, and Tara brought her a glass of water.

After a few sips, she began to speak, her voice shaking a little. "I've never been so viciously and personally insulted.

The man must be mental. He came at me out of nowhere, right in front of the hotel. What kind of neighborhood is this?"

"Ma'am, can you describe the man who attacked you?" George asked.

A diamond bracelet flashed on the woman's wrist. Her expression was uncomprehending. "He was a street person." She shuddered. "Grimy clothes. Body odor. Scraggly beard."

George shot Tara a grim glance over the woman's head.

"He shoved me. That's assault. I had to grab my purse, and he yelled vile things at me. He said *he* was a vet and *I* should show respect."

Tara shook her head at George's grim look. He was ready to blame Eddie for the incident, but Tara knew Eddie. True, Eddie was a vet, like the man their guest had encountered, but Eddie stayed away from the hotel, and he would never yell at a woman. The woman's assailant was likely one of the shouters, someone off his meds and inclined to take out his frustrations on anyone in his path.

"Excuse me." The woman shot Tara a sharp look. "Don't shake your head. Do you people think this is some kind of joke? I assure you this is no joke. I expect you to call the police. I want charges filed against this man."

At that moment Arturo hurried over to them. "Ms. Ralston, how may we help you?" He gave both Tara and George a look that said he was seriously displeased.

The woman started in again on her complaint. Arturo assured her the hotel regarded the situation as deeply serious and would do everything in its power to make up to her for the distress she had suffered.

"Well, you can call the police for starters. I won't tolerate being attacked and insulted in this way."

Arturo nodded to Tara. "Ms. Keegan will get right on it.

And call security."

Tara made the calls from the concierge desk. A uniformed security guard appeared instantly, spoke briefly to Arturo, and left the hotel.

As she expected, at SFPD, the sergeant she spoke with told her that his precinct would send a patrolperson around the area to see whether any of the local characters were acting out. She wished she knew where Eddie was, but she told herself that she should not worry about him. He had not attacked a guest, and he must be somewhere else in the city at this time of day.

As soon as the woman had gone up to her room, Arturo strode over to the concierge desk to demand that Tara tell him where Eddie's camp was. "And don't tell me you don't know. We do not tolerate incidents of this kind at the Belmont."

"I do not know where Eddie's camp is, but I do know that Eddie is not the man involved in the incident." She said it without hesitation.

Tara saw at once that in defending Eddie, she had gone too far, but Arturo was being unjust, condemning Eddie without any investigation. Arturo hadn't asked the first question that a just person had to ask—is it true?

Arturo's frown cut deep lines in his brow. "Apparently, Ms. Keegan, what you don't understand is the meaning of loyalty. You received a direct order, with which you have not complied. If we were not stretched to capacity this weekend, you'd be gone today. As it is, you have until the last of the Lynch party checks out. Then you're done."

Chapter Three

The rehearsal dinner guests began to assemble as Tara's shift ended. She prepared to leave and let the next concierge take over. In the staff room she took off her badge, retrieved her bag, and touched up her make-up, trying for a normalcy she did not feel. As she applied fresh lip gloss, she caught the flash of the ring's green gem in the mirror. *Some life changer!* The thing had spoken three times, and she'd lost her job.

She stretched out her hand. *Well, do you have anything to say? What should I do? Cave in to Arturo? Find Eddie?* She waited, but the ring was silent.

Instead, Jennifer entered the staff room. "Oh, you're still here. So what's going on? Did you quit, or what?"

"Neither. Arturo ordered me to tell him where my friend Eddie sleeps. I didn't, so he's going to fire me on Monday."

Jennifer reached out with a quick hug, than backed away with a grave look. "Really, Tara? Are you going to blow it at the Belmont over some homeless guy? I mean I know they're people and they're down on their luck, but working at the Belmont is not just any job. You love this job, and you just got engaged."

Tara zipped her lip gloss back into its plastic case. She did not trust herself to speak. The loss was big, and Jennifer was a friend who meant well, but she didn't feel like going back on her decision. Maybe she was being stubborn, or maybe the whole thing had not yet sunk in, but it felt right to stand up for a friend.

"I know. We should take you out to celebrate!"

"Celebrate my getting canned?"

"No, your getting engaged. I'll text Hadley. Hold on." Jennifer whipped out her phone. "Where should we go? That pizza place you like near the square. Romina is just the person to cheer you up."

"Do I need cheering up?"

Jennifer peered at her. "Hey your boss is threatening you, and your boyfriend's in Sweden. You need someone right here."

"Jennifer, thank you, but I should look for Eddie to warn him."

"Listen, security is not going to look for him tonight. So you can wait until morning. You know where he sleeps, right?"

But what kind of friend am I if I let security pick Eddie up?

"Come on. You've got a ring on your finger. Let Arturo and your friend Eddie worry their worries. You should do something fun."

The three friends squeezed in the front corner booth of their favorite pizza place and ordered. The proprietress, an ex-dancer who had learned to make pizza in her native Rome, brought them red wine and admired Tara's ring.

"Why haven't we met this young man? Doesn't he eat pizza?"

Tara gave her usual explanation of Justin's work schedule, but it sounded hollow in her ears as she held out her hand to have her ring admired. The fantasy should be perfect—a woman surrounded by friends celebrating happy news. She didn't know how she had let it go so far. There was no way she could confess what she'd done now. It would be too humiliating when they were all being so nice to her. It would be like having all one's junior high fantasies revealed, those dreams of making eye contact with the cutest boy at the dance and having him choose you.

While her friends joked and chatted, she thought back to the moment when she'd first invented Justin after a series of spectacularly bad Internet dates. He had seemed like the best solution to a bad situation, her own private joke. She had taken the "Justin" from Justin Timberlake, and the Wright, from her grandmother's lawyers, and once she'd had a name, her fake boyfriend had come to life in her imagination. In the beginning she had known just how to play the whole thing cautiously. When asked about her status, she'd simply said she'd started seeing someone and it was too early to make much of it. Gradually, when pressed, she'd admitted to having a regular thing going with Justin.

She had wanted someone smart and funny and generous, someone taller than she was at five seven with room for her to wear heels. She had made him a little bit adventurous, willing to travel for his work, unafraid of heights or driving a stick shift in San Francisco with its precipitous hills. She had made him a confident guy who knew his baseball and football, but who was not into sports twenty-four seven. He was never awkward ordering or paying for a meal. Unlike Daniel, Justin actually knew her preferences for wine and food, flowers and film.

"Where do you think you'll be married?" Hadley asked.

"Oh, we haven't decided yet."

Jennifer raised her glass in a toast. "To Tara, one lucky girl."

"Amen." Hadley chimed in. "And may there be more Mr. Wrights out there for us."

Tara raised her glass. Suddenly, being engaged to Justin seemed as satisfying as having a conversation with Bingo Bear, and Tara wanted to end it. She gave the ring a suspicious look. The thing was messing with her mind for sure.

Their salads came, and Tara was able to tuck her ring hand in her lap and encourage other conversation. Both Jennifer and Hadley promised to check their contacts to see where there were concierge openings in the city. Tara was close to receiving her *Clefs d'Or* membership, the sign of the elite concierge who always went the extra mile for her guests, but besides hotels, lots of businesses now employed a concierge to manage customers' needs. She would find another job.

After pizza, Hadley insisted the celebration would not be complete without gelato. Even on a foggy January weeknight, North Beach drew tourists. The friends joined the evening crowd, passing in opposing streams up and down Columbus, dodging advertising stands, planter boxes, and little outdoor tables for hardy diners. The fog swirled about making yellow halos around the streetlights. A dozen women from a bachelorette party wearing fake tiaras, holding pink balloons, and whirling noisemakers giggled by in heels.

"That's you next!" Hadley offered her a high five. Tara wondered how soon she could start looking for Eddie.

The next moment, she bumped into a stranger, catching him smack in the kneecap with her bag. An automatic *excuse me* sprang to her lips as a pair of strong hands gripped her shoulders. She looked up into steady blue eyes, and felt a jolt of recognition.

"You."

"Hey, bag lady. How are you?"

They looked at one another for a moment, then someone else called. "Jack, come on, man. We've got to make our reservation."

The hands released her shoulders. "See you around." He flashed her that confident grin.

Jack? She turned to look over her shoulder as the flow of the crowd carried him off.

"I hope Justin's really hot," Jennifer said, "because that guy was seriously good looking."

He might be, but Tara pulled herself together. A flirtatious smile from a passing stranger was exactly nothing. It was like smelling a bakery at the end of a morning run, a whiff of goodness that did not fill one's stomach. Still, she figured twice in one day meant the stranger was probably local and she might see him again. A little voice sounded in her ear saying, *after you break up with Justin, of course.*

There was no way the ring, with her hand tucked in her pocket, was speaking to her over the noise of city traffic, and it had to be coincidence that the stranger's name was Jack, like Eddie's friend.

She had no intention of taking Eddie up on his offer. Eddie's Jack was probably a fellow vet in his forties, in recovery, divorced with children he never saw, someone with whom she would have nothing in common, but it suddenly hit her that Eddie might be at a meeting. She halted mid-stride. There were hundreds of meetings in the city for recovering addicts of every sort. She fished in her bag for her phone and used it to find the nearest meeting for recovering alcoholics. She found nothing listed for a Thursday night in North Beach. There were only daytime meetings in the neighborhood of the Belmont, so if Eddie was at a meeting, he was on the other side of town, which, with security after him, would be a good thing.

She slipped her phone back into its pocket in her bag. She actually didn't know that Eddie had ever been an addict. She didn't even know how he had ended up on the streets. She had been accepting Eddie's cheerful support on her way to work each day ever since her grandmother had died. Now she was ashamed to realize that Eddie knew a great deal more about her job troubles than she knew about his more perilous circumstances.

The gelato was delicious, and she told herself there could not be any calories in something that dissolved in salty sweetness on the tongue. Didn't research show that if you didn't have to chew, a food could not be fattening? Once she broke up with Justin, she supposed she would have to diet in earnest and start running if she meant to go back to dating. The whole idea was depressing.

Jennifer asked for another cough drop, and Tara warned her not to let Arturo catch her coming to work with a cold.

Their cappuccinos came, and Hadley saluted her with the white cup. "I'm so glad for you that Justin came through before your ex showed up with his girlfriend. I'm sure it would be awkward and painful watching the whole Daniel proposal drama without a fiancé of your own."

Jennifer added, "Even more important, you are lucky to catch this guy Justin now before you turn thirty-five. I mean, after thirty-five, a woman's profile doesn't even show up in the searches."

"Hey, that's what Tinder is for." Hadley took out her phone. Jennifer and Hadley had both joined Tinder, convinced that the new smart phone app approach to dating would be better than the old matching done by algorithms that took no account of chemistry. As they sat around the tiny marble table in the gelato shop, Hadley clicked on a picture and got an answering click. There was a guy out there within a five-mile radius who thought Hadley was cute enough to meet.

While her friends high-fived each other, Tara stood. It was time to look for Eddie.

Suddenly serious, Hadley looked up. "Do you think this person is really a friend, or is he some guy that's figured out how to get something out of you? I mean you bring him coffee every day."

Jennifer added her concern. "Isn't he sort of like a pet or a mascot?"

Tara shook her head. Her friends ended by urging her not to go looking for Eddie on her own so late, but Tara held firm. She promised to text them both and take a cab later. She walked back to the Belmont, thinking about the way truth and fiction had become mixed up in the last seven hours from the time she'd put the crazy ring on her finger. Her friends wanted to celebrate her relationship with Justin and doubt her friendship with Eddie. Even if they were right about Eddie taking advantage of her, when Tara examined her own feelings, she found them sincere. Eddie had come into her life right after her grandmother's death. He had stepped into an empty space in her heart and filled it. He made her laugh, and he made her believe she could do her job. She liked him. She would look for him out of loyalty to her own feelings.

Her only hope of finding him was to return to the alley where she'd seen him that morning. If she was going to lose her job, at least she could let Eddie know that Arturo had Hotel Belmont security looking for him.

The glow of the city lit the fog above, but when she peered into Eddie's alley, it had turned ghostly, all shadows and black fathomless recesses. Holding her pink LED flashlight, with her bag in front of her like a shield, she ventured into the dark. She inched her way along close to a wall of lava-like bricks until a black plastic trash bin jutting across her path forced her into the open alleyway. The place smelled of compost bins and car fumes. Her tiny light wobbled in her hand. Eddie's pale green Victorian doorway should be just ahead of her, but darkness and fog turned all shades the same and obscured the shapes of the buildings. She took another cautious step forward.

The next moment a flashlight beam like a searchlight caught her in its glare. She threw up a hand to cover her eyes. The blast of light came from a hulking figure advancing toward her, whose shadow stretched across the alley from side to side.

Her heart gave a start as if the gun had fired for a race, but her brain recognized the light as belonging to someone in authority, a cop or...a security guard. Her light caught the Belmont badge clipped to the man's belt.

"Hi there," she called. "Thank goodness you have that light." She turned her own puny light toward the ground. "Maybe you can help me. I dropped something here."

"Lady, you're nuts!"

Tara turned slightly to dip her free hand into her bag. She let her fingers close around the first item she found, her ear bud cord, and using her purse as a shield, she managed to lower the cord to the ground. She flashed her light around in wide swings and made as much noise as she could with her heels.

"My ear buds. I must have lost them running this morning. I'm sure they're somewhere around here."

The big man stepped up beside her and turned his beam onto the ground illuminating a patch of pavement big enough to park an SUV. Almost instantly, his light caught the white plastic cord.

"Oh thank you." Tara bent and scooped up the cord. She swirled her light around. "I guess I needed a bigger light."

"Yeah, right. Just tell your scumbag pal to beat it, or he'll get his ass jailed."

"Thanks again." Tara emerged from the alley, heart pounding, and kept walking toward the hotel. She did not know whether she had led security to Eddie's place, or whether the man had found the spot on his own. Worse, she did not know where Eddie was or whether he was safe. Her day had gone down hill each step of the way from the moment she'd put the ring on her finger.

She turned left along a quiet retail block off the tourist track and all closed up for the night. Half way down the block, as her heart started to slow its crazy beat, a shadow stepped from a doorway and fell into step next to her. She clutched her bag and held back a yelp.

"It's me," the shadow whispered.

Tara dared a glance his way. "Eddie! You gave me a total scare."

"What are you doing out alone so late, Tara?"

"Looking for you."

"Here I am." He had traded his daytime hat for a dark wool cap.

She glanced over her shoulder, but no one seemed to be following them. "Listen, I have to tell you something."

"You broke up with Justin?"

"Justin? No. Justin and I are actually engaged, sort of."

"But he's in Sweden."

"We Skyped."

Eddie halted under a streetlight. "I'm not buying it."

"I've got a ring and everything." She wanted him to keep

moving in case the security person was following, but Eddie didn't budge.

"How did he give you a ring over Skype?"

"Well...he..."

"Let me see this ring."

Tara held out her hand. Eddie's hand was cold and rough, but the little green heart flashed as bright as a traffic light at the contact. She caught her breath, waiting for it to speak. *Nothing.* When she looked up, Eddie shook his head.

"Not buying it. This ring is something else." He tapped the green stone with his finger. The next moment he turned his face into his sleeve and doubled over in a cough.

"Listen, I don't want to talk about the ring or Justin. I came to warn you. There was an incident outside the hotel today, and there's one hostile hotel security person camped out in your alley."

"Yeah, I spotted him. The guy goes heavy on the Old Spice. You need to get a cab home."

"Have you found another place?"

"Not a problem." The words ended in another burst of coughing.

Tara waited a minute while Eddie controlled the cough. She would bring him cough syrup in the morning.

"Can I use your phone to text Jack? He'll help me out."

Tara fished her phone out of her bag, relieved that Eddie could call his friend. He needed to get inside for the night. The phone lit up his face as he tapped in a number and a brief message. He looked ghastly. He handed the phone back, saying, "Thanks. That'll do the trick."

She pressed two cough drops into his palm, and his fingers curled around them.

"Where will I find you in the morning? You need some cough syrup."

"Never touch the stuff. Just roll with the punches, Tara girl."

Tara took a cab home from the Belmont to the back unit of her grandmother's house. The front unit with its view over the waterfront tourist attractions and the bay was leased to a couple from France, friends of her mother's who brought French paintings to San Francisco to sell. Sometimes her mother came, too, not often. As her mother pointed out, the point of sending Tara to the French school was precisely so that she could visit her mother in France.

Technically, her grandmother's property now belonged to her dad, but he was not interested in leaving southern California, so Tara managed the place and lived in the back unit. The front unit might be the more spectacular of the two, but for a single woman in the city, Tara could not complain. Her living room had a window seat that framed a view of trees and sky. Sometimes the wild parrots of Telegraph Hill swooped in and set up their chatter in those trees.

She dropped her bag on the window seat where Bingo Bear leaned against the pillows. She picked him up and held him in her lap as she sat looking out at the fog. She had forgiven him long ago for not living up to her expectations. It had not been Bingo's fault that she had imagined him capable of a kind of friendship he could not provide. She had learned to manage her expectations a lot better now. Bingo reminded her why Justin was perfect for her—no expectations, no disappointments.

Today she had lost her job. She had not realized it until now, but she had turned out to be like her parents after all. Love and friendship and loyalty were great ideals, but a job well done was life's real satisfaction. Since her break up with

Daniel, she had chosen work over marriage.

The thing was that one didn't really choose knowing all the options. Life wasn't like shopping or signing up for courses or ordering from a menu with all the choices in front of you. It was more like stepping from stone to stone in a rushing stream, concentrating on each precarious step, and discovering later that you had crossed from one side to the other. In her case the side she was on was the Belmont side, the career side. It was still a good side, better than the side she'd been on when she'd lived with Daniel.

If she'd had a setback today in one job, she'd get another one and carry on. She was good at what she did. She glanced at her ring. In the dim light on the window seat it seemed to have lost its glow. She shook her hand, but the color did not revive. Maybe she had misunderstood the directions in the little box. She took it out of her bag and put it on her window ledge, but she didn't open it.

She got up and tucked Bingo back in among the pillows. *No point in moping*, her grandmother would say. *Roll with the punches*, Eddie would say. Both were right. Be resilient, bounce back. It was only when she went to charge her phone that she realized why she wasn't moping. In fact, she was humming. She had chosen Eddie over her job, and it felt right.

Maybe that was what the ring meant to say when it sounded like Eddie. She glanced at it again, and the thing flashed with the surprising brightness of the moment under the streetlight with Eddie. What had he said? *That'll do the trick.* She saw the moment again clearly. He had been handing her the phone, not pocketing the cough drops. She checked her message queue, and there was Eddie's message—*Jack, now you've got her number, and she's got yours.*

Chapter Four

Through the Friday morning fog Tara spotted another concrete-faced hotel security guard lurking at the entrance to Eddie's alley. She kept walking through the mist. She told herself that Eddie was okay, but she had her doubts. She could see the headline: *Hotel Security Guard Shoots Homeless Vet.*

She offered Eddie's coffee and socks to the next homeless man she passed, who swore at her that he didn't need her stinking charity. She wished him good day and kept going. The more she thought about it, the more it worried her that Eddie hadn't used her phone to ask for his friend's help at all. Two cough drops were not going to fix that cold, and instead of seeking help, Eddie had set her up with his friend when she showed him her "engagement" ring. The ring was certainly changing her life, but it wasn't exactly like winning the lottery or getting a Publishers' Clearinghouse check for life. She tried not even to think of the "D" word, but she felt the day might be headed straight for disaster.

As soon as she reached her desk, the requests started coming. Even though it was low season, the Belmont was at nearly full occupancy. She helped two couples from the bridal party rent bikes and found the right tux in the right size for a six-four groomsman who had left his on a plane. Next she arranged for a departing guest to ship boxes of See's candy to everyone who helped care for her husband who had been hospitalized during their stay. As she made call after call, she was tempted to text the number Eddie had planted in her phone. Just to see whether Eddie and the mysterious Jack had connected.

As the morning passed, she also grew conscious of a lingering unease over Daniel's vision of the proposal moment. He wanted perfection, but he didn't seem to know anything about Nicola's tastes and preferences. The time on her phone told her the flower mart was long closed, so the florist would be committed to red roses, but now the color seemed all wrong to her.

Jack had a full day of patient appointments. He had no time for Eddie's games, and the text he'd received after midnight seemed like a game, a dare, the kind of taunt that fearless older Eddie had often tossed at Jack's younger self. He ignored it for most of the morning. People with real problems needed his attention. But the text kept popping into his mind.

Eddie had sent it from the girl's phone. Most nights, Jack was pretty sure, Eddie tucked himself away in a secure place by midnight. He had learned the lesson of that past beating well. Darkness made the homeless invisible to respectable citizens, but not to thugs who preyed on them. Jack wanted to think that Eddie had done the sensible thing and checked into a shelter, but he knew better. Eddie would stubbornly insist on his independence no matter the cost. Jack could not imagine the girl giving Eddie a place to stay. She might bring him coffee and socks, but she had a job at the upscale Belmont Hotel, and no high-end concierge would encourage a guy like Eddie to come near the guests.

By the time these thoughts had become a familiar refrain in his head, Jack had memorized the girl's number. All morning he held off calling, but when he didn't find Eddie in any of the usual places at lunch, he decided to try the number stuck in his brain.

Nicola Solari did look like Scarlett Johansson, sort of. She had Disney princess golden hair, pansy brown eyes, and a knockout figure. It took Tara less than a minute to realize why Daniel's red rose theme was all wrong. Nicola's favorite color was yellow, her fragrance was Chanel No. 5, and she liked bees. Tara glanced at Daniel. If he was oblivious of his beloved's tastes, it was not because she hid them.

Nicola wore a chrome yellow sleeveless bandage dress tighter than a mummy's wrapping that emphasized her curves. A gold honeycomb bracelet encircled one wrist, and an amber bee with golden wings dangled from a chain around her neck. The bee theme did not stop there, and Tara doubted that Nicola's bag could hold both a credit card and a postage stamp. *Where did she keep her phone?* Nicola might have an eleven-year-old fashion sensibility, but supported by an income in the one percent range, on her it looked terrific.

Tara had to admit that Daniel looked good, too. He had the right haircut for his longish face, a bit of masculine ruggedness in his facial hair, and the perfect green silk V-neck sweater for his hazel eyes and toned abs. It all looked a little calculated, but there was no question that Daniel looked good.

Clinging to Daniel's arm, Nicola looked around the hotel lobby and declared it, "Magic, just magic."

"You just wait, baby," Daniel promised. "It's going to be a perfect weekend."

Scratch the red roses. Tara had a true concierge challenge on her hands if Daniel's Tower Room proposal scene was going to wow his girlfriend.

While Arturo greeted them and Noah hovered at Nicola's side to organize their luggage, underlings loaded garment bags and suitcases onto a cart. As soon as the couple stepped over to the registration desk, Tara texted Hadley to have housekeeping change the duvet and pillows in their suite to pale gold. She called her florist to see what could be done to change the flowers for the proposal scene, and alerted Josephine in the kitchen that their most important guest was a big fan of yellow and of bees.

She thought she managed the encounter quite well. Daniel and Nicola might look photo-shoot perfect, but Tara didn't feel as bad as she'd expected to feel. After all, she had Justin.

While Arturo escorted Nicola up to their suite, Daniel took Tara aside. Her phone buzzed in her hand, and she glanced at the text on her screen. *Jack, here. Do you know where Eddie is?*

Daniel closed his hand over her phone. Nothing a guest did was supposed to shock her, but her immediate thought was decidedly un-concierge-like. She put her phone away with a smile, resisting the impulse to say what she thought. "Yes?"

"So, here's the plan, Keegan. We've got this afternoon to see some of the city and get some things done. Then tomorrow Nicola is competing for a spot on the runway in that big charity fashion show. She'll get her spot no problem, but that's your opportunity. While she's at the Fairmont, you can get everything set up here."

"Thanks, Daniel, we'll handle it. It's what we do." Her phone buzzed again. This time she ignored it.

"Did you get that Goorin Bros. appointment for me?"

"I did."

"Great." Daniel took off.

Her phone buzzed a third time, and Tara sent a quick text. *Don't know. Busy right now.*

From her desk, in between helping other guests, Tara checked with the florist, musicians, housekeeping, and the kitchen. She listened to a torrent of abuse from the florist about the impossibility of changing flowers eight hours after the flower mart closed, until she reminded him that it was Nicola Solari for whom he was rethinking his plans and calling in favors.

"Safeway," she told him. "Great roses." And hung up on his further pungent commentary.

Josephine, the consummate professional in the Belmont kitchen, simply called back with a new menu that included a pale yellow chardonnay, savory corn cakes, and chocolate cups with yellow sugar blooms and candied bees.

You're the best, Tara texted.

Am I? came a return text, and Tara realized she'd accidentally replied to Eddie's Jack person. *Still busy,* she texted.

She waved to Daniel as he left for his hat appointment and sent Hadley off at Nicola's request to help with the dress decision she was making. Still Jack's texts kept coming.

How busy?
Can't find Eddie in the usual places.
Hello. Where did you see him last?

She texted her persistent caller to try her at three and blocked the contact. One thing at a time. First fix Nicola's dream proposal scene, then think about Eddie. She was making headway at last with the florist when Daniel returned sporting a new fedora, winked at her, and went upstairs.

In five minutes he was back, hatless and distraught. "We have a problem. Your friend Hadley told Nicola that you are one of my exes."

"Does it matter?" *You have a problem.*

"Yes. It does. She needs to know that you are no competition for her."

"Really? Daniel, I'm sure you've explained that I'm no threat to her."

He paced in front of her desk, disarranging his perfect hair. Guests in the lobby looked their way, and she encouraged him to step into the area behind her desk so that she could shield their conversation from public notice. Behind her George talked with a male guest, and she sensed that the man wanted her attention. She told herself to be patient. One guest at a time, and Daniel was a guest.

"Daniel, you can tell her that I'm...engaged to someone else. Look, a ring." She waved her hand under his nose.

His monologue stopped abruptly. "Hey, wait a minute. So you are engaged now?"

Tara nodded. "Just yesterday. To my longtime significant other, Justin Wright." She extended her ring hand to show him the ring. *Okay, pay back was a little satisfying.*

His gaze flicked to the ring and glanced away unmoved. "Justin Wright? I've never heard of him. What does this guy do?"

"Daniel, it doesn't matter. What matters is that you can tell Nicola that you and I are over."

"Right. Right. But maybe I should meet this guy. No, I know. I've got it. Nicola has to see you with this Wright guy. When she sees you all tight with him, she'll relax."

"Daniel, as much as I would like to accommodate you in this matter, I really can't. Nicola will be occupied all day tomorrow; the hotel will have everything ready for your big moment; and you'll have to take it from there."

"Keegan, you don't get it. I've worked too hard to nail this thing. I'm not going to have the deal blown now."

Tara wondered whether Nicola knew that she was a *deal* that had to be *nailed*. "You could try a different hotel. That would show her that she's first in your affections."

He shook his head. "We have to have that view. That view is..." he struggled for a word...

"Magic?"

He nodded. "Seriously, call this guy, text him."

"She already has." The deep, slightly familiar voice came from behind her.

Tara and Daniel turned. And once again Tara tried to keep from gaping. The voice belonged to the tall stranger named Jack with the steady blue eyes. He stuck out his hand toward Daniel and looked to Tara for help. "Hi, hon, got your text."

"My text?" *Hon? He was that Jack? Eddie's Jack?*

"Texts, actually. I came as soon as I could. I know you wanted to see me." His look told her to play along.

"Right. Sorry. Let me introduce you." She stepped up beside him, hoping he knew what he was doing. "This is..."

"Justin, Tara's fiancé."

Oh, he was smooth and gorgeous. And she had to be grateful. Daniel was definitely more impressed by Jack than by the ring.

The two men shook hands in that measuring way that men had of sizing up a competitor or a rival. She could see Daniel's mental process in his eyes. He didn't like being replaced by a tall good-looking man, but a tall good-looking man would convince Nicola. Jack merely looked amused.

"Justin Wright, Daniel Lynch." Tara finished. The stranger drew her into a hug against his side. She felt his height, his very solid person, and his strength. She had not made Justin quite so tall or such a good hugger. She had to admit that a fake boyfriend definitely lacked in the hug department.

"Great," said Daniel. He plainly did not like looking up to *Justin*. "Do you two have plans?"

"Well," the stranger looked at Tara. "We have something to do when Tara gets off, and then we're going…" Tara waited to hear what he would say. Daniel was paying close attention. Jack would not say that they were going to search for a lost homeless man. "…kayaking."

Tara could not have heard him right. She turned, and he put his fingers under her chin and tilted her face up to his, smiling down at her, slightly amused, as if he had not just suggested that they were going to take to the bay's treacherous waters in the equivalent of a nautical endive canapé, a vessel so small it would be no more than a floating emery board to passing tankers and cargo ships. The bay had bigger sharks and sea lions.

Daniel frowned. "Just hang on a few minutes, will you? You've got to meet Nicola."

The stranger winked at Tara and looked at his watch. "Gotta run. We've got only about an hour of daylight left."

Daniel was thinking, hesitating. "Huh, kayaking. I don't think that's Nicola's thing."

"It's a two-man boat." The stranger's voice made the non-invitation plain.

"Right. Let me just get Nicola."

Daniel dashed for the elevator, and Tara stepped out of the stranger's hold, and immediately missed it. "Kayaking?"

"You don't want him to come with us, do you?"

"Us?"

"While we look for Eddie." He seemed to feel that she understood the plan.

Oh, they were not actually kayaking. "You're Eddie's Jack?"

"Yes. Hello." He shook her hand. "At the moment, I'm your Justin. You seemed to be in need of Justin. And he's away, according to Eddie."

"Right, but..."

"Any idea where Eddie is?"

"None." She was worried about him, but she was also worried that Jennifer or Hadley would show up any minute and recognize this man as the man she'd bumped into the night before.

"He could be playing a game with us, but..."

Another guest appeared at her desk, and Tara helped him with theater tickets and dinner reservations while Jack watched. Her brain kept thinking about Hadley with Nicola. If Daniel explained that he wanted Nicola to meet Justin in the lobby, Hadley would find a way to get downstairs.

Tara could see the headline: *Lovelorn Lady Concierge Creates Fake Boyfriend. Fraud Exposed.*

She heard the elevator doors open and turned to see Daniel and Nicola coming across the lobby. Nicola had changed into a sweet, pale yellow dress suitable for tea with British royalty, and Daniel had a possessive hand at the small of her back.

Tara stole a glance at Jack as his gaze took in the pair. His expression suggested nothing more than polite curiosity. Daniel did the introductions, and Jack smiled and shook Nicola's hand, as if his brain were still working. In fact, Nicola seemed more interested in Jack than he in her.

"I think we must have met." She plainly expected him to

agree.

Jack shook his head. "Unlikely. I'm a consultant. I travel a lot. It's tough on Tara." He squeezed her against his side again. He was taking advantage, but his hugs were dangerous. They woke up a slumbering tactile sense in Tara that craved more.

Nicola frowned. She obviously had little experience with being contradicted. "No. You don't have a fiancée," she told him.

"I beg your pardon." Jack might be smiling, but she heard the steel in his voice. "Tara and I are engaged."

Tara held up her hand with the Claddagh ring to back him up. It looked like nothing, twisted to one side so the stone was hidden between her fingers.

Nicola shook her head at Jack, ignoring Tara. "Never mind, I'll remember you."

Daniel took over. "Congratulations, both of you. Good to meet you, Wright," he said, putting a pointed end to the conversation. He drew Nicola toward the elevators and leaned to whisper in her ear.

As soon as the other couple crossed the lobby, Tara stepped away from Jack. "You have to leave now. I don't want anyone to see you."

His eyes turned cold and distant, as if she'd slapped him, and his mouth tightened into a grim line that made her take a step back. His face without the grin had a harsh knowing quality, not mocking exactly but penetrating and disapproving. She was letting him down.

"Right. So much for *thank you*. You were with Eddie at midnight. Just tell me where you last saw him."

"I'll draw you a map." She drew a quick street map on a hotel note pad and handed it to him.

He glanced at it and tossed it back on the desk. She felt

the buzz of her phone receiving another text. Hadley could show up any minute. She needed him to leave now, but she hated the look in his eyes. He had just done her a favor, and she'd let him down. She stuck out her hand. "Good luck finding Eddie."

He ignored her hand, turned without another word, and was gone before she could understand his parting look. It felt like that wild moment of driving down the hill with the fire chasing them when everything was about to be lost.

She pressed her hands together to stop the crazy feeling. The stone heart bit into her finger. She twisted the ring back into place. *What are you doing?* The emerald was the color of cactus. She would be crazy to listen to the thing, but she was in motion before she finished the thought.

Jack felt like a prize idiot. When he'd seen his beautiful bag lady in trouble, being harassed by the guy with the super-sized ego, he'd stepped right into the fray. The softly rounded face, with the slightly flustered look of a woman who'd misplaced some vital possession, had already caught his attention twice. Each time he saw her, some protective instinct kicked in, and if he were totally honest, a possessive one. He'd tried to be a hero and instead he'd fallen for an Eddie game.

It was clear the girl wasn't in on it. She was in the middle of her job, satisfying the whims of the rich and the beautiful. But she had made things worse by accepting Jack's help one minute and then turning on him the next. Against his side she had felt so right, an armful of sweetness. He had expected Daniel to produce a beautiful, shallow girlfriend. Five minutes with the guy made that clear, but he hadn't expected his sweet bag lady to turn on him. When she stepped back, her expression told him plainly that she was in command, dealing with the city's elite, and that he was in the way. He would bet that whoever her absent fiancé was, he was not a farm boy who'd worked his way from overalls to scrubs.

Jack wasn't usually so wrong about people, but apparently Eddie's disappearance had clouded his judgment. He realized he was wandering hopelessly in the fog. He needed to bring some method to his search. Even if Eddie was messing with him, his gut said that Eddie needed help.

Outside the fog lay so low the tops of buildings disappeared. Tara caught up with Jack on the steps of the big white church of Saints Peter and Paul on Washington Square in the heart of North Beach. He was looking out across the square of lawn and trees in front of the church. A class of elderly people moved in the slow motion of Tai Chi to the mournful strums and plinks of ancient instruments. Dog walkers gathered in companionable groups, and a few huddled figures claimed the benches. There was no sign of Eddie.

"Hello." She halted at the base of the steps, looking up.

He frowned down at her.

"Can we start over? I want to help."

"Why?" He came down a step. "A concierge at a fancy hotel is the last person to care about Eddie."

"He's my friend, or at least, I'm his friend." Cold air swirled around them while she waited for his reply.

"I tried all the places I usually find him." It was a confession of frustration.

"Did you try the libraries? There's a branch in North Beach and one in Chinatown."

He was down the steps in a flash, taking her arm and asking her the way. They headed down Columbus, the main thoroughfare of the city's Italian neighborhood.

He cast her a measuring glance. "It's not easy to be Eddie's friend."

"Actually, Eddie has been a friend to me. Most days he makes me feel like I can take on the world. I met him after my grandmother's death. He sort of took her place as wise older person."

"You do know that's a bit ironic."

"Because he doesn't have his own life together?"

"Something like that."

A librarian at the North Beach branch library knew Eddie, but had not seen him for several days. "He comes in to read the *Times*," she told them.

Outside again, it was already dark. A crowded cable car made the turn from Columbus onto Mason. They reversed their steps and headed back up into the heart of North Beach. Jack's furrowed brow and hurried stride told her how concerned he was for their missing friend.

"Why do you care about Eddie?" *So much.* He was not at all what she had expected in a friend of Eddie's. Eddie made no secret of his blue-collar roots, while his friend was perfectly at ease in a suit and tie.

They worked their way through a group of tourists before he answered. When he did, his easy manner of speaking had changed, become clipped, the humor gone. "We lived together for awhile when he came back from the army in Iraq."

Tara guessed the arrangement had not worked well. The confident professional beside her seemed to come from an entirely different world from the one Eddie inhabited. She could not conceive how they met, or rather she could conceive of Eddie initiating a conversation, but not Jack, the employed one, inviting Eddie to live with him. "Was he injured in Iraq?"

"He had been concussed a lot, like those pro football players you hear about, and he saw stuff that's hard to forget."

"It didn't work out, your living together?"

"Ended badly."

"So he went on the streets?"

"Yes, and he got beat up." His pace seemed to pick up as they spoke.

She was probing, but instinct told her he needed to be pushed on this. "And you blame yourself?"

"I do."

Tara swung around in front of him and put a hand to his chest, stopping him. She needed to catch her breath from their charge up Columbus. Their gazes collided, and she read the depth of self-blame in his. "I know Eddie would take his share of the blame."

"Maybe, but I'm supposed to be the…"

"The what?" Her question came out through chattering teeth.

"Never mind. There's another place I want to try, but first, you're freezing."

"I'm okay." Her whole body shuddered.

"Come on."

He stopped at a known tourist trap restaurant and stuck her under an outdoor heat stand by a cluster of tables. "Stay." He disappeared into the shop and came out minutes later with a black hooded sweatshirt, a red restaurant logo emblazoned across the front. He made her put her bag down.

"Lift your arms."

She complied, and he pulled the sweatshirt down over her head. The thing came down to her knees and it felt blissful, soft and warm. She looked up to thank him, and he looked down at her with a look that acknowledged a new togetherness between them. He pulled the hood up over her hair, tucking in a few loose strands, his fingers warm against her cold cheeks. His hands cupped her face and lingered there.

Then he let them fall. "Onward?"

She nodded.

They checked the famous Beat bookstore and then the café where so many waves of San Francisco's Bohemian writers and poets had lingered over espressos. Jack's suit and tie looked professional, but his easy way of disarming people and entering into conversation with them was something else. It made her believe that he and Eddie could have been roommates after all. Jack had the same affable manner that had drawn her to Eddie. She supposed she shouldn't wonder at their friendship. Eddie seemed capable of making friends with anyone, except, of course, George or Arturo.

"A few of these guys know Eddie, but no one's seen him today." Jack thrust his hands into his slacks pockets, out of ideas. "He's a mechanic, you know. He can fix anything with moving parts. When his hands aren't shaking."

They stood looking into the deepening gloom with the bright glow of the café behind them. Eddie was out there somewhere. Coughing.

Tara pictured him as she'd last seen him with his worn coat and his wool cap, his backpack on his back. "Eddie always makes me think of a backpacker headed for the mountains. He could be up in the trees around Coit Tower. We haven't tried there."

That grin she was coming to know flashed on Jack's face. "You're on." He grabbed her hand, and they headed back through North Beach up Telegraph Hill. He was in a hurry again, and she struggled to keep up, stumbling as their quick pace kept jolting her bag off her shoulder, down her arm.

He stopped abruptly at the base of a steep block and glared at her bag.

She clutched it to her chest.

"You're carrying Santa's pack there. You'll never make it to the tower."

She shook her head. "We're almost there. I've got it."

"Come on," he said, reaching for the bag. "Think you can lighten the load?"

Tara closed her arms tighter around the bag. She shook her head. "What if something happens?"

He let his hands fall to his sides, studying her. "Anything irreplaceable in there?"

"I don't like to lose things."

"Lost a lot, have you?"

She swallowed. "My house in a fire."

Once again Jack studied her, and she had the sensation of being seen and understood.

"All right then. Give me the bag."

She found herself letting go, passing it over to him, trusting him.

He thrust his arm through the straps and headed up the street. Tara started after him, feeling remarkably light footed.

From the top of Telegraph Hill, Coit Tower shone eerily in the fog like some Star Wars special effect. A few tourists still lingered to look at the murals and peer into the mist at distant lights across the bay. Tara took back her bag and extracted her flashlight, handing it to Jack. They walked the perimeter of the grounds peering into and under the foliage.

Tower security approached to question them, and Jack said, "We're looking for a lost cat. A calico."

Once they had gone completely around the area, Tara admitted to feeling discouraged. The tourists were gone; the place closed up. She was cold from the inside out. "We aren't going to find him, are we?"

"Not tonight. I think that's what he wants."

"He wants us to wander around worried to death that he's ill or injured or freezing?"

Jack took her cold hands in his warm ones and held them. He rubbed his thumb over the ring on her finger. "That's not quite how I would put it. He wanted us to meet, to work together, to get to know each other." He laughed. "I don't know why he wanted that. He told me you had a boyfriend."

"What did he tell you?"

"That he had the girl for me." He straightened the ring on her finger. "I guess he didn't know your guy had proposed."

"Actually, I showed him the ring. Last night." *And he sent the text because of the ring. He sent the text to stop my engagement.*

"I'm glad that guy's out of town. I'm glad I got to be your fake fiancé for a day, Tara Keegan."

Fake fiancé. The ring felt warm, almost hot, under Jack's thumb. She looked up into those eyes of his. She could not see the blue of them, but she did not need light to see the warmth in them.

Tell him. He's the one.

It was her moment, her chance to confess. She leaned toward him. *Actually, there is no Justin. I made him up. I'm free. We could start something.* But she couldn't do it. He looked so confident and competent and honest and good, and she felt like such a fraud, and so unworthy of him with her made-up fiancé and her bag of hedges against disaster.

He didn't seem to realize how foolish she was. He seemed to take her leaning toward him as an invitation.

"Hell," he said, "Sorry, Justin. This one's for me." His hands slid up her arms and closed around her shoulders. And he kissed her. His kiss consumed the cold and disappointment of the moment before. It erased worry and doubt. It claimed the time they'd spent together for them and no one else, forever.

It was her first kiss in years. Tara told herself not to lose her head, not let her brain melt and dribble out her ears. It was a goodbye kiss after all, even if it felt like a hello.

He released her. She wasn't cold anymore; she was burning up, her face aflame with embarrassment. She ducked her chin into the sweatshirt hood. At least it was dark. He couldn't see her flushed cheeks. Making up Justin, lying to everyone seemed like the dumbest thing she had ever done. If he knew, he would look at her with mocking contempt.

"Listen," he said. "Let's get you home. Do you have to work tomorrow?"

She nodded.

"I'll text you when I find him."

"Yes, please. And may I text you if I see him?"

"Sure."

"Good." Her bag felt heavy on her shoulder.

Hours later Tara sat in her window seat, holding her bear, trying to figure out how she had gone so wrong in her search for happiness. Before now it had never seemed wrong or harmful to pretend she had a boyfriend. Justin had been her strategy for deflecting her friends' sympathy and concern. He had been her way of entering conversations about men or relationships, and avoiding having her hopes dashed at the end of a promising evening. She had met no one who made her regret inventing him. Now the pretense came with a price.

Daniel was going to have his "magic" moment. She had settled for illusion. The green stone looked like a dead leaf, a withered green. She ought to put it back in its box and get on with her life. She pinched it between her thumb and forefinger and pulled, but the thing stuck on her knuckle.

Well, she could wear it two more days, until they found Eddie, and until she saw her last Belmont guests out the door, and then she would dump Justin and start over. If she had missed her chance with Jack, that was the price she had to pay for her deception. She looked at the ring to see whether it had brightened at her new plan.

Nope.

Chapter Five

Tara received two texts before seven a.m., neither of them from Jack. The first was from Jennifer saying she was out sick, and asking if Tara could do part of her shift. The second was from Arturo telling her to be at the hotel for Jennifer's shift. At the registration desk, she checked departing guests out while sneaking frequent peaks at her phone. She had unblocked Jack, so he could let her know when he found Eddie. She knew he had not stopped looking.

During a lull, Hadley insisted that Tara come upstairs to look at the Tower Room, where the florist had come through with dozens of yellow roses and banks of yellow and white primroses making a garden path to the view of Coit Tower in the fog.

"Imagine having a boyfriend who spends a fortune to give you all your favorite things. He must be so in love with her." Hadley's Tinder guy was already history.

At three Arturo switched Tara from registration to her usual station at the concierge desk. He was treating Daniel's proposal party as a coup for the hotel and insisted that she double-check all the preparations. He clapped his hands to hurry any bellmen not moving their lingering guests along fast enough.

As the last of the hotel's other guests checked out, Daniel's friends and family began to arrive. Arturo hustled them into concealment in the conference room where they were to wait over wine and cheese for the signal to join the engaged couple in the Tower Room. He made a special effort for Nicola's prominent parents, and Tara kept her head down as Daniel's parents arrived. Arturo emerged from the conference room beaming with the triumph of having gathered such illustrious guests in his hotel. No one seemed to think that Nicola might say no. By four the fog had lightened just enough to promise a red and gold sunset. Tara had not heard from Jack.

The lobby was dead about thirty minutes before sunset when Tara got a text from Daniel that he and Nicola were on their way. Tara relayed the message to Arturo. Everyone got into position out of sight but ready to assist.

At fifteen minutes to sunset, right on schedule, Daniel's town car pulled up. Tara slipped into the background next to Arturo. George held the door open as Daniel and Nicola, absorbed in each other, passed through a lobby as empty as the Beast's castle. In the hush, the buzz of a text on Tara's phone made Arturo turn and glare. Tara looked at the message feeling instant relief then confusion.

Eddie's at your door.

She looked through the open lobby door to the street. *Eddie? Here?*

Daniel and Nicola had reached the middle of the lobby. Once they turned for the elevators, Tara could slip behind them for the door. Even as the thought occurred, she saw Eddie, framed in the doorway, poised to come in. She wanted to shout to him to wait, that she would come out, but he slipped past George and lurched into the lobby.

Tara took a step toward him, a hand outstretched, causing George's gaze to flicker her way. Arturo grabbed her wrist and hissed at her. Oblivious, Eddie angled his unsteady steps her way, until a cough doubled him over. At the sound of the cough, George turned and lunged for Eddie, a gloved hand reaching for his collar. Eddie simply crumpled, as quietly as if he were made of rags. George's hand closed on air. Eddie hit the rug with a thump.

Tara shook off Arturo and went down on her knees at Eddie's side.

"I brought Jack to you." Eddie's voice croaked in the perfectly silent lobby, and his eyes rolled back in his head. Tara called to him and leaned down to check his breathing.

Arturo stood over her. "Move aside, Ms. Keegan." She looked up as he signaled George to move to Eddie's feet. "George, call security. Let's get this fellow out of here."

With her hands on Eddie's shoulders keeping him in place, Tara looked straight at George. "Call 9-1-1." She did not break eye contact until George punched the number into his phone.

She hunched over to check Eddie's breathing again. "Can you hear me?"

"Ms. Keegan," Arturo insisted. "This man does not belong here. You will move aside." George stood at Eddie's muddied boots in his immaculate Belmont uniform. Arturo, reaching for Eddie's shoulders, hesitated, with an obvious reluctance to touch him.

A security man arrived, his shoulders the width of an SUV. He pushed Arturo aside and reached down to grab Eddie beneath the arms. "Back to the street you go, buddy."

Tara leaned over Eddie. They would have to toss her out, too.

Jack passed through the untended hotel door. One glance

took in the scene. Eddie lay in a heap on the expensive carpet with leaves in his hair and salty lines of dried sweat down the sides of his face. His body twitched, but he was breathing. Tara Keegan had flung herself across his trunk, in her eyes a fierce flash of determination to protect him from the three men who stood ready to heave his unconscious body out onto the pavement.

Jack took a careful step forward, a volatile mix of love and anger churning in him, aware that he might hit someone if he moved any faster. "Move that man, and you answer to me."

All pairs of eyes turned to him. The security man dropped his hold. The uniformed functionary raised his hands and backed away. The guy in the suit sputtered something about the hotel not being responsible for trespassers.

Jack stared them down. "I'm a doctor. I say when this man may be moved."

He waited for them to retreat and make enough space around Eddie and Tara for him to go to work. The lobby was oddly empty except for the couple, Daniel and Nicola. Jack could not conceive what they were doing, standing there watching. The atmosphere felt charged with anticipation.

His gaze met Nicola's, and he saw recognition there.

She pointed at him, shaking her head, and then at Tara. "He's not her fiancé, you know. He's single. He's from the Mr. Single San Francisco contest. I saw his picture. His name is Jack Reeder, Doctor Jack Reeder."

"He's breathing, Jack." Tara's voice drew his gaze back to Eddie.

Jack knelt at her side. He opened Eddie's coat and checked the pulse in his throat. Eddie was alive. Jack steadied himself. He just had to find the injury or illness. He ran his hands lightly over Eddie's head, keeping his movements both calm and assessing. He talked to Eddie the whole time, telling him what he was doing.

From the other side of the room he heard Daniel speak in an urgent whisper to Nicola. "Baby. Whatever. It's not our concern. I've got something I want you to see upstairs. It's...magic."

His pleading voice seemed to reach her. "Magic?"

Daniel's voice came again. "It's a surprise. Let me show you."

Jack kept his concentration on Eddie. "Help me get him on his side."

Together they rolled Eddie over, and Jack tilted his head back, checking once more for breathing. He lifted Eddie's eyelids and continued his examination of Eddie's limbs and trunk.

When the paramedics arrived, Jack again identified himself as a doctor, and explained what he'd observed. For a few minutes they worked together. Then they had Eddie on a gurney, hooked up to an IV, and ready to move.

With a glance at her badge, one of the paramedics turned to Tara. "Does anybody know who this guy is?"

She started to answer, but Jack was first. "His name is Edward Reeder. He's my brother."

His gaze met her shocked one over the gurney. He could imagine what she thought, the woman to whom Eddie had turned in his illness, the woman who hadn't hesitated to throw her body over his brother's, while he, who was supposed to be his brother's keeper, had failed to keep him from the streets. The naked exchange of glances between them ended, and Jack followed the gurney to the waiting ambulance.

***

Tara did not know what had just happened. She and Jack had been working together, hands and hearts focused on Eddie. Then the gurney had been between them, and Jack had confessed his true connection to Eddie. They should be closer than ever, and yet he'd looked at her as if an ocean of regret separated them.

She stood staring after them until Arturo stepped in front of her and snatched the badge from her lapel. "You no longer need this, Ms. Keegan," he said through clenched teeth. He drew himself up, his shoulders back, head high. "You're done here. Finished. At the Belmont we have the highest standards of hospitality. Our duty is to our guests. We offer romance. We do not permit homeless trespassers to bring sickness and filth into our hotel. We don't tolerate any interference with our guests' comfort and security."

Tara could see the ambulance doors closing. Arturo believed every word he said. It was the code he lived by, but he didn't really get hospitality, after all. "Eddie was a guest, Arturo. He was my guest. He needed and deserved my hospitality, so I gave it to him. Keep the badge."

She grabbed her phone, and dashed for the curb. A red-orange sunset lit up the windows of North Beach and the slender white tower on the hill. Daniel would be proposing to Nicola. Tara hoped that the view, the cascade of yellow roses, the pretty tables, the delicious food were all the magic they needed. But she did not envy them. They needed *things* to make their romance happen. She needed something else, some*one* else.

She banged on the side of the ambulance. The hunky paramedic in the passenger seat lowered his window. "Sorry, miss. No one rides in the ambulance but family."

"Where are you taking him?"

He shouted an answer as the ambulance pulled away.

Behind her the sun had set, leaving the west-facing windows of Telegraph Hill gray again in the fog. From the hotel a cheer went up. She glanced back and saw Daniel's friends swarm through the lobby toward the elevators, like sports fans celebrating a victory.

George closed the hotel door on the happy din.

Waiting for Jack, Tara had lots of time to think, and an ER waiting room was precisely the place to realize she wanted something quite different from the Mr. Wright she'd created in her head. The ER was as shabby and functional as the Belmont was elegant and luxurious. The harassed woman checking people in was a concierge in a way, helping people get their needs met. She didn't get to wear a chic suit or sit at a Chippendale desk. Instead she listened to people and met their needs with linoleum squares under her feet, perforated ceiling tiles overhead, and the smell of strong cleaning solution like a miasma over all. The only glamor about the place was in the glossy photos of celebrities on the tattered covers of last month's magazines.

Emergency room hospitality looked and smelled different from Belmont hospitality, but Tara recognized it as genuine hospitality. The ER took in everybody from Eddie to Daniel. You didn't need designer clothes or endless wealth to get a room. You just needed to be a human being in need. That was your ultimate claim on other people's compassion and help. Arturo's standard of hospitality was not the highest after all.

The ER was also a good place to realize that she wanted an ordinary man, a man without fancy labels or big deals to make him important in the world, a man who would buy a girl a sweatshirt when she was cold and shoulder her too-heavy bag, a man who needed her help and wanted to work with her, a man who could be harder on himself than on others. She wanted Jack.

She glanced at the ring on her finger. She had never seen it flash so bright. Its green was about hope, about fresh blades of grass, new leaves, the first buds of elm trees, and traffic lights that blinked *Go!* after eons of gridlock.

When Jack emerged from the examining rooms hours later, he looked dazed and surprised to see her, but she had never felt more clear. She stood and went to him.

"How is he?"

"He's dehydrated, which is probably why he passed out. And he has pneumonia, with a complication called pericarditis, an inflammation of the sac around the heart."

"Which means?"

"They've admitted him. They'll give him fluids and antibiotics, and he'll get better." He gave her a smile as tired as the wrinkled suit he had been wearing for twenty-four hours. She wanted to see him in jeans and a sweater, with his grin restored.

"Did you talk to him?"

"He wants to talk to you." He sank into one of the orange plastic chairs. "I let him down again."

The waiting room was momentarily empty. She sat beside him and considered what to say. He had not let anyone down. He couldn't. He was a man who took action, a man who wouldn't quit on a friend, or back down, or leave anyone behind, not even his homeless brother.

"Tell me," she said.

Jack leaned forward, his hands dangling between his knees. "I'm a doctor. I have knowledge and skills. I help people every day, but I couldn't help my brother. Instead I lost him to the streets." He looked at his hands as if they disgusted him. "It makes me feel..."

"Helpless?"

He nodded.

"What makes you think you let him down?" She reached over and pulled one of his hands into her lap.

He looked up. "He went to you, not me."

Tara let out a long slow breath. Jack had no idea. She was going to have to tell him the truth, and maybe she would lose him yet. She started with the easy part. "It's easy for Eddie to come to me. Eddie knows I need him. He knows I don't have it all together."

"You?" His look was plainly incredulous. "With your suits and your job, and that bag that has more stuff in it than an Ikea store."

She nodded. "Eddie thinks *you* don't need *him*. He's the one who feels useless. He is supposed to be the older brother, isn't he? He was your hero, once, wasn't he?"

Jack nodded. "In high school. He was a three-sport, all league, MVP kind of guy, and a flirt as well."

"But now he can't be your hero because you're successful and confident and capable, and he's a homeless guy."

He shot her a sharp glance. "I thought that once. That was part of the problem between us, but I was wrong. You didn't judge him by his circumstances. You didn't ever see him as just a homeless guy, did you?"

"I did for about thirty seconds that first day before we started talking. He sized me up in minutes. With me, he's always been the honest one, the fearless one. If he wants to see me now, it's because he wants me to be that way too."

He looked to her for explanation.

"Let's go find him. You'll see."

They had no trouble finding Eddie's room. People on the

hospital staff greeted Jack and pointed the way. Most offered to look in on his brother in the heart unit.

In Eddie's room Jack checked his chart.

"How do I look, doc?" Eddie leaned back against the pillows of the raised bed surrounded by blinking machines that hummed and beeped. Someone had combed the leaves out of his hair.

"You're hooked up to an IV wearing a hospital gown— you've looked worse. What were you thinking?"

"Desperate times call for desperate measures." Eddie didn't lift his head, but he looked closely at them. "I got you two together."

They nodded in sync, and Jack pulled her against his side. *Ooh, it felt good to be there.*

Eddie looked straight at her. "Did you tell him the truth?"

"I plan to. How did you know?"

"About your phony Mr. Wright? Mr. Wrong, I'd say. Give me some credit for brains, girl. All the time you were sending Justin around the globe, you never looked like a woman who was giving or getting any loving."

"Wait." Jack turned Tara's face up to his. "There's no Justin?"

"So there's a look?" Tara tilted her head toward Eddie, trying to keep her cool, but Jack's expression did unsettling things to her female parts.

"There's a glow." Eddie reached out his hand with its orange plastic ID strip and IV port. "Show me that ring."

Tara offered him her hand. Jack watched her closely.

"There we go." Eddie's excitement caused his bed to beep like a backing truck. "That's the ticket. Look at that thing, lit up like a ballpark for a night game."

They got the bed to stop beeping, and as they turned to

leave, Eddie called out, "Hey, get my brother into bed. He's exhausted."

Good idea.

Tara had no trouble convincing Jack to come to her place. He stumbled over the threshold, caught himself, and apologized for falling asleep in the cab. He had spent the previous night going from ER to ER in his search for Eddie. Inside she steered him through her little living room and into the bedroom. She pushed him and he collapsed on the bed. "Sleep," she commanded.

"I will, but don't think I've forgotten that there's no Justin and that you have explaining to do."

"It can wait until morning."

His eyes drifted down. "I'm not sleeping alone."

"You're not?"

He reached out and snagged her hand. "No more elevator doors closing or ambulances driving off. You're with me now."

"I am," she confirmed, and let him pull her down on the bed. He rolled her into his embrace and kissed her thoroughly until she felt his arms go slack as sleep claimed him.

He woke once more as Tara was arranging a quilt over him, and took hold of her hand. "We won't make love until you're ready, but if you could feel ready by tomorrow, that would not be too soon."

When Tara came out of her kitchen in the morning, she found Jack in her window seat, examining Bingo with the same attentive, curious touch he'd used on Eddie. She felt suddenly awkward with her untold truth and the desire he'd confessed about wanting to make love to her.

"Tell me about the fire," he said. He patted the bench beside him. She had forgotten that she'd mentioned the fire to him. She started to sit primly on the edge of the bench, but he pulled her into his arms, so that she leaned back against him, nestled between his legs. She admired his bare feet.

"I was eleven," she began and then could hardly stop. The story tumbled out of her from the first wisp of smoke to their last visit to the ashy ruins of their house. His arms held her the whole time.

"Did you get a new bike?"

She shook her head. "My mother said I could make a list of twenty-five things I'd lost, for the insurance claim. I kept playing with the list, remembering things. In the end, I didn't put the bike on the list. I didn't think I would ride it in the city."

"And this guy?" He held her bear. "Why did you pick him?"

"Oh, Bingo didn't come from the fire. He was here with my grandmother. She had given him to me one Christmas, and I'd rejected him for not matching my fantasy of a talking animal friend."

"So he was here after the fire." Jack pulled the string on Bingo's back, and his recorded voice said, *I want a hug.*

"He was the Justin of my childhood." It was the closest she had come to the truth she still had to tell him.

"Ah." He put the bear aside and closed his arms around her, holding her, waiting. She didn't know how much he'd figured out, but the moment had come.

"There is no Justin. I made him up."

"What do you mean, you made him up?"

"He's a fiction. I was no good at dating. It felt so up and

down, like investing in an emotional stock market, where I was bound to lose every time. I'd come home from a date with my hopes raised and a text would dash them the next time I looked at my phone. Even if I had five dates in a row with the same man, the whole relationship would suddenly collapse with no explanation. I decided to invent a romance that went the way it should go."

She should feel mortified at the revelation of the lie, the silly pretense that she'd clung to for so long, but she felt free, as if she'd stepped out of hiding into the open. She waited a suspended heartbeat for Jack to speak.

"So what was Justin like?"

And just like that, Jack let her know that he understood.

"Why do you want to know?"

"I just want to know what I'm up against. What if he was a Justin Timberlake clone, or a super chef?"

"He did dance. He took me to lots of great restaurants. He sent me my favorite chocolates and flowers. Are you worried?"

"No. If that's all he's got, I think I've got the edge, a secret advantage." His arms tightened around her.

"What?" She twisted in his hold to look at him.

"I'll tell you later." He took her hand in his. "So where did the ring come from?"

From the window ledge she took the red box and handed it to him. He opened it and read the little paper. She leaned back against his shoulder. The parrots arrived and set up their squawking.

He lifted the hand that wore the ring and kissed the green stone. "I owe this little heart a lot."

Later they took the muni across town to feed Jack's dog, a yellow lab, whom Jack introduced as his secret advantage. Watson squirmed to be petted by Jack, and Tara understood how the dog felt to be on the receiving end of Jack's touch. Jack sent an email to his partner about some contest he had to bow out of. He showered and changed into jeans and a sweater while Tara explored his apartment and befriended his dog. Then they walked Watson and visited Eddie, who was sitting up, eating, and making plans to get out of the hospital as quick as he could. He and Carol, the night nurse, were great friends. One of the aides, Lynn, had helped him wash his hair and shave, and he winked at Tara and vowed to make a conquest of the no-nonsense day nurse, Barbara.

Then Jack proposed kayaking, and somehow Tara agreed, floating along without any resistance to his plans on a current of happiness, until they actually stood on the dock looking down into the bright yellow shell bobbing in the water.

Jack took in the doubtful look on her face. "It's a kayak. My kayak."

"I know what it is." What had she agreed to? She realized she stood between him and a floating coffee stirrer. A surfboard was wider. She clutched her bag to her chest.

"You can't take a cargo container on a kayak."

"Are you referring to my bag?"

"That's not a bag. It's a storage locker. You don't need it. You can never lose the things you keep in your heart."

She glanced over her shoulder. He understood her so well. "What happens if the thing tips over?"

"We get wet."

"What about sharks and hypothermia and drowning?"

"Try not to let them spoil the fun."

"Seriously, there must be safety lessons."

"There are. You learn to roll with the—"

"—punches?"

"Actually," he took her by the hips, "the thing you have

to learn is called a hip snap." His hands applied a gentle pressure, and she felt her hips tip as if she were doing a Hawaiian dance, then back. "Only quicker. Under water."

His hands on her hips almost made her forget that they could drown. Then she remembered. And something more, something she'd locked away and kept inside for so long that she'd forgotten it was there, something that she had denied for far too long, had to come out.

"Wait. There is something I have to say before...before we take off."

"I'm listening."

He looked so good then, so real and honest and brave. She liked the way the faint brightness of sun through the fog brought out the squint lines around his eyes and the way the cold air pressed the worn denim of his jeans against his lean, muscled legs. There was a risk she had to take, a hope she had to go for.

She put her bag down on the dock. "People can say what they like about marriage as a failed institution. Moms and dads can divorce each other. Novelists can write that marriage is the 'death of self and possibility.' But I want it. I want a dog and a porch, and a bicycle and babies. I want a union of true hearts, friendship, loyalty, and love, like this crazy ring." She waved the ring in front of his face.

Jack caught her by the shoulders in a tight grip. "Are you proposing to me?"

A distant foghorn sounded its deep bass note. A gull cried. Tara laughed. "No. You are supposed to propose to me."

"Well, then, Tara Keegan, you'd better stop talking so I can get on with it."

"Wait. You can't be proposing to me. We've known each other less than three days."

"Listen to your heart." He released her shoulders and took her hand, the hand with the magic ring and pressed it close to her heart, and closed his own big warm hand over hers.

She closed her eyes and let the sounds of the city around her fade into the white nothing of the fog itself, opening her ears for that inner voice, the one she couldn't quite hear whenever she demanded that the ring speak. But under the ring where she felt its ridge against her chest, she felt her own heart beat. When she opened her eyes, he was still there, real and solid, even though everything around them was as insubstantial as mist.

"Do you want to know why I can propose to you?"

She nodded.

"Because even though you expect disaster and carry more gear than went down with the Titanic, you are incapable of not helping people, incapable of walking away from the truly helpless. And when I'm with you, I'm alive. I'm not just going through the motions. Are you ready now?"

She could only nod.

Jack took her hand and knelt on the wet boards of the dock. "Tara Keegan, I love you. Will you marry me?"

She nodded, and Jack pulled her down into a kiss. It was a Jack kiss, the kind she was beginning to know, a kiss that could face anything, lose anything, and still believe in goodness and happy endings, a kiss to build a life on. When she opened her eyes, there were no rose petals, no tower views, no musicians, or bottles of champagne, only a man's steady blue eyes and an extraordinary green flash.

In the end they did not drown or get eaten by sharks. Tara did not learn the hip snap, but Jack promised they would work on it.

Epilogue

Tara left her bed. Jack did not move. He lay on his stomach, his dark hair tousled, his jaw shadowed, lashes down over those blue eyes. He looked so at home in her bed. She checked the ring on her finger. *Yep, it glowed brightly.*

In minutes she had her running clothes on, gray, cropped T-shirt, black yoga pants, and a favorite red sweatshirt tied around her hips. She gathered her phone and her keys and retrieved the burgundy ring box from the window seat. It was time to pass the Claddagh on to another woman. She didn't know how she knew, but she knew. She stopped to write Jack a quick note explaining that she'd be back with coffee and a treat. She felt his scrutiny and looked up.

"You have no idea what you do to me," he said.

They had made love twice the night before, but she started to pull the cropped top down over her rounded belly.

"Don't!" She froze at the intensity of the command.

Jack threw back the covers and rolled out of bed, crossing to her, grabbing her, and whirling her around in his arms. He put her down and cupped her belly in one hand. She loved his hands. "That's one of the happy parts of you."

"Happy?"

"Well, all of you makes me happy."

Several distracting kisses later, she pushed back in his arms.

"Where are you off to?" He glanced at her unfinished note and the box.

"Well, a morning run, but…" She held out her ring hand. He would understand. "It feels as if I should start looking for the next woman who needs the ring."

"Ah." She could see he approved of the idea. He let her go, and she stepped back. She tugged on the ring, and it slipped easily from her finger. For a moment her finger looked naked.

Jack took her hand in his. "You know I am grateful to that ring, but now…" his thumb and forefinger encircled her ring finger…"there's a space for my ring, the one we pick out together." Jack's smile made her blink like looking into bright sun. His thumb caught the moisture from her eyes.

She gave the ring a kiss for luck, placed it back in its well-worn box, and tucked the box in the pouch of her sweatshirt.

Leaving her grandmother's place, Tara headed down Hyde to Aquatic Park and turned east. Passing through the touristy Fisherman's Wharf area until she reached the long curving sweep of the Embarcadero, she felt so light she could run forever.

A tangerine sun was coming up on her left over the Oakland hills, healed now from the fire, and the windows on the hill on her right were catching the light in a coppery blaze of morning. She felt so alive as if she were really seeing people, seeing the world. She kept an eye out for that woman who needed the ring. She wasn't sure she would recognize her. It was early, and there were few people about, but Tara had certainly learned to trust the ring. She had not understood how it worked at first in spite of the carefully worded instructions. She had been skeptical and demanding, only gradually discovering how the ring opened her up to listen to her own heart.

Now she knew that when the moment was right, there would be someone who needed to learn from it, as she had learned. For her the lessons had been about letting go. She had had to let go of all the past hurts and fears that she had been carrying in her absurdly heavy bag. She had had to let go of the protective fantasy of Justin Wright. She had had to let go of her perfect job. And she had had to do it all without any guarantees. That was how hope worked. Now she had a last bit of letting go to do, letting go of the ring. It would pass to someone else, but Jack had taught her the secret of letting go—that the things one kept in one's heart could never get lost.

She could see a white and blue Marin ferry approaching across the bay and thought she would take a look at the passengers as they disembarked, so she angled to the left along the water, and halted on the wharf side of the Ferry Building to watch the crowd hurrying to work. She realized that the ring was still guiding her.

And suddenly there she was. Tara knew her instantly, the one who must receive the Claddagh. And she realized the final lesson of the ring, that it would keep on giving, that the miracle would be repeated. Tara smiled and knew that her smile was, like the one she had received from the woman at the cable car stop, the smile of a woman who knew her own heart.

Social Media

For more about Ciji Ware and her books:

Visit Ciji at her website: **www.cijiware.com**
Like Ciji on Facebook:
www.facebook.com/CijiWareNovelist
Follow Ciji on Twitter: **www.twitter.com/CijiWare**
View images of her research at Pinterest:
www.pinterest.com/CijiWare

For more about Diana Dempsey and her books:

Visit Diana at her website: **www.dianadempsey.com**
Like Diana on Facebook:
www.facebook.com/DianaDempseyBooks
Follow Diana on Twitter: **www.twitter.com/Diana_Dempsey**

For more about Kate Moore and her books:

Visit Kate at her website: **www.katemoore.com**
Like Kate on Facebook:
www.facebook.com/KateMooreAuthor
Follow Kate on Twitter: **www.twitter.com/MooreKate0**

That Autumn in Edinburgh

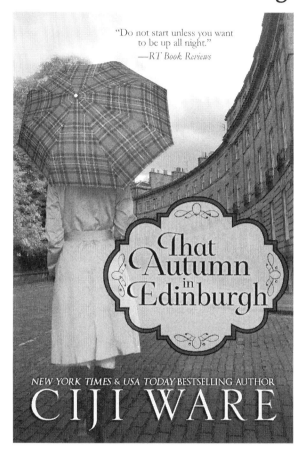

by Ciji Ware

250 years later…a contemporary, stand-alone sequel to Ciji Ware's award-winning historical novel *Island of the Swans*.

Can memories of a tragic, eighteenth century love triangle be passed down through a descendant's DNA?

A compelling, almost mystical attraction draws American designer Fiona Fraser into the force field of visiting

Scotsman, Alexander Maxwell, through an eerie happenstance one steamy summer's day in New York City. When Fiona's mercurial boss dispatches her to Edinburgh to create a Scottish Home Furnishings Collection, the chemistry deepens as she and Alex discover their ancestral bonds to the star-crossed lovers Thomas Fraser—the "Lost Lieutenant"—and Jane Maxwell, the flamboyant 4th Duchess of Gordon who died in 1812.

From the cobbled streets of Edinburgh's Royal Mile to the tartan and cashmere mills of the Scottish border country, the modern lovers grapple with the imminent threat of financial ruin to their respective firms, along with ancient wounds echoing down through time—and a heartbreaking mystery, hidden for more than two centuries, that will dictate their own destinies...

Available now in print and digital editions

Falling Star

by Diana Dempsey

"A Perfect 10!...Debut author Diana Dempsey soars with *Falling Star*, a powerful, moving, riveting tale of greed and betrayal, love and self-discovery..." *Romance Reviews Today*

Natalie Daniels' husband just dumped her. Her boss is scheming to replace her. And she's falling in love with her sexy Australian TV news agent—who's about to propose to somebody else. What's a woman to do? Dig deep and show what she's made of—which just might land her both the job and the man of her dreams.

This full-length novel was originally published by Penguin's New American Library, and was nominated for a RITA award for "Best First Book" by the Romance Writers Association.

Available now in print and digital editions

A Prince Among Men

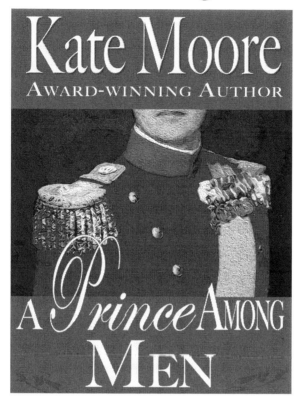

by Kate Moore

Library Journal Best Genre Fiction 1997 (New Edition for Kindle): An incognito prince and an intelligent, independent heroine find unexpected love in this story. Willful duke's daughter Lady Ophelia Brinsby, resists her parents' plans to marry her to a dull man of rank. She'd rather spend time with her bright and witty best friends who have no rank at all. When her father's strict orders to her new groom Alexander stand in her way, she must find a way to outwit the one man clever and charming enough to stir her heart. As their clash of wills reveals their kindred spirits, they soon overstep the boundaries of servant and mistress. But their new trust and understanding is tested when Alex is unmasked and his engagement to another is announced. Suddenly he is in the fight of his life—to win back the woman he loves.

Available now in print and digital editions

Authors' Notes

Author's Note from Ciji Ware

My first thank-you goes to the two other authors in this trilogy, Diana Dempsey and Kate Moore, for the honor of being part of this literary effort. It's been an inspiring and exhilarating experience, to say nothing of being just plain fun!

Thanks, too, to talented San Francisco chef, Clare Molla, for sharing her world with me at local food events and over a few terrific lunches. The wonderful Harry Chapman has my gratitude for lending me his name as the CEO in this work. I also owe a huge debt to the "Ciji Betas" Diane Barr, Cynthia Mason, Linda Hammond, Donna Christie Kolkey, and my sister, Joy Ware—who gave this "draft writer" their early feedback on Version 1, and to my husband, Tony Cook, my loving partner in life's adventures.

Every writer needs a safety net of friendship and support, and in addition to my family and friends just mentioned, the Women's Dog Walking Group and members of the Sausalito Women's Club make life in the maritime village where I live a joy.

And finally, my deepest appreciation to the Bradley family, owners of Amphora Nueva Berkeley Olive Oil Works, as well as McEvoy Ranch manager Dick Neilsen and his wife Linda who have hosted me numerous times among the spectacular olive groves and lavender fields of Petaluma, California. This one's for *you...*

Author's Note from Diana Dempsey

In 1993, my sister Debbie adopted a year-old baby girl from Kazakhstan. Three years later, she adopted a four-month-old girl from Moscow. Those delightful infants have grown into my lovely nieces Alyssa and Jacinda, and because of them I have long wanted to write an adoption story.

No two adoptions are the same, but at their core all share loss, heartbreak, joy, fulfillment, and love. For every orphan who is placed with a family, there are hundreds, thousands of children whose dreams come to naught. International adoptions have plummeted by fifty percent in the last decade, largely due to more restrictive policies by foreign governments. My heart aches as the number of orphaned children overseas only continues to rise.

I traveled with my sister to pick up tiny Alyssa, and our journey to Moscow and Akmola (now known as Astana) is one I will never forget. I hope Veronica's tale will shed some light on the anguished yet wondrous path birth parents, adoptive parents, and adopted children tread.

I would like to thank my wonderful husband Jed for his help with my novella. He always has to slog through the roughest drafts. Thank you, too, to my dear friend and marvelous writer Bill Fuller for his insights. I am also grateful to my fellow author in this anthology, Kate Moore, who proved she is not only a splendid storyteller, but a perceptive reader, too. And many thanks to the very talented Ciji Ware, who invited me to participate in this project and also made a key introduction when it came time to research the world of opera. Thank you, Ciji! As it happens, my best source prefers to remain anonymous; but she knows who she is, and I thank her.

Author's Note from Kate Moore

This little story grew and took shape with inspiration from many sources. First, a big thank you to my fellow authors, Ciji Ware and Diana Dempsey, for inviting me to join them in the project. It's been great fun. My thanks, as always, go to a group of brainstorming authors—Carol Culver, Diana Dempsey, Barbara Freethy, Lynn Hanna, and Barbara McMahon. Further thanks go to Hank Biddle, Senior Vice President, Western Region, Ritz-Carlton Hotels, who provided invaluable information about hotel staffing and operations. And a final thank you to my son Kevin for showing me how a thirty-something person experiences San Francisco.

About the Authors

About Ciji Ware

In addition to the novella "The Ring of Kerry Hannigan," Ciji Ware is the *New York Times* and *USA Today* bestselling author of eight novels and two nonfiction works. She is the daughter, niece, and descendant of writers (including William Ware, author of the historical romance *Zenobia*, 1836; Henry Ware, author of *On the Formation of the Christian Character*, 1831), so the writing profession is just part of the "family business."

Among her many accolades, she has been honored with the Dorothy Parker Award of Excellence and a *Romantic Times* Award for Best Fictionalized Biography for *Island of the Swans*, and as a result of that book, was made a Fellow of the Society of Antiquaries of Scotland (FSA Scot), a tribute she treasures. In 2012, she was a finalist in the prestigious WILLA (Cather) Literary Award for *A Race to Splendor*.

Ware is also an Emmy-award winning television producer, former radio and TV on-air broadcaster for KABC in Los Angeles, as well as a print and online journalist. She received a BA in History from Harvard University and has the distinction of being the first woman graduate of Harvard College to serve as the President of the Harvard Alumni Association, Worldwide.

The author lives in the San Francisco Bay Area and can be contacted at **www.cijiware.com**.

About Diana Dempsey

Diana Dempsey traded in an Emmy Award-winning career in TV news to write fast, fun romantic fiction. She is the author of eight women's fiction and mystery novels. Her debut novel, *Falling Star*, was nominated for a RITA award for Best First Book by the members of Romance Writers of America. The Ms America mysteries introduce beauty queen and budding sleuth Happy Pennington.

In her dozen years in television news, the former Diana Koricke played every on-air role from network correspondent to local news anchor. She reported for NBC News from New York, Tokyo, and Burbank, and substitute anchored such broadcasts as *Sunrise*, *Today*, and *NBC Nightly News*. In addition, she was a morning anchor for KTTV 11 Fox News in Los Angeles. She started her broadcast career in the anchor chair for Financial News Network.

Born and raised in Buffalo, New York—Go, Bills!—Diana is a graduate of Harvard University and the winner of a Rotary International Foundation Scholarship. She enjoyed stints overseas in Belgium, the U.K., and Japan, and now resides in Los Angeles with her husband and a West Highland White Terrier, not necessarily in that order.

Diana loves to hear from readers. Visit **www.dianadempsey.com** to email her, and be sure to sign up for her mailing list while you're there to hear first about her new releases.

About Kate Moore

Kate Moore is a Readers' Crown winner and three-time RITA finalist who has been reading and writing romance fiction since she was ten. Her historical fiction takes readers to the dark side of Regency London and the triumphant side of love. Her contemporary fiction, on the lighter side, is set in the San Francisco area where Kate lives in a little town north of the Golden Gate with her surfer husband and her children's dogs. Kate can be contacted at:
www.katemoore.com.

Authors' Book Lists

Available from Ciji Ware

Historical Novels

Island of the Swans
Wicked Company
A Race to Splendor

"Time-Slip" Historical Novels

A Cottage by the Sea
Midnight on Julia Street
A Light on the Veranda

Contemporary Novels

That Summer in Cornwall
That Autumn in Edinburgh
That Winter in Venice – coming 2015
That Spring in Paris – coming 2016

Contemporary Novellas

Ring of Truth : "The Ring of Kerry Hannigan"

Nonfiction

Rightsizing Your Life
Joint Custody After Divorce

Available from Diana Dempsey

Women's Fiction

Falling Star
To Catch the Moon
Too Close to the Sun
Chasing Venus

Mystery

Ms America and the Offing on Oahu
Ms America and the Villainy in Vegas
Ms America and the Mayhem in Miami
Ms America and the Whoopsie in Winona

Novellas

Ring of Truth: "A Diva Wears the Ring"

Available from Kate Moore

Regency Romances

To Kiss a Thief
Sweet Bargain
The Mercenary Major
An Improper Widow

Regency Historicals

Winterburn's Rose
A Prince Among Men
To Tempt a Saint
To Save the Devil
To Seduce an Angel
Blackstone's Bride

Contemporary Novels

Sexy Lexy

Contemporary Novellas

"Once Upon a Ring" in *Ring of Truth* anthology

Made in the USA
Charleston, SC
07 September 2015